ARMADILLO

'Unabashedly enjoyable'   *Observer*

'Darkly comic, beautifully paced, the novel is
crammed with an almost Dickensian sense of
atmosphere and turbulence, yet blessed with the
deftness of Waugh. Full of great moments, it
also succeeds in being momentous'
Tom Adair, *Scotsman Weekend*

'An outstanding comic novel . . . with some characters
who are masterpieces of grotesque invention'
Andrew Biswell, *Literary Review*

'Boyd barely puts a foot wrong – the flat, blowy
wastes of Silvertown, pretentious city wine bars, the
prosperous squalor of Pimlico are all cleanly
caught . . . a book that is a pleasure to read'
Robert Hanks, *Independent on Sunday*

'As entertaining as anything he has written . . . brisk
farce and dialogue that can be finger-licking good'
David Profumo, *Spectator*

William Boyd was born in 1952 in Accra, Ghana, and was brought up there and in Nigeria. He was educated at Gordonstoun School and at the universities of Nice, Glasgow and Oxford. Between 1980 and 1983 he was a lecturer in English literature at St Hilda's College, Oxford. He is the author of *A Good Man in Africa*, which won the Whitbread Literary Award for the Best First Novel in 1981 and a Somerset Maugham Award in 1982; *On the Yankee Station* (1982), a collection of short stories; *An Ice-Cream War*, which won the John Llewellyn Rhys Memorial Prize for 1982 and was shortlisted for the Booker Prize; *Stars and Bars* (1984); *The New Confessions* (1987); *Brazzaville Beach*, which won the James Tait Black Memorial Prize for 1990 and for which William Boyd was awarded the McVitie's Prize for Scottish Writer of the Year; *The Blue Afternoon*, which won the 1993 *Sunday Express* Book of the Year Award and the 1995 *Los Angeles Times* Book Prize for Fiction; *The Destiny of Nathalie X* (1995), a further collection of short stories. *Armadillo* was first published in 1998. Nine of his screenplays have been filmed, the latest of which, *The Trench*, he also directed. All of his books are published by Penguin.

William Boyd is married and lives in London.

WILLIAM BOYD

Armadillo

PENGUIN BOOKS

PENGUIN BOOKS

Published by the Penguin Group
Penguin Books Ltd, 80 Strand, London WC2R 0RL, England
Penguin Putnam Inc., 375 Hudson Street, New York, New York 10014, USA
Penguin Books Australia Ltd, Ringwood, Victoria, Australia
Penguin Books Canada Ltd, 10 Alcorn Avenue, Toronto, Ontario, Canada M4V 3B2
Penguin Books India (P) Ltd, 11 Community Centre, Panchsheel Park, New Delhi – 110 017, India
Penguin Books (NZ) Ltd, Cnr Rosedale and Airborne Roads, Albany, Auckland, New Zealand
Penguin Books (South Africa) (Pty) Ltd, 24 Sturdee Avenue, Rosebank 2196 South Africa

Penguin Books Ltd, Registered Offices: 80 Strand, London WC2R 0RL, England

www.penguin.com

First published by Hamish Hamilton 1998
Published in Penguin Books 1998
This film and TV tie-in edition published 2001

1

Copyright © William Boyd, 1998
All rights reserved

Set in 10.5 on 12.5pt Monotype Baskerville
Typeset by Intype London Ltd
Printed in England by Clays Ltd, St Ives plc

for Susan

Armadillo. (āɪmădi·lo). 1577 [– Sp. *armadillo*, dim of *armado* armed man, so lit. 'little armed man':– L. *armatus*, pa. pple. of *armare* ARM v.]

We and other animals notice what goes on around us. This helps us by suggesting what we might expect and even how to prevent it, and thus fosters survival. However, the expedient works only imperfectly. There are surprises, and they are unsettling. How can we tell when we are right? We are faced with the problem of error.

W. V. QUINE, *From Stimulus to Science*

Chapter 1

In these times of ours – and we don't need to be precise about the exact date – but, anyway, very early in the year, a young man not much over thirty, tall – six feet plus an inch or two – with ink-dark hair and a serious-looking, fine-featured but pallid face, went to keep a business appointment and discovered a hanged man.

Lorimer Black stared aghast at Mr Dupree, his mind at once clamorous with shocked alarm and curiously inert – the warring symptoms of a form of mental panic, he supposed. Mr Dupree had hanged himself from a thinly lagged water pipe that crossed the ceiling in the little anteroom behind reception. A small set of aluminium folding steps lay on its side beneath his slightly splayed feet (his tan shoes needed a good clean, Lorimer noticed). Mr Dupree was simultaneously the first dead person he had encountered in his life, his first suicide and his first hanged man and Lorimer found this congruence of firsts deeply troubling.

His eyes travelled reluctantly upwards from Mr Dupree's scuffed toecaps, pausing briefly at the groin area – where he could discern no sign of the fabled, impromptu erection of the hangee – and moved on up to his face. Mr Dupree's head was hunched too far over and his expression was slumped and sleepy, like that worn by exhausted commuters who doze off in overheated railway carriages, propped upright by badly designed banquettes. If you had seen Mr Dupree snoozing opposite you on the 18.12 from Liverpool Street, his head canted over in that awkward position, you would have ached presciently for the stiff neck he was bound to experience on awakening.

Stiff neck. Cricked neck. Broken neck. Christ. Lorimer carefully placed his briefcase on the floor, stepped past Mr Dupree and moved quietly to the door at the end of the anteroom. He opened it and peered out over the devastated expanse of the factory. Through the blackened and carbonized joists and beams of the roof he could see the low, unrelieved pewter of the sky; the floor was still covered with the charred and melted naked bodies of a near-thousand plastic mannequins (976, according to the documentation, a consignment destined for a chain of stores in the USA). All that mangled and ruined 'flesh' provoked a shiver of ersatz disgust and horror (ersatz because they weren't real; after all, he told himself, no pain had been suffered) but here and there was preserved a head of cartoon handsomeness, or a tanned girl smiling a smile of preposterous welcome. The unchanging good nature of their expressions lent a certain touching stoicism to the scene. And beyond, Lorimer knew from the report, lay the torched workshops, the design studios, the clay and plaster sculpture rooms, the moulding lines. The fire had been unusually fierce and typically thorough. Apparently, Mr Dupree had been insistent that nothing would be touched, not a melted model budged, until he received his money and, Lorimer could see, Mr Dupree's word had been steadfast.

Lorimer exhaled and made little popping noises with

his lips. 'Hmmm', he said out loud, then, 'Jesus H. Christ', then 'Hmmm' again. He realized his hands were shaking slightly, so he thrust them in his pockets. The phrase 'a bad business' began to repeat itself moronically, mantrically, in his head. He speculated vaguely and reluctantly about Hogg's reaction to the Dupree suicide: Hogg had told him about 'toppers' before and Lorimer wondered what the procedure was . . .

He closed the door, worried for a second about fingerprints, and then thought: why would they dust for a suicide? It wasn't until he was back in reception and reaching for the phone that another thought entered his mind that possibly, just possibly, it might not have been suicide after all.

The detective who came as the result of his call to the police, Detective Sergeant Rappaport, seemed not much older than Lorimer but called him 'sir' regularly, and a little needlessly, all the same. 'Dennis P. Rappaport' it had said on his ID.

'You say you had an appointment with Mr Dupree, sir.'

'Yes. It had been booked for over a week.' Lorimer handed over his business card. 'I was here promptly at 10.30.'

They were standing outside now, beneath the cursive red plastic sign that read 'Osmond Dupree Display Mannequins est. 1957'. Police and other officials busied themselves with Mr Dupree's mortal remains inside. A constable diligently wound fluttering striped tape around lamp-posts and railings, notionally sealing off the front of the factory and banning access to half a dozen cold, expressionless bystanders curiously looking on. Waiting for the body bag, Lorimer thought: charming. Detective

Sergeant Rappaport carefully studied the business card and then performed a histrionic pouching mime.

'May I, sir?'

'By all means.'

From his leather jacket Rappaport produced a fat wallet and slipped Lorimer's card inside.

'Not your average beginning to your average sort of day, sir, I would imagine.'

'No . . . Most distressing,' Lorimer agreed, watchfully. Rappaport was a burly fellow, beefy and blond with cornflower-blue eyes, the sort of looks unsuitable in a detective, Lorimer thought, for some reason, thinking instead that Rappaport should have been a surfer or a tennis pro, or a waiter in a Los Angeles restaurant. Furthermore, Lorimer wasn't sure if Rappaport's deference was meant to unnerve, reassure or to be subversively ironic in some way. On balance he thought it was probably the last: Rappaport would have a chortle about its effect later in the mess or canteen or the pub or wherever it was the detectives gathered to natter and moan about their respective days.

'Now we know where to find you, sir, we won't trouble you any further. Thank you for your assistance, sir.'

More than ironic, the blatant overuse of 'sir', Lorimer thought, was clearly and deliberately patronizing, there was no doubt about that, but at the same time a conversational irritant, a covert sneer, impossible to protest against.

'Can we run you back anywhere, sir?'

'No thank you, Detective Rappaport, my car's round the corner.'

'The "t" is silent, sir. *Rappapor.* Old Norman name.'

Old Norman smug bastard, Lorimer thought, as he walked back to his Toyota in Bolton Place. But you wouldn't be quite so pleased with yourself if you knew what I had in my briefcase, he reflected, cheering himself up somewhat as he turned into the square. The improved mood was transitory, however. As he unlocked his car door he felt a depression settle on him like a shawl, almost physically there, across his back and shoulders, as he considered Mr Dupree's desperate, humble demise: what drove a man to tie a washing line to a water pipe, slip a noose around his neck and kick away the aluminium steps that supported him? It was the memory of his scuffed shoes hanging three feet off the ground that stayed with Lorimer rather than the grotesque loll of the head. That and the miserable January day – bleak and dull – and Bolton Place. Its naked plane trees with their Gulf War camouflage, the struggling, tarnished light, the cold – a wind had freshened – and the morning's rain had left the sooty brick of the entirely acceptable Georgian houses almost charcoal-coloured. A child in a padded moss-green jacket tottered here and there on the central rect-angle of lawn, vainly seeking distraction, first among the sodden cropped flowerbeds, then with a wily thrush, then scuffing up a few remaining dead leaves and flinging them aimlessly about. In a corner on a bench its nanny or child-minder or mother watched, smoking a cigarette and swigging something from a lurid can. City square, venerable buildings, a patch of tended green, an inno-cently happy toddler, a concerned supervising adult – in any other context these ingredients might have conspired to form a more joyous symbolism. But not today, Lorimer thought, not today.

He was pulling out of the square on to the main road when a taxi passed a little too close to the front of his car and he was forced to lurch abruptly to a stop. The wobbly

5

diorama of Bolton Place slid along the taxi's glossy black side and his oath caught in his throat as he saw the face framed in the rear window. This happened to him from time to time, occasionally several times in one week – he would see a face in a crowd, through a shop window, going down the escalator of the Underground as he went up, that was of such luminous, transfiguring beauty that it made him both want to shout in exultant surprise and weep with frustration. Who was it who said that 'a face in the Tube can ruin an entire day'? It was the glance that did it, the glance with its swift, uncertain apprehension, its too hurried analysis of the optic phenomena available. His eyes rushed to judgement; they were too keen to see beauty. Whenever he had a chance for a second look the result was nearly always disappointing: the studied gaze was always a severer arbiter. And now, here, it had happened again – but this one, he thought, would survive sober reassessment. He swallowed; he recognized the authentic symptoms: the slight breathlessness, increased pulse, the sensation of a packed thoracic cavity. The girl's wan, perfect, oval face – the woman's face? – had been eager, hopeful, leaning forward to the window, long-necked and wide-eyed with pleasurable anticipation. It came and went so rapidly that the impression, he told himself, so as not to ruin his entire day, couldn't fail to have been an idealized one. He shivered. Still, it had been a form of benign random compensation, erasing the image of Mr Dupree's suspended scruffy shoes for a moment or two.

He turned right and headed for Archway. In his mirror he could see that the small crowd around Dupree's Display Mannequins lingered on balefully. The girl's taxi had become stuck behind the ambulance and he saw a policeman gesticulating at the driver. The rear door opened – but that was all, because he was away, off down Archway and Holloway Road, down Upper Street to the Angel, along City Road to Finsbury Square to see, soon appearing ahead of him, the rain-lashed, jagged towers and dripping walkways of the Barbican.

He found a meter near Smithfield Market and strode briskly back up Golden Lane to the office. Some sort of stingy, sleety rain was falling diagonally – he could feel it, despite his bowed head, smiting his cheeks and chin. Freezing, foul day. Shop lights glowing orange, pedestrians hurrying, heads down like him, suffering, clenched, concerned only about reaching their destination as quickly as possible.

At the door he keyed in his code and stamped up the pine stairs to the first floor. Rajiv saw him through the reinforced glass panel, the door buzzed and Lorimer pushed through.

'Brass monkeys out there, Raj.'

Rajiv stubbed out his cigarette. 'What're you doing here?'

'Hogg in?'

'What d'you think this place is? Holiday camp?'

'Humorous, Raj. Very satirical.'

'Idle damn bastards.'

Lorimer hefted his briefcase on to the counter and clicked it open. The neat rows of new bills always gave him a small shock – their unreal latency, their strange mint purity, unfingered, not crumpled or folded, yet to be exchanged for goods or services, yet even to function as money. He started stacking the trim wads on the counter top.

'Aw, fuck,' Rajiv said and strolled to the back of his den to open the big safe. 'Police called, asking about you. Thought it might be trouble.'

'Not the best start to the day.'

'Bleater?' Rajiv filled his palms with money.

'I should be so lucky. Topper.'

'Ouch. I'm going to have to get security back, aren't I? Doesn't make Rajiv happy.'

'I'll take it home, if you like.'

'Sign here.'

Lorimer signed the money back in. £500,000. Twenty wads of five hundred fifty-pound notes, fresh with their astringent, chemical, paper smell. Rajiv hitched his trousers over his belly and lit another cigarette as he checked the docket. As he bent over the page the overhead strip light was reflected down the middle of his shiny, perfectly bald pate. A lucent Mohican, Lorimer thought.

'Want me to call Hogg?' Rajiv asked, not looking up.

'No, I will.' Hogg always claimed that Rajiv was the best accountant in the country; he was even more valuable to the firm, Hogg said, because he didn't know it.

'Damn bore,' Rajiv said, slipping the docket into a file. 'Hogg was expecting you to have this one sorted, what with the new chappie coming.'

'What chappie?'

'The new director. For God's sake, Lorimer Black, how long've you been away?'

'Oh, yeah,' Lorimer said, remembering.

He waved vaguely and airily at Rajiv and headed down the corridor to his office. The set-up here reminded him of his college: small, identical, boxy rooms off an overlit corridor, each door fitted with a rectangle of reinforced glass so that absolute privacy was denied. Pausing at his hutch, he saw that Dymphna was installed opposite, her door ajar. She looked tired, her eyes weary, her big nose blown raw. She smiled lethargically at him and sniffed.

'Where've you been?' he said. 'Sunny Argentina?'

'Sunny Peru,' she said. 'Nightmare. What's up?'

'Had me a topper.'

'They are bastards. What did the Hogg-man say?'

'Haven't told him yet. I had no idea it was likely. Never suspected. Hogg never told me anything.'

'He never does.'

'Likes surprises.'

'Not our Mr Hogg.'

She made a knowing, resigned face, hoiked up her heavy bag – one of those squared-off ones with many internal compartments reputedly favoured by airline pilots – and set off past him down the corridor, home-wards. She was a big, solid girl – haunchy, buttocky – lugging her heavy bag with ease. On her feet she wore surprisingly fine, high-heeled shoes, all wrong for this weather. She did not turn round as she said, 'Poor old Lorimer. See you at the party. Wouldn't tell Hoggy straight away, though, he'll not be a happy camper, what with this new director coming.' Rajiv laughed in loud agreement at that. 'Night, rascal Raji,' Dymphna said, and was gone.

Lorimer sat at his desk for an aimless ten minutes, pushing his blotter about, selecting and rejecting various pens before deciding that perhaps a memo to Hogg was a bad idea. He hated memos, Hogg. Face to face was what he liked. Nose to nose, even better. Hogg must surely understand in this case: everyone had a topper sometime, it was a risk in this job. People were at their weakest, their most fallible and unpredictable – Hogg was always telling

9

you that – going over the edge was an occupational hazard.

He drove home to Pimlico, turning off Lupus Street into Lupus Crescent and finally finding a parking space a mere hundred yards from the house. It had grown decidedly colder and the rain now had a heavy spittley look as it angled through the tangerine glare of the street lights.

Lupus Crescent was not crescent-shaped, though the street of standard basement and three-storey, cream stucco and brown brick terraced houses did have a slight bend in it, as though it had aspired to crescenthood but did not have the energy to go the full distance. When he'd bought his flat in number 11 he had been put off by the name, wondering why anyone would want to christen a street after a particularly unpleasant ailment, a 'disease of the skin, usually tubercular or ulcerous, eating into the substance and leaving deep scars', according to his dictionary. He was relieved when his downstairs neighbour, Lady Haigh – a slim, spry octogenarian, genteelly impoverished – explained that Lupus had been the family name of an Earl of Chester, something to do with the Grosvenor family, who had owned the whole of Pimlico at one time. Still, Lupus was an unfortunate surname, given its medical connotations, Lorimer considered, and was one he would have thought seriously about changing, had he been the Earl of Chester. Names were important, which was all the more reason for changing them when they didn't suit, or irked in some way or gave rise to unpleasant associations.

Lady Haigh's television set mumbled loudly through her front door as Lorimer sorted through the post in the hall. Bills for him and one letter (he recognized the handwriting); *Country Life* for Lady H; something from the *Universität von Frankfurt* for 'Herr Doktor' Alan Kenbarry up top. He pushed the magazine under Lady Haigh's door.

'Is that you, Alan, you jackanapes?' he heard her say. 'You woke me up this morning.'

He changed his voice. 'It's, ah, Lorimer, Lady Haigh. I think Alan's out.'

'I'm not dead yet, Lorimer, darling. No need to worry, my sweet.'

'Glad to hear it. Night-night.'

The magazine was tugged effortfully inside as Lorimer padded up the stairs to his flat.

As he closed the door behind him, hearing the new aluminium and rubber seals kiss shut, he felt an immediate sense of relaxation rinse through him. He laid his palm ritually on the three helmets that stood on the hall table, feeling their ancient metal cool beneath his skin. Buttons were pressed, switches flicked, low lights went on and a Chopin nocturne crept through the rooms following him, his feet soundless on the rough charcoal carpet. In the kitchen he poured himself two fingers of ice-cold vodka and opened his letter. It contained a polaroid photograph and on its reverse side, scrawled in turquoise ink, the following message: 'Greek Helm. *c.* 800 BC. Magna Graecia. Yours at a very special discount – £29,500. Sincerely, Ivan.' He studied the picture for a moment – it was perfect – then he slipped it back into the envelope and tried not to think about where he could lay his hands on £29,500. Glancing at his watch, he saw he had at least an hour to himself before he would need to prepare for the party and head off to the Fort. He slid *The Book of Transfiguration* out of its drawer, spread it on the counter and, taking a tiny, lip-numbing sip from his glass and selecting a pen, he settled himself down to write. What pronoun should he use, he wondered? The reproachful, admonitory second person singular, or the more straightforwardly confessional first? He moved between 'you' and 'I' as his mood took him, but today, he considered, he had done nothing untoward or recriminatory, there was no need for harsher objectivity – 'I' it would be. '379', he wrote, in his tiny, neat hand. 'The Case of Mr Dupree'.

*379. **The Case of Mr Dupree.** I had spoken to Mr Dupree only once, when I called to make the appointment. 'Why isn't Hogg coming?' he had said immediately, neurotically, like a lover, disappointed. 'Had enough fun, has he?' I told him Mr Hogg was a busy man. 'Tell Hogg to come himself or the whole thing's off,' he said and then hung up.*

I relayed all this to Hogg, who made a sick-looking face, full of contempt and disgust. 'I don't know why I bothered, why I took the trouble,' Hogg said. 'He's squatting in the palm of my hand,' he said, holding out his broad palm, callused like a harpist's, 'with his trousers around his ankles. You finish it off, Lorimer, my lad. I've got bigger fish to fillet.'

I did not know Mr Dupree, which is why my shock was so short-lived, I suppose – still disturbing to think about, but not profoundly so. Mr Dupree had existed for me only as a voice on the telephone, he was Hogg's case, one of Hogg's rare sorties into the market, as he liked to put it, to sample the wares and the weather, just to keep his hand in, and then passed him on to me, routinely. That's why I felt nothing, or, rather, what genuine shock I felt was so brief. The Mr Dupree I encountered had already become a thing, an unpleasant thing, true, but had a flayed cow carcase been hanging there, or, say, I had been confronted by a pile of dead dogs, I would

*have been equally upset. Or would I? Perhaps not. But Mr Dupree,
the human being, had never impinged on me, all I had to go on
was the importunate voice on the phone; he was merely a name on a
file, merely another appointment as far as I was concerned.*

*No, I don't think I am a cold person, on the contrary I am too
warm and this, in fact, may be my problem. But why am I not
more shattered and distressed by what I found today? I do not lack
empathy but my inability to feel anything lasting for Mr Dupree
disturbs me rather. Has my job, the life I lead, given me the emotional
responses of an overworked stretcher-bearer on a crowded battlefield
blankly noting and enumerating the dead only as potential burdens.
No, I'm sure of it. But the case of Mr Dupree was something that
should never have happened to me, should never have become part
of my life. Hogg sent me there on his business. But did he know
something like this might occur? Was it his insurance to send me
there instead?*

The Book of Transfiguration

He cabbed to the Fort. He would drink too much, he knew,
they all would, they always did at these rare gatherings of
the entire team. Sometimes if he drank a lot he slept at
night but it didn't always work, though, otherwise he
would have embraced alcoholism with a convert's zeal.
Sometimes it kept him up, jangled and alert, mind going
like a train.

Getting out of the cab, he saw that the Fort was agleam,
all aglow tonight, spotlights picking out its full twenty-
four floors. Three swagged, gilded commissionaires stood
at the *porte cochère* below the aquamarine neon sign. Solid,
emphatic, classical roman font – FORTRESS SURE.
Something grand must be going on in the boardroom,
he thought, all this is not for the likes of us. He was

checked, saluted and directed across the lobby to the
escalators. Second floor, Portcullis Suite. There was a
full-sized catering kitchen on the twenty-fourth, he had
been told, and a chef. Someone had said it could have
doubled as a three-star restaurant: it probably did, for all
he knew – he had never risen to those heights. He smelt
cigarette smoke first, then heard the ebb and flow of too-
loud conversation and chorused male laughter, feeling
the transient electricity of excitement that free drink
always provoked. He hoped some canapés had made
their way down here to the proles. Mr Dupree had
made him miss lunch, he realized, and he was hungry.

Dymphna's breasts were momentarily visible as she
stooped to stub out her cigarette. Small with pale pointy
nipples, he noticed. She really shouldn't wear such low –

'– He's fucking livid,' Adrian Bolt was saying to
Lorimer with enthusiastic relish. Bolt was the oldest
member of the team, an ex-police inspector, a Mason
and an aspiring martinet. 'Steam coming out of his ears.
Course, you can't tell with Hogg. That control, that
discipline –'

'Isn't the steam a bit of a giveaway?' Dymphna said.

Bolt ignored her. 'He's impassive. Like a rock, Hogg.
A man of few words, even when fucking livid.'

Shane Ashgable turned to Lorimer, his square face
sagging with false sympathy. 'Wouldn't like to be in your
shoes, compadre.'

Lorimer turned away, a sudden acid sting of nausea in
his throat, searching the busy room for Hogg. No sign.
He saw that a microphone was being attached to the
moulded pine dais at the far end and thought he could
make out the oiled grey-blond hair of Sir Simon

Sherriffmuir, Fortress Sure's chairman and chief executive, in the midst of a cluster of beaming acolytes.

'Another drink, Dymphna?' Lorimer asked, needing something to do.

Dymphna handed him her warm, empty, smeared glass. 'Why thank you, lovely Lorimer,' she said.

He pushed and eased his way through the drinking throng, all drinking avidly, quickly, glasses held close to their mouths, as if someone was likely suddenly to snatch them away, confiscate the booze. There were very few he knew here any more, just a sprinkling from his own days at the Fort. They were a young crowd, early to mid-twenties (trainees?), newly suited, loudly tied, flushed, cheery faces. Friday evening, no work tomorrow, arse-holed by midnight, rollocked, well bevvied. The women were all smoking, confident in their minority status, laughing as the males grouped and regrouped about them, sure of themselves, sought-after. Lorimer ruefully reflected that he hadn't really been fair to –

His elbow was gripped, hard. He barely had the strength to hold on to Dymphna's glass. He felt obliged to utter a small gasp of pain as he was wheeled round, effortlessly, as if on a dance floor, being masterfully led.

'How's Mr Dupree?' Hogg asked, his big, lumpy face bland, and very close to Lorimer's. His breath smelt most odd, a mix of wine and something metallic, like Brasso, or some other powerful cleansing agent, or as if every cavity in his teeth had been freshly filled an hour ago. Hogg had also, improbably, tiny ruby jewels of shaving cuts on his left earlobe, his upper lip and another two centimetres down from his left eye. He must have been in a hurry.

'Mr Dupree in the pink, is he?' Hogg went on. 'Tip top, hale and hearty, full of piss and vinegar?'

'Ah,' Lorimer said weakly, 'you heard.'

'From the fucking POLICE,' Hogg said in a throat-grating whisper, his big simple features looming ever closer, almost out of focus. Lorimer held his ground: it was important not to flinch in the brunt of Hogg's verbal batterings, even though, if he thrust his face any further forward, they might as well be kissing. Hogg's mineral breath wafted off his cheeks, fanned his hair gently.

'I had no idea,' Lorimer said, resolutely. 'He agreed to meet. I figured I'd have it tied up –'

'– Nice choice of vocabulary, Black.' He prodded Lorimer in the chest with some force, hitting his right nipple square on, as if it were a bell-push. Lorimer winced, again. Hogg stepped back, his face a mask of loathing, of profound, metaphysical disgust. 'Sort it out. And keep it squeaky.'

'Yes, Mr Hogg.'

Lorimer swiftly gulped two glasses of wine at the bar, inhaled and exhaled deeply a few times, before heading back towards Dymphna and his colleagues. He saw Hogg across the room pointing him out to a fleshy-looking man in a hand-made pin-stripe suit with a pink tie. The man began to make his way towards him and Lorimer felt his throat tighten suddenly – What now? Police? No, surely not in bespoke tailoring? – and he ducked his head to suck at some of his wine as the fellow approached, smiling a thin, insincere smile. The face was puffy, strangely weather-beaten with the roseate, burny glow of burst capillaries around the cheeks and nostrils. Small, bright, unfriendly eyes. Closer to he saw that the man was really not that old after all, not much older than he was, he just seemed older. The motif on the man's pink tie, he noticed, was of tiny yellow teddy bears.

'Lorimer Black?' the man said, raising his deep voice, a lazy patrician drawl, to compete with the babble around them. Lorimer noticed that his lips barely moved, he spoke through his teeth, like an inept ventriloquist.

'Yes.'

'Stalk hilly virgin.' His mouth had opened a slit and these sounds had issued forth. These were the words Lorimer aurally registered. He proffered a hand. Lorimer juggled glasses, slopped wine, managed a brisk, damp shake.

'What?'

The man looked at him fixedly and the insincere smile grew marginally wider, marginally more insincere. He spoke again.

'Thought we'll heave the gin.'

Lorimer paused for the briefest of moments. 'Excuse me. What exactly do you mean?'

'Torn, we'll lever chain.'

'Look, I don't know what –'

'TALK, OR WE'LL LEAVE HER, JANE.'

'Jane who, for God's sake?'

The man looked about him in angry incredulity. Lorimer heard him say – this time quite distinctly – 'Jesus fucking Christ.' He fished in his pocket and produced a business card which he offered to Lorimer. It read: Torquil Helvoir-Jayne, Executive Director, Fortress Sure PLC.

'Tor-quil-hell-voyre-jayne,' Lorimer read out loud, as if barely literate, realizing. 'I'm so sorry, the ambient noise, I couldn't –'

'It's pronounced "heever",' the man said contemptuously. 'Not "hellvoyre". Heever.'

'Ah. I get it now. Torquil Helvoir-Jayne. Very pleased to –'

'I'm your new director.'

Lorimer handed Dymphna her glass, thinking only that he had to leave this place now, pronto. Dymphna did not look drunk but he knew she was, knew in his bones that she was deadly drunk.

'Where've you been, *mein Liebchen*?' she said.

Shane Ashgable leered over at him. 'Hogg was here looking for you.'

There was the sound of a gavel being beaten vigorously on a wooden block and a stertorous voice bellowed. 'A-ladies and a-gentlemen, pray silence for Sir Simon Sherriffmuir.' Genuinely enthusiastic applause appeared to break out from those crowded round the dais. Lorimer glimpsed Sir Simon stepping up to the podium, slipping on his heavy tortoiseshell half-moons and peering over them as he held up one hand for silence, the other producing a tiny slip of notepaper from a breast pocket.

'Well . . .' he said – pause, pause, theatrical pause – 'It's not going to be the same old place without Torquil.' Energetic laughter greeted this modest sally. Beneath its reverberations Lorimer edged towards the twin doors of the Portcullis Suite only to have his arm gripped at the elbow for the second time that evening.

'Lorimer?'

'Dymphna. I'm off. Must dash.'

'D'you fancy supper? Just the two of us. You and me.'

'I'm dining with my family,' he lied quickly, still moving. 'Another time.'

'And I'm going to Cairo tomorrow.' She smiled and

raised her eyebrows as if she had just provided the answer to a ridiculously easy question.

Sir Simon started talking about Torquil Helvoir-Jayne's contribution to Fortress Sure, his years of tireless service. Lorimer, filled with despair, gave Dymphna what he hoped was a forlorn, hey-life's-like-that smile and shrug.

'Sorry.'

'Yeah, another time,' Dymphna said, flatly, and turned away.

Lorimer requested that the taxi-driver actually raise the booming volume of the football match that was being broadcast on his radio and was thus driven – thunderously, stridently – through an icy and deserted City, over the black, surging, tide-turning Thames, south of the river, his head echoing and resonant with the commentator's raucous tenor voice detailing the angled crosses, the silky skills of the foreigners, the scything tackles, the grip on the game loosening, the lads giving it one hundred and ten per cent all the same. He felt alarmed, worried, stupid, embarrassed, surprised and achingly hungry. And he realized he hadn't drunk nearly enough. In such a state, he knew from past experience, the melancholy silent cell of a black cab is not the best place to be. Then a new and welcome sensation stealthily infiltrated itself into his being – as the sands of time drew to a close and the final whistle beckoned – drowsiness, lassitude, languor. Perhaps it would work tonight, perhaps it really would. Perhaps he would sleep.

114. Sleep. What was his name, that Portuguese poet who slept so badly? He called his insomnia, if I remember correctly, 'indigestion

*of the soul'. Perhaps this is my problem — indigestion of the soul —
even though I'm not a true insomniac? Gérard de Nerval said,
'Sleep takes up a third of our lives. It consoles the sorrows of our
days and the sorrow of their pleasures; but I have never felt any rest
in sleep. For a few seconds I am numbed, then a new life begins,
freed from the conditions of time and space, and doubtless similar
to that state which awaits us after death. Who knows if there is not
some link between those two existences and if it is not possible for
the soul to unite them now?' I think I know what he means.*

The Book of Transfiguration

'Dr Kenbarry, please,' Lorimer said to a suspicious porter.
He always over-articulated the name, unused as he was
to referring to Alan in this way. 'Dr Alan Kenbarry, he'll
be in the Institute. He's expecting me, Mr Black.'

The porter pedantically consulted dog-eared lists and
made two phone calls before he allowed Lorimer any
further into the Social Studies Department of the University of Greenwich. Lorimer rode the scuffed and litter-
strewn lift to Alan's demesne on the fifth floor, where he
found Alan waiting for him in the lobby, and then they
walked together through the dim passageways towards
the double swing doors blazoned with the inscription (in
a lower-case Bauhaus-style font) 'the institute of lucid
dreams', and on through the darkened lab towards
shrouded cubicles.

'Are we alone tonight, Doctor?' Lorimer asked.

'We are not. Patient F. is already installed.' He opened
the door to Lorimer's cubicle. 'After you, Patient B.'
There were six cubicles side by side in two rows of three
at the end of the laboratory. Wire rose from each to be
gathered centrally at a metal beam in a loose braid which

looped its way across the ceiling to the control area with its banks of tape recorders, stacks of winking monitors and EEGs. Lorimer had always used the same cubicle and had never encountered a fellow lab-rat. Alan liked it that way – no symptom-sharing, no exchange of placebos or special tricks. No gossip about that nice Doctor Kenbarry.

'How are we?' Alan asked, a solitary strip light somewhere turning his spectacle lenses into two white coins as he moved his head.

'We're quite tired, actually. The day from hell.'

'Poor baby. Your jim-jams are ready. Do we need to go to the loo?'

Lorimer undressed, carefully hung up his clothes and pulled on the clean cotton pyjama trousers. Alan reappeared a moment later with a flourished tube of ointment and a roll of transparent sticking plaster. Lorimer stood patiently as Alan busied himself with the electrodes: one to each temple, one below the heart, one on the wrist at the pulse.

Alan taped down the electrode on his chest. 'I think another little shave might be in order, before the next time. Bit bristly,' he said. 'There we are. Sweet dreams.'

'Let's hope so.'

Alan stood back. 'I've often thought we should attach one to the patient's cock.'

'Ha-ha. Lady Haigh said you woke her up this morning.'

'I was only putting the rubbish out.'

'She was cross. She called you a jackanapes.'

'The Jezebel. That's because she loves you. Everything OK?'

'Fine and dandy.' Lorimer crawled into the narrow

bed, while Alan stood at its foot, arms folded, smiling at him like an affectionate parent, the tableau marred only by his white coat – a complete affectation, Lorimer thought, wholly unnecessary.

'Any requests?'

'Waves on the beach, please,' Lorimer said. 'I won't need an alarm, I'll be out of here by eight.'

'Night, Big-Boy. Sleep well. I'll be here for an hour or so.'

He switched out the lights and left, leaving Lorimer in absolute darkness and in almost absolute silence. Each cubicle was thoroughly insulated and the noises that filtered through were so indistinct as to be unrecognizable. Lorimer lay in the dazzling darkness waiting for the photomatic flashes in front of his eyes to subside. He heard the tape of ocean breakers come on, the lulling susurrus of foam smashing on rock and sand, the plash and rattle of the pebbles in the undertow, as he settled his head deeper in the pillow. He *was* tired, what a disastrous day . . . He tried to keep his head clear of images of Mr Dupree and found instead that they were replaced by the unsmiling face of Torquil Helvoir-Jayne.

Now that was something else. A director, he had said, looking forward very much, challenging times, exciting developments ahead, and so on. Leaving the Fort to come to us. And he had always thought Hogg was the sole director, the big tuna – or at least the only visible one. Why would Hogg agree to that? It was Hogg's show, why would he tolerate someone like Helvoir – sorry, 'heevor' – Jayne? He seemed all wrong. Embarrassing moment, that. Lazy speaker, elocution lessons required, especially with a name like that. Torquilheeverjayne. Arrogant sort of shit. Snotty. Ego at large. Strange having someone like him about the office. Not quite our type. Seems all wrong. Torquil. Somehow foisted on Hogg? How could that happen? . . . This had to stop, he realized, or he'd never sleep. Change of subject required. That was why he was here. What to think about. Sex? Or Gérard de Nerval? Sex. Sex it was. Dymphna, sturdy, broad-shouldered, small-breasted Dymphna and her candid invitation. Right out of nowhere, that. Never would have dreamt. Trying to imagine Dymphna naked, the two of them making love. Those silly shoes. Strong, shortish legs. As he felt himself slipping away, going under, another image replaced that of Dymphna – a sliding diorama on a taxi's glossy door and above it a girl's face, a girl's wan, oval, perfect face, eager, hopeful, long-necked and wide-eyed –

Brutal knocking on the door, two harsh iron-knuckled raps, jerked him awake, alarmed. He sat upright, heart kicking, in impenetrable darkness, to the sound of notional waves breaking on a notional shore.

The lights went on and Alan came in, a resigned smile on his face, a printout in his hand.

'Woah,' he said, showing Lorimer a jagged mountain range. 'Almost broke a rib there.'

'How long was I out for?'

'Forty minutes. Was it the knock-on-the-door thing?'

'Yep. Someone's fist on that door. Bam-bam. Loud.'

Lorimer lay back, thinking that more and more often it was – for some unknown reason – the heavy noise of knocking, or of doorbells ringing or sounding that woke him these nights. Experience told him that this sort of awakening was a brusque portent of an end to sleep as well; he never seemed to drift off again, as if the shock of that rousing had so rattled and shaken his system that it required a full twenty-four hours to settle again.

'Absolutely fascinating,' Alan said. 'Tremendous hypnopompic reveries. Love it. Two knocks, you said?'

'Yes. Glad to be of help.'

'Were you dreaming?' He gestured at the dream diary by the bed. All dreams were to be logged, however fragmentary.

'No.'

'We'll keep on monitoring. Try and get back to sleep.'

'Whatever you say, Doctor Kenbarry.'

The waves rolled in. The darkness resumed. Lorimer lay in his narrow cell and thought this time about Gérard de Nerval. It did not work.

Chapter 2

As he turned the corner into Lupus Crescent, Lorimer saw Detective Sergeant Dennis Rappaport spring agilely from his car and take up a studied, lounging position, his back against a lamp-post, as if to indicate that this was a casual encounter, with little of the official about it. The day was one of pronounced greyness and coldness, with a low sky and a dead light that made even Detective Rappaport's unlikely Nordic looks appear drab and under attack. He was happy to be invited to come inside.

'So, you didn't come home last night,' Rappaport observed genially, accepting a mug of steaming, well-sugared, instant coffee from Lorimer – who managed to suppress his quip about the detective's uncanny powers of deduction.

'That's correct,' he said. 'I was participating in a research project, about sleep disorders. I'm a very light sleeper,' he added, pre-empting the detective's next observation. In vain.

'So, you're an insomniac,' Rappaport said. Lorimer noticed he had dropped his obsequious use of 'sir' and he wondered whether this was a good or bad sign. Rappaport smiled at him, sympathetically. 'Sleep like a top, I do. A spinning top. No problem. Out like a light. Head hits the pillow, out like a light. Sleep like a log.'

'I envy you.' Lorimer was sincere, Rappaport had no idea how sincere he was. Rappaport went on to enumerate some epic sleeps he had enjoyed, citing one sixteen-hour triumph on a white-water rafting holiday. He was a regular eight-hour-a-nighter, it transpired, so he claimed with some smugness. Lorimer had observed in the past how a confession of sleep dysfunctions often provoked this good-natured bragging. Few other ailments elicited a similar response. An admission of constipation did not engender proud boasts of regular bowel movements. A complaint about migraine, or acne, or piles, or a bad back generally produced sympathy, not a swaggering testimonial about the interlocutor's own good health. Sleep disorders did this to people, he noticed. It was almost talismanic, this guileless braggadocio, as if it were a form of incantation, protection against a profound fear of sleeplessness that lurked in everyone's lives, even the soundest of sleepers, such as the Rappaports of this world. The detective was now expounding on his ability to enjoy restorative catnaps if the demands of the job ever interrupted his restful, untroubled nights.

'Is there anything I can do for you, detective?' Lorimer asked gently.

Rappaport removed his notebook from his jacket pocket, and flicked through it. 'This is a very nice flat, you've got here, sir.'

'Thank you.' Back to business, Lorimer thought. Rappaport frowned at something he had written.

'How many visits did you make to Mr Dupree?'

'Just the one.'

'He had you booked in for two hours.'

'Quite normal.'

'Why so long?'

'It was to do with the nature of our business. It's time-consuming.'

'You're in insurance, I take it.'

'No. Yes. In a manner of speaking. I work for a firm of loss adjusters.'

'You're a loss adjuster, then.'

And you are a credit to the force, Lorimer thought, but he said merely, 'Yes. I'm a loss adjuster. Mr Dupree had made an insurance claim as a result of the fire. His insurance company —'

'Which is?'

'Fortress Sure.'

'Fortress Sure. I'm with Sun Alliance. And Scottish Widows.'

'Both excellent firms. Fortress Sure felt — and this happens all the time, it's almost routine — that Mr Dupree's claim was on the high side. They employ us to investigate it to see if the loss is in fact as great as it is claimed, and, if not, then to adjust it, downwards.'

'Hence the name "loss adjuster".'

'Exactly.'

'And your firm — G G H Ltd — is independent from Fortress Sure.'

'Not independent but impartial.' This was written in letters of stone. 'Fortress Sure does pay us a fee, after all.'

'Fascinating line of work. Thank you very much, Mr Black. That is most useful. I won't trouble you no further.'

Rappaport is either very clever or very stupid, Lorimer thought, standing hidden at the side of his bay window looking down at the detective's blond head as he descended the front steps, and I cannot decide which. Lorimer watched Rappaport pause in the street and light a cigarette. Then he stared frowning at the house

27

as if its façade might hold some clue to Mr Dupree's suicide.

Lady Haigh clambered up from her basement with two gleaming empty milk bottles and as she set them down by the dustbin at the top of the basement steps Lorimer saw Rappaport engage her in conversation. He knew, from the way Lady Haigh nodded her head in vigorous assent, that they were talking about him. And, although he also knew that his character would receive nothing but the staunchest backing from her, the discussion – it had moved on, Lady Haigh was now pointing crossly at a gigantic motorbike parked opposite – for some reason made him strangely uneasy. He turned away and went to wash out Rappaport's coffee mug in the kitchen.

37. Gérard de Nerval. On my first visit to the Institute of Lucid Dreams Alan asked me what I was currently reading and I told him it was a biography of Gérard de Nerval. Alan then instructed me that, as a conscious sleep-inducing device, I should either concentrate on the life of de Nerval or else indulge in sexual fantasies – one or the other. These were to be my choice of 'sleep triggers' and I should not deviate from them during my treatment at the Institute – it was to be de Nerval or sex.

Gérard de Nerval, Guillaume Apollinaire or Blaise Cendrars. Any one of them would have been apt. I am unnaturally interested in these French writers for one simple reason – they had all changed their names and reinvented themselves under new ones. They started out their lives, respectively, as Gérard Labrunie, Wilhelm-Apollinaris de Kostrowitzky, and Frédéric-Louis Sauser. Gérard de Nerval was closest to my heart, however: he had serious problems with sleep.

The Book of Transfiguration

Lorimer bought a hefty leg of lamb for his mother and then threw in two dozen pork sausages as well. In his family a gift of meat was prized above all others. Coming out of the butcher's, he hesitated in front of Marlobe's flower stall – just enough time, as it turned out, for Marlobe to catch his eye. Marlobe was talking to two of his cronies and smoking his horrible pipe with the stainless steel stem. As he spotted Lorimer he broke off his conversation in mid-sentence and, holding out a flower, called over, 'You won't find a sweeter-smelling lily in the country.'

Lorimer sniffed, nodded in agreement and resignedly offered to buy three stems, and Marlobe set about wrapping them up. His flower stall was a small, complicated wheeled contraption of folding doors and panels which, when opened, revealed several rows of stepped shelves filled with flower-crammed zinc buckets. Marlobe loudly claimed to believe in quality *and* quantity but interpreted this homily to mean lots of limited choice and consequently kept the range and type of flower he sold very small, not to say disappointingly banal. Carnations, tulips, daffodils, chrysanthemums, gladioli, roses and dahlias were all he was prepared to offer his customers, in or out of season, but he provided them in overwhelmingly large quantities (you could buy six dozen gladioli from Marlobe without clearing the stock) and in every colour available. His only concession to exoticism were lilies, in which he took particular pride.

Lorimer enjoyed flowers and bought them regularly for his flat but he disliked Marlobe's selection almost exclusively. The colours, also, were primary or lurid wherever possible (Marlobe was loudly derogatory of all pastel shades) on the assumption that vividness of hue was the main criterion of a 'good flower'. The same value system determined price: a scarlet tulip was more expensive than a pink one, orange rated higher than yellow, yellow daffodils fetched more than white and so on.

'You know,' Marlobe went on, rummaging in his pocket for change with one hand and holding the lilies with the other, 'if I had a Uzi, if I had a fucking Uzi, I'd fucking go into that place and fucking line them up against the wall.'

Lorimer knew he was talking about politicians and the Houses of Parliament. It was a familiar refrain, this.

'*Gnakka-gnakka-gnakka-gnak*,' the imaginary Uzi bucked and chattered in his hand, once Lorimer had relieved him of the lilies. 'I'd shoot every last fucking one of them, I would.'

'Thanks,' Lorimer said, accepting a palmful of warm coins.

Marlobe smiled at him. 'Have a nice day.'

For some bizarre reason, Marlobe liked him and always took the trouble to pass bitter comment on some aspect of contemporary life. He was a small, burly man, quite bald with a few traces of sandy, gingery hair around his ears and the nape of his neck and he had the permanent, faintly surprised, innocent look of the pale-lashed. Lorimer knew his name because it was painted on the side of his mobile flower cabana. When not selling flowers he would be engaged in loud, profane conversation with an odd selection of cronies, young and old, solvent and insolvent, who occasionally departed on mysterious errands for him or fetched him pints of lager from the pub on the corner. There was no floral competition within half a mile, and Marlobe, Lorimer knew, earned a handsome living and took holidays in places like the Great Barrier Reef and the Seychelles.

Lorimer bussed to Fulham. Up Pimlico Road to Royal Hospital Road, along King's Road, then Fulham Road to the Broadway. He avoided the tube at weekends – it seemed wrong somehow: the tube was for work – and there would be nowhere to park his car. He stepped off at some traffic lights on the Broadway and strolled up Dawes Road, forcing himself to recall details of his childhood and youth in these narrow and car-choked streets. He even detoured a quarter of a mile so he could contemplate his old school, St Barnabus, with its smirched, high, brick walls and its pitted asphalt playground. It was a valuable exercise in painful nostalgia and was really the primary reason why he sometimes accepted his mother's standing invitation to Saturday lunch (never Sunday lunch). It was like picking a scab off a sore; he actually wanted scar-tissue, it would be quite wrong to try and forget, to blank it all out. Every fraught memory that lurked here had played its role: everything he was today was an indirect result of the life he had led then. It confirmed the rightness of every step he had taken since his escape to Scotland . . . No, this was all becoming a little overblown, a little high-cheekboned and intense, he thought. It wasn't fair to burden Fulham and his family with all the responsibility of who he was today – what had happened in Scotland also carved out a sizeable slice of that particular cake.

Yet, as he turned off Filmer Road he felt a familiar heat, a searing, in his oesophagus – his indigestion problem, his heart burning. One hundred yards from his family home, his natal home, and it kicked in, the stomach acids started to bubble and seethe. For some people, for most people, he fondly supposed, such a return home would be signposted by a familiar tree (much shinned-up in childhood), or a carillon of church bells from across the green, or a cheery greeting from an elderly neighbour . . . But it was not for him: he sucked on a mint and gently punched his sternum and he rounded the corner to face the thin, wedge-shaped terrace. The small, mean parade of shops – the post office, the off-licence, the Pakistani grocer, the shuttered, out-of-business butchers, the estate agent – tapering to the pointed apex, number 36, with its dust-mantled pride of double-parked saloon cars and, on the ground floor, the frosted windows of 'B and B Mini-cabs and International Couriers'.

Some new fancy plastic name tag had been screwed above the bell-push since his last visit – black copperplate on smoked gold: 'FAMILY BLOCJ'. 'The J is silent' would have been the motto blazoned on the Blocj family escutcheon, if such a crest could be imagined, or alternatively, 'There is a dot under the C'. He could hear, coming through time, his father's patient, deep, accented voice, at innumerable post-office counters, holiday hotel reception desks, car rental franchises: 'The J is silent and there is a dot under the C. Family Blocj.' Indeed, how many times had he himself apologetically muttered the same instructions in his life? It did not bear thinking of – it was all behind him now.

He rang the bell, waited, rang again and eventually heard small feet pattering rhythmically down the stairs in irregular anapaests. His little niece, Mercy, opened the door. She was a tiny girl, bespectacled like every female member of his family, who looked about four years old, though in fact she was eight. He worried unceasingly for her, for her diminutiveness, her unfortunate name (short for Mercedes – which he always pronounced the French way, trying to forget that it was because her father, his brother-in-law, was the co-partner in the mini-cab firm) and her dubious destiny. Hugging the door, she stared at him, shy-curious.

'Hello, Milo,' she said.

'Hello, darling.' She was the only person he ever called 'darling', and then only when others were out of earshot. He kissed her twice on each cheek.

'Have you got anything for me?'

'Lovely sausages. Pork.'

'Oh, lovely.'

She stamped up the stairs and Lorimer followed wearily. The air in the flat seemed tart and briny with steam and spices. Apparently a TV, a radio and another source of rock music were playing simultaneously some-where. Mercedes preceded him into the long triangular front room, filled with light and sound, at the sharp end of the terrace directly above the 'B and B Mini-cabs and International Couriers' control room and the bull pen for the drivers. The music (middle-of-the-road country/ rock fusion) was playing in here on a dark, winking stack of audio equipment. The radio (shouting advertisement) emanated from the kitchen to his left, accompanied by the clatter and bang of energetic cookery.

'It's Milo,' Mercedes announced and his three sisters looked round lazily, three pairs of eyes dully register-ing him through three pairs of lenses. Monika was sewing, Komelia was drinking tea and Drava (Mercy's mother) was eating – astonishingly, given they were ten minutes away from lunch – eating a nut and chocolate bar.

As a child he had parodically burlesqued his three older sisters as, respectively, 'Bossy', 'Silly' and 'Sulky', or alternatively as 'the big one', 'the thin one' and 'the short one', such crude appellations strangely becoming ever more apposite as he and they aged. Being the baby of the family, he was routinely ordered around and importuned by these, to his memory, always-women. Even the youngest and prettiest, sullen, petite Drava, was six years older than him. Only Drava had married, produced Mercedes and then divorced; Monika and Komelia had always lived at home, working intermittently in the family businesses or part-time jobs. They were now full-time carers and, if either or both of them had a love life, it was lived secretly, somewhere far afield.

'Morning, ladies,' Lorimer said with feeble jocularity. They were all so much older than him: he saw them more as aunts rather than sisters, reluctant to believe the blood tie was so proximate, trying vainly to establish some genetic distance, some congenital breathing space.

'Mum, it's Milo,' Komelia bawled into the kitchen, but Lorimer was already heading that way, toting his solid bag of meat. His mother's wide frame blocked the doorway as she wiped her hands on a dishcloth, beaming moistly at him through the fogged lenses of her spectacles.

'Milomre,' she sighed, the love in her voice palpable and overwhelming, and she kissed him vigorously four times, the plastic frames of her glasses smiting his cheekbones two glancing blows each. Behind her, amongst the shuddering, steaming pans, Lorimer could see his grandmother chopping onions. She waved the knife at him, then pushed up her spectacles to knuckle away tears.

'See how I cry for joy to seeing you, Milo,' she said.

'Hello, Gran. Lovely to see you, too.'

His mother already had the lamb and sausages out on the work top, weighing the leg admiringly with her coarse rosy hands.

'He's a big joint that, Milo. Is they pork?'

'Yes, Mum.'

His mother turned to her mother and they spoke quickly in their language. By now Grandmother had dried her eyes and shuffled forward for her kisses.

'I say to her, ain't you looking smart, Milo. Ain't he smart, Mama.'

'He's a handsome. He's a rich. Not like them milkcow out there.'

'Go and see your papa,' his mother said. 'He'll be pleased to see you. In his parlour.'

Lorimer had to ask Mercy to move so he could open the door, as she was kneeling in front of it playing a computer game. As she slowly shifted Drava took the opportunity to sidle up to him and ask in a petulant, graceless voice if she could borrow forty pounds. Lorimer gave her two twenties but she had seen the slim wad in his wallet.

'Couldn't make it sixty, could you, Milo?'

'I need the money, Drava, it's the weekend.'

'It's my weekend too. Go on.'

He gave her another note and received a nod of acknowledgement, no word of thanks.

'You handing out, Milo?' Komelia called. 'We'd like a new telly, thanks.'

'Tumble drier, please, while you're at it,' Monika added. They both laughed shrilly, genuinely, as if, Lorimer thought, they could not take him seriously, that the person he had become was a subterfuge, one of Milo's curious games.

35

He had a short panic attack in the hall, practised his restorative breathing again. The television was also hollering from his father's 'parlour' down the corridor. Six adults and a child lived in this house ('Six females in one house,' his older brother Slobodan had said, 'it's too much for a man. That's why I had to get out, Milo, like you. My masculinity was suffocating'). He paused at the door – a sports programme, loud Australian voices on satellite (had he paid for that?) thundered beyond. He bowed his head, swearing to himself that he would not break down, and pushed the door open quietly.

His father seemed to be watching the screen (on which the green-blazered experts loudly debated); certainly his armchair had been placed squarely in front of it. He sat there motionless, in shirt and tie, trousers sharply creased, palms flat on the chair-arms, his unchanging smile framed by his trimmed white beard, his specs slightly askew, his thick, springy grey hair damp and flattened on his scalp.

Lorimer stepped forward and turned the volume low. 'Hello, Dad,' he said. His father's unreflecting, uncomprehending eyes stared at him, blinking once or twice. Lorimer reached forward and straightened the spectacles on his nose. He was always amazed at how dapper he looked; he had no idea how they did it, his mother and sisters; how they ministered to every need, bathed and shaved and pampered him, walked him about the house, parked him in his parlour, attended (with huge discretion) to his bodily functions. He did not know and he did not want to know, content to see this smiling homunculus the odd weekend in three or four, ostensibly happy and well cared for, distracted by daylong television, tucked up in bed at night and gently roused in the morning. Sometimes his father's eyes would follow you as you moved, sometimes not. Lorimer stepped to one side and Bogdan Blocj's head turned as if to contemplate his youngest son, tall and smart in his expensive blue suit.

'I'll put the volume back up, Dad,' he said. 'It's cricket, I think. You like cricket, don't you, Dad.' His mother claimed he heard and understood everything, she could see it in his eyes, she said. But Bogdan Blocj hadn't spoken a single word to anyone in over ten years.

'I'll let you get on then, Dad, take care.'

Lorimer stepped out of the parlour to find his brother Slobodan standing there in the hall, swaying slightly, his gut tight against his stretched sweat shirt, a smell of beer off him, his long silvered hair lank, the loose switch of his ponytail lying on his shoulder like a flung tie.

'Heyyyy, Milo.' He opened his arms and hugged him. 'Little bro. City gent.'

'Hi, Lobby,' he corrected himself. 'Slobodan.'

'How's Dad?'

'Seems fine, you know. You having lunch?'

'Nah, busy day. Match at Chelsea.' He put his surprisingly small hand on Milo's shoulder. 'Listen, Milo, you couldn't lend me a hundred quid, could you?'

17. A Partial History of the Blocj Family. Imagine some ancient fragments of stone unearthed in the desert, eroded, windblasted, sunbleached, upon which can be discerned some cryptic, runic lettering in a forgotten alphabet. Upon such tablets of stone might have been incised the history of my family, for the effort of deciphering them, of reconstructing meaning, has proved almost impossible to attain. Some years ago I embarked on months of dogged questioning of my mother and grandmother which allowed the story to advance a little further, but it was hard work, the oral history of my family was recalcitrant, barely comprehensible, as if uttered with huge reluctance in a language barely understood, with many gaps, solecisms and demotic errors.

We should start, because I can go no further back, in World War II, in Romania, Adolf Hitler's favourite ally. In 1941 the Romanian army annexes Bessarabia, on the northern shore of the Black Sea and renames the region Transnistria. It is used for the permanent resettlement of tens of thousands of Romania's Gypsy population. Forced transportation begins almost immediately and amongst the first to be dispatched is a young Gypsy girl in her late teens called Rebeka Petru, my grandmother. 'Yes, I am in train, in truck,' my grandmother told me, 'and I become Transnistrian. My papers say Transnistrian but in fact I am Gypsy, Tzigane, Rom.' I have never been able to glean any information at all about the pre-Transnistrian phase of her life, it is as if consciousness only evolved, her personal history began, the moment she jumped out of the cattle-truck that day on the banks of the river Bug. In 1942 she gave birth to a daughter, Pirvana, my mother. 'Who was her father, Gran?' I ask and watch with alarm as the tears form in her eyes. 'He's a good man. He killed by soldiers.' The only other fact I could learn about him was his name – Constantin. So Rebeka Petru and little Pirvana live out the war in routine terror and discomfort along with tens of thousands of other Transnistrian Gypsies. In order to survive they formed alliances of mutual help and support with other Rom families, prominent amongst whom were two orphaned brothers named Blocj. The youngest of the two brothers was called Bogdan. Their parents had died of typhus in the first transportations from Bucharest to Transnistria.

Then the war was finally over and the Gypsy diaspora was further dispersed in the massive, dispiriting migrations of populations in 1945 and '46 that occurred all over Europe. The Petrus and the Blocjs found themselves in Hungary, ending up in a small village south of Budapest, where the Blocj boys showed some elementary initiative as 'merchants', enabling the Rom in that corner of Hungary to survive, if not flourish. Ten years later, in 1956, Bogdan, now in his early twenties and an enthusiastic revolutionary, exploited the chaos of the Hungarian uprising to flee to the West with Rebeka and the fourteen-year-old Pirvana. 'What about his brother?' I questioned once. 'Oh, he stay. He happy to stay. In fact I think he go back to Transnistria,' my grandmother said. 'What was his name?' I asked. 'He was my uncle after all.' I remember my grandmother and my mother looked sharply at each other. 'Nicolai,' said my grandmother. 'Gheorgiu,' said my mother simultaneously, then added disingenuously, 'Nicolai-Gheorgiu. He was a bit . . . funny, Milo. Your dad was the good brother.'

In 1957 Rebeka, Pirvana and Bogdan arrived in Fulham via Austria as part of a quota of refugees from the Hungarian revolution given a home by the British government. Bogdan wasted no time in resuming his entrepreneurial activities, establishing a small import-export business with the communist states of Eastern Europe called EastEx, trading in whatever meagre toing-and-froing of goods that was permitted – cleaning fluids, aspirins and laxatives, kitchen utensils, tinned food, vegetable oil, tools – a clapped-out reconditioned lorry making the difficult run to Budapest, initially, and then expanding modestly over the years to Bucharest, Belgrade, Sofia, Zagreb and Sarajevo.

It was inevitable that Bogdan should marry Pirvana after what they had been through together. And it was Pirvana who stood by his side in the early days of EastEx, wrapping cardboard boxes in brown paper, stacking them on pallets, loading the truck, labelling the cartons, supplying the Thermos of clear soup to the driver, while above them in the tiny flat Rebeka cooked meat, stews and goulash, salted hams and made a spicy variation of blood sausage which she sold to other immigrant families in Fulham who yearned for an authentic taste of home.

Slobodan arrived in 1960, duly and speedily followed by Monika, Komelia, Drava and, eventually, after a longish gap, little Milomre.

EastEx gamely flourished in an unexceptional way and over the years Bogdan diversified, adding a small haulage division, a smaller van and truck hire company and a mini-cab firm to the EastEx's roster. A larger apartment was required for the growing family and the kids were fervently encouraged to become English men and women. Bogdan decreed that no Hungarian or Romanian was to be spoken – although Pirvana and Rebeka would still chat covertly to each other in their special dialect which even Bogdan could not understand.

And this is how I remember it: the big, crowded, triangular flat, the ever-present smell of cooking meat, the frowsty, chilly reek of the EastEx warehouse, school in Fulham, promise of a role in one of the family's always somewhat struggling businesses, the constant incantation of, 'Now you are English boy, Milo. This is your country, this is your home.' But what of the enigmas that remained? My grandmother's early youth, grandfather Constantin, my shady uncle, Nicolai-Gheorgiu? I read a rare history of the Transnistrian Gypsies and came to understand a little of the horrors and the hardships they must have endured. I read also of the gendarmerie commanders in Transnistria, cruel, petty tyrants who dominated and exploited their transplanted populations, and who 'lived in debauchery with beautiful Gypsy women'. I looked at my wily old grandmother and thought of the beautiful teenager who must have stumbled from the cattle-trucks by the banks of the river Bug wondering what had happened to her life and what fate lay in store for her . . . Perhaps to be confronted by a handsome young gendarmerie officer named Constantin . . . I will never know, I will never know more than this. All my questions were met with shrugs or silences or sly deflections. My grandmother would say to me as I pestered her for more information: 'Milo, we have saying in Transnistria: when you eat the honey do you ask bee to show you the flower?'

The Book of Transfiguration

Ivan Algomir's shop was on the north side of Camden Passage, behind the arcade, to the left. Its two windows contained one spotlit object each – a studded painted chest in one, and a small brass cannon in the other. The shop was called VERTU and emanated such a daunting aura of the exquisite and pretentious that Lorimer wondered how anyone dared to cross its threshold. He remembered his first visit well, how he had dithered, hummed and hawed, visited the Design Centre, circled back, searched for excuses to go elsewhere, but had finally surrendered to the irresistible lure of the dented Norman basinet (£1,999) which stood on its high pedestal, starkly lit in the sepulchral gloom of the vitrine (which he had sold last year, finally and reluctantly, but for a considerable profit).

He had not planned to come up to Islington; it had been a long and tedious ride from Fulham, landing him with a £23.50 taxi fare, impeded and harassed by Saturday shoppers, football fans, and those strange souls who chose to take their cars out only on weekends. Up Finborough Road to Shepherd's Bush roundabout, on to the A40, past Madame Tussauds, Euston, King's Cross, along Pentonville Road to the Angel. Half way through the journey, as the cab driver gamely tried and abandoned a route north of Euston, he had wondered why he was bothering, but he sorely needed cheering up after his lunch at home (a meal that had cost him, in various loans and donations, some £275, he had calculated) and, furthermore, Stella didn't want him to come over until after nine. Turning north and then south, accepting the taxi-driver's baffled apologies for the traffic ('Nightmare, mate, nightmare'), he realized that, increasingly, his life was composed of these meandering trajectories across

this enormous city, these curious peregrinations. Pimlico-
-Fulham, now Fulham–Islington, and two more awaited
him before the journeying could stop: Islington–Pimlico,
then Pimlico–Stockwell. Up North of the Park and then
South of the River – these were boundaries, frontiers he
was crossing, not merely itineraries, names on the map;
he was visiting city-states with their different ambiences,
different mentalities. This was how a city routinely
appeared to its denizens, he considered, rather than to
its visitors, its transients and tourists. If you lived in the
place it existed for you as a great matrix, an ever-more-
complex web of potential routes. This was how you
grappled with its size, how you attempted to make it
submit to your control. Come to dinner in . . . There's a
meeting at . . . Pick me up from . . . See you outside . . .
It's not far from . . . And so on. Each day threw up its set
of route conundrums: how to get from A to B, or F, or
H, or S, or Q – a sophisticated formula that factored-
in local knowledge, public or private transport, traffic
conditions, roadworks, time of day or night, priorities of
speed or calm, brutal expediency or more relaxed
sagacity. We are all navigators, he thought, quite pleased
with the romantic associations of the metaphor, millions
of us, all finding our individual ways through the labyrinth. And tomorrow? Stockwell–Pimlico, and then
perhaps he should stay put, though he knew that he
should really go further east, to Silvertown, and start
thinking about the décor and furnishing for the new
flat.

Ivan had spotted him and stuck his death's head out
of his smoked glass door.

'Lorimer, my dear fellow, you'll freeze.'

Ivan was wearing a biscuity tweed suit and a floppy,

oyster-grey bow-tie ('You have to dress the part for this job,' he had said slyly, 'and I think you know exactly what I mean, don't you, Lorimer?'). The shop was dark, walls covered with chocolate-brown hessian or else darkly varnished exposed brick. It contained very few, hilariously expensive objects – a globe, a samovar, an astrolabe, a mace, a lacquered armoire, a two-handed sword, some icons.

'Sit down, laddie, sit down.' Ivan lit one of his small cigars and shouted upstairs, 'Petronella? Coffee, please. Don't use the Costa Rica.' He smiled at Lorimer, showing his awful teeth and said, 'Definitely the time of day for Brazil, I would say.'

Ivan was, to Lorimer, the living, breathing representation of the skull beneath the skin, his head a gaunt assemblage of angles, planes and declivities somehow supporting a pendulous nose, large, bloodshot eyes and a thin-lipped mouth with a partial set of skewed brown teeth that seemed designed for a larger jaw altogether, an ass's or a mule's, perhaps. He smoked between twenty and thirty small, malodorous cigarlettes each day, never seemed to eat and drank anything on a whim – whisky at 10 a.m., Dubonnet or gin after lunch, port as an aperitif ('*Très français*, Lorimer') and had a rare, distressing, body-racking cough that seemed to rise from his ankles and made its appearance at roughly two-hourly intervals, after which he often went and sat quietly alone in a corner for some minutes. But those rheumy, bulging eyes were alive with malice and intelligence and somehow his feeble frame endured.

Ivan began to enthuse about 'almost an entire garniture' he was assembling. 'It'll go straight to the Met or the Getty. Amazing the stuff coming out of Eastern

Europe – Poland, Hungary. Turning out the attics. Might have a couple of things for you, old chum. Lovely closed helm, Seusenhofer, with beavor.'

'I'm not so keen on the closed.'

'Wait till you see this. I wouldn't wear a white shirt with that tie, my dear old china, you look like an undertaker.'

'I was having lunch with my ma. Only a white shirt will convince her you're in gainful employ.'

Ivan laughed until he coughed. Coughed until he stopped, swallowed phlegm, patted his chest and drew heavily on his cheroot. 'God love me,' he said. 'Know exactly what you mean. Let's have a look at our little treasure, shall we?'

The helmet was of average size and the bronze had tarnished and aged to a dirty jade, encrusted and flaky, as if it were covered by a vibrantly coloured form of lichen. The curved cheek plates were almost flush with the nose guard and the eye holes were almond-shaped. It was more like a mask than a helmet, a metal domino, and Lorimer supposed that was another reason why he instantly coveted it, why he desired it so. The face beneath would be almost invisible, just a gleam from the eyes and the lines of the lips and chin. He stood staring at it, some ten feet away from where it had been placed on a thin plinth. A small two-inch spike rose from the centre of the cranium.

'Why's it so expensive?' he asked.

'It's nearly three thousand years old, my dear friend. And, and it's got some of its plume left.'

'Nonsense.' Lorimer approached. Some strands of horsehair trailed from the spike. 'Come off it.'

'I could sell it to three museums tomorrow. No, four. All right, twenty-five. Can't say fairer. I'm making almost nothing.'

'Unfortunately, I've just bought a house.'

'Man of property. Where?'

'Ah . . . Docklands,' Lorimer lied.

'I don't know a soul who lives in Docklands. I mean, isn't it just a teensy bit *vulgaire*?'

'It's an investment.' He picked the helmet up. It was surprisingly light, one cut sheet of bronze, beaten thin, then shaped to fit a man's head, to cover everything from the nape of the neck and the jawbone up. He knew infallibly whenever he wanted to buy a helmet – the urge to put it on was overpowering.

'Funerary, of course,' Ivan said, breathing smoke at him. 'You could chop through this with a bread knife – no protection at all.'

'But the illusion of protection. The almost perfect illusion.'

'Fat lot of good that'd do you.'

'It's all we've got in the end, isn't it? The illusion.'

'Far too profound for me, dear Lorimer. It is a lovely thing, though.'

Lorimer replaced it on its stand. 'Can I think about it?'

'As long as you don't take for ever. Ah, here we are.'

Petronella, Ivan's remarkably tall, plain wife, with a rippling swathe of thick, dry, blonde hair down to her waist, came percussively down the stairs with a tray of coffee cups and a steaming cafetière.

'That's the last of the Brazil. Good afternoon, Mr Black.'

'We call him Lorimer, Petronella. No standing on ceremony.'

270. *The current collection: a German black sallet; a burgonet (possibly French, somewhat corroded) and, my special favourite, a*

barbute, Italian, marred only by the absence of the rosette rivets and
so ringed with holes. It was the strange music of this lost vocabulary
that drew me first to armour, to see what things these magical words
actually described, to discover what was a pauldron, a couter, a
vambrace and fauld, or tasset, poleyn and greave, beavor, salleret,
gorget and besague. I derive a genuine thrill when Ivan says to
me: 'I've an interesting basinet with letten fleurons and with,
astonishingly, the original aventail – though of course the vervelles
are missing,' and I know exactly – exactly – what he means. To
own an armour, a suit entire, is an impossible fantasy (though I
once bought a vambrace and couter of a child's armour, and a
shaffron from a German horse armour) so I settled instead for
armour of the head, on helms and helmets, developing a particular
taste for visorless helmets, the sallets and kettle hats, basinets,
casques, spangenhelms and morions, burgonets, barbutes and –
another dream, this – the frog-mouthed and the great helms.

The Book of Transfiguration

Stella shifted beside him, her knee touching his thigh,
making it hot almost immediately, so he slid another
couple of inches away from her. She was asleep, soundly,
deeply, a small snore gently emanating from time to time.
He squinted at the luminous figures on his watch dial.
Ten to four: the endless dark centre of the night, that
period of time when it is too early to get up, too late to
read or work. Perhaps he should make a cup of tea?
It was at moments like these that Alan had told him
consciously to note and analyse what was going on in his
mind, systematically, one by one. So what was going on
in there? . . . The sex had been good enough, sufficiently
prolonged to send Mrs Stella Bull off to sleep almost
immediately, Lorimer reflected. He had been intensely

irritated by the visit to his family but that always applied, and, equally true, seeing his father like that always unsettled him, but that was hardly out of the ordinary . . . He enumerated other subject headings. Health: fair. Emotional? Nothing, as it should be. Work? Mr Dupree's death – very bad. Hogg, Helvoir-Jayne – all a bit uncertain, unresolved, there. Hogg seemed more than usually on edge and that communicated itself to everyone. And now the Dupree business . . . Solvency? There would be no bonus now on the Dupree case even if Hogg had been prepared to share it with him; Hogg wouldn't let him deal with the estate – that was normal practice, it would go through now, unadjusted. The house in Silvertown had swallowed up almost all his capital, but there would be more work along shortly. So what was it? What was there in that macédoine of niggles and worries, shames, resentments and preoccupations that left him alert and tireless at four in the morning? Standard anxiety-insomnia, Alan would say, too much going on.

He slipped out of bed and stood naked in the bedroom dark wondering whether to half-dress or not. He pulled on Stella's towelling dressing gown – the sleeves ended in mid-forearm and his knees were showing but it would do as precautionary decency. Stella's daughter Barbuda was still away at school so the coast was clear, in theory. Barbuda had walked into the kitchen late one night, sleepy and pyjamaed as he had searched the fridge, naked, looking urgently for something savoury to eat. It was not an encounter he wanted to repeat and it was fair to say that things had never been quite the same between them since then, in fact he thought Barbuda's previous indifference had turned, after that chance meeting, to a peculiar form of hate.

47

Waiting for the kettle to boil, he tried not to think of that night nor of what degree of tumescence he had or had not displayed. He stared out at a corner of the brightly lit scaffolding yard visible through the kitchen window. A tight row of flat-bed lorries, the enormous shelves of planks and pipes, the skips filled with clamps and extenders . . . He remembered his first visit here, on business, one of his early 'adjusts'. Stella walking him coldly round the yard, £175,000 worth of material stolen. Everything had been painted the Bull Scaffolding colours, 'cerise and ultramarine', she had assured him. She had been away on a Caribbean holiday. The security guard had been pounced on, bound up and had watched helpless as the team of villains had driven off three trucks laden with the requirements of next day's scaffolding job, an entire tower block's worth in Lambeth.

It was an obvious con, a clear scam, Lorimer had decided, a cash-flow problem needing to be speedily resolved, and with anyone else he would have been confident that the £50,000 cash he was carrying in his briefcase would have proved too tempting. But it soon became equally obvious that this small, wiry, blonde woman with the hard but oddly pretty face was, in loss adjuster's parlance, 'nuclear' through and through. 'Nuclear' from 'nuclear shelter' – impermeable, unyielding, impregnable. She was proud: a single woman, no support, her own business, a ten-year-old daughter – all bad signs. He returned to Hogg and reported his conclusions. Hogg had openly scoffed and had gone back himself the next day with £25,000. 'Just you watch,' he had said, 'those lorries are parked up in a warehouse in Eastbourne or Guildford.' The next day he called Lorimer in. 'You were right,' he said, chastened somehow.

'A grade-A nuclear. Don't get many like that.' He allowed Lorimer to be the bearer of the good news. Rather than telephone (he was curious, he wanted to check her out further, this genuine grade-A nuclear) he drove back to the Stockwell depot and told her Fortress Sure would honour her claim. 'I should fucking well think so,' Stella Bull had said, and then asked him to supper.

He sipped at his scalding tea, one sugar, slice of lemon. They had been sleeping together, off and on, for nearly four years now, Lorimer reflected. It was by far and away the longest sexual relationship of his life. Stella liked him to come to her house (Mr Bull, an obscure figure, was long ago divorced and forgotten), where she would cook a meal, drink a lot, watch a video or late-night television, then go to bed and make fairly orthodox love. The visits sometimes extended into the next day: breakfast, shopping 'up West', or lunch in a pub – a pub on the river was what she particularly liked – and then they would go their separate ways. They had spent perhaps five weekends together in three years and then Barbuda went to boarding school near Reigate. Since then, during term-time, Stella had taken to calling more regularly, once or even twice a week. The routine did not change and Lorimer was intrigued to note that its increased regularity had made nothing pall. She worked hard, did Stella Bull, as hard as anyone he knew – there was good money to be made in scaffolding.

He exhaled, feeling suddenly sorry for himself, and switched on the television. He caught the end of a pro-gramme devoted to American football – the Buccaneers against the Spartans, or something similar – and watched it uncomprehendingly, happily diverted. He brewed up again when the commercials came on. This time it was the music that drew him back to the screen, a familiar piece, both surging and plangent – rejigged Rachmaninov or Bruch, he guessed – and as he tried to remember he found his attention drawn by the images, pondering vaguely what on earth this clip could be advertising. An ideal couple at expensive play. He: dark, Gypsy-ish; she: laughing blonde, forever tossing and flicking her big hair. Sepia, then heightened colour, much camera tilt. Yacht, skis, scuba-diving. Holidays? A sleek motor on an empty autobahn. Cars? Tyres? Oil? No, now restaurant food, tuxedos, meaningful looks. Liqueur? Champagne? His hair was luminously shaggy. Shampoo? Conditioner? That smile. Dental floss? Plaque detector? Now the fellow – bare-chested, in morning light – smilingly waves off his beauty in her nippy sports car from his mews pad. But turns away, suddenly miserable, angst-ridden, full of self-loathing. His life, despite all this expensive sex, fun, play and consumerism, is clearly a sham, empty, bogus to the core. But then, at the end of the mews, another girl appears with a suitcase. Dark, seriously pale, chic, simply dressed, shorter glossy hair. Music soars. They run to each other, embrace. Lorimer was completely obsessed by now. Sonorous, throaty voice, caption fades up: 'IN THE END THERE IS ONLY ONE CHOICE. STAY TRUE TO YOURSELF. FORTRESS SURE.' Good God Almighty. But in the whirling, slow-motion embrace he had seen something that both disturbed and moved him in its serendipity. The slim, dark girl at the end of the cobbled mews. The girl returning to the morose hunk. He had seen her not forty-eight hours ago, he was sure of it: she was, indubitably, mystifyingly, the girl in the back of the taxi.

Chapter 3

The phone on Lorimer's desk rang: it was Hogg, bluntly ordering, 'Up here, sunshine.' Lorimer took the fire stairs to the floor above, where he discovered that the configuration of the place had been altered over the weekend: Hogg's secretary, Janice – a plump, cheerful woman, with enormous green joke spectacles, iron-wool hair and a jangling charm bracelet on each wrist – and her typing-pool (an ever-changing cycle of temps) had been moved across the hall from her boss, and three large grey filing cabinets, like standing stones, were now parked in the corridor outside her new office. Rajiv and his young assistant Yang Zhi had also been displaced – neat stacks of cardboard boxes with cryptic serial numbers stencilled on their sides were being carried to and fro. The ambience was one of mild chaos and peppery irritation. Lorimer could hear Rajiv shouting at his secretary with unfamiliar emotion.

'One sugar and a slice of lemon, isn't it, Lorimer? Digestive or Garibaldi?'

'Yes, please. But no biscuits, thanks, Janice. What's going on?'

'Mr Helvoir-Jayne moving in.' She emphasized the 'heever' with some vehemence. 'He needed a bigger office so I've moved, Rajiv's moved, and so on.'

'Musical chairs.'

'I think that would be altogether more jolly, Lorimer, if I may be so bold. He's ready for you.'

Lorimer carried his tea into Hogg's office, a large but spartan place, as if furnished from some 1950s, low-grade, civil-service catalogue, everything at once solid but nondescript, apart from a vivid orange sunburst carpet on the floor. The dusty reproductions on the ivory walls were Velazquez, Vermeer, Corot and Constable. Hogg was standing at a window, gazing fixedly down at the street.

'If that stupid arsehole thinks he can park there . . .' he said, musingly, without turning.

Lorimer sat and sipped quietly at his tea. Hogg wrenched open the window, admitting a keen draught of wintry air.

'Excuse me,' he shouted. 'Yes, you. You cannot park there. It's reserved. You cannot park there. Do you speak English? Well, understand this: I am calling the police now. Yes, YOU!'

He closed the window and sat down, his pale face dead, and took a cigarette – untipped – from a silver box on his desk, tapped an end a couple of times on a thumb-nail and lit it, inhaling avidly.

'There are some stupid fucking bastards loose on this earth, Lorimer.'

'I know, Mr Hogg.'

'As if we don't have enough to cope with.'

'Exactly.'

Hogg dipped a hand into a drawer and pitched a green file at him across the desk. 'Get your incisors into this. A right shagger.'

Lorimer reached for the folder and felt a small hammer

of excitement vibrate through him. What do we have here? he thought, admitting that this curiosity was one of the few reasons he stayed in the job, this thrill of unknown encounters and experiences ahead – this and the fact that he couldn't think what else he might do with his life. Hogg stood up, tugged fiercely at his jacket and began to pace steadily up and down the length of his vivid carpet. He smoked his cigarette rapidly, with a small flourish, a little shooting of the cuff of the smoking arm as he brought the cigarette to his lips. Hogg, rumour had it, had been in the services in his youth; certainly, he always praised military types and virtues, and Lorimer wondered now if it might have been the navy – he smoked very strong navy cut cigarettes and there was something of the captain on the poop deck about the way he paced his ground.

'Hotel fire,' he said. 'Severe damage. Twenty-seven million.'

'Jesus.'

'And I don't think we should pay a penny. Not a red cent. Smells bad to me, Lorimer, nasty, nasty pong coming off of this one. Nip down and see what you think. It's all in the dossier.' He skipped nimbly over to the door, opened it and closed it again.

'Did you, ah, meet our Mr Helvoir-Jayne?' Hogg's stab at ingenuousness was laughable, as he studied the smouldering end of his cigarette intently.

'I did. Just a few words. Seems a very amiable –'

'I'm convinced his arrival here as co-director and this hotel fire are connected.'

'I don't understand.'

'Nor do I, Lorimer, nor do I. The mist clears in the

53

paddy field but we still do not see the leopard. But just you bear my observation in mind.' Hogg leered at him, 'Softly, softly catchee monkey.'

'Who's the monkey? Not Mr Helvoir-Jayne?'

'My lips are sealed, Lorimer.' He edged closer. 'How can you drink English tea with lemon? Disgusting. I thought there was an alien smell in this room. You want to put milk in your tea, Lorimer, else people will think you're a nancy boy.'

'People have only been milking their tea for a hundred years.'

'Raw bollocks, Lorimer. Heard anything on the Dupree front?'

'Nothing.' Reminded, Lorimer asked him about the Fortress Sure advertisement. Hogg had never heard of it, or seen it, but he said he did remember some recent campaign that had not pleased the board (Hogg had some connection with the board of Fortress Sure, Lorimer recalled) and it had either been rejected or consigned to less prominent slots while a staider or less flashy message was developed. It had cost an arm and a leg, Hogg said, and somebody had been royally shafted. Perhaps that was the one? Lorimer considered that indeed it might have been and he thought pleasantly about the girl again, thought about the luck of him rising that early, the pleasing coincidence.

Hogg settled a large haunch on the corner of his desk. 'Are you an aficionado of television commercials, Lorimer?'

'What? Ah, no.'

'We make the world's best television commercials in this country.'

'Do we?'

'At least we can be proud of something,' Hogg said with some bitterness, swinging his leg. Lorimer saw that Hogg was wearing slim loafers, very un-naval, no more than slippers, really, which made his feet look small and delicate for such a burly, hefty man. Hogg noticed the direction of his gaze.

'What the hell are you looking at?'

'Nothing, Mr Hogg.'

'You got anything against my shoes?'

'Not at all.'

'You shouldn't stare at people's feet like that, it's damned insolent. The height of rudeness.'

'Sorry, Mr Hogg.'

'You still got your sleep problems?'

'Yes, afraid so. I'm going to a sort of clinic, sleep disorder thing, see if I can get it analysed.'

Hogg walked him companionably to the door. 'Take care of yourself, Lorimer.' He smiled one of his rare smiles at him – it was as if he were trying out a recently learned facial gesture. 'You're an important, nay, a key member of G G H. We want you in tip-top condition. Tip-top, man, tip-top.'

257. *Hogg rarely compliments you, and you know that when he does you accept it gracelessly, suspiciously, as if you are being set up in some way, or as if a trap has started to spring.*

The Book of Transfiguration

Lorimer saw from his map that the hotel was just off the Embankment, just back from the river between Temple Lane and Arundel Street with, perhaps, an angled view of half the National Theatre on the far bank. According to the file it was a development of a property company called Gale-Harlequin PLC and was to be known, improbably, as the Fedora Palace. The building had been three-quarters completed when fire had broken out on the eighth and ninth floors late one night in what was to be the duplex gym and sauna facility. It quickly spread, completely destroying three other furnished and finished floors below with considerable collateral damage due to smoke and the thousands of gallons of water needed to extinguish it. The claim was in for £27 million. A structural engineer's report indicated that it might be cheaper to demolish the building and start again. This was the new way with insurance: repayment in kind. You 'lose' your watch on holiday and make a claim – we give you a new watch, not money. Your hotel burns down and you call the company – why, we rebuild your hotel for you.

Lorimer decided to walk down to the river; it was still cold but there were shreds of lemony sunshine breaking through the ragged clouds that were being bustled westwards across the city by a stiffish breeze. He strode briskly down Beech Street rather enjoying the cold on his face, collar up, hands deep in his flannel-lined pockets. Should have a hat on, eighty per cent of heat lost through the head. What kind of hat, though, with a pin-striped suit and a covert coat? Not a brown trilby, look like he was going to the races. A bowler? He must ask Ivan, or Lady Haigh. Ivan would say a bowler, he knew. In summer you could wear a panama, or could you?

It was round about Smithfield Market that the sensation crept up on him, the strange feeling that he was being followed. It was like those times when you're convinced someone has called your name, you say 'Yes?' and turn but no one steps forward. He sheltered in a shop doorway, looking back the way he came. Strangers hurried by – a girl jogger, a soldier, a beggar, a banker – and continued on their ways. But the sensation was undeniable, all the same: what alerts you? he wondered, what sets it off? A particular pattern of footstep, perhaps, persistently in your aural range, neither overtaking nor falling back. He moved out of his doorway and made for the Fedora Palace – there was no one following him. Fool. He smiled at himself – Hogg's paranoia was infectious.

From the outside the hotel didn't look too bad, just blurry soot scorches on the window embrasures up high, but when the site manager showed him round the scarred and blackened gymnasium space, the buckled and blistered floor, he had acknowledged the sheer efficiency of fire, the potency of its destructive force. He peered into the central service and lift shaft: it looked like a smart-bomb had swooped down and detonated itself. The heat had been so intense that the concrete cladding of the shaft had actually started to explode. 'And concrete is not normally noted for its percussive qualities,' the manager observed soberly. It was worse on the burnt-out, completed floors: here the damage was recognizably domestic – charred beds, sodden, blackened shreds of carpet and curtain – and, somehow, more pathetically relevant and wasteful. Overlaying it all was the sour, lung-penetrating stink of damp soot and smoke.

'Well,' Lorimer said, feebly. 'About as bad as it gets. When were you meant to open?'

'Next month, or thereabouts,' the site manager said cheerfully. He was not a worried man, it wasn't his hotel.

'Who were the contractors?'

It turned out that the fitting-out of various floors had been subcontracted in the interests of speed: the upper floors were being done by a firm called Edmund, Rintoul Ltd.

'Any problems with them?'

'Some hassle with a stack of Turkish marble. Delayed. Quarry on strike or something. Usual cock-ups. They had to fly out there theirselves, chase it up.'

Down below in a Portakabin Lorimer was given copies of the relevant contracts, just to be on the safe side, and surrendered his hard hat. Hogg was right: there was a smell off this one and it wasn't smoke damage. One visit to Edmund, Rintoul Ltd should confirm it, he reckoned. This had the air of an old, familiar scam, some ancient chicanery, but the scale was all wrong – perhaps a modest bit of routine deceit that had gone hideously out of control, exploding into something from a disaster movie. Hogg was over-confident in one area, though: they would be paying out a few red cents on this one; the question was, how much?

He heard the soft chirrup of his mobile phone in his jacket pocket.

'Hello?'

'Lorimer Black?'

'Yes.'

'Fraught, we'd seal the drain.'

'Hello there.'

'You free for lunch? I'll pop down to you. Chol-mondley's?'

'Ah. All right. Sounds good.'

'Brilliant. See you at one.'

Lorimer beeped Helvoir-Jayne back into the ether and frowned to himself, recalling Hogg's ambiguous suspicions. First day in the office and he wants lunch with Lorimer Black. And where do I happen to be?

Cholmondley's looked like a cross between a sports pavilion and an oriental brothel. Dark, from the rattan blinds that shrouded the windows and copious date palms in every corner, it boasted roof fans and bamboo furniture warring with battered sporty memorabilia – peat-brown cricket bats and crossed oars, wooden tennis racquets, sepia team photos and ranked split-cane fishing rods. The staff, men and women, wore striped butcher's aprons and boaters (could you wear a boater with a city suit?). Country and Western ballads thudded almost inaudibly from hidden speakers.

Helvoir-Jayne was already at the table, half way through a celery-sprouting bloody mary and unwrapping the cellophane from a pack of cigarettes, just brought to him by a waitress. He waved Lorimer over.

'Do you want one of these? No? Well, we'll have a bottle of house red and house white.' A shocking thought seemed to occur to him, and he froze. 'It's not English wine, is it?'

'No, sir.' She was foreign, Lorimer heard, a thin, somehow stooped young girl with a sallow, tired face.

'Thank Christ. Bring the wine then come back in ten minutes.'

Lorimer held out his hand.

'What's going on?' Helvoir-Jayne looked at him, baffled.

'Welcome to GGH.' Lorimer kept forgetting they didn't like to shake hands so he rolled his wrist vaguely, creating a standard gesture of welcome, instead. 'Missed you at the office.' He sat down, refusing Helvoir-Jayne's

59

offer of a cigarette. Automatically, he did a quick inventory: maroon, motif-sprinkled, silk tie, off-the-rail pale pink cotton shirt, badly ironed, but monogrammed THJ, on the lip of the breast pocket, oddly, French cuffs, gold cufflinks, no silly braces, signet ring, tassled loafers, pale blue socks, slightly too small, old, off-the-peg, double-breasted pin-stripe dark blue suit with twin vents, designed for a thinner Helvoir-Jayne than the one opposite him. They were both dressed almost identically, right down to the signet ring; apart from the socks – Lorimer's were navy blue – and both his double-breasted pin-striped suit and his shirt were hand-made. Furthermore, his shirt had no breast pocket and his monogram – LMBB – which had been discreetly placed on his upper arm, like an inoculation scar, had been removed since the day Ivan Algomir had told him that monogrammed shirts were irredeemably common.

'Sorry to bug you on day one,' Helvoir-Jayne said. 'By the way, you must, simply must, call me Torquil. Anyway, I had to get out of that place. What a bunch of fucking geeks.'

Torquil. Torquil it would be, then. 'Who? What geeks?'

'Our lot. Our colleagues. And that girl, Dinka, Donkna? Where do they dig them up from?'

'Dymphna. They're all very good at their job, actually.'

'Thank God for you, that's all I can say. Red or white?'

Torquil was eating spicy Cumberland sausages with mash; Lorimer was pushing bits of over-dressed, char-grilled Thai chicken salad around a black papier mâché bowl when the waitress approached with a jar of mustard on a saucer.

'We'll have another bottle of red,' Torquil said, accepting the mustard, then, 'Hold your horses, my lovely. This is French mustard. I want English.'

'This is only one we have.' She sounded Eastern European to Lorimer's ear. She seemed to be carrying a whole history of weariness on her back. She had a thin face with a pointed chin, not unattractive in its enervated way, with dark shadows under her big eyes. A small mole high on her left cheek oddly exoticized the drabness and the fatigue she seemed to personify. Lorimer felt a thin lariat of kinship snake out, joining him to her.

'Go and get some English mustard.'

'I telling you we don' have no –'

'OK, bring me some bloody tomato sauce then. Ketchup? Red stuff in a bottle? Fucking ridiculous.' Torquil sawed off a plug of sausage and ate, not fully closing his mouth. 'Call the place Cholmondley's, staff it with foreigners and don't serve English mustard.' He stopped chewing. 'Don't you know Hughie Aberdeen? Weren't you engaged to his sister, or something?'

'No. I don't –'

'I thought you were at Glenalmond. Hogg said you went to school in Scotland.'

'Yes. Balcairn.'

'Balcairn?'

'Shut down now. Near Tomintoul. Smallish place. Catholic. Run by a bunch of monks.'

'You a left-footer, then? Monks, suffering Christ. Give me the creeps.'

'Lapsed. It was a funny old place.'

'I think my wife's a Catholic. Catholic-ish. Keen on Gregorian chants, plainsong, that sort of thing. No I don't want the ketchup. Take it away. Yes, I have finished.'

The waitress silently, stoically removed their plates, Torquil still chewing as he reached for his cigarettes. He set fire to one, squinting after the waitress.

'She's actually got quite a nice little bum, for such a sourpuss.' He took a deep breath, inflating his chest hugely. 'Balcairn. I think I might have known someone who went there. I went to a place called Newbold House. In Northoooomberland. Sure you don't want some of this red? What do you make of your man Hogg?'

'Hogg is a law unto himself,' Lorimer said carefully.

'Fearsome reputation in the Fort, I must say. No. Take them away. I will call you when we want menus. Take them *away*. What is she? Some sort of Polish, German, Hungarian or what?' He leant forward. 'No, seriously, I'll be relying on you, Lorimer, in the early days, just to, you know, steer me right. Specially regarding Hogg. Not totally clear on this loss adjustment lark. Don't want to fall foul of him, that's for sure.'

'Absolutely.'

Lorimer was only certain of one thing – that he did not want to be this man's ally; riding shotgun for Torquil Helvoir-Jayne did not appeal. He looked across at him now as he sat there, picking at his teeth for shreds of spicy Cumberland sausage. He was overweight and had straight, thinning brown hair brushed back from his frowning brow.

'You got kids, Lorimer?'

'I'm not married.'

'Wise man. I've got three. And I'll be forty in six weeks. What's it all about, eh?'

'Boys or girls?'

'Jesus. Forty years old. Practically falling off the perch. Do you shoot?'

'Not any more. Bust an ear-drum. Doctor's orders.'

'Shame. My father-in-law has a decent place in Gloucestershire. Still, you must come and have dinner.'

'With your father-in-law?'

'No. No, me and the wife, me trouble-and-strife. Hello! Yes, you. Menu. Men-you. Fucking hell.' He turned amiably to Lorimer. 'Well, maybe it'll be all right after all. Two of us against the world. D'you want a port or brandy? Armagnac or anything?'

44. The Short Curriculum Vitae.
Name: Lorimer M. B. Black.
Age: 31.
Current employment: Senior Loss Adjuster, GGH Ltd.
Education: St Barnabus, Fulham. 11 GCSEs, 4 A-levels (Maths, Economics, English Literature, History of Art).
Foundation modular BSc degree course in Applied Mathematics and Fine Art at the North Caledonia Institute of Science and Technology (now the University of Ross and Cromarty).
Employment history: Trainee Insurance Assessor, Clerical and Medical (3 yrs); Insurance Valuer, Fortress Sure (2 yrs); Loss Adjuster, GGH Ltd (5 yrs).
Hobbies: collecting antique helmets.

The Book of Transfiguration

It was dark by 4.30 and Marlobe's flower cabin had its lights on – a warm, brilliantly coloured cave, all shades of red and yellow, mauves and flame-orange – when Lorimer paused to buy a rare bunch of white tulips. Marlobe was in loud and cheery humour as he talked to one of his regulars, a thin young man with an oddly dished face caused by the absence of all top teeth. As

Marlobe selected and wrapped the bouquet, Lorimer divined that the topic for discussion this evening was 'The Ideal Wife'. Marlobe could hardly get the words out for laughing.

'– No, no, I tell you she has to be stacked, right? Dead heat in a Zeppelin race, yeah? And she's got to be three foot tall, right? For easy blow-jobs. And she's got to have a flat head – right? – so I can put me beer bottle down while she's sucking me off.'

'That's disgusting, that is,' the young man slushed.

'Wait on. Also, also, she'd have to own a pub, right? The pub would be hers. And, after sex, she'd have to turn into a pizza.'

'Gaw, that's disgusting, that is.'

'Those do not merit the designation "flower", mate,' Marlobe said to Lorimer, still chortling. 'I wouldn't wipe me arse on those. Don't know how they crept in.'

'I get it: turn into a pizza,' Slushing-Voice said. 'So you can eat her, right? What about a kebab? Kebab would be great. I love a kebab.'

'A steak pie,' Marlobe bellowed, 'even better.'

'I happen to like white flowers,' Lorimer said, bravely, impassively, but he could not be heard above the general merriment.

92. No Deep Slumber. After your first few visits to the Institute of Lucid Dreams Alan had a better idea of your problem. The electroencephalogram – the EEG – is the tool that unlocks the sleeping persona, is how we discover the electrophysiology of sleep. The printout of your EEG patterns shows us what is the nature of the activity going on in your head. Alan told you that when you are asleep your EEG patterns show that you seem to be in a near

permanent pre-arousal state, that it is very rare to see any EEG
stage 4.

– EEG stage 4? you asked, alarmed.

– What we call deep slumber.

– No deep slumber? I have little or no deep slumber? Is that
bad?

– Well, nothing worth writing home about.

The Book of Transfiguration

Lady Haigh ambushed him as he was going through
the post in the hall. Bill, bill, circular, freesheet, bill,
circular . . .

'Lorimer, dear, you really must come and see this, it's
extraordinary.'

Lorimer obediently entered her flat. In the sitting room
her ancient dog, Jupiter, lolled panting on a hair-clogged
velvet cushion in front of a soundless black and white
TV. Lady Haigh's imposing, cracked-leather, winged
armchair was flanked by two single-bar electric fires and
lit by an early-model cantilevered reading lamp. The rest
of the furniture was almost invisible beneath piles of
books and sheaves of magazine and newspaper clippings
– Lady Haigh was an avid snipper-outer of articles that
caught her interest, and loath to throw them away.
Lorimer followed her through into the kitchen, its anti-
quated components burnished and scoured to museum-
standard levels of cleanliness. Beside the thrumming
fridge was a plastic basin full of Jupiter's dog food – giving
off an astringent, gamey smell – and beside it a cat-litter
(for Jupiter, also, he supposed; Lady Haigh detested cats,
'Selfish, selfish creatures'). She wrestled with the
numerous locks and chains on her back door, opened

them and, picking up a battery torch, led Lorimer out into the night, down the iron steps over the basement well to her patch of rear garden. Lady Haigh, Lorimer knew, slept in the basement but he had never ventured or been invited down there. From here the one window he could see was stoutly barred, the glass opaque with grime.

The garden was bounded by the angled walls and recent extensions of the abutting houses, and at its end was overlooked by the rear elevations and small curtained windows of the houses in the parallel street. Great brittle tangles of clematis teetered on the rotting wooden fences that marked the garden's narrow rectangular boundary, and in one corner a gnarled acacia gamely grew, each year producing noticeably fewer leaves and more sterile boughs, though it added, in summer, a hopeful, trembling presence of pale green leaves against the dirty, crumbling brickwork. Lorimer had a view of the small garden from his bathroom and he had to admit that, when the acacia was in leaf and the clematis was out, and the hydrangeas, and the sun angled down to strike the green turf, Lady Haigh's little verdant rectangle did possess a form of wild invitation that, like all green things growing in the city, did console and modestly enchant.

But not tonight, Lorimer thought, advancing into his condensing breath as he squelched across the lawn following the torchbeam, his shoes rapidly dampening from the unkempt grass (Lady Haigh disdained lawnmowers of any variety – when she couldn't use sheep, she used hedge clippers, so she claimed). At the foot of the acacia the sepia coin of light illuminated a small patch of ground.

'Look,' Lady Haigh said, pointing, 'a fritillary, now isn't that astonishing?'

Lorimer crouched and peered and sure enough there was a tiny bell-shaped flower, almost grey in the torch light, growing out of the scumbled earth, but with a distinct darker checkerboard pattern on the thin, papery flute.

'Never seen one so early,' she said, 'not even at Missenden, and we had masses there. And we didn't have any last year – I thought the frost had got them.'

'You must have a little micro-climate going here,' Lorimer said, hoping that was the sort of intelligent comment one made. 'It certainly is a beautiful little flower.' Not up Marlobe's street, he couldn't help thinking.

'Ah, fritillaries,' she said with touching nostalgia, then added, 'I did put a mulch down for the acacia, you see. Nigel gave me a couple of buckets from his border. That may have encouraged it.'

'Nigel?'

'That very nice Santafurian in number 20. Sweet man.'

Back in the kitchen Lorimer gently declined her offer of tea, pleading work that was waiting for him.

'After you with the *Standard*, if I may,' she asked.

'Please take it, Lady Haigh. I've flicked through it already.'

'What a treat,' she exclaimed. 'Today's *Standard*!' Jupiter chose this moment to waddle effortfully through from the sitting room; he sniffed once or twice at his basin of food and then just stood there, staring at it.

'Not so hungry.'

'He knows, you see,' Lady Haigh said with a sigh. 'The condemned man. He can tell. Won't touch his hearty meal.' She folded her arms. 'You'd better say goodbye to Jupiter, he won't be here tomorrow.'

'Why on earth not?'

'I'm having him put to sleep, taking him to the vet. He's an old dog set in his ways and I don't want anyone interfering with him when I'm gone. No, no,' she would hear nothing of Lorimer's protests, 'the next cold or flu will carry me off, you'll see. I'm eighty-eight years old, for heaven's sake, should have gone ages ago.'

She smiled at him, her pale blue eyes shining – with pleasant anticipation, Lorimer thought.

'Poor old Jupiter,' he said spontaneously. 'Seems a bit harsh.'

'Fiddlesticks. I wish someone would take *me* to the vet. It's driving me loopy.'

'What?'

'All this hanging about. I'm bored stiff.'

At her door she put her hand on his arm and drew him close. She was tall, despite her stoop, and Lorimer supposed that once she had been an attractive young woman.

'Tell me,' she said, lowering her voice, 'do you think Dr Alan might be a tiny bit of a pansy?'

'I should think so. Why?'

'I don't see any gels coming or going. But then again, I don't see any gels coming or going for you, either.' She laughed at him, a breathy giggle, and covered her mouth. 'Only teasing, Lorimer dear. Thanks for the paper.'

Lorimer worked late, doggedly going through the Gale-Harlequin contracts, paying special attention to the paperwork relating to the Edmund, Rintoul deal. They confirmed his suspicions, as he suspected they would, but the work could not distract him from the dark seep of melancholy that seemed to be penetrating his soul like a stain.

So he spent two and a half hours surfing the channels on his cable TV before he caught the Fortress Sure advertisement once more. He quickly switched on his video and managed to record the last forty seconds. Replaying it, and freezing the frame at the end, he stared at the girl's gently shuddering face for some moments. Now he had her, caught fast, and it was indeed her, without doubt. And surely, he thought, cheered suddenly, there must be some straightforward way of finding out her name.

At half past four he padded quietly downstairs and slipped a note under Lady Haigh's door. It read: 'Dear Lady Haigh, is there any way I can prevent Jupiter's last journey to the vet? What if I promise solemnly to look after him in the unlikely event of something happening to you? It would greatly please me. Yours ever, Lorimer.'

Chapter 4

Lorimer's surveillance of Edmund, Rintoul Ltd had lasted two days and he did not anticipate it requiring much longer duration. He waited in a café across the Old Kent Road from their offices, a suite of rooms above a carpet warehouse. At the rear was a small builder's yard, garlanded with razor wire and containing a couple of battered vans and, unusually, the firm's own skip-lorry (which was also for hire). Lorimer turned in his seat to signal for another cup of tea, eventually catching the eye of the surly, unhappy patron who was swiping margarine on to a leaning tower of white bread slices. It was 10.45 in the morning and St Mark's café was not busy: apart from himself there were a nervy, chain-smoking girl with lip, nose and cheek studs and a couple of old blokes in raincoats annotating the *Sporting Life*, doubtless waiting for the pub or the bookie's to open.

The St Mark's was unpretentious in the extreme, not to say unequivocally basic, but Lorimer took a perverse pleasure in the place – these caffs were steadily dying out and soon they'd be distant memories, or else lovingly recreated as temples of post-modern kitsch, serving cocktails along with *sandwiches aux pommes frites*. There was one long counter, a chilled display unit, a lino floor and a dozen formica-topped tables. Behind the counter was a huge handwritten menu laboriously detailing the dozens of combinations available from a few central ingredients – eggs, bacon, chips, toast, sausages, beans, mushrooms, gravy and black pudding. The windows facing the Old Kent Road were fogged and teary with condensation and the display unit contained only three ingredients for sandwiches – ham, tomato and chopped boiled eggs. Tea was served from an aluminium teapot, coffee was instant, the crockery was Pyrex, the flatware plastic. Such brutal frugality was rare, almost a challenge to its clientele. Only the boldest, the poorest or the most ignorant would seek shelter and sustenance here. Lorimer felt it could easily qualify for his Classic British Caffs series – an informal log he kept in *The Book of Transfiguration* of similar establishments that he had encountered on his wanderings across the city. Forget pubs, he reasoned, this was where the country's true and ancient culinary heritage resided; only in these uncompromising estaminets would you find the quintessence of a unique way of English life, fast disappearing.

His dark brown steaming tea was poured, he milked and sugared it (Hogg would have approved) and he gazed across the road through the bleary porthole of clarity he had smeared in the condensation.

As far as he could tell, Dean Edmund was the builder of the partnership and Kenneth Rintoul the front man who dealt with the clients and contractors. They were both in their late twenties. Parked up on the cracked and weedy pavement in front of the graffitied shutters of the carpet warehouse were two shiny new motors – a Jaguar and a BMW – worth approximately £150,000 between them, so Lorimer had calculated, and Rintoul's (the BMW) also had a personalized number plate – KR 007. Edmund lived with his wife and three children in a large new house in Epping Forest; Rintoul's pad was a converted warehouse loft in Bermondsey with a distant view of Tower Bridge – there was clearly a deal of money swilling around. Rintoul sported a small ponytail and both men were neatly goateed. Lorimer had an appointment with them at eleven o'clock but he always thought it advisable to be ten minutes late – meetings tended to go better, he found, if they started with apologies.

*174. **The Recurring Lucid Dream**. It is night and you are walking down a corridor, cool lino under your bare feet, heading towards a door. From behind this door comes the noise of many people whooping and cheering and the indistinct blather of a TV set with the volume high. You are vexed and aggravated, the noise is bothering you, angering you, and you want it to cease.*

Just as you reach the door you realize you are naked. You are wearing only an unbuttoned shirt (pistachio green, unironed) and its tail floats above your naked buttocks as you stride down the corridor. It is not clear whether you are fully tumescent or not. You reach for the door knob (just as an extra-loud mass screech of delight followed by gulping ululations erupt in the room beyond) – but you suddenly withdraw your hand. You quickly turn and retrace your steps to your small boxy room, where you dress immediately and with care, before going out again into the night.

The Book of Transfiguration

'This way, sir. Mr Rintoul and Mr Edmund will see you right away.'

'Sorry, I'm a bit late,' Lorimer said to the rear view of the young, black and heavily perfumed receptionist who led him down a short corridor to Rintoul's office. The day before Lorimer had had his hair cut and this morning had lightly gelled it flat. He was wearing a fawn leather blouson jacket, a pale blue shirt and striped knitted tie, black trousers and Italian loafers. He had removed his signet ring and had replaced it with a tooled gold band which he wore on his right middle finger. His briefcase was new, shiny brass and polished leather. All specialist loss adjusters had their own approach to the job – some were aggressive, some cynically direct, a few bullied, or set out to inspire fear, others came in strong and hostile like hit-men, some were neutral apparatchiks emotionlessly executing orders – but Lorimer was different: he was much more interested in the absence of threat. He dressed this way not to disguise himself but – crucially, deliberately – to reassure: these were expensive clothes but they would not threaten the likes of Edmund or Rintoul, they did not hint at other worlds, strata of society alien or hostile or sitting in judgement – in theory they shouldn't even notice what he was wearing, which was, in fact, their designed effect and the *modus operandi* of his personal and particular loss adjusting method. No one knew about this approach – methodology was never discussed or shared amongst the adjusters – and Hogg only judged by results, he did not care how success was arrived at.

Hands were warmly shaken: Rintoul was smiley, chipper, agitated, matey; Edmund tenser and more circumspect. Coffees were ordered, Priscilla, the receptionist, enjoined to use the espresso machine this time – not instant ('We can tell the difference, darling') – and Lorimer began his apologies, blaming the delay on the diabolical traffic. They talked for some time on this subject, while the coffee was made and served, and the merits of alternative routes in and out of the East End were discussed in precise detail.

'Deano lives in Epping Forest,' Rintoul said, pointing a thumb at his partner. 'Murder, isn't it, Deano? Traffic.' Rintoul moved constantly, as if he could not decide which body position to adopt, as if he were testing them all out. His facial muscles too were similarly mobile, Lorimer noticed – was that a smile forming or a pout, a frown or an expression of surprise?

'M11, is it? Blackwall Tunnel?' Lorimer said. 'Got to be fucking kidding. Every day, there and back?'

'Fucking nightmare,' Edmund admitted, reluctantly, with a sniffing toss of the head. He was a gruffer, slower, heavier man, not entirely at ease in the office, off the site. His hairy wrists looked thick and clumsy projecting from the fine striped cotton of his snazzy shirt cuffs; his goatee was badly, half-heartedly shaved, as if he had grown it as the result of a dare rather than a genuine hirsute affectation.

'Yeah, well,' Lorimer said, winding up the traffic discussion, 'all part of life's rich pageant.' Polite chuckles at this. Lorimer was rounding his vowels, as well as swearing, and introducing the hint of a glottal stop. Click, click – he sprang the locks on his briefcase. 'Well, gentlemen, shall we ponder the fire at the Fedora Palace?'

Incredulity mingled with regret (it had been the firm's biggest contract to date), ritual cursing of the truly rotten filthy luck that so often attended those who toiled in the building trade ('Try finding decent plumbers,' Edmund said with real anger and resentment, 'they've gone, like they're extinct. There ain't any.'). Lorimer listened, nodded, winced, then he said, 'There was a ten-grand-a-week penalty clause if you were late.'

A silence here: Edmund said, defiantly, too quickly, 'We were on target.'

'Seems a bit steep,' Lorimer said, sympathetically, 'steepest I've seen on a job like this.'

'Fucking right,' Rintoul said, bitterly. 'But it's the only way people like us get jobs like that, these days. They screw you on the penalty clause.'

'It makes no sense: you have to work so fast, can't guarantee the same quality, surely?' Lorimer oozed sympathy, now.

Rintoul smiled. 'Exactly. That's how it works, see. You bust a gut, you finish on time. Then they fuck you on the snagging – "This isn't right, that's not right." Refuse to pay the last instalment.' He turned to Edmund. 'We didn't get our full whack on what? Last three jobs?'

'Four.'

'See? They got you. Short and curlies.'

Lorimer looked at his notes. 'You say you were on target to complete at the end of the month.'

'Definitely.'

'Absolutely.'

Lorimer paused. 'What if I put it to you that you were actually running late, well late?'

'We was a bit late on account of the fucking Turkish marble,' Edmund said, 'but we had a waiver for that. All in order.'

'The quantity surveyors say you were looking at a ten-to-fifteen-day penalty.'

'Whoever told you that,' Rintoul said evenly, his voice quieter, 'is a fucking liar.'

Lorimer said nothing: silence could be so eloquent, silence could work like a rising tide on a sandcastle. Rintoul leaned back in his chair, folding his hands behind his head; Edmund stared at his lap. Lorimer put his notes away.

'Thank you, gentlemen. All seems very clear. I won't trouble you no further.'

'I'll walk you down,' Rintoul said.

Outside the carpet warehouse Rintoul turned his back to the wind and hunched his jacket to him, leaning close to Lorimer.

'Mr Black,' he said, with quiet vehemence, 'I know what's going on.' Lorimer thought he could detect a faint West Country burr beneath the East End twang, a sedimentary trace of Rintoul's early life in Devon or Dorset, perhaps.

'Oh yeah? What is going on, Mr Rintoul?'

'I know you insurance people,' Rintoul continued, 'you just don't want to pay out, so you're going to fucking shaft us with this fire business so you don't have to pay the claim to Gale-Harlequin. We were on time to finish, Mr Black, no way we'd of been late. This is our life here, our livelihood. You could mess it all up for us, easy, you could ruin everything. I see the way you're thinking, I see where this is heading . . .' He smiled again. 'Please don't go down that road, Mr Black.' There was no entreaty in his voice, but Lorimer was impressed – he was very nearly convincing.

'I'm afraid I can't discuss my report with you, Mr Rintoul. Like you, we just try to do our job as professionally as possible.'

Lorimer drove away from the meandering mean street that was the Old Kent Road, his head busy, away from the giant new petrol stations and the unisex hair salons, the cash 'n' carrys, the tyre and wheel depots and the karaoke pubs. 'Houses cleared' signs told him, and he saw the evidence in the landscape everywhere. Timber merchants, panelbeaters, lorry parks and closed-down electrical goods merchants behind dusty diamond mesh grilles passed by until he drove beneath the river and emerged on the north bank, swerving east through Lime-house and Poplar and Blackwall towards Silvertown. Lorimer put in a call to the office to book an appointment with Hogg. Janice told him when he could come in, then added, 'I got a call from Jenny, PR at the Fort, about that advert. They think the name you're looking for is Malinverno. I'll spell it: Flavia Malinverno. F-L-A-V-I-A –'

Lorimer stood in his empty sitting room looking at the view through curtainless windows. He had a clear sight of the City Airport across the choppy blue-grey waters of Albert Dock and beyond that, dark against the sky, the industrial alp of the Tate & Lyle sugar factory, wisps of steam emanating from various pipes and funnels, a steel Krakatoa threatening to blow. To his right, in the distance, stood the immense obelisk of Canary Wharf, its blinking eye on its summit flashing at him like a beacon across Canning Town, Leamouth and the Isle of Dogs. The light was cold and harsh, the horizons bulldozed flat, bereft of houses, crisscrossed by the elevated concrete ribbons of the spine roads and the MII link and the stalky modernity of the tracks and stations of the Docklands Light Railway loftily picking its way from Beckton to Canning Town. Everything old was going here, or being transformed, cast out by the new. It seemed a different, pioneering city out here in the east, with its emptiness and flatness, its chill, refulgent space, its great unused docks and basins – even the air felt different, colder, uncom-promising, tear-inducing – not for the faint-hearted or uncertain. And further over to the east, beyond the gas and sewage works, he could see the full mass of a purple and gunmetal cloudscape, a continent of cloud bearing down on the city, gilded with the citrus clarity of the estuarine light. Snow coming, he thought, all the way from Siberia.

His house was small and detached, and was set in the centre of a raked rectangle of mud, part of a tentative development called Albion Village established by an optimistic builder. On the ground floor there was a garage, kitchen and dining room, and above, a sitting room and bedroom with a bathroom off the landing. Another atticy bedroom with an en suite shower lurked under the roof tiles, lit by skylights. The place smelt of paint, putty and builder's dust and the honey-coloured cord carpet had been recently laid, strewn with offcuts. On either side of him, forming a rough arc, were the six other houses of Albion Village, all of similar but, tastefully, not identical design, some occupied, some with the builder's tape still crisscrossing the windows. A small, pseudo-community, awaiting its members, with its newly sown green grass and spindly wind-thrashed saplings, purpose-built on the very eastern fringe of the city, another small encroachment on the wastelands.

And it was all his, bought and paid for. His little home in Silvertown . . . He began to note down the very minimum he would need to make it habitable – bed, sheets, pillows, blankets, sofa, armchair, desk and chair, TV, sound system, pots and pans. The kitchen was fitted, no dinner parties were envisaged, so a few tinned and frozen foods would suffice. Curtains? He could live awhile with the complimentary roller blinds. The odd table lamp would be welcome but they, by definition, required tables and he wanted to have the house ready as quickly as possible, with as little fuss and distracting choice. Why did he need another place to live? Good question, Lorimer. Insurance, he supposed. Same old story.

So, it was Flavia Malinverno. The name itself couldn't be better, couldn't be more perfect. And how would you be pronouncing that, Miss? Flahvia? Or Flayvia?

Marlobe brandished a newspaper at him, the headline exposing some government U-turn on its tax and pension plans.

'Looks like snow,' Lorimer said.

'This country needs a fucking revolution, mate. Sweep them away – politicians, financiers, fat cats, civil servants, toffs, nobs, TV personalities. String 'em up. Get the people back running things. Hard-working people. You and me. Our sort. Fucking violent bloody revolution.'

'I know what you mean. Some days –'

'Got some white carnations for you, mate – special. Fiver. Ta.'

Suspended from his door, held by a strip of festive Xmas sticky tape, was a folded note. It read: 'My Dear Lorimer, One day soon Jupiter will be all yours. Thank you so much. Yours ever, C. H.'

Lorimer felt useless regrets crowd around him as he read it through again, weighing the consequences of his generosity. If only he had not been so precipitate . . . Still, he supposed it was a 'good thing' he had done. At the very least Jupiter might find his appetite had returned, now his execution had been forestalled.

In his hallway he ritually rested his palm on his three helmets in turn and wondered, suddenly, if Ivan would take them as part-exchange for the Greek one. A swift computation of their collective value told him he would still be some way short of the requisite amount but it would certainly be a leap forward towards his goal. Thus cheered, he put King Johnson Adewale and his Ghana-beat Millionaires on the CD and poured himself a small tumblerful of vodka. Lady C. Haigh. Curious, he had never wondered about her Christian name, never even imagined her with one. 'C' – what could it stand for? Charlotte, Celia, Caroline, Cynthia, Charis? A young girl's name, conjuring up the 1920s and '30s, Oxford bags, bright young things, trophy hunts, illicit weekends in provincial riverside hotels . . . As the vodka hit and the highlife rhythms gently thudded through the flat he allowed himself a small smile of self-congratulation.

Chapter 5

Lorimer set his alarm for an early rise – a mere gesture, this, as he tossed and turned and was wide awake by 4.45. So he read doggedly for a while, managed to doze off again and woke at 7.00 feeling drugged and stupid. He bathed and shaved and changed the linen on his bed, then, like an automaton, he hoovered the flat, wiped down the surfaces in his kitchen, took his shirts and smalls to the laundry, and two suits to the dry cleaners, visited the bank and bought some food at the ShoppaSava on Lupus Street. These mundane rituals of bachelordom did not depress him, rather he saw them as proud domestic testimony to his independence. What was it Joachim had said to Brahms? *Frei aber einsam*, 'Free but lonely.' Brahms was, perhaps, the greatest bachelor the world had known, he thought now, as he selected some freesias from the ShoppaSava's newly installed flower stand. Brahms with his genius, his unshakeable routines, his huge dignity and his ineffable sadness. There was the exemplar, this was what he should aspire to, he reflected as he bought some lemony ranunculus and spotted tall apricot tulips, assorted pot plants of the most vivid green, ferns, eucalyptus, gypsophila and ranked boxes of daffodils at one-third the price Marlobe charged. Well enough stocked, he thought, when did they put this in? No carnations, though, that franchise was still securely Marlobe's.

At the checkout counter he turned and surveyed the patient queues of customers waiting to pay their money – there was no one he recognized, but again he had felt that strange sensation of being observed, as if someone who knew him was lurking near by just out of sight, playing a game with him, seeing just how much time could pass before he was discovered. He waited at the door a while by the news-stand, buying some papers and magazines, but no one emerged who was familiar.

He decided to breakfast at the nearby Café Matisse (Classic British Caffs no. 3), where he ordered a fried egg and bacon sandwich and a cappuccino, and flicked through his weighty pile of reading matter. He preferred the Matisse at this time of day to all others, early, before the shoppers trooped in for elevenses, when the place was mopped and swabbed and relatively smoke-free. He had been coming here for four years, regularly, and had yet to receive even a nod of welcome from the staff. Mind you, he had outlasted them all: the turnover of personnel at the Matisse was extraordinary. He saw that the rangy South African girl was still here and the lugubrious Romanian too. He wondered vaguely if the tiny Portuguese one had left, the one who flirted with the bikers – the wealthy middle-aged men, paunchy in their leathers, who descended in a group at prearranged times of the week to drink coffee and stare lovingly at their immaculate Harleys, all spangling chrome, parked up on the pavement in full view. Maybe she had indeed gone, perhaps she'd trapped one of these portly, well-heeled free-spirits into marriage? For he saw there was a new girl doing the front half: she looked darkly Latin, with long, wiry hair, the slim body of a sixteen-year-old but the face of a haughty duenna.

'Thanks,' he said to the Romanian as she suddenly clattered his sandwich down in front of him. She swept off as ever, wordlessly, with a toss of her blue-black hair.

The Matisse owed its name to a single reproduction of that Master's work, a late-period blue nude which hung on the wall between the ladies' and gents' lavatories. Its cuisine was notionally Italian but the menu boasted many a familiar English standard – cod and chips, lamb chops and roast potatoes, apple pie and custard. As far as he could discern, not a single Italian currently worked in the place but it must have been the traces of that influence, perhaps lingering on in the basement kitchen, that ensured at least the coffee's surprising excellence. He ordered another cappuccino and watched the customers come and go. Everyone smoked in the Matisse, apart from him; it almost seemed to be a condition of entry. The counter staff and the waitresses smoked during their breaks and every customer, young and old, male or female, fervently followed suit as if they used the place as a brief smoking respite from their otherwise smokeless days. He looked around him now at the types scattered around the big gloomy rectangular room. A middle-aged couple – style: Eastern European intellectual – the man looking uncannily like Bertolt Brecht, both bespectacled, both in drab zip-up waterproof jackets. A table of four consumptive hippies, three men with lank hair and poor beards and a girl (rolling her own), bead-swagged with a flower tattooed on her throat. In one of the booths down the side was the obligatory lost-waif couple, two chalk-faced girls, black-clad, talking worriedly in furious whispers – too young, in trouble, pimp-fodder. And behind them a man smoking a tiny pipe who looked like a member of the International Brigade in the Spanish Civil

War, tangle-haired with big muddy shoes, unshaven, wearing a collarless shirt and baggy corduroy suit. At the counter two unnaturally tall girls were smoking and paying. Breastless, hipless, they had swan necks and tiny heads – models, he assumed, there must be an agency near by – they drifted in and out of the Matisse all day, these lanky, freakish females, not beautiful, just differently made from all the other women in the world. All human life ventured into the smoky interior of the Matisse at some stage; if you sat long enough you would see everyone, every prototype the human species had to offer, every product of the gene pool, rich or poor, blessed or afflicted – which was the key to the place's strange and enduring allure, in his opinion. Even he, he realized, must sometimes attract such idle speculation – who is the quiet young man in the pin-stripe suit? A journalist on an upmarket weekly? A lawyer? A Eurobond dealer? – with his dry cleaning and pile of newsprint.

'Fancy a drink this evening? Torquil asked, leaning round Lorimer's office door. Then coming in and mooching about as they talked, fingering a picture frame (Paul Klee) and leaving it a degree or two awry, touching the leaves of his potted plants, drumming a rhythm on the flat top of his PC.

'Great,' Lorimer said with scant enthusiasm.

'Where is everybody?' Torquil said. 'Haven't seen you for days. Never known an office like it, all this coming and going.'

'We're all on various jobs,' Lorimer explained. 'All over the place. Dymphna's in Dubai, Shane's in Exeter, Ian's in Glasgow –'

'I don't think our Dymphna likes me at all,' Torquil

said, then grinned. 'A cross I shall just have to bear. What're you up to?'

'Tidying up a few things,' Lorimer said ambiguously – Hogg was very against discussion of their respective adjustments.

'Hogg's given me this Dupree job to finish off. Seems pretty straightforward. Paperwork, really.'

'Well, it is, now that he's dead.'

'Topped himself, didn't he?'

'It happens. They think their world has been destroyed, and, well . . .' He changed the subject. 'Look, I've got an appointment with Hogg. Where shall we meet?'

'El Hombre Guapo? You know, Clerkenwell Road? Six?'

'See you there.'

'Don't mind if I bring someone along, do you?'

Hogg was standing, scarfed and coated, in the middle of his orange carpet.

'Am I late?' Lorimer asked, perplexed.

'See you in Finsbury Circus, in ten minutes. I'm going out the back way, give me five minutes. Leave by the front door – and don't tell Helvoir-Jayne.'

Hogg was sitting on a bench beside the bowling green in the small oval square when Lorimer arrived, his chin on his chest, looking thoughtful, his hands thrust in his pockets. Lorimer slid himself down beside him. All around the neat central garden were the leafless plane trees with their backdrop of solid, ornate buildings with a few frozen workers smoking and shivering in doorways. The old city, Hogg always said, as it used to be in the great days – which was why he so liked Finsbury Circus.

Twenty yards away a man expertly juggled three red

balls to an audience of none. Lorimer realized Hogg was staring fascinatedly at the juggler, as if he'd never seen the trick done before.

'Bloody marvellous,' Hogg said, 'sort of mesmerizing. Run over there and give him a pound, there's a good lad.'

Lorimer did as he was told, dropping the coin in a woollen hat at his feet.

'Cheers, mate,' the juggler said, the balls still following their apparently tethered trajectories.

'Bloody marvellous!' Hogg shouted from across the square, and gave the juggler the thumbs up. Lorimer saw him rise to his feet and stride off without a backward glance. Sighing, Lorimer followed briskly but had still not caught him up by the time he entered a modern pub set incongruously in the corner of an office block with a good view of the giant ochrous waffle iron of the Broadgate Centre opposite.

Inside, the pub smelt of old beer and yesterday's cigarette smoke. A row of lurid computer games winked and clattered, thundered and swooshed, trying to entice players, the technobarrage competing successfully with some jazzy orchestral muzak emanating from somewhere or other. Hogg was having a pint of pale, frothy lager drawn for him.

'What'll it be, Lorimer?'

'Mineral water. Fizzy.'

'Have a proper drink, for God's sake.'

'Half of cider, then.'

'Jesus Christ. Sometimes I despair, Lorimer.'

They carried their drinks as far away as possible from the squawking and beeping machines. Hogg drank two-thirds of his pint in four huge swallows, wiped his mouth and lit a cigarette. Neither of them removed their coats – the vile pub was cold as well.

'OK, let's have it,' Hogg said.

'Standard torching. The subcontractors were running late, facing a big penalty, so they started a fire in the gymnasium. It must have got out of control. There was no way they wanted to destroy five floors and all the rest.'

'So?'

'So I still can't see 27 million quid's worth of damage. I'm not an expert but the place wasn't trading, wasn't finished. I can't see why the claim is so large.'

Hogg reached inside his coat and drew out a folded photocopy and handed it to Lorimer.

'Because the place is insured for 80 million.'

Lorimer unfolded the copy of the original Fortress Sure policy and leafed through it. He could not make out the signature on the final page.

Lorimer pointed at the scrawl. 'Who's that?'

Hogg drained his pint and stood up, ready to fetch another.

'Torquil Helvoir-Jayne,' he said, and headed for the bar.

He came back with a packet of beef and horseradish crisps and another foamy pint. He munched at the crisps carelessly, causing a small shrapnel fall to dust his coat front. He swilled lager round his clogged teeth.

'So Torquil over-insured.'

'Way over.'

'Big premium. They were prepared to pay.'

'Everything was dandy until those arseholes started their fire.'

'It'll be a hard job proving it,' Lorimer said, guardedly. 'Those guys, Rintoul and Edmund, there's a kind of desperation there. Semi-nuclear, I would say.'

'It's not their problem – or rather,' Hogg corrected himself, 'let's make it Gale-Harlequin's problem. Pass the buck. Say we suspect foul play and won't cough up.'

'We'll have to pay something.'

'I know,' Hogg said venomously. 'As long as it's nowhere near 27 mil. Pitch it low, Lorimer.'

'Me?'

'Why not?'

'Well . . . I've never done anything this size. We could be talking millions of pounds.'

'I hope we are, Lorimer. Big bonus for you, my son. Big day for GGH. Big smiles at Fortress Sure.'

Lorimer thought about this a moment.

'Torquil has fucked up,' Lorimer said, reflectively.

'Big time,' Hogg said, with almost glee, 'and we have to pull the baby out of the burning bush.'

Lorimer admired both the mixed metaphor and the use of the first person plural.

'Go to Gale-Harlequin,' Hogg said. 'Tell them we suspect arson. Police, fire brigade, inspectors, hearings, eventual prosecutions. Could take years. Years.'

'They won't be happy.'

'It's a war, Lorimer. They know it. We know it.'

'They paid the big premium.'

'They're property developers. My heart bleeds.'

Despite his instinctive alarm Lorimer felt his heart quicken at the prospect. Applying the arcane formulae that calculated, graded and further refined the amount of the loss adjuster's bonus, Lorimer considered that he could be looking at six figures. There was one other matter that troubled him, however.

'Mr Hogg,' he began slowly, 'I hope you don't mind

my asking, but why, after all this, has Torquil come to work at G G H?'

Hogg gulped lager, noisily expelled carbonated breath.

'Because Sir Simon Sherriffmuir asked me, as a personal favour.'

'Why would he do that? What's Torquil to Sir Simon?'

'His godson.'

'Ah.'

'Yeah. As clear as a gnat's chuff, eh?'

'Do you think Sir Simon knows something?'

'Have another cider, Lorimer.'

*12. **The Specialist**. Hogg says to you: 'It's a big world, Lorimer. Let your mind play with the concept "armed forces" for a moment. That concept contains your army, your navy and your air force, not to mention ancillary or subsidiary services – medics, engineers, cooking, sanitary, police, etcetera. These larger sub-divisions are divided in turn into battle groups, army corps, regiments, wings, battalions, flotillas, squadrons, troops, flights, platoons and so on. All very organized, Lorimer, all very neat and proper, all very above board and as obvious as a warm white loaf, sliced. Thoroughly thought-through, plain for all to contemplate and analyse.*

'But in your armed forces you've also got your specialist élite units. Very small in number and with vigorous and highly demanding selection procedures. Many fall by the wayside. The choice is fundamental, is absolute, membership very restricted. SAS, SBS, Navy Seals, your Stealth bombers, spy planes, saboteurs, your FBI and MI5, agents and sleepers in the fields. Secrecy shrouds them, Lorimer, like a shroud. We've all heard of them, but we know next to fuck-all about them, in brutal reality. And why is this the case? Because they do vital jobs, jobs of vital importance. Covert operations. Counter-insurgency. Still part of the larger concept of "armed forces", yes – but a tiny sub-sub-sub-section, and, also to be borne

in mind, one of the armed forces' most deadly and violently effective components.

'That is us, Lorimer. This is the analogy to hold on to. Like them we are specialists, the specialist loss adjusters. Everyone knows what a loss adjuster does in the wider, above-the-board, larger world. But, just like the élite forces, no one really knows what us specialists get up to. But that large world needs us, Lorimer. Oh, yes. Just as the armed forces have to rely in certain circumstances on the SAS or the bomb-makers or the assassins. You see, only we can do certain jobs, the difficult jobs, the discreet jobs, the secret jobs. That's when they call the specialist loss adjusters in.'

The Book of Transfiguration

'Mr Rintoul?'

'Yeah.'

'Lorimer Black. GGH.'

'Oh yeah. How you doing?'

'Fine. I thought I should let you know that we are going to contest the claim on the Fedora Palace.'

'Oh. Right.' Rintoul paused. 'What's that got to do with me?'

'It's got everything to do with you.'

'Don't get you.'

'You set fire to that hotel because you didn't want to pay the penalty charge.'

'Fucking lie. Lies.'

'We are going to contest the Gale-Harlequin claim on the grounds of your arson.'

Silence.

'I thought it only right to let you know.'

'I'll kill you, Black. Fucking kill you. Say nothing or I'll kill you.'

'This conversation has been recorded.'

The phone was slammed down and Lorimer hung up, his hand trembling slightly. However many death threats he had received in this job – a good half-dozen or so – they still unnerved him. He took the cassette from his answer machine and popped it in an envelope, marking it 'Fedora Palace. Rintoul. Death threat'. That would go up to Janice for the master file which was kept in Hogg's office. On the tape Rintoul had not actually admitted he had started the fire so it would not stand as legal evidence – it did not explicitly incriminate him. The death threat was unequivocal, though, and Lorimer hoped that would make him safe – it usually did. When they knew they had been recorded it stayed their hand. It was a useful bit of extra insurance.

93. Two Types of Sleep. I have learned through my conversations with Alan that there are two types of sleep: Rapid Eye Movement sleep (REM) and Non-Rapid Eye Movement sleep (NREM). REM sleep is paradoxical, NREM sleep is orthodox. Alan told me, after studying my EEG patterns, that I was experiencing far more REM sleep than is the norm, which, he said, makes me very paradoxical indeed.

He told me about the stages of NREM sleep. Stage 1 – sleep onset. Stage 2 – deeper, we see changes in the EEG patterns, sleep-spindles, K-complexes, but you are still aware of outside stimuli, your brain activity taking the form of short sequences of waves. Stages 3 and 4 plunge you ever deeper, showing decreased vigilance, this is what we call 'deep slumber'. We believe, Alan said, that NREM sleep in the deep slumber phase is essential for body repair. REM sleep is for brain repair.

The Book of Transfiguration

El Hombre Guapo was a large tapas bar just off the Clerkenwell Road, lined with sheets of carefully distressed stainless steel. The floor was stainless steel too and portions of the Berlin Wall were hung horizontally in chains from high beams creating a distinctly different kind of false ceiling. The staff wore grey boiler suits with many zips (of the sort favoured by combat fighter pilots) and the driving, relentless music was played punishingly loud. It was popular with young journalists from the style pages of broadsheet newspapers and with futures and derivatives traders – Lorimer thought it a strange place for Torquil to choose.

As ever, Torquil was already installed at the bar and half way into his drink – whisky, judging by the smell on his breath. He offered Lorimer one of his cigarettes and was politely turned down. Lorimer ordered a triple vodka and soda with plenty of ice – Rintoul's last words were still echoing in his inner ear.

'That's right, you don't smoke,' Torquil said incredulously. 'Why not? Everybody smokes.'

'Well, not everybody. Two-thirds of us don't.'

'Rubbish. All smoking statistics are lies, I tell you, Lorimer. Every government in the world lies about them, they have to. Smoking's on the increase worldwide and it suits them fine, though they daren't admit it. So they routinely churn out these figures. But take a look around you.'

'You're probably right,' Lorimer conceded. True enough, of the fifty or so people in El Hombre Guapo, ninety-eight per cent were smoking and the other two per cent looked like they were about to smoke any minute, rummaging in pockets and handbags for their cigarettes.

'How was your day?' Torquil asked, lighting up himself. 'I hope it was more exciting than mine.'

'Same old stuff.'

'What?'

'SAME OLD STUFF!' Lorimer raised his voice to a half-shout. Everyone was obliged to talk louder in order to be heard above the music.

'I tell you, Lorimer, if it wasn't for the money I'd be out of this game in a shot.'

Torquil ordered another whisky and a plate of *croquetas* which he proceeded to eat one after the other in rapid order, offering none to Lorimer.

'No sups for Torquil,' he said, leaning close. 'Binnie's with her ma and pa.'

'Binnie?'

'My darling wife.'

'In Gloucestershire?'

'Absolutely.'

'Kids with her?'

'They're all away at school, thank Christ.'

'I thought your youngest was seven.'

'He is. He's at a prep school near Ascot. But he comes home at weekends.'

'Oh, fine.'

'Well, it's not fine actually.' Torquil frowned. 'It sort of unsettles him. Started wetting his bed. Not fitting in. I keep telling Binnie it's all this coming home at weekends. He doesn't want to go back, you see. I say he should stick it out.'

Lorimer looked at his watch. 'Well, I should be –'

'There she is.'

Lorimer turned to see a young girl in her early twenties, wearing a suede coat buttoned up to her neck, pushing her way cautiously through the raucous crowd. She had thin sandy hair and heavily made-up eyes. She looked vaguely familiar.

'Lorimer, this is Irina. Irina, young Lorimer, m'colleague.'

Lorimer shook her weak hand, trying not to stare as he sought to place her. Then he had it: the waitress from Cholmondley's.

'You remember Lorimer, don't you?'

'No, I don't think. How are you?'

Torquil ignored her and turned away to order her a beer while Lorimer reminded her of their first meeting and asked a few polite questions. It turned out Irina was Russian, over here studying music. She said Torquil had assured her he could help with her work-permit application. She accepted one of Torquil's cigarettes and dipped her head to have it lit. She plumed smoke at the ceiling and held the cigarette awkwardly, her beer bottle in the other hand. Lorimer felt her melancholy soul reach out to encircle him. Then she said something but neither of them could hear.

'What?'

'I say this is nice place,' she yelled. 'Where is ladies' room?'

She edged off in search of it and Torquil watched her go, before smirking at Lorimer, and leaning forward to put his mouth uncomfortably close to Lorimer's ear.

'I thought I'd been a bit grumpy at lunch,' Torquil explained. 'So I went back the other day to apologize, asked if I could buy her a drink. She's a flautist, apparently. Firm, pliable lips I should imagine.'

'She seems nice. Something intrinsically sad about her, I feel.'

94

'Bullshit. Listen, Lorimer, you wouldn't mind sort of buggering off now, would you? I think I've done the decent thing. I'll say you were called away.'

'Got to go, as it is.'

Relief propelled him out of the bar but Torquil caught him at the door.

'Almost forgot,' he said. 'What're you doing next weekend? Come to dinner, Saturday, stay the night. And bring your golf clubs.'

'I don't play golf. Look, I –'

'I'll get the Binns to drop you a line with the details. Not far away, Hertfordshire.' He slapped Lorimer affectionately on the shoulder and pushed his way back to the bar, where Irina was now waiting, shrugging herself out of her suede coat. Under the bluey lights of El Hombre Guapo Lorimer glimpsed pale arms and pale shoulders, white as salt.

Chapter 6

That night he slept, even by his reduced standards, badly. Alan had told him he was alone in the Institute and normally that information helped. Also, following Alan's instructions, he had pondered lengthily on Gérard de Nerval's fraught and difficult life but his mind refused to obey, dithering skittishly between images of Flavia Malinverno and the prospective adjust at Gale-Harlequin. He forced his mind back to poor tormented Gérard and his hopeless love for Jenny Colon, the actress. De Nerval had hung himself one freezing winter's night – the 25th January 1855. Now that was the sort of fact one read in a biography with little pause, unless you had seen a hanged man yourself. Mr Dupree, Gérard de Nerval. Rue de la Vieille Lanterne, hung himself on some railings, apparently . . . Jenny Colon broke off with de Nerval and married a flautist. Irina was a flautist . . . Were these coincidences or signs? Subtle parallels . . . There was a photograph by Nadar of de Nerval at the end of his life – he'd never seen such a wrecked, ravaged face . . . *visage buriné*, the French called it, a whole lifetime of grief and mental anguish etched there . . . He must have slept at some stage because he did dream . . . he dreamt about Flavia and Kenneth Rintoul. It was Rintoul who was waiting, dishevelled and glum, at his dinky mews house, Rintoul who ran to embrace Flavia . . .

Lorimer had woken and had dutifully jotted the facts down in the dream diary by the bed. Then he had dozed and drifted for a while, his mind intermittently involved with pragmatic details of his work, wondering whether to spend more time backgrounding Gale-Harlequin or simply to march in and play it by ear. At around 4.30 a.m. he made himself a strong cup of tea – two tea bags, a three-minute steep – and somehow managed an hour of dreamless slumber.

'Just the one dream,' Alan said to him later that morning, disappointment heavy in his voice.

'I've got a lot on my mind,' Lorimer protested. 'You're lucky I slept at all, lucky to have anything. Jesus.'

'This fellow,' Alan looked at the dream diary, 'Rintoul. You don't like him?'

'Well, he doesn't like me. He threatened to kill me.'

'Interesting. But you couldn't eradicate him from the dream, this nemesis-figure?'

'It wasn't a lucid dream, Alan.'

'What about the girl? Do you know her?'

'I've seen her in a taxi. She's in a TV ad. I found out her name.'

'You couldn't sexually interpose yourself in this dream?'

'It wasn't a lucid dream, Alan. The last thing I want to see is this Kenneth Rintoul bloke with this Flavia Malinverno girl in his arms.'

'Damn. Damn and shit. These are promising ingredients, Lorimer. Next time concentrate on them.'

'I gave de Nerval a whirl, like you said.'

'Leave Gérard on the sub's bench, next time around. Next time I want you to fantasize about this girl. Strong sexual fantasies, as perverse as you like. Can you come in tonight?'

Lorimer said no. He was beginning to have his doubts about Alan's lucid dream programme. It had all sounded fine initially but now it seemed not to be helping him at all. Light sleepers, Alan claimed, had fifty per cent more lucid dreams than ordinary people and claimed further that in the machinations of the lucid dream – the way it was controlled and influenced by the dreamer – lay the solution to one's sleep disorder. But at this juncture the theory grew a little vague, links in the causal chain sundered, and Lorimer ceased to understand what Alan was talking about, the jargon was too opaque. What was more irritating was that, after six weeks of participation in the Institute's programme, it was ever more clear to Lorimer that the dream segment of the research, rather than the curative outcome, most intrigued Dr Kenbarry.

'You don't really care if I ever sleep normally, do you?' Lorimer accused him as they walked downstairs to the entrance.

'Nonsense,' Alan said, emphatically. 'If you don't end up sleeping normally my work is worthless, that's the whole point.'

His breezy confidence was encouraging and Lorimer felt a little flutter of hope shiver through him as they walked through the building. Corridors were being swept and polished and the air was loud with the plaintive hum of industrial machinery. There was also a fresh smell of mass catering emanating from some canteen or cafeteria and the day's first sleepy, lank-haired students were assembling wordlessly by the revolving doors, swigging sugary colas from two-litre bottles, patiently rolling their thin fags.

'How can you be so sure this is working, Alan?' Lorimer said, scepticism returning again. 'Because I'm not sure, not sure at all.'

'I can see the signs,' he said, cryptically. 'You're my best light sleeper ever, Lorimer. Seven bona-fide lucid dreams in five weeks.'

'Six.'

'Six weeks already? Don't let me down, son. Don't quit while you're ahead.'

'Yeah, but I –'

'Once I work out your lucid dream triggers, you'll be laughing. Physician heal thyself, sort of thing.' He smiled. 'Come back soon, we're on the verge of great things, my child. Mind how you go.'

It was an abnormally dark morning, the mass of cloud seemed to have settled, still and unmoving, about fifty feet above the surrounding rooftops. It did not threaten snow or rain but the light was absurdly feeble for the time of day, tired and puny, greying everything it touched. Perhaps he was suffering from Solar Deprivation Syndrome, or S A D – Seasonal Absence Deficiency or whatever it was called, Lorimer thought, easing himself into his car. Perhaps he should sit for an hour in front of a high-wattage light bulb as, reputedly, melancholy Scandinavians did to revive themselves from their hibernal torpor, a blast of ultra-violet dispelling their winter blues? . . . At least it wasn't raining.

As he drove back to Pimlico – up Church Street and Creek Road, crossing the river at Tower Bridge and on to Lower Thames Street, across Parliament Square to Vauxhall Bridge Road – he wondered again about the credibility and validity of Alan's programme. True, it was highly, not to say impressively, funded: the sleep lab and the monitoring machines had all been paid for by a Department of Education research fund and Alan had two postgraduate assistants logging and collating the data as well as a contract from a university press for the eventual book – *Timor Mortis: The Lucid Dream Phenomenon* (working title). There were even whispered hints of a television documentary. Yet Lorimer still could not rid himself of this feeling of aggrievedness: for Alan he was simply an interesting specimen, an exemplary set of symptoms. He felt as he imagined rats in a psychiatrist's maze might feel, or Pavlov's salivating pooches, or a chimp being soused with perfumes and aftershave. Frankly, Alan did not really care about his troubled nights, in fact as far as he was concerned the more troubled the better.

At the front door in Lupus Crescent a thin black man with waist-length dreadlocks, thick as coaxial cables, was talking animatedly to Lady Haigh. He was introduced as Nigel – the Santafurian from number 20, Lorimer surmised, the mulch-provider. Lady Haigh said she was considering an herbaceous border and Nigel knew where to lay his hands on some excellent compost. Nigel, it turned out, worked for the Westminster Council's Parks Department, tending Pimlico's few forgotten squares – Eccleston, Warwick, St George's, Vincent – its floral roundabouts and roadside plantations. He seemed amiable enough, Lorimer thought, as he clambered up the stairs to his flat, realizing that he really should quell his instant suspicion of all those who worked for municipal parks departments. It was unjust: one rotten apple did not spoil the whole barrel, not every local authority gardener was like Sinbad Fingleton, after all.

54. *The House at Croy.* *I went to Scotland to escape, to be alone and, I suppose, as convention dictates, to find myself. All I knew, after I left school, was that I had to go far away, far from Fulham and the family Blocj. So I sought out the most distant institution of higher education in the land that offered a course I was qualified to take and, after some research, decided that the North Caledonia Institute of Science and Technology provided me with the perfect geographical and academic conditions I required. I took the train north and travelled eagerly six hundred miles to the neat and tidy city of Inverness, with its castle, its cathedral and its clear, shallow river and the enfolding purple hills beyond. It was, for a while, everything I had asked for.*

I lost my virginity in my second term at college to Joyce McKimmie, a mature student (mid-twenties) who sat in on some of the art history seminars I attended. Joyce was a fresh-faced, blowzy redhead who looked full of confidence but in fact was the opposite, her answers to questions in the seminar rooms beginning in an uncertain small voice and swiftly diminishing to a hushed whisper or sometimes even terminating in total inaudibility, leaving us all straining to hear, or creatively interpreting her almost-silence and rounding off her sentences on her behalf. She wore voluminous, improbable combinations of clothes, long, lacy skirts with cleated trainers and a nylon anorak, or in summer went bra-less beneath a man's waistcoat with blue pedal-pushers and flip-flops on her dusty feet. She had a three-year-old child, a boy, Zane, who lived with her mother in Stonehaven during term-time. While she was at college she rented and sub-let rooms in a fair-sized house in a village called Croy to an odd selection of tenants.

Joyce, like many shy people, found liberation in alcohol and our first coupling took place – while we were both drunk – in a back room at someone else's party. We bussed back to Croy at dawn and I spent the next three days there. Joyce seemed to have more money than the rest of us – child benefit? Zane's absent father contributing?

– and this had allowed her to rent the house, which she ran, surprisingly, as a kind of prissy, strict commune, introducing washing-up rotas, waste recycling, a partitioned fridge with prominently labelled milk bottles and coffee jars as well as permitting a tolerant attitude towards sexual activities, alcohol- and drug-consumption. At the centre of this routine was the evening meal, served promptly at eight o'clock, which all members of the house currently present beneath the roof were expected to attend. Amongst the shifting tenants was a hard-core of regulars, two genial, moon-faced brothers from the Isle of Mull, Lachlan and Murdo, a postgraduate Japanese girl called Junko (studying life sciences, to which mysterious end she spent many days out at sea on fishing boats quantifying and analysing catches), Joyce's cousin Shona (thin, wiry, promiscuous) and Sinbad Fingleton, the feckless, gormless son of a local laird, recently expelled from his public school with one GCSE in biology to his credit, who worked for the Inverness Town Council Municipal Parks Department. To my vague surprise I found I liked Joyce's uncomplicated company and the curious regimen in the House at Croy with its blend of licence and order and preferred to spend more time there than alone in my boxy cell in the college hall of residence, with its drab view of muddy football pitches and the dark, impenetrable green of the pine-clad hills beyond.

The Book of Transfiguration

Gale-Harlequin PLC resided in a new granite and polished steel building off Holborn. There was abstract art in the lobby and dark clumps of palm, fern and weeping fig. Uniformed security guards sat behind a rough-hewn ziggurat of slate. The harlequin logo was subtly present in the canvases on the walls, variations on its theme painted by eminent contemporary artists, two of whom Lorimer could identify through the plate-glass from the street. This was not going to be a simple adjust, he felt with small tremors of foreboding, there was a whiff of moneyed respectability about this place, the solid heft of solvency and success.

He checked his notebook: Jonathan L. Gale, chairman and managing director, and Francis Home (pronounced 'hume', doubtless), finance director, were the men he had to see, a far cry from Deano Edmund and Kenny Rintoul, he had to admit, but also, he had to admit further, on occasions these sophisticated types could match anyone in the cupidity and venality stakes. He turned away and strolled off in the direction of Covent Garden, trying to clear his mind of worries: the appointment was scheduled for the next day and he had done as much backgrounding as he was prepared to do. This adjust had to be done newborn, slick and shiny – so the expression ran in GGH – just sprung from the womb, innocent, untarnished, slick and shiny.

Stella had called and left a message on his answering machine: could they meet, with Barbuda, no less, in Covent Garden for a pre-shopping lunch? Her voice had sounded unusually hesitant, not pleading so much as apologetically urging this rendezvous. Lorimer wondered vaguely what was afoot, trying to keep further foreboding at bay – his future was dark enough with foreboding as it was, he had to maintain some light in his life.

He was far too early he saw, as he stepped down the wide circular staircase into the huge basement room that was the Alcazar. Beyond the generous horseshoe of the bar tables were still being set up and there was a clatter and rattle of glasses and bottles being stacked on shelves or slammed into racks, like shells into breeches, ready for the day's offensive. A barman (shaven head, chin beard) looked up from his glass-fronted fridge and said he would be with him in a couple of ticks, chief.

Lorimer sat on a bar stool, sipped at his tomato juice, and selected a newspaper from the layered pile made available to clients. He wondered what the Alcazar had been before its new incarnation as bar-restaurant. Probably a failed bar-restaurant, or nightclub, or storeroom. Yet the ceiling was high and elaborately moulded, the cornice picked out in lime-green and indigo. He enjoyed being in these establishments as they prepared themselves for their day's business. He watched a young guy, wearing a suit but tieless, carrying a copy of the *Sporting Life*, come shiftily in and order a bottle of champagne – one glass. He looks even more tired than I do, Lorimer thought. Another light sleeper, perhaps? Should he introduce him to Alan Kenbarry's Institute of Lucid Dreams, have his sleep disorder solved? Then two other young men sauntered in, fit-looking, also suited but oddly out of sorts in formal wear, as if their bodies were more accustomed to shorts and sweatpants, T-shirts and track suits. They ordered pints of extra-strength lager with a dash of citron vodka – an interesting variation on an old theme, Lorimer thought, making a mental note to try the mix himself when he felt particularly close to the end of his tether. A Japanese family entered, two elderly parents with teenage daughters, and asked to be sat down immediately for an absurdly early lunch. Slowly, the Alcazar accommodated itself to its incoming customers: the music was switched on, the empty crates cleared from behind the bar, the last lemons quartered. Two young women with cold faces and harsh make-up (style: Berlin cabaret 1920s) took up position by the wrought-iron lectern at the restaurant's entrance and pored frowningly over the register like cryptologists close to a solution. Sporting Life was joined by a male friend who also ordered his own bottle of champagne. Lorimer consulted his watch: Stella had stipulated between 12.45 and 1.00, the table was booked in her name, she had said, and Lorimer wondered if, given the chilly demeanour of the two seaters, he should confirm that at least one –

Flavia Malinverno walked in.

Flavia Malinverno walked in and there was a rushing in his ears as of surf foaming and fizzing on a sandy beach. Curious portions of his body – his nostril flanges, the little webs of skin between his fingers – seemed to grow unnaturally hot. For an instant he felt – stupidly – that he should avert his face, before remembering in a second instant that she would not know him, would not know him from Adam. So, covertly, innocently, shifting slightly on his bar stool, he watched her over the top of his newspaper. Watched her have a brief word with the ice maidens at their lectern and watched her take a seat in a far corner of the bar area and order something to drink. Meeting somebody? Obviously. Early like me, over-punctual, good sign. He shook out his newspaper ostentatiously, turning and flattening a flapping page. Extraordinary coincidence. To think that. In the flesh. At more leisure he took her in, drank her in, imprinted her permanently on his memory.

She was tall – right, good – slim, wearing different shades and textures of black. A black leather jacket, sweater, black shawl-scarf thing. Her face? Round, almost blandly even-featured. She seemed neat and clean. Her hair parted, straight, shortish, cut sharp to just below the jawline, glossy dark brown hair, chestnut shot with a purplish-red – some sort of henna? In front of her on the table a fat leather notebook diary, a packet of cigarettes, dull silver block of a lighter. Her drink comes, big glass of yellow wine. She drinks but does not smoke, interesting. Something faintly tomboyish about her. Flat black cowboy boots, small raked Cuban heels. Black jeans. She was looking round the room and he felt her gaze wash over him like the beam of light from a lighthouse and keep on going.

He loosened his tie, very slightly, and with his fingertips mussed his hair, untidying it. Then, to his astonishment, he found he was crossing the room towards her, a voice in his ear – the inner man – shouting, YOU ARE OUT OF YOUR FUCKING MIND, as he heard his own voice saying to her, quite reasonably:

'Excuse me, are you by any chance Flavia Malinverno?'

'No.'

'I'm so sorry, I thought –'

'I'm *Flavia* Malinverno.'

Ah. Flahvia, not Flayvia. Idiot. Fool.

'I'm sorry to bother you,' he proceeded, 'but I saw you on television the other night and –'

'In *Playboy of the Western World*?'

What the hell –? Quickly now.

'Ah, no. An advertisement. A Fortress Sure advertisement. That, ah, advertisement you did.'

'Oh, that.' She frowned. He liked her frown immediately, enormously. A serious, unequivocal buckling of the forehead, an inward coming-together of her eyebrow ends registering huge doubt. And suspicion.

'How do you know my name, then?' she said. 'I don't think they run credits on ads, do they?'

Jesus Christ. 'I, ah, I work for Fortress Sure, you see. P R department, marketing. There was a screening, a presentation. Um, these things stick in my mind, names, dates. I saw it on cable the other night and I thought how good it –'

'Have you got the time on you?'

'Five past one.' He saw her eyes were brown like unmilked tea, her skin was pale, untanned forever and her nails were bitten short. She looked a little worn out, a little tired, but, then again, didn't everybody? We all look a bit tired, these days, some more than others.

'Hmm,' she said, 'I'm meant to be meeting someone here at half twelve.' It seemed to signal a change of tone, this change of subject, a partial admission of him into her own day's routines.

'I just wanted to say you were great, I thought, in that ad.'

'You're most kind.' She looked at him flatly, sceptically, mildly curious. Her accent was neutral, unplaceable, the city's demotic middle-class voice. 'I must have been on screen for a whole five seconds.'

'Exactly. But some presences can –'

'Lorimer.'

He turned to see Stella waving at him from the lectern. Barbuda stood beside her, looking at the ceiling.

'Nice meeting you,' he said, weakly, hopelessly. 'Just thought, I'd, you know –' He spread his palms, smiled goodbye, turned away and crossed the bar area to join Stella and Barbuda, feeling her eyes on his back and hearing in his head an inarticulate, strangely joyous jabber of accusation and exhilaration, of shame and pleasure and regret – regret that the moment was past, was gone forever. Happy – amazed – at his audacity, though. Furious, seething, that he had forgotten to look at her breasts.

He kissed Stella and half waved at Barbuda, as he suspected strongly she did not like being kissed, by him or any male over twenty.

'Hello, Barbuda, half-term, is it?'

85. The Seven Gods of Luck. *At the end of one term in Inverness Junko gave me a present. She gave all the household gifts (she was returning home to Japan for the holiday), gifts of food or articles of clothing that were markedly personal, the result, one assumed, of Junko's particular assessment of the character of the recipient. Shona received a single earring, for example, Joyce a full set of thermal underwear including a thermal bra, while Sinbad was given two bananas. 'Why two?' he asked, wrinkling his nose with a baffled smile, flicking back the corkscrew tendrils of hair that he liked to have fall in front of his eyes. 'One for each hand,' Junko said with a polite smile, which silenced him.*

She gave me a postcard, bought in Japan, stiff and shiny, a bright picture of seven symbolic figures aboard a junk in an extravagantly stylized choppy sea.

'Who are they?' I asked.

'The Shichifukujin. *The seven gods of luck,' she said. 'What you must do, Milo, is put this picture under your pillow on the night of January first and in this way your first dream of the year will be lucky.'*

'This will bring me luck?'

'Of course. I think you are a person who has much need of luck, Milo.'

'Haven't we all?'

'But for you, Milo, I wish you special luck.'

She told me who the seven gods were and I wrote down their names: Fukuro kujo and Jurojin, the gods of long life; Benzaiten, the only female, goddess of love; Bishamonten, warlike, armoured, god of war and good fortune; Daikokuten, god of wealth; Hotei, god of happiness with his bulging belly; and finally Ebisu, the god of self-effacement, carrying a fish, the deity of one's job or career.

Junko said, 'Ebisu is my favourite.'

That New Year I did as she suggested and slipped the card under my pillow and tried to dream a lucky dream, endeavoured to force good luck into my life with the help of the seven gods. I dreamt of my father – was that good luck or bad luck? The year turned out to be a bad one for him and a momentously bad, life-changing one for me. The seven gods of luck. Not the seven gods of good luck. Luck, you must remember, like many things in life, is two-faced – good and bad – something I think the seven gods implicitly recognized, adrift in their little boat on their stormy sea. I left my card from Junko behind during my harassed and rushed departure from Inverness. For a while that loss perturbed me more than it ought to have done.

The Book of Transfiguration

He sensed her leave just as their first courses arrived, he glanced over and saw in the corner of his eye a fleeting dark figure for an instant at the stairs' beginning. He looked around but she was gone.

Stella was talking: she seemed upbeat, cheery today. 'Isn't this nice?' she kept saying. 'The three of us.' At one stage she reached under the table and surreptitiously ran her hand up his thigh until it touched his cock.

'Barbuda's going to her first proper party –'

'Mum, I've been to tons of –'

'And I think there's going to be a certain young man

present. Mmm? So we have to find something very ultra mega glamorous, don't we?'

'Mum, for God's sake.'

Lorimer refused to join in. He remembered this mortifying adult banter all too well from his own hellish adolescence. It was only the impending purchase of expensive clothes, he knew, that explained Barbuda's sullen tolerance of this leering speculation at all. In his own case he recalled similar hours of prurient inquiry from Slobodan about his non-existent sex life, but with no promise of reward to sweeten the pill: 'Who *do* you fancy then? Got to be someone. What's her name, then? She got specs? It's Sandra Deedes, isn't it. Doggy Deedes. He fancies Doggy Deedes. Disgusting.' And so, endlessly, on.

He smiled over at Barbuda in what he hoped was an understanding, non-patronizing, non-avuncular way. She was an ungainly girl, made more lumpy by pubescence, with dark hair and a sly, pointy face. Her small, sharp breasts caused her huge embarrassment and she was always swathed in the baggiest of jumpers, layers of shirts and jackets. She was wearing make-up today, he noticed: a smear of grey above the eyes and a violet lipstick that made her small mouth smaller. She looked a darker, bitterer version of her mother, whose strong features spoke instead of confidence and will-power. Perhaps it was the mysterious Mr Bull's genetic contribution that brought this out in her – hints of low self-esteem, a mean spirit, destined to find life a disappointment.

'Mum, tell Lorimer, will you?'

Stella sighed theatrically. 'Load of nonsense,' she said. 'Still, listen to this. Barbuda doesn't want to be called Barbuda any more. She wants to be called – wait for it – Angelica.'

'It's my middle name.'

'Your middle name is Angela, not Angelica. Barbuda Angela Jane Bull. What's wrong with Jane, eh, Lorimer? I ask you.'

Jane Bull, Lorimer thought, bad idea.

'The girls at school all call me Angelica. I hate being called Barbuda.'

'Rubbish. It's a beautiful name, isn't it, Lorimer?'

'It's the name of an island not a person,' Barbuda/ Angelica said with passionate loathing.

'I've been calling you Barbuda for fifteen years, I can't suddenly change to Angelica.'

'Why not? More people call me Angelica than Barbuda.'

'Well, you'll always be Barbuda to me, young lady.' She turned to Lorimer for support. 'Tell her she's being silly and stupid, Lorimer.'

'Well, actually,' Lorimer said, carefully. 'You know, I sort of understand where she's coming from. Excuse me, I must make a phone call.'

As he rose from the table he caught Barbuda/Angelica's stare of candid astonishment. If only you knew, girl, he thought.

At the payphone by the stairs he punched out Alan's number at the university.

'Alan, it's Lorimer . . . yeah. I need a favour. Do you know anyone at the BBC?'

'I know them all, darling.'

'I need to find out the telephone number of an actress who was in *Playboy of the Western World* the other night. BBC 2, I think.'

'It was Channel Four, actually. Fear not, I have my sources. An actress, eh? Who's she sleeping with?'

Lorimer was inspired. 'It's the girl in the dream. From the ad. Turns out she was in this play. I think I may be on to something, Alan, dreamwise. If I could see her, meet her, talk to her, even. I think I could lucid dream all night.'

'And I thought you were going to say you'd fallen in love.'

They both laughed at this.

'I just have a hunch. She's called Flavia Malinverno.'

'I shall "procure" her for you. In a jiffy.'

Lorimer hung up the phone suffused by a strange feeling of confidence, confident that if there were one motive force likely to galvanize Alan Kenbarry it was the prospect of a spouting silver fountain of lucid dreams.

381. Market Forces. *This evening Marlobe said to me, pointing the wet stem of his pipe at my chest, 'It's dog eat fucking dog, my friend. Market forces. You cannot buck the market. I mean, face it, we are all, like it or not, capitalists. And the amount I pay in fucking taxes justifies me, personally, in saying to those whingeing fucking scroungers – PISS OFF. And you, matey, fuck right off to your own sad fucking stinking country, wherever it is.' Two old women waiting for a bus moved huffily away, saying loudly they were going to a nicer bus stop. Marlobe appeared not to hear this. 'You understand these matters,' he said. 'You in your business, just like me in mine. We got no choice. Market fucking forces rules. If you go to the wall, you go to the wall.' So I decided to ask him what he felt about the recently installed flower stand in the ShoppaSava. 'Load of fucking rubbish,' he said, although his grin looked a little sick. 'Who wants to buy a flower from a checkout girl? You want personal service. Someone who knows flora, the fluctuations of the seasons, the proper nurture and attention of the flower. I'll give it a month. They'll lose a fortune.' I made a worried face and said, I* *thought, bravely, 'Well . . . Market forces? . . .' He laughed and showed me his surprisingly strong-looking white teeth (are they false?). 'I'll give them market forces,' he said. 'You wait.'*

The Book of Transfiguration

Chapter 7

His mother passed him a small circular tray of piled white bread sandwiches.

'Here, Milo, take this down to Lobby, darling, will you?'

He thought there were probably twenty or thirty sandwiches, cut into triangles, with various fillings of meat and all neatly laid out in concentric circles as if to be handed round at an office party or working lunch.

'They're not all for him, surely?'

'He's a growing young boy,' his grandmother said.

'He's nearly forty years old, Gran, for heaven's sake.'

His grandmother spoke to his mother in their language, saying something that made them both chuckle.

'What's that?' Lorimer asked.

'She say: if a man eat too much fish he don't got enough meat.'

'Go on, go on, Milo. Lobby don't like to wait for his lunch.'

From the hall he could see his father being walked gently along the angled walls of the living room by Komelia, her hands carefully supporting an elbow. His father was wearing a blue blazer with a badge on the breast pocket and a pair of pale blue slacks. His white beard had been recently trimmed, its edges razored sharp against his pink skin.

'Look, Dad, there's Milo,' Komelia said, as the circuit brought him round to face the open doorway to the hall. His father's creased bright eyes twinkled, the permanent smile never faltered.

'Give him a wave, Milo.'

Lorimer raised his hand for a second or two and let it fall. It was all too fucking sad, he thought, desperately. Komelia led him off again, his father's feet moving busily in short shuffling steps.

'Isn't he doing well? Hello, Dad. Look, Milo's here.' Monika had appeared silently from somewhere in the house to stand beside him. She helped herself to one of Slobodan's sandwiches. 'Tongue?' she exclaimed, chewing. 'Since when does he get tongue?'

'He seems fine,' Lorimer said, inclining his head in his father's direction. 'How's he doing?'

'He's sixty-five years old, Milo, and he's not as regular as he should be.'

'What does that mean?'

'Doctor's coming. We think he needs a wee enema.'

Lorimer carried Slobodan's tray downstairs and along the street to the B and B office. There was a gusty cold wind blowing with a misty fine rain mixed up in it and Lorimer held his spread palm an inch above the sandwich rings in case one of them might be flipped away by the stiff breeze. In the office Drava sat in front of a VDU making up the accounts; beyond her on two shiny, bum-worn sofas lounged half a dozen drivers, reading the papers and smoking. There were mutters of welcome.

'Milo.'

'Cheers, Milo.'

'Hi, Milo.'

'Dave, Mohammed, Terry. Hi, Trev, Winston. How you doing?'

'Brilliant.'

'Smashing.'

'You off to a wedding, Milo?'

'This is Mushtaq. He's new.'

'Hi, Mushtaq.'

'He's Lobby's little bro.'

'He's the brains in the family, ha.'

'Give us one of Lobby's sarnies, then,' Drava said, taking off her specs and pinching the bridge of her nose, hard. 'How are you, Milo? Look a bit done in. They working you too hard? Very smart, I must say.'

'It's the weight of that wallet what he has to carry around, ha,' Dave said.

'I'm fine,' Lorimer said. 'Got a meeting in town. I heard Dad was poorly, said I'd drop by.'

'He's got awful constipation. Rock solid. Won't budge. Hang about, that's tongu .'

'Get your mucky paws off of my lunch,' Slobodan said, wandering out of his control room. 'Trev, take over, will you? Mohammed? Parcel at Tel-Track. How are you, Milo? Looks a bit tired, don't he, Drava?'

Slobodan relieved him of the tray, winked at him and started eating a sandwich. 'Tongue,' he said appreciatively, 'nice one,' and stuck his own out at Drava. 'Back in half a mo. Anything you want me to tell Phil?'

'Nothing printable.'

'I'll tell him that and he won't be well pleased, Drava. Come on, Milo. Have a word in my office.'

Lorimer followed his brother out into the street and round the corner to his small terraced house. He noticed that Slobodan had plaited his ponytail and as he walked it bumped unpliantly from shoulder to shoulder as if it were stiffened with wire. The house was a product of Slobodan's brief (six months) marriage some eight or nine years ago. Lorimer had only met his sister-in-law, Teresa, once – at the wedding, in fact – and could dimly bring to mind a feisty, lisping brunette. The next time he returned home the marriage was over and Teresa had left. But the purchase of the nuptial home had at least ensured Slobodan's quitting of the Blocj household and he had lived in impoverished but seemingly contented bachelorhood around the corner ever since. He was always keen to volunteer confidences about his sex-life and occasional partners ('Can't do without it, Milo, it's not natural') but Lorimer did not encourage such revelations.

Slobodan, to give him credit, Lorimer thought, kept the place tidy. He had gravelled the thin strip of front garden and had trailed a clematis over the front door. He paused now at the gate, munching, and gestured with his tray of sandwiches at his shiny car, an ancient, much-loved burgundy Cortina.

'Looking good, eh?'

'Very shiny.'

'Waxed her yesterday. Come up lovely.'

There were no pictures on the walls in Slobodan's immaculate house and only the absolute minimum of furniture sparsely occupied the rooms. A persistent smell of air freshener lingered about the place as if someone regularly wandered upstairs and down with a can of aerosol scooshing wafts of 'Forest Glade' or 'Lavender Meadow' into the corners. Above the fireplace in the living room was the house's sole ornament, a large crucifix with a quarter-life-size, writhing, blood-drizzled Christ.

The television was on and watching the lunchtime news was Phil Beazley, a can of beer in hand, Drava's ex-husband and Slobodan's partner in B and B Mini-cabs and International Couriers.

'Hey, Milo,' Phil said, 'my main man.'

'Hi, Phil.'

'What you drinking, Milo?' Slobodan stood by his crammed drinks trolley – over fifty beverages on offer, was his proud boast. Lorimer passed; Phil had his beer replaced and Slobodan fixed himself a Campari and soda. Phil knelt forward and turned down the volume on the television. He was a small, thin man – dangerously thin, Lorimer thought – with sunken cheeks and jutting narrow hips. He dyed his fine hair blond and wore an earring. His blue eyes were slightly astigmatic and he cultivated a jolly, laddish demeanour that seemed entirely false. One's first and lasting impression of Phil Beazley was one of suspicion. For example, Lorimer suspected strongly that Beazley had only married Drava – a hunch that was reinforced by the christening of Mercedes – for the euphonious motoring associations of her name.

'Good to see you, Milo,' Phil Beazley said, regaining his seat. 'Been a while. Looking terrific, isn't he, Lobby?'

'Smart as a new pin, Phil.'

'You handsome bastard. I can see life's treating you well, no worries,' Beazley said.

Lorimer felt a weariness descend on him and simultaneously a concomitant, metaphorical weightening of his cheque book in his breast pocket, as if its leaves had turned to lead.

It duly turned out that B and B's cash-flow problem was insignificant and temporary, so Slobodan and Phil warmly informed him. A valued account customer had gone bankrupt, leaving four months' unpaid bills. This valued account customer had turned out to be a fucking bastard evil cunt because even though he knew he was going to go belly-up he was still ordering cars like 'they was going out of fashion'. Cars here, cars there, cars to take packages to Bristol and Birmingham, cars for wait-and-returns clocking up idle hours outside pubs and nightclubs. Phil said he wanted to sledgehammer the valued account customer's kneecaps or do a 'chesterfield' on his back with an industrial stapler but Lobby here had dissuaded him. They were taking on more drivers to make up the shortfall but in the interim, temporarily, through no fault of their own, they were in need of an injection of capital.

'Above board, Milo, no favours, here's what I propose. I, me, am going to sell you the Cortina.'

'How much?'

'Three K.'

'I have a car,' Lorimer said. 'What do I want with your Cortina? You need it.'

'I've got a new motor, a Citroën. The Cortina is a classic car, Milo. Look on it as an investment.'

On the television set were mute images of a burning village in Africa. Boy soldiers brandished Kalashnikovs at the camera.

Lorimer reached for his cheque book. 'Three grand will cover it?'

Phil and Slobodan looked at each other as if to say: shit, we should have asked for more.

'You can't do it cash, can you, Milo?'

'No.'

'That going to be a problem, Phil?'

'Ah. No. Could you make it out to my dad? Anthony Beazley. Great. Terrific, Milo, ace.'

'Diamond,' Slobodan agreed. 'Diamond geezer.'

Lorimer handed over the cheque, trying to keep the resignation out of his voice. 'Pay me back when you can. Keep the car for the firm. Find another driver, use it, make it work for you.'

'Nice idea, Milo. Good thinking, Phil, isn't it?'

'That's why he's the City gent, Lobby, not like us daft cunts. Nice idea, Milo.'

As he drove east – New King's Road, Old Church Street, along the Embankment, along the sunken, torpid, mud-banked river, past the bridges – Albert, Chelsea, Vauxhall, Lambeth – on to Parliament Square and its honey-coloured, busily buttressed and fretted palace (focus of Marlobe's unquenchable bile), an uncharitable thought edged its way into his mind: how had Slobodan known he was coming that day and so contrived to have Phil Beazley present? Answer: because when he, Lorimer, had called his mother she had said his father was unwell and he had immediately arranged a visit. But his father had seemed unchanged, or at least much as usual, despite all the loud diagnosis about the state of his bowels. And this business with the sandwiches – his mother and grandmother practically pushing him out of the kitchen ... It was as if he had been set up, set up by his own family for a three grand sting to help Lobby Blocj out of a jam.

214. Lorimer Black. *If you want to change your name, the solicitor said, simply do so. If enough people call you by, or know you under, your new name then you have effectively, to all intents* *and purposes, changed your name. As an adult you are perfectly free to do this, as the case of many actors and artistes demonstrates.*

But this seemed too easy to you, too ephemeral. What about documents, you asked? What about driving licence, passport, insurance, pension plan? What if you wanted all the documentation of your life to bear your new name?

Then that will require formalizing, the solicitor said. Either by deed poll or by what is called a statutory declaration, witnessed by a lawyer. You submit the statutory declaration as formal evidence of your change of name.

This was what you wanted, you wanted your new name to be in all the record banks and computer mainframes, in the files and phone books, the voting registries, in your passport and on your credit cards. Only in this way could you truly possess your different identity. Your old name is deleted, becomes an endangered species, then, eventually, extinct.

This was what was dominating your thoughts when you returned so suddenly from Scotland. A clear and distinct schism had to be established. Milomre Blocj would not be rubbed out entirely but would live on quietly, known to a handful of people in a corner of Fulham. But to the rest of the world he would cease to exist: your statutory declaration would see to that, from now on you could and would become Lorimer Black.

You came back suddenly from Scotland to change your name and life and found your father ill.

He was lying in bed, his skin grey, his beard untrimmed, whiter and thicker than you remembered.

'What's wrong, Dad?' you asked. 'Working too hard?'

'I keep thinking I fainting,' he said. 'Everything going like misty. The noise too, I don't hear the noise proper. I feel tired. Maybe I got virus.'

'Take it easy, Dad.'

'You come home, Milo. Everything all right?'

'I need to get a job, Dad. I need your help.'

'What you want to do? EastEx is not so good now. You could work with Slobodan on the cars.'

'I need something different. Something safe. Something ordinary.'
You were thinking: nine to five, Monday to Friday, an office, steady, anonymous, routine, grey, calm. You were thinking: accounting, a bank, civil service, telephone sales, credit control, assistant manager, personnel . . .

'You tell me, Milo, I got plenty friends. I can get you job. But be quick, OK? I don't think I very well man. What job you want to do, Milo?'

You said, quite spontaneously, 'Insurance.'

The Book of Transfiguration

Lorimer parked in the multi-storey off Drury Lane, where he sat in his car quietly for five minutes gathering his thoughts, calmly rehearsing the phrases he would use and the inflections he would give them. Then he changed his tie – silk, but very subdued – put the waistcoat on under his jacket and changed his tassled loafers for lace-up brogues. As a final touch he recombed his hair and placed the parting an inch further to the left. Most of these small signifiers would be undetected by ninety-nine per cent of the people he met; the remaining one per cent who almost unreflectingly registered them would regard them as a norm, and thus entirely unexceptional. And this was what he was after, really: the minute alter-ations in his appearance were designed primarily for himself, they were for his own peace of mind, encouraging confidence in the persona he had decided to wear. They functioned, in a way, as a form of almost invisible armour and, thus protected, he was ready to do battle.

Jonathan L. Gale's capacious corner office looked down Holborn towards St Paul's cathedral and beyond to the tall scattered towers of the City. The day was fresher, the blue sky populated with a dense flotilla of clouds, spinnakering north. The wink of sunflash on high windows, as he turned his head.

'If you can believe it,' Gale was saying, sawing at the vista with the edge of his palm, 'I'm actually going to spoil my own view. Our new development is going to block out about three-quarters of the dome of St Paul's . . .' He shrugged. 'It is a rather super building, I must say.'

'I think Wren is the master, finally,' Lorimer said.

'What? Oh no, I mean our new development.' He went on proudly to name a firm of architects he was employing of whom Lorimer had never heard.

'You could always move office,' Lorimer ventured.

'Yeees. Can I get you some coffee, tea, *acqua minerale*?'

'No, thank you.'

Jonathan Gale sat down behind his desk, taking care not to crease his jacket. He was a slackly handsome man in his fifties with an even sunbed-bronzed look to him and thinning, oiled-back chestnut hair. Lorimer was relaxed, Gale was in the ninety-nine per cent, he had overcompensated. Gale was also a little too well-dressed, in Lorimer's verdict. Savile Row suit, yes, but the cut was slightly too tightly waisted, the lapels a little wide, the rear vents a little too long. Also the vibrant cobalt blue shirt with the white collar and cuffs, the pillar-box red of the tie were distinctly lurid – all this and the unfamiliar knobbled leather (mamba? iguana? komodo dragon?) and pointedness of the shoes hinted at *dandysme*, the ultimate sin in Ivan Algomir's book, the worst sort of pretension. The watch was ostentatious, heavy, gold, rising half an inch off the wrist with many dials and projecting winders. This chronometer was consulted and there ensued some speculation about the tardiness of Francis, whereupon he presently arrived, apologizing.

Francis Home was olive-skinned, wearing a dollar-green suit that only the French and Italians can get away with. He had dark, crinkly hair and a fine gold chain around his right wrist. He smelt of some faint coniferous, cedary aftershave or cologne. Cypriot? Lebanese? Spanish? Egyptian? Syrian? Greek? Like himself, Lorimer knew, there were many types of Englishmen.

Lorimer shook the hand with the gold chain. 'Mr *Hume*,' he pronounced carefully, 'how do you do? I'm Lorimer Black.'

'Homey,' Home said with a slight guttural rasp on the 'h'. 'The "e" is not silent.'

Lorimer apologized, repeated his name correctly, coffee was ordered and fetched and they took up their positions.

'We are simply devastated by the fire,' Gale said. 'Shocked. Aren't we, Francis?'

'It is a most serious matter for us. The knock-on effect to our operations is . . . is . . .'

'Disastrous.'

'Precisely,' Home agreed. He had a very slight accent, quasi-American, Lorimer thought. 'The claim is in,' Home went on. 'I assume everything is in order,' he added, knowing full well it wasn't.

'I'm afraid not,' Lorimer confirmed, sadly. 'It turns out that the fire in the Fedora Palace was a deliberate one. Arson.'

Gale and Home looked sharply at each other, eyes beaming messages in unfeigned alarm, Lorimer thought.

He continued: 'It was started by one of your subcontractors, Edmund, Rintoul, to avoid paying penalty charges. Of course they deny it, categorically.'

Gale and Home's surprise deepened. They wanted to speak, to curse, to exclaim, Lorimer guessed, but some profound level of caution silenced them. They glanced at each other again, as if waiting for a sleepy prompter: the mood in the room grew darkly serious, stakes increasing by the second.

'Deliberately? Are you sure?' Gale managed to say, forcing a baffled smile.

'It happens all the time. A week or two's delay is all they're after, a rescinding of the penalty clause. *Force majeure*, sort of thing. The trouble with the Fedora Palace was that it all got out of hand, badly out of control. A little bit of damage to the gymnasium would have sufficed – they'd no intention of destroying five floors and the rest.'

'This is outrageous. Who are these men? They should be in prison, for God's sake.'

'They deny everything.'

'You should prosecute them,' Home said brutally. 'Sue. Destroy them. And their families.'

'Ah, but it's not our problem, Mr Home. It's yours.'

There was a silence. Home began to look genuinely troubled, rubbing his hands together persistently to produce an irritating slippery rasp of moist flesh.

'You're saying that this will affect payment of the claim in some way,' Gale ventured.

'Yes, I'm afraid so,' Lorimer said. 'In a significant way.' He paused. 'We will not be paying.'

'It's not a question of disagreeing with the valuation?' Gale asked, still civil.

'No. But in our opinion it has become a criminal matter. It's no longer a straightforward claim for fire damage. One of your own contractors has deliberately destroyed a fair proportion of the building. We can't simply reimburse arsonists, you must understand. The whole city would be ablaze.'

'What do the police say?'

'I've no idea. These conclusions are a result of our own investigations, carried out by us on behalf of your insurer.' Lorimer paused. 'I have no alternative under these circumstances but to advise them – Fortress Sure – not to honour this claim.' He paused once more, giving a trace of a saddened smile. 'Until these matters are satisfactorily resolved. It could take a long time.'

Gale and Home looked at each other again, Gale making an effort to keep his features composed.

'You'll have to pay us in the end. Good God, man, did you see our premiums?'

'The premiums are nothing to do with our firm. We are simply loss adjusters. Our advice is that this is a criminal matter and in view of this it would be most inappropriate –'

It went on for a while in this clipped and politely hostile way, the subtext – Lorimer was sure – emerging plain and lucid for all to see. Then he was asked to leave the room for a while and was served a cup of tea by a brisk, matronly woman who made small effort to disguise the utter loathing she held him in. After twenty minutes he was summoned back – Home was no longer present.

'Is there any way you can see that might get us out of this ... this fix?' Gale asked, more reasonably. 'Any compromise we might reach in order to avoid endless delay?'

Lorimer met his gaze unflinchingly: it was vital to avoid all sense of embarrassment, of covert shamefulness, of tacit admission of guilt.

'It's possible,' Lorimer said. 'Our clients are normally keen to find a solution – some sort of median figure that is acceptable to both parties is usually the best way forward.'

'You mean if I agree to take less?'

'If you see the difficulties this sort of case presents us with and if you decide in the interests of expediency –'

'How much?'

This was too bold, so Lorimer decided to press on, formally: '– you decide in the interests of expediency that the full claim should be reduced. If I go back to my client with this information, I'm sure a compromise can be reached.'

Gale looked at him coldly. 'I see. And what sort of a figure do you think Fortress Sure will be able to live with?'

This was the moment: Lorimer could feel the pulses pumping in his wrists – 20 million? 15 million? He looked at Gale and his instincts spoke loud and clear.

'I should think,' he frowned as if making swift mental calculations, but he had already decided, 'I should think you'd be safe with 10 million.'

Gale let out a throaty half-laugh, half-expletive.

'You owe me £27 million and you offer me 10? Jesus Christ.'

'Remember this is no longer normal business, Mr Gale. Your contractors started this fire deliberately. We would be entitled to walk away from this.'

Gale stood up, walked to the window and contemplated his soon-to-be-spoilt view of the ancient cathedral.

'Would you put that in writing? The offer of 10 million?'

'You are the one making the offer,' Lorimer reminded him. 'I'm sure that if it's acceptable you will be formally notified.'

'Well, I'll make the offer formally, you get me an "acceptance" in writing, Mr Black, and we'll take it from there.' He bowed his head. 'If 10 million seems the way of least resistance, then I will – with huge reluctance – reduce my claim on the Fedora Palace.'

At the door Gale turned to face him, blocking his exit. His tan face was flushed with blood, his anger turning him brick-coloured.

'People like you are filth, Black, you're scum. You're no better than thieves, lying fucking villains. You'll happily take our money but when it comes to paying out –'

'Would you please let me leave.'

Gale continued to swear harshly at him in a low voice as Lorimer stepped back.

'As soon as we have your communication we'll be in touch, Mr Gale. Tomorrow, probably.'

As Lorimer hummed down in the lift towards the lobby, towards its lush greenness and discreet lighting, he felt his head throbbing slightly, felt his chest fill and lighten, as if packed with effervescing bubbles and – strangely, this was a first – his eyes smarted from unshed tears. But beneath his exhilaration, his buoyant sense of triumph, a keener warning note sounded. Gale had seemed angry, sure – he had just lost £17 million that he might reasonably have thought were coming to him – but he hadn't been nearly angry enough, in Lorimer's opinion, not nearly, that was the trouble. Why not? This was worrisome.

117. The First Adjust. *You flourished in 'insurance' in those early years. Your father's connections delivered a lowly but secure actuarial job, you diligently worked and were duly rewarded and routinely promoted. As part of a diversification and work-experience scheme in your first company you were sent on attachment to a firm of loss adjusters. Your first adjust was at a shoe shop in Abingdon whose stock had been ruined as a result of a burst pipe, inundating the basement, unnoticed over a bank holiday weekend.*

How did you know the owner was lying? How did you know that the grief and handwringing was sham? Hogg said later it was pure instinct. All great loss adjusters, Hogg said, can spot a liar at once because they understand, at a fundamental level, the need to lie. They may be liars themselves – and if they are they are excellent liars – but it is not necessary. What is necessary is this understanding of the philosophy of a lie, the compulsive urge to conceal the truth, its complex grammar, its secret structures.

And you knew this man was lying about his soaked and sodden stock, and you knew his wife was lying too as she tried gamely to hold back the tears while they contemplated, alongside you, the destruction of their family business. Mr Maurice, that was the name.

You looked at the papier maché litter of hundreds of drenched shoe boxes, the shining puddles on the floor, smelt the stench of wet leather in your nose and something made you turn to Mr Maurice and say, 'How do I know you just didn't turn your hose on the rest of the stock that weekend, Mr Maurice? It seems tremendous damage for one burst pipe.'

It is the quality of the rage that gives them away. The rage is always there, it always erupts, and Mr Maurice's rage was impressive, but something about the pitch and tone of an indifferent liar's rage rings false, troubles the inner ear, like the whine of a mosquito in a darkened bedroom, unmistakable, unerringly disturbing.

So you told Mr Maurice that you were going to advise his insurers to refuse to honour his claim on the grounds of fraud. Shortly after, Mr Maurice was prepared to accept a cash payment of £2,000 as compensation. You saved the insurance company £14,000, you earned your first bonus, it was inevitable that you became a loss adjuster and your continuing, remarkable success in your chosen field brought you, eventually, to the attention of George Gerald Hogg.

The Book of Transfiguration

'Well, well, well,' Hogg said sonorously, and lit a cigarette with his usual little flourish. 'Well, well, well. Ten million.' Hogg raised his pint of lager. 'Cheers, son, well done.'

Lorimer toasted himself with his half of Guinness. He had calculated as thoroughly as he could on the way over and, as far as he could tell, on the basis of a £17 million adjust, the bonus due to him was £134,000, give or take a few hundred. A standard 0.5 per cent up to one million and then a complex scale of exponentially diminishing fractions of one per cent as the amount grew. He wondered what the company's commission would be – Hogg's commission. Well into seven figures, he guessed. This was a big one: only Dymphna dealt routinely in sums like these with her botched dam projects, unbuilt power stations and disappearing jumbo jets. This was a straight and simple 'save' for Fortress Sure. No risk had been laid off. A good day at the office for all concerned, so why wasn't Hogg happier?

'Any trouble?' Hogg asked. 'Missiles? Screamers?'

'No. Just the usual insults and oaths.'

'Sticks and stones, chummy. Still, I take my hat off to you, Lorimer,' Hogg said. 'I don't think even I'd have dared pitch it quite that low myself. So – the question looms large – why did he go for it?'

Lorimer shrugged. 'I don't know,' he said. 'I couldn't really figure it out. Cash-flow problems? Doubt it. A little of something better than all of nothing? Perhaps. They seem a pretty secure organization.'

'They are,' Hogg said, reflectively. 'Funny that. I thought there would have been more of an explosion. A few writs, threats, telephone calls . . .'

'I must say I was a bit surprised too,' Lorimer admitted.

Hogg looked at Lorimer, shrewdly. 'You cut along to the Fort. See Dowling in Finance, be the bearer of good news.'

'Me?' Lorimer said, puzzled. This was normally Hogg's prized and privileged role.

'You deserve the credit, son. Drink up. I'll get another round in.'

Dowling was genuinely pleased, however. A genial, plump man with a big belly and a capric stink of lunchtime cigars about him, he shook Lorimer's hand warmly and talked a lot about appalling oversights, damage-limitation and the valued saving to the firm. Then he excused himself and left the room, returning in two minutes with Sir Simon Sherriffmuir himself. Up close, Sherriffmuir's face was fleshier and more seamed than had appeared the night of Torquil's farewell party. But Lorimer could not fault his clothes: a black pinstripe just shy of ostentation, butter yellow shirt and a big-knotted, pale-pink, self-coloured tie. Everything bespoke, Lorimer knew instantly, even the tie. He wore no watch, Lorimer noticed and wondered if there was a fob somewhere. Interesting: he was not up on the protocols of fobs – perhaps he should affect one? – he would have to check with Ivan.

'This is the young man', Dowling was saying, 'who's saved us all that money.'

Sherriffmuir smiled automatically, his handshake was firm and brisk. 'Best news I've had all day. And you are?'

'Lorimer Black.' He just managed to prevent himself adding a servile 'sir'.

'So, you're one of George's brilliant young samurai,' Sherriffmuir mused, looking at him almost fondly. 'It's been a bit of a bloody cock-up, this Fedora Palace business, I'm most grateful to you. Can you wrap it up quickly? We want to get the whole mess behind us.'

'I've agreed we'll OK the new claim,' Dowling interjected.

'Good, good . . .' Lorimer felt Sherriffmuir still studying him, with some mild curiosity. 'You're not Angus Black's youngest, are you?'

'No,' Lorimer said, thinking: I'm Bogdan Blocj's youngest, and feeling a small, rare flush of shame.

'Send my love to your pa, will you? Tell him we've got to get him south of the border soon,' Sherriffmuir said, not listening and turning to Dowling. 'Peter, see you at –?'

'– Half five. All arranged.'

Sherriffmuir moved easily to the door, slightly round-shouldered like many tall men, the hair on the back of his head curling up above his collar, Lorimer noticed.

He gave Lorimer a loose, parting wave. 'Thanks, Lorimer, fine work.'

Despite his better instincts Lorimer felt pride in himself, as if he had been suddenly ennobled, vindicated by Sir Simon's praise and the familiar use of his Christian name. For God's sake, he rebuked himself almost instantly: the man's not God Almighty, he just works in insurance, like the rest of us.

Rajiv was leaning on his counter, smoking, tie off, his shirt unbuttoned almost to his navel, as if he were on holiday.

'Hail to the conquering hero,' he said, not smiling.

'Thanks, Raj,' Lorimer said. 'You lose some, you win some.'

Rajiv slipped his hand inside his shirt and massaged a plump breast. Now he did smile, a slight puckering of his round cheeks.

'Don't get too big for those boots,' he said. 'Hogg's in your cubicle.'

As Lorimer wandered down the corridor Shane Ashgable poked his head out of his office, jerked a thumb and mouthed 'Hogg' at him. Such rare solidarity, Lorimer thought, can only mean one thing: Hogg is in one of his black moods.

Pausing at his door, Lorimer could see through the glass rectangle Hogg openly going through the files and correspondence in his in-tray. He glanced towards Dymphna's door – she was sitting at her desk crying, dabbing at her eyes with a corner of tissue. Bad, bad omens, Lorimer thought. But why the mood change? What had happened? The first wave of Hogg's wrath had evidently broken on poor Dymphna: he would have to be nicer to Dymphna, he thought suddenly, charitably, perhaps he would ask her for a drink after work.

Hogg did not look round, nor desist from his investigation of Lorimer's paperwork, when he entered.

'You heard any more from the police about that suicide?' Hogg asked.

'Just a follow-up visit. Why?'

'Has there been an inquest?'

'Not yet. Will there be one?'

'Of course.'

Hogg stepped round the desk and lowered himself slowly into Lorimer's chair and scrutinized him aggressively.

'Go all right with Dowling?'

'Fine. Sir Simon came in.'

'Ah. Sir Simon, himself. Very honoured.'

Lorimer could see there was a torn-out sheet from a message pad in the middle of his desk blotter. Reading it upside down he saw that it said 'Dr Kenbarry' and was followed by a number. A telephone number, and, below that, an address. He felt his throat go dry, tight.

Hogg was wrestling angrily with something stuck in his jacket pocket and cursing silently. Finally he removed it and handed it over to Lorimer – it was a compact disc, still wrapped in its tight cellophane sheath. On a plain white field in jagged child's handwriting the cover read 'David Watts. Angziertie.' Along the bottom of the square was a photograph of three dead bluebottles on their backs, their sets of six legs brittle, half-clenched.

'Angziertie,' Lorimer read slowly. 'Is that German? Or bad spelling?'

'For the love of Mike, how should I know?' Hogg said, angrily.

He *is* in a filthy mood, Lorimer remarked to himself, and wondered again what harshness had been visited on Dymphna.

'Who is David Watts?' Lorimer tried again.

'Your next job,' Hogg said.

'Who is David Watts?'

'Sweet suffering Christ, even I've heard of David Watts.'

'Sorry.'

'He's a singer. A "rock" singer. D'you know his music?'

'The only contemporary music I listen to these days is African.'

'Right, that does it.' Hogg stood up, furiously, abruptly, to attention. 'You know, Lorimer, sometimes I think you're fucking barking mad. I mean, for God's sweet sake, man.' He began to pace angrily about the office. Lorimer pressed himself against the wall. 'I mean, Jesus Christ, how old are you? What's the point of employing young people? You should have this popular culture stuff at your fingertips. He's a bloody rock singer. Everyone's heard of him.'

'Oh, yes. Rings a bell, now. That David Watts.'

'Don't fucking interrupt me when I'm talking.'

'Sorry.'

Hogg stopped in front of him and stared, balefully, frowningly at him.

'Sometimes I think you're not normal, Lorimer.'

'Define "normal" —'

'Watch it, right?' Hogg jabbed a blunt, nicotined finger at him, then he sighed, allowed his features to slump, tutted, and shook his head. 'I don't know, Lorimer, I just don't know . . . I'm not a happy matelot at the moment. My life is lacking in joy. Janice has got the file on this David Watts character. Sounds right up your alleyway.'

He paused at the door, made sure it was shut and then in a curious crabwise fashion shuffled back towards him, still keeping half an eye on the corridor visible through the glass panel. He smiled now, showing his small yellow teeth through the slit in his lips.

'Know what I'm going to do Monday? First thing Monday morning?'

'No, Mr Hogg. What?'

'I'm going to sack Torquil Helvoir-Jayne.'

388. A Glass of White Wine. *Torquil is not a particularly proud or vainglorious man; I would not say 'pride' was listed among his many vices, but he is fiercely defensive about what he considers his sole claim to lasting fame, and he defends his rights to this obscure celebrityhood with adamant passion. He claims, he insists, he demands to be credited, acknowledged to be the originator, the only begetter of a piece of apocrypha, a snippet of contemporary folklore that he himself spawned but which, to his continuing fury, has now passed unattributed into common currency.*

It happened at a weekend house party in Wiltshire (or Devon or Cheshire or Gloucestershire or Perthshire). On the Saturday night, copious alcohol had been consumed by the guests, all in their twenties (this was a while ago, in the 1980s), young men and women, couples, singles, a few marrieds, escaping to the country for their precious weekends, fleeing their city homes, their jobs, their humdrum weekday personae. Torquil had been possibly the drunkest that Saturday night, knee-walking drunk, he said, mixing drinks with abandon, whisky following port following claret following champagne. He had risen late on the Sunday morning, after midday, when the other guests had already had breakfast, been for a walk, read the Sunday papers and were now forgathering in the drawing room for pre-Sunday lunch drinks.

'I arrived downstairs,' Torquil says, taking up the story, 'feeling like total shit, serious bad news, hill-cracking headache, mouth like an ashtray, eyes like pissholes in the snow. And they're all standing there with their bloody marys, gins and tonics, vodkas and orange juice. There's a bit of jeering, bit of ribbing as I stumble in, feeling like death, and the girl whose house party it was – forget her name

– comes up to me. Everyone was looking at me, you see, because I was so late and I looked like absolute death warmed up, all laughing at me, and this girl comes up to me and says, "Torquil, what're you going to have to drink? G and T? Bloody mary?" Actually, to tell the truth, the thought made me want to puke and so I said, quite seriously, quite spontaneously, "Ah, no thank you, I couldn't possibly touch a drop of alcohol, I'll just have a glass of white wine."

At this point he stops and stares at me long and hard and says, 'Now, you've heard that story before, haven't you?'

'Yes,' I remember I said. 'I have. I can't think where. It's an old joke, isn't it?'

'No. It was me,' Torquil protests, helplessly, voice cracking. 'That was me. I said it: I was the first person who said it, ever. It was my line. Now any old smart-arse bounds down the stairs on a Sunday morning and gets a cheap laugh. It's not an "old joke", it was something I said. I said it first and everyone's forgotten.'

The Book of Transfiguration

He punched out the telephone number that Alan had given him, realizing that he was functioning on a kind of personal automatic pilot; he was acting on pure whim, without reflection or analysis or thought of any consequences beyond the present moment. The phone rang, rang again, rang again.

'Yeah?'

A man's voice. He was jerked out of his robotic reverie: he thought fast.

'Hello, could I speak to Mr Malinverno?'

'Speaking.'

'Oh good. I'm calling from –'

Lorimer hung up. Why had he not thought of this before? How could this probability, or possibility, not even have entered his calculations? So, she was married. No – it could have been a brother, or even a father, or even an uncle (just). All feeble, self-deluding stuff, he realized: a Mr Malinverno had answered the phone – the odds were that this was the man in her life.

To clear his mind, and calm himself down, he turned to other more pressing matters: he dictated a letter into his pocket memo for Gale-Harlequin confirming that a reduced claim of £10 million would be acceptable to his clients, Fortress Sure. Janice would arrange to have it typed up and sent off in the morning – at least some sort of satisfactory full-stop had been appended to that chapter of his life.

Dymphna's eyes were still heavy and pink-rimmed but she seemed to have regained her usual animated and genial mood, he thought. Appropriately, it was happy hour and they were in The Clinic, a newly themed, large pub off Fleet Street – Dymphna's choice. The barmen wore white coats and the serving waitresses were dressed in skimpy nurses' uniforms. Dymphna was drinking a cocktail called a Soluble Aspirin which, as far as Lorimer could tell, was made up of a random selection of white spirits (gin, vodka, white rum, triple sec) topped off with a dash of coconut milk. The music was full-throatedly loud and the place was hectic with suited young men and women weary from work and looking for fun. Dymphna lit a cigarette and puffed smoke into the low grey haze that shifted and eddied above their heads. Lorimer had a slight tension headache, the epicentre located an inch above his left eyebrow.

'He's a complete bastard,' Dymphna said. 'He just wanted to make me cry, for some reason. Kept going on at me. Do you know what made me break? I'm so pissed off with myself. Furious.'

'You don't need to tell me —'

'He said, please don't come in wearing skirts of that length any more.'

'Bloody nerve.' Lorimer looked down at Dymphna's caramel skirt, its hem an orthodox couple of inches above her somewhat pudgy knees.

'He said I had fat legs.'

'Jesus Christ. Well, if it's any consolation he said I was barking mad. He was in a filthy mood.'

Dymphna drew heavily and thoughtfully on her cigarette. 'I don't have fat legs, do I?'

'Course not. He's just a mean bastard.'

'Something's really bugging him. He's always rude when he's unsettled.'

Lorimer wondered if he should tell her the news about Torquil's impending demise. Then with a shock of clear vision he realized that this was exactly what Hogg was expecting him to do — it was one of the oldest traps in the book and he had almost walked right into it. Perhaps he had told everyone, perhaps it was a test of loyalty, who would leak the news first?

'Another Soluble Aspirin?' he asked, then added, innocently, 'I think the presence of Torquil may have something to do with it.'

'That wanker,' Dymphna said harshly, handing him her cloudy glass. 'Yes please. One more and you can have your way with me, lovely Lorimer.'

That was what happened when you tried to be 'nice', Lorimer thought, as he ordered another Soluble Aspirin and a low-alcohol beer for himself. He was pretty sure Dymphna knew nothing about the firing but, all the same, he would have to snuff out her amorous tendencies pretty –

Flavia Malinverno was across the room. He stood on tiptoes and peered – someone's head was in the way. Then she moved and he saw it wasn't her at all, nothing like her. Good God, he thought, it showed what was on his mind – practically hallucinating with wishful thinking.

Dymphna sipped at her white drink, her eyes firmly on him over the glass's rim.

'What is it?' Lorimer said. 'Too strong?'

'I really like you, Lorimer, you know? I'd really like to get to know you better.'

She reached out and took his hand. Lorimer felt his spirits begin their slow slide.

'Give us a kiss, then,' she said. 'Go on.'

'Dymphna. I'm seeing someone else.'

'So what? I just want a fuck.'

'I'm . . . I'm in love with her. I can't.'

'Lucky you.' She gave a bitter little laugh. 'It's hard, meeting someone you like. Then when you do, you find they've got someone else. Or they don't fancy you.'

'I do like you, Dymphna, you know that.'

'Yes, we're great "chums", aren't we.'

'You know what I mean.'

'Who is this damn girl, then? Do I know her?'

'No. She's an actress. Nothing to do with us, our world.'

'Wise. What's her name?'

'Flavia. Listen, have you heard of a singer, a rock singer called David Watts?'

'Flavia . . . What a horribly attractive name. Is she very la-di-da? David Watts? I *love* David Watts.'

114. REM Sleep. *You have a lot of REM sleep, much more* *than the average person. Could this be because your brain is in need of more repair each night?*

REM sleep. The brain wave patterns are on a far faster frequency, there is a higher heart beat and respiration, your blood pressure may rise and there is significantly more motility of the facial muscles. Your face may twitch, your eyeballs move behind your closed eyelids, there is increased blood flow to the brain, your brain becomes hotter. Sometimes in REM sleep your brain is firing more neurons than when you are awake.

But at the same time your body experiences a form of mild paralysis: your spinal reflexes decline, you have heightened motor inhibition and suppressed muscle tonus. Except in one area of your body. A further identifying characteristic of REM sleep is penile erection or clitoral engorgement.

The Book of Transfiguration

The steel crescents set in the toes and heels of his shoe soles clicked militaristically on the concrete floor of the multi-storey carpark, the white fluorescent bulbs leaching the primary colours from the rows of shiny cars, the noise of his shoes contributing to the mood of incipient threat which always appeared to brew amongst these stacked decks after dark, with their unnatural luminosity, their oppressively low ceilings, their bays crowded always with empty cars but unpopulated by their drivers or passengers. He was thinking about Hogg and his mood swings, his bully-boy provocations. Behind the bluffness and the banter he and Hogg had always got along and there was in their exchanges an implicit sense – often jocularly remarked on by his colleagues – that Lorimer was the golden boy, the chosen one, the *dauphin* to Hogg's Sun King. But today that had not been the case: the huge confidence that allowed Hogg to swagger through his little fiefdom had been absent – or rather, it had been there, but forced and strained for, and therefore uglier. He had seemed, frankly, worried, and Lorimer had never before associated Hogg with that particular state of mind.

But what was troubling him? What could Hogg see coming down the pike that he couldn't? There was a bigger picture here but Lorimer was not staring at the whole canvas. He was right, too: the news about Torquil's sacking was an attempt at entrapment, a blatant one. Hogg was waiting to see whom he told, waiting to see, Lorimer realized, if he would tell Torquil himself. But why would Hogg think this of him, his golden boy? Why would Hogg test him in this way?

Lorimer's steps slowed as the answer came to him. Hogg, troubled, unsettled, aware of these larger dimensions that Lorimer could not yet grasp, saw – or thought he saw – a role in them that was being played by Lorimer himself. Hogg, Lorimer realized with a genuine shock, was suspicious of him. He stood still now, some yards from his car, his brain working. What was it? What could Hogg see that he could not? Something was eluding him, some pattern in recent events . . . This uncertainty was alarming and it was even more alarming when he considered the natural consequences of suspicion: if Hogg was suspicious, then that implied only one thing – George Gerald Hogg no longer trusted Lorimer Black.

Someone had done something to the front of his car. Most curious. He saw as he drew near that letters had been made from sand, sand poured on to the bonnet and moulded into two-inch-high ridges to spell – BASTA.

He looked around him. Had the perpetrator been alerted by the martial click of his shoe steels and fled, or was he, or she, still hiding somewhere near by? He saw no one, nothing stirred, so he swept the cold sand from the gentle slope of the bonnet. How to explain this? Was this directed at him or was it random, his bad luck? BASTA – it meant 'enough' in Italian. Or was it an incomplete slur on the marital status of his mother? *Basta*. Enough. Enough already. Enough questions. He hoped he would sleep tonight, but he doubted it, his mind was already full of his next project: he was going to telephone Flavia Malinverno in the morning.

Chapter 8

'Hello?'

'Could I speak to Flavia Malinverno?'

'You are?'

'Hello. This is Lorimer Black. We met –'

'Who?'

'Lorimer Black. We –'

'Do I know you?'

'We met very briefly the other day. In the Alcazar. I was the one who was so taken with your performance. In the Fortress Sure advertisement.'

'Oh, yeah.' Pause. 'How did you get my number?'

'I told you – I work for Fortress Sure. All that information is on file.' He was floundering a bit. 'From the company who made the film. You know, call sheets, ah, transportation records . . .'

'Really?'

'They're very keen on files. They're an insurance company, remember. Everything filed away somewhere.'

'Oh. You don't say.'

'Yes.' In for a penny. 'I was wondering if we could meet? Drink, buy you lunch or something?'

'Why?'

'Because . . . Because, I'd like to, is the honest answer.'

Silence. Lorimer swallowed. No saliva in his arid mouth.

'All right,' she said. 'I'm free Sunday evening. Where do you live?'

'Pimlico. In Lupus Crescent,' he added, as if that made him sound more alluring and upscale.

'That's no good. I'll meet you at the Café Greco in Old Compton Street. 6.30.'

'6.30, Café Greco, Old Compton Street. I'll be there.'

'See you then, Lorimer Black.'

175. Sinbad's Folly. *Sinbad Fingleton had unruly mid-brown hair, frequently unwashed, that formed itself into thick corkscrews, like planed shavings off a plank of wood, and that hung forward over his narrow brow to just below eye-level. He had a chronic sinus problem which meant he sniffed a great deal and was obliged to breathe through his mouth. Consequently his mouth was open most of his waking day, and indeed his sleeping night. He enjoyed simple physical exertion – chopping, mowing, clipping, digging, carrying – which was why his despairing father (phoning a crony on the town council) had managed to swing him a menial job in the Parks Department. His other pleasure was marijuana and its derivatives and from the tales he recounted it sounded that his colleagues shared similar tastes, passing their working hours tending to the lawns and borders, shrubs and saplings of Inverness in an agreeable drug haze. Sinbad was happy to experiment with other drugs and when a friend sold him some tabs of LSD he had driven off in a Parks Department Land Rover and tripped out in the craggy isolation of Glen Affric for thirty-six hours (necessitating a further round of mollifying phone calls from his father, more markers being called in). It had been, Sinbad told the household, the most, you know, amazing experience of his life and he would like to offer – free of charge – some LSD to any fellow tenants who wished to sample the intensity of perceptual change the stuff provoked. Lachlan and Murdo accepted, saying they would take it back to Mull to try.*

The rest of us indifferently, but politely, declined (Joyce doing so on Shona's behalf – Shona was keen).

Sinbad was disappointed by this reticence and so one evening, as Joyce was preparing our communal meal – a large shepherd's pie – Sinbad dropped three tabs of acid into the simmering mincemeat to ensure that we did not miss out on the mindbending experience he felt sure, really, that in our heart of hearts we wanted. It was one of the evenings when I happened to be staying over.

The Book of Transfiguration

Ivan Algomir looked at Binnie Helvoir-Jayne's scrawled note, her huge, looping handwriting giving instructions about the dinner party.

'Black tie?' he said. 'That's a bit naff, isn't it?' He sniffed. 'I suppose it's *just* allowable these days, there must be someone grand coming.'

'I wouldn't know.'

'If it's just a bunch of friends then it's unforgivable. Where the hell is Monken Hadley?'

'It's in the borough of Barnet,' Lorimer said, 'believe it or not.'

'Priddion's Farm, Monken Hadley? You could be in darkest Gloucestershire.'

'It's about a mile from the beginning of the AI.'

'Sounds very dodgy to me. Well, if you've got to go black tie, remember: no wing collar; a proper bow tie that you tie, a black one too, absolutely no colours; no silly velvet slippers; no cummerbund; no frilly shirts; no black socks; no handkerchief in the pocket. Velvet coat's all right. I know,' he said, smiling suddenly and showing his big ruined teeth, 'you can go in a kilt. Perfect. Black Watch tartan. Ideal, Lorimer.'

'Can I wear a dirk?'

'Absolutely not.'

'What's wrong with black socks?'

'Only butlers and chauffeurs wear black socks.'

'You're a genius, Ivan. What do you think about fobs? I rather fancy one.'

'No gentleman wears a fob, ghastly affectation. If you don't want physically to wear a wristwatch then just carry it in your pocket. Far more the thing to do, believe me.'

'Right,' Lorimer said. 'Now, about this helmet.' He spread out three polaroids of his helmet collection and handed Ivan the list of their provenances. Ivan glanced at them and pushed them away.

'Not interested in the burgonet or the barbute, but this fellow looks good. I'll give you five thou for him. Oh, all right, seven thousand for all three.'

'Done.' Lorimer was making a profit but it was irrelevant – he never bought his helmets to make a profit. 'I've got them in the car.'

'Write me a cheque for £13,000 and he's yours,' Ivan said, reaching over to a table where the Greek helmet stood on its stand and setting it in front of Lorimer. 'I'm barely covering my costs on this.'

Lorimer thought. 'I can write you a cheque,' he said, 'but you'll have to hold on to it until I say. I've got a rather nice bonus coming in but it's not through yet.'

Ivan smiled fondly at him. Lorimer knew the affection was genuine, and not just because he was a regular customer. Ivan enjoyed his role as *consigliere* and general fount of all wisdom about matters sartorial and social. Like many Englishmen he cared little for what he ate or drank – a gin and tonic and banana sandwich would suit at any hour of the day – but in matters of decorum

Lorimer treated him as positively oracular, and Ivan was amused and rather flattered to be consulted. It also helped that Lorimer never challenged a single opinion Ivan expressed or statement he made.

'I'll pack it up and you can take it away with you,' he said, turning and shouting up the stairs. 'Petronella? Champagne, darling, we've made a sale. Bring down the Krug.'

32. George Hogg's Philosophy of Insurance. What does insurance do, really do? Hogg would ask us. And we would say, diligently echoing the textbooks, that insurance's primary function is to substitute certainty for uncertainty as regards the economic consequences of disastrous events. It gives a sense of security in an insecure world. It makes you feel safe, then? Hogg would follow up. Yes, we would reply: something tragic, catastrophic, troublesome or irritating may have occurred but there is recompense in the form of a preordained sum of money. All is not entirely lost. We are covered, after a fashion, protected to a degree against the risk – the bad luck – of a heart attack, a car smash, a disability, a fire, a theft, a loss, things that can, and will, affect us all at some or many times in our lives.

That attitude, Hogg would say, is fundamentally immoral. Immoral, dishonest and misleading. Such an understanding promotes and bolsters the fond notion that we will all grow up, be happy, healthy, find a job, fall in love, start a family, earn a living, retire, enjoy a ripe old age and die peacefully in our sleep. This is a seductive dream, Hogg would snarl, the most dangerous fantasy. All of us know that, in reality, life never works out like this. So what did we do? We invented insurance – which makes us feel we have half a chance, a shot at achieving it, so that even if something goes wrong – mildly wrong or hideously wrong – we have provided some buffer against random disaster.

But, Hogg would say, why should a system that we have invented not possess the same properties as the life we lead? Why should insurance be solid and secure? What right do we have to think that the laws of uncertainty which govern the human condition, all human endeavour, all human life, do not apply to this artificial construct, this sop that affects to soften the blows of filthy chance and evil luck?

Hogg would look at us, contempt and pity shining from his eyes. We have no right, he would say solemnly. Such an attitude, such beliefs were deeply, fundamentally unphilosophical. And this was where we – the loss adjusters – came in. We had a vital role to play: we were the people who reminded all the others that nothing in this world is truly certain, we were the rogue element, the unstable factor in the ostensibly stable world of insurance. 'I am insured – so at least I am safe,' we like to think. Not so, Hogg would say, shaking a pale finger, uh-uh, no way. We have a philosophical duty to perform when we adjust loss, he told us. When we do our adjustments of loss we frustrate and negate all the bland promises of insurance. We act out in our small way one of the great unbending principles of life: nothing is sure, nothing is certain, nothing is risk-free, nothing is fully covered, nothing is forever. It is a noble calling, he would say, go out into the world and do your duty.

The Book of Transfiguration

Priddion's Farm, Monken Hadley, turned out to be a sizeable 1920s stockbroker's villa, brick and pebble-dashed, complete with decorative half-timbering and steepling mock-Elizabethan chimneys. It was set in a large garden of several terraced lawns with a view of a golf course, the Great North Road, and the distant rooftops of High Barnet. Even though Monken Hadley was still a part of the huge city, perched on its very northern fringe, it looked and felt to Lorimer like a toy village, with a village green, a flinty ashlar church – St Mary the Virgin – and a venerable manor house.

Priddion's Farm was partially screened from the road and its neighbours by dense clumps of laurel and rhododendron and there was an assortment of mature trees – cedar, chestnut, maple, monkey puzzle and weeping ash – strategically scattered about the lawns, doubtless planted as saplings by the wealthy man who had paid for the house to be built.

Lorimer drew his car up beside three others on the gravelled sweep before the front porch and tried to square this bourgeois palace with the Torquil Helvoir-Jayne he thought he knew. He heard laughter and voices and wandered round the side of the house to find a croquet lawn upon which Torquil and another man in pink corduroy trousers were playing a boisterous, profane game of croquet. A thin young woman in jeans, smoking, looked on, laughing nasally from time to time, giving a whoop of encouragement as Torquil first lined up and then powerfully hammered his opponent's ball away across the lawn and through a border out of sight where it could be heard thumping dully along the paving stones of a lower terrace.

'You fucking bastard,' the man in pink trousers bellowed at Torquil, trotting off to find his ball.

'You owe me thirty quid, you anus,' Torquil yelled back, lining up his own next shot.

'Pay up, pay up,' the young woman shouted, heartily. 'And make sure you get it in cash, Torquie.'

'Sounds like fun,' Lorimer said to the young woman, who turned to look at him incuriously.

'Potts, say hello to Lorimer,' Torquil encouraged, 'there's a good girl.'

Lorimer unreflectingly offered his hand which, after a surprised pause, was feebly shaken.

'Lorimer Black,' he said. 'Hi.'

'I'm Potts,' she said. 'Don't you love croquet? Oliver's useless, such a bad sport.'

'And this shambling cretin's Oliver Rollo,' Torquil said as the young man in pink trousers returned, strolling back with his ball. 'Lorimer Black. Lorimer was at Glenalmond with Hugh Aberdeen.'

'How is old Hughie?' Oliver Rollo said. He was tall, long-armed and quite overweight, twin pink spots on his cheeks, flushed from his short walk back up from the lower terrace. He had a big, loose jaw, thick, dark, hard-to-comb hair and the flies of his pink corduroys gaped undone.

'I haven't the faintest,' Lorimer said. 'Torquil won't let go of this idea that I know him.'

'Right, cuntface, you've had it,' Oliver said, Lorimer quickly realizing he was talking to Torquil. He dropped his ball on the grass and seized his mallet.

'If you're going to take a piss in my garden do you mind not fucking exposing yourself,' Torquil said, pointing at Oliver's fly. 'Bloody pervert. How do you stand it, Potts?'

''Coz 'e's a larverly boy,' Potts said in the voice of a cockney crone.

'Because I've got a ten-inch dick,' Oliver Rollo said.

'Dream on, darling,' Potts said, acidly, and a cold glance flew between them.

A cheerful-looking, matronly young woman bounced out of the French windows that gave on to the croquet lawn. She had a big, shapeless bosom beneath a baggy, bright jumper covered in blue stars and dry blonde hair held off her face with an Alice band. Her cheeks were flaky with what looked like mild eczema and she had a waning cold sore at the side of her mouth. But her smile was warm and genuine.

'Lorimer Black, I presume,' she said, shaking his hand in orthodox manner. 'I'm Jennifer – Binnie.'

There was a full-throated roar of disappointment from behind as Torquil missed a sitter. 'Fuckfuck FUCK!'

'Boys,' Jennifer-Binnie called. 'Neighbours, remember? And language, please.' She turned back to Lorimer. 'Your girlfriend's just called from the station. Do you want me to collect her?'

'Sorry? Who?'

Before Lorimer could ask further, Torquil was by his side, a hand squeezing his shoulder.

'We'll pick her up,' he said. 'Come along, Lorimer.'

As they drove to High Barnet in Torquil's car Torquil apologized. He seemed excited, Lorimer thought, coiled and tense with a kind of manic energy.

'I should have checked first, I suppose,' he said, unconvincingly. 'I had no time to clear things with you. Thought we'd be able to busk it. I told Binnie you'd only just started going out.' He grinned, salaciously. 'Don't worry, you won't be sleeping together.'

'And just who is my girlfriend this weekend?'

'Irina. The Russian bint. You remember?'

'The sad one.' Lorimer frowned.

'I couldn't ask her on her own, could I? What would Binnie think?' He patted Lorimer's knee. 'Don't worry, I only got the idea yesterday. I didn't have you lined up as chaperon all along.'

'Fine.' Lorimer wasn't so sure about this. But it explained Torquil's unnatural glee.

'She seemed a bit lonely, you know. Friendless. I thought this would cheer her up. But obviously I had to come up with something more persuasive for the Binns.'

'Obviously.'

'Oh, and I should apologize that the dinner's black tie. One of Binnie's little fads.'

'No problem.'

'And I apologize for the house too, while I'm in contrite mood.'

'Why?'

'You see, it was left to Binnie by an uncle of hers, a distant uncle.' He stopped talking and looked at Lorimer with an expression close to shock. 'You don't seriously think I'd choose to live in Barnet, do you? As soon as the market recovers I'm flogging it.'

He pulled up outside High Barnet tube station and they saw Irina waiting alone at the bus stop, wearing a duffle coat and carrying a red nylon backpack. Lorimer sat and watched Torquil go to greet her, kiss her on each cheek and talk urgently for a few minutes, Irina nodding wordlessly at his instructions, before he led her back to the car.

'You remember Lorimer, don't you?' Torquil said, smiling benignly as Irina climbed into the back seat.

'I think you were in restaurant,' she said, anxiously.

'Yes,' Lorimer said. 'That's me. Good to see you again.'

Lorimer buckled on the sporran and checked its positioning over his groin in the full-length mirror. He was pleased to be wearing a kilt again after so many years and surprised, as he always was, by the transformation it wrought on him – he almost didn't recognize himself. He squared his shoulders, contemplating his reflection: the short black jacket with its silver buttons, the dark green of the tartan (Hunting Stewart, there was no Black Watch at the dress-hire agency), the knee-length white socks and their gartering of laces, criss-crossed above his ankles. This was, to his mind, as close to the Platonic 'Lorimer Black' as he had ever desired, as complete a metamorphosis as he could ever have wished for. His pleasure in his appearance momentarily dispelled the depression that was gathering within him at the prospect of the evening ahead.

He was sleeping in a room at the end of a long L-shaped corridor on the house's second floor, under the eaves, a big atticy room with two dormer windows and with clearly unnecessary beam work supporting the ceiling but designed to foster an impression of antiquity. Torquil had apologized for the beams and for the half-timbering outside, for the brass sconces in the passageways and for the plum-coloured bathroom suite and the bidet when he had shown Lorimer his room. He continued to blame everything on the execrable taste of Binnie's distant uncle ('*Nouveau riche*, lived in Rhodesia half his life'), taking no responsibility at all for the appearance of his own home. Lorimer paced back from the mirror and turned sharply on his heel, admiring the perfect way the pleats of his kilt fanned out and swirled as he swung his hips.

He stepped out into the corridor and saw that Torquil was at the far end, minus his dinner jacket, holding the hand of a small, fair-haired boy in pyjamas who looked about seven years old.

'This is Lorimer,' Torquil said. 'Say hello to Lorimer, he's sleeping next door to you.'

The little boy's eyes were wide at Lorimer's Caledonian resplendency.

'Hello,' Lorimer said. 'I know who you are, you're Sholto.'

'Sholto, the famous bedwetter,' said his father, whereupon Sholto started to cry.

'It's not fair, Daddy,' Lorimer heard him wail as Torquil bustled his son into his bedroom. 'I can't help it, Daddy.'

'Don't be such a sissy. Take a joke, can't you? Jesus Christ.'

Downstairs in the drawing room curtains were closed, candles were lit and there was a fire going, a real fire, Lorimer noticed, and gathered in front of it were Binnie, Potts, Oliver and another couple, introduced as Neil and Liza Pawson, the headmaster of a local school and his wife. Everyone was smoking except for Neil Pawson.

'I do love a man in a kilt,' Liza Pawson said, with forced bravura as he came in. She was a lean, bespectacled woman with a long, stretched neck, whose massive tension was clearly visible, a cursive blue vein throbbing in her temple. Her dress was daintily floral, spruced up with a homemade hint of evening lace added at neck and wrists.

'You've got to have the right arse for a kilt,' said Oliver Rollo, throwing his cigarette end into the fire. 'That's essential.'

Lorimer could have sworn, inwardly, that at the mention of the word 'arse' a sudden coolness seemed to spread across his buttocks.

'Och aye, he's a true Scot,' Potts said, standing behind him, the pleated hem of his kilt held high in her hands, 'he's no wearing knickers.'

Somehow Lorimer's smile stayed pasted to his face, his scorching embarrassment was covered by the explosion of nervous laughter that followed and the loudly genial chiding of the irrepressible Potts and her famously naughty pranks. Lorimer's hand was still shaking slightly as he poured himself a huge vodka at the drinks table, tucked slightly out of sight behind a baby grand covered in framed photographs.

'I understand your friend is from Russia,' Neil Pawson said, padding over for a refill. He seemed a blurry, indistinct, fair man, freckled, with dense blond eyebrows and a boyish lick of pepper and salt hair swept across his forehead.

'Who?'

'Your, ah, girlfriend. Binnie tells me she never wants to go back to Russia.'

'Probably. I mean, probably not.'

Neil Pawson smiled at him, amiably. 'Binnie says she's over here studying music. What's her instrument? I'm a bit of an amateur musician myself. What does she play?'

Lorimer quickly ran through an entire orchestra of instruments before settling on the saxophone, for some reason.

'The saxophone.'

'Unusual choice. I'm a clarinet.'

He had to get away from this man. 'She plays many instruments,' Lorimer said, recklessly. 'Almost all of them: violin, timpani, bassoon. Strings, generally, ah, and oboe. The flute,' he said with relief, remembering. 'The flute is her instrument.'

'Not the saxophone, then?'

'No. Yes. Sometimes. Ah, there she is.'

Lorimer went enthusiastically to greet her, but saw

Torquil was right behind, solicitous palm at the small of her back, saying, 'Now who hasn't met Lorimer's young lady, Irina?' She was wearing a silvery satin blouse that made her skin appear even more blanched and bloodless, despite the lurid gash of her lipstick and the heavy blue shadow on her lids. In the subsequent shiftings and displacements that took place with these new arrivals being admitted to the circle, Lorimer found himself in a corner beside Binnie, glowing warmly pink, larger and more substantial somehow, in a voluminous dress made of quilted maroon velvet fitted with a bizarre short cape-effect around the shoulders, heavily embroidered. It made him feel hot just looking at her and he spread his legs slightly beneath his kilt, feeling his balls hang free, cooling. Marvellous garment.

'– So pleased you could come, Lorimer,' Binnie was saying, tiny pearls of sweat trapped in the downy hair of her upper lip. 'You're the only person I've ever met from Torquil's work. He says you're his only friend in the office.'

'I am? He does?'

'He says no one else has anything in common with him.'

He glanced over at Torquil who was handing round a bowl of quail's eggs, leering at Potts, who had removed the shimmering, chiffony scarf that had been draped around her shoulders earlier, to reveal her modest cleavage.

'I say, tits out, Potts,' Lorimer heard Torquil observe, genially. 'Oliver's in luck tonight, eh?'

'Have a good look,' she said and with a finger hooked forward the front of her dress. Torquil took full advantage.

'Damn, you're wearing a bra.'

'Isn't Potts a scream,' Binnie said to Lorimer, beneath the ensuing laughter. 'Such a sweet girl.'

'Why does everyone call her Potts? Because she's potty?'

'It's her name – Annabelle Potts. How long have you and Irina been going out?'

'Who? Oooh, not long.'

'Torquil says he can hear the distant chiming of wedding bells.' Binnie looked sideways at him, mischievously.

'Does he? Bit premature, I would say.'

'Such a pretty girl. I do love that Russian look.'

At dinner Lorimer was placed between Binnie and Potts; Torquil was flanked by Irina and Liza Pawson. An absurdly tall girl called Philippa was introduced to the company as the cook and she also served and cleared plates, with help from Binnie. They started with a tasteless, still partially frozen vegetable terrine and progressed to over-cooked salmon and new potatoes. There were eight open bottles of wine, four white and four red, placed randomly about the table and Lorimer found he was drinking almost uncontrollably, taking every opportunity to top up Binnie and Potts before refilling his own empty glass. Gradually, the desired anaesthetizing of the senses began to creep over him and an attendant mood of indifference replaced his earlier social terror. He was not relaxed but he ceased to care any more, ceased to worry.

Potts was rummaging for another cigarette in her handbag so Lorimer reached over for a candle. To his astonishment he saw Torquil place another four open bottles – two white, two red – on the table as Philippa cleared the remains of the salmon. There were now so many bottles on the table that he could only see the heads of the people opposite. Potts waved her cigarette negatively at the cheese, so Binnie set it down in front of him.

'– Couldn't stand Verbier any more, too many grockles,' Potts was saying, 'so I said to Ollie, what about Val d'Isère? But he can't stand the French schoolkids barging the queues. I said give me French schoolkids to German schoolkids – or do I mean Swiss? Anyway, I said, what about the States? And he practically had a fit. So we're going to Andorra – anyway, peace at last.'

'Yeah. Thank God we both like Italy,' Oliver Rollo said.

Potts turned deliberately to Lorimer. 'Where do you go?'

'To do what?'

'Ski.'

'I don't. Not any more – I broke my leg very badly. Doctor's orders.'

'Shame. Thanks.' She finally lit her cigarette from his proffered candle. 'I must say, you've got a lovely, hairy bum, Lorimer.'

'I heard that,' Oliver boomed from across the table. 'You leave his bum out of it. What's wrong with my bum?'

'It's fat and pimply.'

Liza Pawson forced her face into a smile. Neither of her partners, Torquil nor Oliver Rollo, had spoken to her for at least twenty minutes, Lorimer had noticed, but now Oliver's interjection had freed up Binnie, who went in search of more bread.

'What exactly do you do?' Lorimer heard Liza Pawson ask Oliver. No, he thought, don't ask them about their jobs, they hate it, it makes them depressed. 'Are you in the same line as Torquil?' she persisted.

'I sell houses,' Oliver said brusquely through a soft mouthful of cheese, turning away immediately. 'Bung down the red, Torq, will you?'

'Do you miss Scotland, Lorimer?' Binnie asked, returning to sit beside him once again.

'Yes, I suppose I do,' Lorimer said, relieved for once not to have to lie but not keen, all the same, to encourage this line of questioning. He brought Potts into the conversation. 'Have you ever skied at Aviemore?'

'I love Scotland,' Binnie said, fondly nostalgic. 'We used to shoot every year in Perthshire. Do you know Perthshire?'

'We're further north,' Lorimer said, as vaguely as possible.

'Aviemore,' Potts said. 'Is that the Grampians?'

'Cairngorms.'

'Do you shoot?'

'Not any more, I ruptured an ear-drum, doctor's orders.'

'You are unlucky with your sports, Lorimer,' Potts said, slyly. 'What about bridge?'

'Whereabouts north, exactly?' Binnie persisted. 'Any more cheese anyone?'

'What's for pud?' Torquil cried.

'Um, Inverness, sort of area, place called Loch –' he urged his dulling brain to work – 'Loch Kenbarry.'

'That's in Ireland, isn't it?' Potts said.

'I understand you play in an orchestra,' Liza Pawson said to him, leaning across the table desperate for conversation, candle flames dancing in the lenses of her spectacles.

'No, not exactly.'

'I heard you and my husband talking about musical instruments. A group of us have formed a small chamber orchestra. I thought he might be trying to recruit you.'

'No, I don't play, it's –' he gestured across the table at his supposed girlfriend, his prospective fiancée, and realized he had completely forgotten her name. 'It's her, she, ah, she's the musician. I work in insurance.'

'No shop!' Torquil yelled at him. 'Fine that man. Who's for some brandy?'

Lorimer's untouched *crème brûlée* was whisked from his place by a looming Philippa.

'Now you're talking, Helvoir-Jayne,' Oliver Rollo said, punching the air.

'Loch Kenbarry,' Binnie frowned, still trying to place it. 'Is that near Fort Augustus?'

'Nearish.'

Potts offered him one of her cigarettes for the seventh or eighth time that evening. He declined again and fetched her a candle. She leaned forward to the flame and lowered her voice, holding her cigarette poised, and said, hardly moving her lips.

'I must say I've found it very exciting with you sitting beside me, Lorimer, naked under your kilt.'

'Binnie,' Torquil said impatiently.

'Sorry, darling.' Binnie stood up. 'Shall we, ladies?'

Lorimer could imagine Ivan Algomir's snorting bray of derision. *The women left the room?* Potts shot to her feet and was away, Liza Pawson moved more uncertainly. Only the Russian girl did not budge.

'Irina?' Binnie said, gesturing towards the door. Irina. That was her name.

'What is? Where are we –' For the first time that evening she looked to Lorimer for help.

'It's a custom,' he explained. 'A British custom. The women leave the men at the end of the meal?'

'For why?'

'Because we tell disgusting jokes,' Oliver Rollo said. 'You got any port in this pub, Torquil?'

Lorimer was pleased with himself. When the ladies had left the room, and as Torquil and Oliver fussed pedantically over the lighting of their cigars, he asked Neil Pawson about his chamber orchestra and the man talked happily about his passion for music, of the difficulties and rewards of running an amateur orchestra and, moreover, spoke at a pedagogic, headmasterly pitch of conversation that brooked no interruption for a full ten minutes. It was only Oliver Rollo's insistent throat-clearings that alerted Torquil to the fact that terminal boredom was setting in and he suggested they withdrew and joined the ladies for coffee in front of the fire.

The evening wound down swiftly: the Pawsons left almost immediately, Lorimer warmly wishing them goodbye, even pecking Liza Pawson on the cheek, confident he would never see them again in his life. Irina said she was tired and Binnie sprang to her feet and fussily showed her to her room. Then Oliver and Potts went upstairs to bed, to much prurient speculation from Torquil. For a strange moment Lorimer and Torquil were alone in the room, Torquil sitting back in his armchair, legs splayed, puffing at the soggy butt of his cigar and swilling an inch of brandy around in his goblet.

'Great evening,' Lorimer said, feeling he had to break the gathering intimacy of the silence.

'That's what it's all about,' Torquil said. 'Old friends. Good food and drink. Bit of a chat. Bit of fun. That's what's life's, you know, makes it go round.'

'I think I'll shoot off,' Lorimer said, trying to ignore the dull headache that was tightening above his eyes.

'Kick that Potts out of your bed if she tries to crawl in,' Torquil said, with an unpleasant smile. 'Cat on a hot tin roof, that one. Real goer.'

'So she and Oliver aren't –'

'Oh yes. They're getting married in a month.'

'Ah.'

Binnie returned. 'You're not going to bed, are you, Lorimer? Good lord, it's ten to two. We are late.'

'Super evening, Binnie,' Lorimer said. 'Thank you so much. Delicious meal. Very much enjoyed meeting everyone.'

'Potts is a scream, isn't she? And the Pawsons are so nice. Do you think Irina enjoyed herself?'

'I'm sure she did.'

'She's a quiet one, isn't she?'

'Thought we'd go for a walk on the common to-morrow,' Torquil interrupted. 'Before lunch. Fresh air. Late breakfast, come down when you like.'

'Do you know Peter and Kika Millbrook?' Binnie asked.

'No,' Lorimer said.

'Friends from Northamptonshire, coming for lunch. With their little boy Alisdair. Company for Sholto.'

'Is he the dyslexic one?' Torquil asked. 'Alisdair?'

'Yes,' Binnie said. 'It's very bad, awful shame.'

'A dyslexic and a bedwetter. Bloody marvellous. They'll make great chums.'

'That's cruel, Torquil,' Binnie said, her voice hard,

suddenly, emotion making it quaver. 'That's a horrid thing to say.'

'I'm off,' Lorimer said. 'Night everyone.'

From his window Lorimer could see the beaded stream of headlights on the Great North Road. Why so many cars, he thought, leaving the city on a Saturday night, heading for the north? What journeys were being started here? What new beginnings? He had a sudden ache of longing to be with them, driving through the dark, putting as many miles as possible between him and Priddion's Farm in Monken Hadley.

221. Driving late at night through the city, you were searching the airwaves, looking for a radio station that was not playing popular music of the late twentieth century. As you fiddled with the dial you heard a melody and a wise husky voice that made you break your rule for a moment and listen. It was Nat 'King' Cole who was singing and the simple lyric lodged effortlessly in your head. 'The greatest thing / You'll ever learn / Is just to love / And be loved in turn.' Why did this make you so unutterably sad? Was it simply the effortless melancholy in Nat's dry, lung-cancery voice? Or did it touch you in another way, search out that small abiding hidden pocket of need we all carry. Then you turned the dial and found some sensuous, delicate Fauré which distracted you. The greatest thing you'll ever learn.

The Book of Transfiguration

An insistent hand on his shoulder shook Lorimer awake. Slowly he realized that his mouth was rank, his body was poisoned with alcohol and his head was gonging with a pure and unreasonable pain. Leaning over him in the darkness, wearing only a dressing gown, was Torquil. From somewhere there was coming a keening half-scream, half-wail, like the ululations from some primitive mourning ritual. For a moment Lorimer wondered if this was the noise of his abused brain, protesting, but then he registered swiftly enough that it emanated from deep in the house: it was another person's problem, not his.

'Lorimer,' Torquil said, 'you've got to go. Now. Please.'

'Jesus.' Lorimer wanted more than anything else to clean his teeth, then eat something salty, spicy and savoury and then clean his teeth again. 'What time is it?'

'Half-five.'

'Good God. What's happening? What's that din?'

'You've got to go,' Torquil repeated, stepping back from the bed as Lorimer rolled out on to his knees, from which position he levered himself upright after a little while and dressed as quickly as he could.

'You've got to take Irina with you,' Torquil said. 'She's ready.'

'What's happened?'

'Well . . .' Torquil expelled his breath, tiredly. 'I went to Irina's room and we –'

'You and Irina?'

'Yes. I snuck in there about three – why the hell do you think I got her here? – and, you know, we, we had it off. We "made love". And then I fucking fell asleep and so did she.' He looked at his watch as Lorimer swept his kilt and sporran into his grip. 'Then about half an hour ago Sholto came into our bedroom – Binnie's and mine. The little bastard had wet his bed.'

'I see.'

'He *never* wets his bed here. Never,' Torquil said with genuine fury. 'I can't think what brought it on.'

Lorimer carefully zipped up his overnight bag, not wanting to say anything, not wanting to interject a plea of clemency on Sholto's behalf.

'So Sholto says, "Where's Daddy?" Binnie gets worried. Binnie looks around. Binnie gets thinking. The next thing I know I wake up bollock-naked beside Irina and Binnie's standing there at the end of the bed with the duvet in her hands screaming. She hasn't stopped.'

'Christ. Where is she?'

'I've locked her in our bedroom. You have to get that girl out of here.'

'Me?'

'Yes.'

'What about Oliver and Potts?'

'I need them. Potts is in there with her. She's Binnie's oldest friend.'

'Really? Is she? Right, I'm ready.'

Irina was crying softly in the hall, dressed, her face strangely bland, free of her paint and powder. She said nothing, allowing Torquil and Lorimer to usher her gently outside to Lorimer's car. Outside it was icy cold, with a frost so heavy that even the gravel beneath their feet did not crunch, it was set so hard. Their breath condensed rather beautifully about them in evanescent lingering clouds.

'Good luck,' Lorimer said, wondering why he wished it. 'I mean, I hope you –'

'She'll calm down,' Torquil said, shivering, pulling his dressing gown tight around him. 'She always has before. Mind you, it's never been quite so . . . graphic, if you know what I mean.'

'You'd better go in,' Lorimer said, 'or you'll catch your death.'

'Fucking freezing.' Torquil peered in at Irina, his expression bland and disinterested as if he were searching an open fridge for a snack. She did not meet his gaze. 'Tell her I'll, you know, be in touch or something.' He reached into the car through the gap in the window and patted Lorimer's shoulder. 'Thanks, Lorimer,' he said with feeling. 'You're a humanitarian and a gentleman.'

This was the last compliment Lorimer wanted to hear from Torquil Helvoir-Jayne.

Lorimer drove carefully along deserted streets, white and deadened by the grip of the frost. It had taken several goes to establish where Irina lived, so intense was her solipsistic sense of misery, so unreal was her grasp of a world beyond her small circle of shame. Eventually she looked up at him, blinked and said croakily, 'Stoke Newington.' So he drove from Monken Hadley to Stoke Newington – through Barnet, Whetstone and Finchley, following signs to the City, then round Archway, past Finsbury Park and on to Stoke Newington. Crossing the North Circular, he suddenly realized that he had only slept a matter of three hours or so and thus, technically, in terms of alcoholic units consumed and not fully absorbed by the body, he was probably classifiable as totally drunk, though he had never felt so uncomfortably, palpably aware of his sobriety. By Seven Sisters Road he remembered that it was Sunday morning and that he had a rendezvous with Flavia Malinverno just twelve hours hence. His joy was mitigated by the sorriness of his physical state. He had to be ready for this meeting, of all the important meetings in his life – he really had to establish some control over the way he was living.

Chapter 9

Driving with pedantic care and attention back from Stoke Newington in the grey dawn, Lorimer had stopped at a petrol station and bought some Sunday papers and a two-litre bottle of Coca-Cola (regular), from which he swigged periodically as he made his way slowly but easily across town through empty miles of streets, arriving in Pimlico with his belly full of sweet gas and his teeth veloured with a rime of sugar. Once home in his flat he took four aspirin, cleaned his teeth and soaked in a hot bath for half an hour. Then he dressed and cleaned his teeth again, grabbed a newspaper and headed out for breakfast.

Lady Haigh was waiting for him downstairs, her pale blue eyes peering at him through the crack in her door.

'Morning, Lady Haigh.'

'How was your weekend? Were they nice people?'

'It was most interesting.'

'I thought you might like to take Jupiter for a walk.'

'I'm just going out for a bite of breakfast.'

'That's all right. He won't mind as long as you give him a bit of bacon or sausage. I thought you two should get to know each other better.'

'Good idea.'

'He will be yours one day soon, after all.'

He nodded, thoughtfully. There really was no suitable

answer to Lady Haigh's bland prognostications about her own death.

'By the way,' she said. 'That man was round again yesterday, looking for you.'

'What man?'

'He didn't leave his name. Quite well-spoken – said he was a friend of yours.'

'Was it the detective? Rappaport?'

'Not that one. He was courteous, though, just like a policeman.' She opened the door fully and led Jupiter out. He was wearing an odd woollen checked coat that covered his body, belted under his belly and across his chest. Jupiter's rheumy eyes contemplated Lorimer with an impressive lack of curiosity.

'He's done his business,' Lady Haigh assured him, lowering her voice confidentially, 'so there should be no problem on the street.'

Lorimer set off up the road with Jupiter plodding steadily beside him: he walked with visible effort, like an old man with hardening arteries, but maintained a regular pace. Unlike other dogs he did not stop and sniff every kerb and car tyre, scrap of litter and turd, nor did he feel the need to cock his leg at each gate or lamp-post they passed; it was as if the effort of getting from A to B absorbed all his attention and he had no time for other canine frivolities. In this way they made good progress through the cold, bright morning to the Café Matisse, where Lorimer tied Jupiter's lead to a parking meter and went inside to order the most calorifically intense breakfast the establishment could concoct. The place was quiet, a few regulars secure behind the rustling screens of their newspapers, and Lorimer found a seat at the front where he could keep an eye on Jupiter. The Spanish duenna waitress impassively took his order for bacon, sausage, two fried eggs on fried bread, grilled tomatoes, grilled mushrooms, baked beans and chips with an extra helping of chips on the side. When it arrived he slathered the brimming plateful with generous rivulets of ketchup and tucked in. Jupiter sat patiently by the parking meter, looking like an old dosser in his tatty checked coat, licking his chops from time to time. Lorimer, guilty, took him out a sausage but he merely sniffed at it and looked disdainfully away. Lorimer placed it on the ground by his front paws but it was still there, untouched and cold, when he emerged twenty minutes later, swollen gut straining at his belt, feeling grotesquely full but with his hangover subdued, a definite fifty per cent better.

He saw Rintoul following him, or rather paralleling him across the street. Rintoul was walking abreast of him, wanting to be seen, and when their eyes met he made an aggressive jabbing, taxi-hailing salutation in his direction. Lorimer stopped, uneasy, reasoning that this was what the gesture demanded and looked about him: the street was quiet, a few early risers hurrying homeward with their newspapers and pints of milk, but surely Rintoul could do nothing violent or untoward here? It would be the height of recklessness – or desperation – and in any event he always had Jupiter to scare him off.

Rintoul strode purposefully across the street. He was wearing a thin leather coat that did not look warm enough for this chilly, frosty morning, and in the low-angled sunlight his face had a pinched, pale look to it. Lorimer said nothing – he assumed Rintoul had something to tell him.

'I wanted you to be the first to know, Black,' Rintoul said, sounding slightly out of breath, facing him, shifting

to and fro, his feet making restless little shuffling movements. 'We're being sued for negligence and criminal
damage by Gale-Harlequin.'

'Their decision, Mr Rintoul, not ours.'

'It gets better. They're withholding all monies owed.
Not paying us for past work. So our company's going
into receivership.'

Lorimer shrugged. 'It's something between Gale-Harlequin and you.'

'Yeah, but you fucking told them.'

'We made a report.'

'How much did Gale-Harlequin settle for?'

'Confidential, Mr Rintoul.'

'We're broke. We're going bust. Do you know what
that means, Black? The human cost? Deano's a family
man. Four young kids.'

'This is what happens when you set fire to expensive
buildings, I'm afraid.'

'We never meant it to go so –' Rintoul stopped, realizing it was too late, that in these circumstances half a
confession is as good as a whole one. He licked his lips
and looked at Lorimer with unequivocal hatred, then
glanced up and down the street, as if searching for an
escape route. Or a weapon, Lorimer thought, something
to bludgeon me with. His wandering eyes finally settled
on Jupiter sitting ever-patiently at Lorimer's feet.

'This your dog?' Rintoul asked.

'In a manner of speaking, yes.'

'I've never seen a more clapped-out, pathetic-looking
animal in my life. Why don't you get yourself a proper
dog?'

'He's called Jupiter.'

'You're going to fucking pay for this, Black. One way

or another you – you, mate – are going to suffer for what you've done to us. I'm going to –'

'One more threat, one more violent word and we will prosecute you in the courts,' Lorimer said, deliberately raising his voice for any passer-by to hear, before launching into the standard G G H response to any public verbal menace, always to be couched in the first person plural. 'You cannot threaten us in this way. We know everything about you, Mr Rintoul, and have you any idea how many lawyers we have working for us? If you so much as lay a finger on us, so much as threaten us once more, we will set them to work on you. You'll be truly finished then, truly washed up. The law will get you, Mr Rintoul, not me, the law. Our law.'

Lorimer saw tears in Rintoul's eyes, tears of frustration and impotence, or perhaps just a response to the icy keenness of the wind that had started to blow. It had to be a finely judged process, this counter-threat – sometimes it had the opposite effect to the one desired, it pushed people too far, to uncontrollable extremes instead of pinioning them, freezing them on the edge of retaliation. But now Rintoul was immobilized, Lorimer saw, his revenge motor stalled, inert between these two competing forces – his own rage, his own urge to strike out, versus the perceived might of Lorimer's awesome reply.

Rintoul turned and walked away, one shoulder oddly hunched, as if he had a cricked neck. Lorimer experienced a form of qualified sorrow for him – the petty thief landed with some real villain's murder rap; the apprentice mugger who jumps the world kick-boxing champion. Lorimer felt oddly besmirched himself – he had rarely used the legal-counter-threat response, his *modus operandi* usually made it unnecessary – but he had crossed through Rintoul's world for a moment, the world of dog eat dog or, rather, of big dog eating smaller dog, and had shared in his terms of reference, spoken a language of unfairness and injustice that Rintoul understood all too well.

But he could not relax, this did not mean he was safe. One dark night Rintoul might have violence visited on him anonymously – after all, Lorimer Black was the only objective correlative he had, the living, breathing symbol of all his woes . . . Lorimer wondered if he should tell Hogg – it was time for an 'oiling', in GGH parlance, another resource available to troubled or worried employees caught in the line of fire. Some 'cod-liver oil' was a pre-emptive frightener, a scarer-away, the details of which he knew very little, as it was something controlled exclusively by Hogg. 'So you need a dose of cod-liver oil,' Hogg would smile, 'to keep the colds and flu away. Leave it to Uncle George.' Lorimer watched Rintoul's hunched, shrinking figure disappear down the street and thought perhaps it might not be necessary after all. At least he knew who had put the sand on his car, now.

'Come on, old boy,' he said to Jupiter, still patiently sitting, 'let's go home.'

211. You sometimes feel your job dirties you, you're unhappy at the levels of duplicity and manipulation the work demands. You feel corrupt and at that moment the world seems a sink where only the powerful and the ruthless flourish and ideas of justice and fair play, of honour and decency, of bravery and kindness are like childish fantasies.

What did you do the last time you felt like that? You went to see Hogg.

'So you want consoling?' Hogg said, with exaggerated, wholly false pity. 'You think the world's a place where only evil-doing and graft get you where you want to be?'

'Sometimes it seems like that,' you admitted.

Hogg said: 'It depends on where you stand. Let me tell you something: there have always been many more decent folk in the world than bastards. Many more. The bastards have always been outnumbered. So what happens is that bastards congregate in certain places, in certain professions. Bastards prefer the company of bastards, they like doing business with other bastards, everything's understood then. The problem for people like you – and people like me – occurs when you find yourself, a decent person, having to live and work in the world of bastards. That can be difficult. Everywhere you look, the world seems a sink, and there seem to be only two options for survival – become a bastard yourself, or surrender to despair. But that's only because you're in your small bastard world. Outside in the wider world, the real world, there are plenty of decent folk and it's run along lines that decent folk can understand, by and large. We've got plenty of bastards in this square mile and that's why you're finding it tough; but move away, change your point of view and you'll see it's not all dark. You'll see the good in the world. It helps.'

You'll see the good in the world. It does work, it worked for you, for a while, until you wondered if Hogg believed a word of what he said.

The Book of Transfiguration

The Café Greco was a small, shadowy place, a thin, dark rectangle wedged between a betting shop and an off-licence, with a counter and the Gaggia machine at one end and some chest-high shelves running along the walls where patrons were meant to stand, drink their coffee quickly and go. There were three stools, all currently occupied when Lorimer arrived at 6.15.

He ordered an espresso and considered what this choice of venue told him. The Café Greco would never merit selection for his collection of 'Classic British Caffs' because of its recycled Europeanism and its strained-for modishness, however tired: black walls, over-familiar reproductions of famous black and white photos, bare floorboards, Latin American salsa on the sound system. Only variations of coffee were served, or soft drinks in cans; there were some pastries under a plastic bell jar and a half-hearted stab at a selection of *panini*. No, the décor and its pretensions told him nothing, he realized with weary worldliness, it was the configuration of the café itself that was important. This was intended to be a *brief* encounter. Couples who met at a place where standing was the norm did not intend to linger. Still, smart thinking on Flavia's behalf, he had to concede; in her shoes he would have done the same.

He had thought carefully about his clothes. The signet ring was off and a thin silver bracelet was on. Under an old black leather jacket he wore a green trainer top with a hood that hung over the jacket collar like an empty pouch, and under that a white T-shirt with the hem of the neckband unpicked to create an inch-long frayed slit. He had on well-washed black jeans that had turned an uneven grey and sensible, unpolished black shoes with a heavy rubber sole. His hair was deliberately mussed and he had deliberately not shaved. The ambiguities and counter-signals were nicely balanced, he calculated – style, and the deliberate avoidance of style; cost present but impossible to evaluate – he could have been any-one – could work in a bookshop or a bar, could be a video-tape editor, an off-duty postman, a pub-theatre actor, the floor manager of a recording studio. Perfectly democratic, he thought, nothing that would surprise Flavia, no unwitting clues.

At 6.35 the doubts began to crowd in. Telling himself that there was probably a perfectly reasonable explanation for her late arrival, he ordered another coffee and read his way diligently, page by page, through an abandoned *Standard*. At 7 o'clock he borrowed a pen from behind the bar and began to do the crossword puzzle.

'Lorimer Black?'

She was standing there in front of him, right there, wearing a big quilted jacket and with a loosely woven oatmeal scarf wound round and round her neck. Her hair was different, darker than the last time, almost aubergine, the darkest ox-blood. She was carrying what looked like a typewritten script. He slid off his stool, a stupid smile breaking on his face.

'You waited,' she said, unapologetically. 'You were serious, then.'

'Yes. What can I get you?'

He fetched them both a cappuccino and stood by her stool as she searched her pockets and failed to find any cigarettes. His heart was punching violently in its socket behind his ribs and he said nothing, content to be beside her and have this opportunity for close-quarter observation.

'Have you got a cigarette?' she asked. White, even teeth. What has she done to her hair?

'I don't smoke.' A hint of an underbite gave a pugnacious edge to her beauty, a slight jut to the jaw. He offered to buy her some cigarettes but she declined.

'It won't kill me.' Strong eyebrows, unplucked, dense. Those brown eyes.

'So,' she said, setting down her coffee cup. 'Mr Lorimer Black.'

He asked her, for politeness's sake, and simply to start conversing, what she had been doing and she said she had just come from a read-through of a friend's play.

'Which is a load of crap, really. He has no talent at all.'

Finally she removed her jacket and scarf and finally he was able to look, guardedly this time, at her breasts. From the pleasing convexities and concavities of her vermilion polo-neck he calculated they were of perfectly average size but flattish, rather than protruding, more grapefruit-halves than anything particularly conic. He was glad to have this atavistic, but essential, male curiosity satisfied and returned his full attention to the animated and luminous beauty of her face, still not quite able to believe his astonishing good fortune, as she continued to run down and generally demolish the aspirations and pretensions of her playwright friend's efforts.

'What's this all about, Lorimer Black?' she said suddenly, more sharply. 'What exactly is going on here?'

'I saw you one day in a taxi and I thought you looked beautiful,' he told her, candidly. 'Then a few days later I saw you in that commercial and thought, "This is Fate" –'

'Fate,' she said with an ironic laugh.

'And when you came into the Alcazar that lunchtime I knew I had to do something about it. I had to meet you.'

'You're saying you fancy me, are you, Lorimer Black?'

Why did she keep repeating his full name, as if it amused her in some way?

'I suppose I am,' he confessed. 'But thank you, anyway, for coming.'

'I'm a married woman, me,' she said, 'and I've got to bum a ciggie off someone.'

The other five people currently drinking coffee in the Café Greco were all smoking, so she was spoilt for choice. A plump woman with spiky ginger hair and an earful of rings parted with one of her cigarettes and Flavia returned triumphant to resume her place on the stool. Lorimer was glad of the opportunity to stare at her figure again, noting her height, the length of her legs, the ranginess of her stride and her slim, almost hipless body. Pretty much ideal, he thought, no complaints here.

'So, you're out of luck, Lorimer Black,' she said.

'I notice you didn't describe yourself as a "happily" married woman.'

'Goes without saying, doesn't it?'

'Does it?'

'I would have thought so. You're not married, I take it.'

'No.'

'In a "relationship", then?'

'Ah. Not any more.'

'So what do you do at Fortress Sure? Sounds a deadly dull sort of life.'

'I'm what they call a loss adjuster.'

'Adjusting loss . . . Someone who "adjusts" loss . . .' She thought about it. 'That could be nice – or it could be fucking spooky.' She looked shrewdly at him, narrowing her eyes. 'Is your job meant to make people happy? People who've lost something, they call on you to adjust it, make the loss less hard to bear?'

'Well, not exactly, I –'

'As if their lives are broken in some way and they call on you to fix it.'

'Not exactly,' he said again, cautiously, unable to fix her tone – whether naïve or heavily ironic.

'No. Sounds too good to be true, I think.'

Ironic, then, Lorimer thought. Profoundly.

He stared at her and she looked him back squarely in the eye. It was absurd, he thought, swiftly analysing his feelings, it was almost embarrassing, but true none the less: he could happily have sat there for hours simply staring at her face. He felt light, also, a thing of no substance, as if he were made of styrofoam or balsa wood, something she could cuff aside with the most casual of backhanders, toss him out of the Café Greco with the flick of a wrist.

'Mmmm,' she said, reflectively. 'I suppose you'd like to kiss me.'

'Yes. More than anything.'

'You've got nice lips,' she said, 'and nice, tired eyes.'

He wondered if he dared lean forward and press his lips to hers.

'And I might have allowed you to kiss me,' she said, 'if you'd taken the trouble to shave before coming out to meet me.'

'Sorry.' A useless word, he thought, for the awful regret he felt.

'Do you ever tell lies, Lorimer Black?'

'Yes. Do you?'

'Have you ever told me lies? In our short acquaintance?'

'No. Yes, well, a white lie, but I had good –'

'We've known each other for about five minutes and you've already lied to me?'

'I could have lied about it.'

She laughed at that.

'Sorry I'm late, honeybun,' a man's voice said at his shoulder.

Lorimer turned and saw a tall man standing there, dark like him, fashionably dishevelled, older by five years or so. Lorimer took in, quickly, patchy stubble, long curly hair, a lean, handsome, knowing face, not kind.

'Better late than never,' Flavia said. 'Lucky my old chum Lorimer was here, stop me dying of boredom.'

Lorimer smiled, sensing the man appraising him now, checking out the look, the presence, weighing him up, subtly.

'I don't think you've ever met Noon, have you, Lorimer?'

Noon?

'No. Hi, Noon,' Lorimer said, keeping his face straight. It wasn't hard, he felt all the mass returning to his body, all his specific gravity, his *avoir dupois*.

'Noon Malinverno, number one husband.'

Malinverno offered a lazy hello then turned back to Flavia. 'We should go, sweetums,' he said.

Flavia stubbed out her cigarette, wound her long scarf about her neck and shrugged on her jacket.

'Nice to see you again, Lorimer,' she said. Malinverno was already moving to the door, his eyes on them both. 'Oh yes,' she said. 'Don't forget to give me Paul's number.'

'Sure,' Lorimer said, suddenly proud of her guile, taking up his pen and writing his telephone number, and his address, on the margin of a page of the *Standard*, which he tore off and gave to her. 'Paul said call any time. Twenty-four hours a day.'

'Ta, ever so,' she said, deadpan. As they left the Café

Greco Malinverno put his arm around her neck and Lorimer turned away. He didn't want to see them together in the street, husband and wife. He was not bothered that she had arranged for Malinverno to meet her there too – her insurance, he supposed – he nursed instead the warm glow of their conspiracy, their complicity. He knew they would see each other again – there is no disguising that charge of mutual attraction as it flickers between two people – and he knew she would call, she liked his nice, tired eyes.

*104. **Pavor Nocturnus**. Gérard de Nerval said, 'Our dreams are a second life. I have never been able to pass through those ivory gates that lead to the invisible world without a shudder.' I know what he means: like everything in life that is good, that nurtures, comforts and restores, there is a bad side, a disturbing, unsettling side, and sleep is no exception. Somnambulism, somniloquy, apnoea, enuresis, bruxism, incubus, pavor nocturnus. Sleepwalking, sleep-talking, snoring, bed-wetting, teeth-grinding, nightmare, night terror.*

The Book of Transfiguration

He barely slept that night: he was not surprised, in fact he did not particularly want to sleep, his head was so busy with thoughts about the meeting with Flavia. He analysed its conflicting currents without much success, making little headway in interpreting its shifting moods and nuances – moments of hostility and compliance, tones of irony and affection, glances of curiosity and diffidence. What did it add up to? And that offer of a kiss, what did it imply? Was she serious or was it bravado, an act of seduction or a cruel form of taunting? He lay in his bed listening to the growing quiet of the night, always approaching silence but never quite achieving it, its progression halted by a lorry's grinding gears, a siren or a car alarm, a taxi's ticking diesel, until, in the small hours, the first jumbos began to cruise in from the Far East – from Singapore and Delhi, Tokyo and Bangkok – the bass roar of their engines like a slowly breaking wave high above, as they wheeled and banked in over the city on their final approach to Heathrow. Then he did fall asleep for a while, his head full of the odd conviction that his life had changed irrevocably in some way and that nothing from now on would ever be quite the same.

Chapter 10

When Lorimer came into the office he heard Hogg down the passageway, singing, boomingly, 'I got a gal in Kalamazoo-zoo-zoo' and he knew that Torquil had been sacked.

He hung back, waiting for him to move on before slipping unnoticed into his room, where he sat quietly and assiduously going through the newspaper clippings in the David Watts file and speed-reading his way through a slackly written, instant biography called *David Watts – Beyond Enigma* that had been published a couple of years previously. The most intriguing fact about David Watts was that 'David Watts' was his stage name. He had been born Martin Foster in Slough, where his father had worked for the Thames Water Board as assistant manager of the vast sewage works to the west of Heathrow airport. It was curious, Lorimer thought, to exchange one bland name for another. All the other details of his life and progression to eminence were unexceptionable. He was a bright, withdrawn only child with a precocious talent for music. He had dropped out of the Royal College and with a friend, Tony Anthony (now, was that a stage name?), had formed a four-man rock band called, first, simply Team, which had metamorphosed into David Watts and the Team. Their first three albums had gone double-platinum; there was a protracted dalliance with a girl called Danielle, who worked on a music paper before becoming David Watts's live-in lover; they had enjoyed two sell-out tours to the USA . . . Lorimer found he was nodding off: so far, so predictable. The biography concluded with a fanfare of bright tomorrows: the world was there for the taking; rumour had it Danielle was pregnant; the creative juices were flowing in veritable torrents. Anything was possible.

That had been two years ago and now the newspaper clippings took up the story where the biography ended. The romance with Danielle hit the reef: she left, became ill, became anorexic, disappeared, probably aborted the baby (this provoked abiding tabloid fodder: the lost child of David Watts). The band split with satisfying acrimony; Tony Anthony sued and settled out of court. Danielle was discovered in Los Angeles, washed-up and haggard, on detox and living with some other unsuitable rock has-been. She denigrated David Watts with routine and tireless venom ('egomaniac', 'control-freak', 'satanist', 'nazi', 'communist', 'martian', 'nerd' and so on). David Watts released his first solo album with a select bunch of the world's best session-musicians, *Angziertie*, which, contrary to all expectations, outsold everything previous to it. A thirty-five-nation, eighteen-month world tour was mooted. Then David Watts had a nervous breakdown.

Here the newspapers gave way to insurance policies. A £2 million claim was filed for costs incurred over the cancellation of the tour. As Lorimer riffled through the documents he came across many affidavits from Harley Street physicians and psychiatrists testifying to the genuine nature of David Watts's *crise*. A series of increasingly angry letters had started coming in from DW Management Ltd, signed by Watts's manager, one

Enrico Murphy, as Fortress Sure's first set of loss adjusters doggedly queried every expense and invoice. A compensatory loss of earnings claim was submitted for £1.5 million and one or two of the larger arenas (a baseball ground in New Jersey, a dry dock in Sydney, Australia) and bona fide foreign impresarios were paid off. By the time Lorimer reached the file's final letter, Enrico Murphy was angrily demanding outstanding settlement to the tune of £2.7 million and threatening litigation as a result of all this 'incredible hassle' which was further undermining his client's fragile health. Moreover, he was ready and willing to go public: the press was permanently avid for news about David Watts.

Shane Ashgable rapped gently on Lorimer's door and sidled conspiratorially into the room. He was a lean, fit man whose relentless work-out programme had squared his face almost perfectly with bulging jaw muscles. He walked as if he had his buttocks permanently clenched (Hogg said once, memorably, 'D'you think Ashgable's got a fifty pence piece held between his cheeks?'). He once confessed to Lorimer that he did a thousand press-ups a day.

'Helvoir-Jayne's been canned,' Ashgable said.

'Jesus Christ! When?'

'This morning. He was in and out of here like shit through a tin horn. Never seen anything like it. Ten minutes.'

'What's going on?'

'No idea. Hogg's like a man pissing on ice. What do you make of it?' Ashgable was no fool, Lorimer knew; he had spent a year at the Harvard Business School, hence his penchant for American slang.

'Haven't the faintest,' said Lorimer.

'Come on,' Ashgable said, with a sly smile. 'He's your friend.'

'Says who?'

'Says Torquil Helvoir-Jayne, constantly. You spent the weekend at his house, didn't you? He must have had wind of it. No one's that insensitive.'

'I swear he never gave a sign.'

Ashgable was clearly sceptical. 'Well, as he left he kept asking for you.'

'Maybe I should see Hogg . . .'

'We want a full report, Lorimer.'

Upstairs there was a cardboard box in the hallway containing bits and pieces from Torquil's rapidly cleared desk. Lorimer caught a glimpse of a studio portrait of a smiling, pearl-collared Binnie and the three scrubbed, plump children.

Janice raised her eyebrows helplessly, and gave a short piping whistle as if that were the only way to illustrate her incredulity. She beckoned Lorimer over and whispered, 'It was brutal and sudden, Lorimer, and the language was unseemly on both sides.' She glanced towards Hogg's closed door. 'I know he wants to see you, he keeps asking if you've left the building.'

'Come,' Hogg barked when Lorimer knocked. Lorimer stepped in and Hogg pointed wordlessly at the chair already placed before his empty desk.

'He had no idea what hit him, not a clue,' Hogg said, manifest pride colouring his voice. 'Most satisfying. That look of total disbelief on someone's face. Moments to cherish, Lorimer, moments to recall in your dotage.'

'I told no one,' Lorimer said.

'I know. Because you're clever, Lorimer, because you're

not thick. But what intrigues me, though, is just how clever you are.'

'I don't understand.'

'Do you think you're so clever you can outsmart us all?'

Lorimer was begining to feel offended and hurt by Hogg's recondite innuendoes: Hogg's paranoia was registering off the dial. Lorimer also sensed his own ignorance once more, a feeling that he was in possession of only a few of the facts, and those not the most crucial.

'I'm just doing my job, Mr Hogg, that's all, as I always have.'

'Then you have nothing to worry about, do you?' Hogg paused, then added breezily, 'How was your weekend with the Helvoir-Jaynes?'

'Ah, fine. It was purely social, purely.'

Hogg clasped his hands behind his head, a faint sense of amusement causing his eyes to crinkle at the edges and his thin lips to twitch, as if there was a laugh behind them trying to bubble forth. What had Ashgable said? Like a man pissing on ice.

Lorimer rose from his chair. 'I'd better get on,' he said. 'I'm working on the David Watts adjust.'

'Excellent, Lorimer, tip-top. Oh and take Helvoir-Jayne's odds and sods with you when you go, will you? I'm sure you'll be seeing him again sooner than I will.'

210. Shepherd's Pie. *We had nearly finished the shepherd's pie, I remember, because I was contemplating putting in an early claim for seconds, when the room went yellow, full of yellows – lemon, corn, sunflower, primrose – and refulgent whites, as in a partial printing process or silk-screening, waiting for the other primary colours to be overlaid. Some sort of aural dysfunction kicked* in too: voices became indistinct and tinny, as if badly recorded some decades before. Turning my head extremely slowly, I registered that Sinbad was telling some rambling and inarticulate story, flinging his big hands about the place, and that Shona had started to cry softly. Lachlan (Murdo was away) seemed to lurch back from his plate as if he'd discovered something disgusting on it but then started to poke fascinatedly around the mince and potatoes with a fork as if he might unearth something valuable like a gemstone or a golden ring.

I took deep breaths as the room and its contents leached to white, all the yellows gone, and then shimmered and stirred into shades of electric, bilious green.

'Oh my God,' Joyce said quietly. 'Oh oh oh.'

'It's fantastic, isn't it?' Sinbad said.

I could hear the blood draining from my head, a bubbly death rattle, like water whirlpooling down a too-small plughole. Joyce reached trembling fingers across the table to me and squeezed my hand. Junko had risen to her feet and was swaying about, as if on the pitching deck of one of her fishing boats. Then Shona seemed to pour, as if molten or boneless, off her chair and reformed in a tight foetal ball, weeping loudly now in clear distress.

'Brilliant,' Sinbad opined. 'Wicked.'

For my part the green had given way to deep interstellar blues and blacks and I was becoming aware of some kind of shaggy fungoid growth forming on the walls and ceiling of the kitchen.

'I've got to get out of here before I die,' I said, reasonably, sensibly, to Joyce. 'I'm going back to the hall.'

'Please let me come with you,' she begged. 'Please don't leave me, my darling one.'

We left them – Shona, Junko, Lachlan and Sinbad – Sinbad laughing now, his eyes shut and his wet lips pouting, his hands fumbling at his fly.

Outside it was better: the cold, the streetlamps' harsh glare *helped, seemed to calm things down. Arms around each other, we waited ten minutes for a bus, not saying much, holding tight to each other like lovers about to be parted. I felt disembodied, muffled; the colour changes modified, shifted, faded and brightened but I could cope. Joyce seemed to be retreating into herself making small mewing kittenish noises. As the bus arrived all sound appeared to cut out and I could hear nothing: no Joyce, no bus engine, no hiss of compressed air as the door opened, no wind noise in the trees. The world became hushed and absolutely silent.*

The Book of Transfiguration

There was something grubbily attractive about the sullen girl who opened the door to him at DW Management Ltd in Charlotte Street, Lorimer had to admit. Perhaps it was just her extreme youth – eighteen or nineteen – perhaps it was the deliberately botched peroxide job on her short hair, or the tightness of the leopardskin print T-shirt she was wearing, or the three brass rings piercing her left eyebrow, or the fact that she was simultaneously smoking and chewing gum? Whatever it was, she exuded a cut-price, transient allure that briefly stirred him, along with a combination of latent aggression and a massive weariness. There were many minor skirmishes ahead, he sensed, only counter-aggression would work here; politesse and civility were a waste of time.

'Yeah?' she said.

'Enrico Murphy.' He added a hint of urban twang to his voice.

'Not here.'

'This is DW Management, yeah?'

'Ceased trading. I'm packing up.'

Lorimer looked around, concealing his surprise: he

had assumed the office was simply a mess but he began to see traces of order amongst the mess, some documents piled, some pot plants in a cardboard box.

'Well, well,' Lorimer said, looking her in the eye. 'Turn up for the books.'

'Yeah, brilliant.' She wandered back to the reception desk. 'David fired him, Sat'day.'

Everybody getting the bum's rush, Lorimer thought. 'Where is Enrico, anyway?'

'Hawaii.' She dropped her cigarette in a styrofoam cup containing an inch of cold tea.

'All right for some, eh?'

She twiddled with a fine gold chain at her neck. 'He must've been in here at the weekend – took a lot of files, took the platinum discs.' She pointed at some darker rectangles marking the hessian walls. 'Even the fucking phones're dead.'

'Enrico do this?'

'No, David. Thought I'd nick 'em, I suppose. Haven't been paid yet this month, see.'

'Who's the new manager, then?'

'He's doing his own management now. From home.'

Lorimer thought: there were always other ways, of course, but this was probably quickest. He took out his wallet and counted out five twenty pound notes on to the desk in front of her, then picked up a pen and a sheet of notepaper and placed them on top of the notes.

'I just need his phone number, thanks very much.'

He looked down at the dark cutting her parting made in her white-blonde hair as she bent her head to scribble the figures on the sheet of paper. He wondered about this young girl's life, what had brought her here, what path it would take now. He wondered what Flavia Malinverno was doing today.

8. *Insurance*. *Insurance exists to substitute reasonable foresight and confidence in a world dominated by apprehension and blind chance. This has a supreme social value.*

The Book of Transfiguration

There were several messages on his answer machine when he returned home that evening. The first went: 'Lorimer, it's Torquil . . . hello? Are you there? Pick up if you're there. It's Torquil.' The second was a few moments of quiet hiss and then a click. The third was: 'Lorimer, it's Torquil, something ghastly's happened. Can you call me? . . . No, I'll call you.' The fourth was from Detective Sergeant Rappaport: 'Mr Black, we have a date for the inquest.' Then followed the date and time in question and various instructions relating to his attendance at Hornsey coroner's court. The fifth was to the point: 'It's not over, it's not over yet, Black.' Rintoul. Damn, Lorimer thought, perhaps the situation did require cod-liver oil after all. The sixth made him stop breathing for its duration: 'Lorimer Black. I want you to take me to lunch. Sole di Napoli, Chalk Farm. I've booked a table, Wednesday.'

He slid *Angziertie* into his CD player and removed it after approximately ninety seconds. David Watts had a reedily monotonous, albeit tuneful voice with no character and the rank pretension of the lyrics was rebarbative. The fatal gloss and polish of the most expensive recording studios in the world stripped the music of all authenticity. He realized this reaction placed him in a tiny minority, was almost freakishly perverse, but there was little he could do about it: it was as if one of his senses had gone, smell or taste or touch, but he simply was unable to tolerate any contemporary British, American or European rock music of recent decades. It seemed fatally bogus, without soul or passion, a conspiracy of manipulated tastes, faddery and expert marketing. He replaced David Watts with Emperor Bola Osanjo and his Viva Africa Ensemble and sat back, brain in neutral, trying to cope with the preposterous sense of elation that was building inside him. He thought of Flavia Malinverno's beautiful face, the way she looked at you, the way she seemed always to be half-challenging you, provoking you . . . There was no question, without doubt she –

The doorbell buzzed and he lifted the speakerphone off its cradle, suddenly worried that it might be Rintoul.

'Yes?'

'Thank Christ. It's Torquil.'

Torquil put his suitcase down and looked about Lorimer's flat in frank admiration.

'Nice gaff,' he said. 'It's incredibly neat and sort of solid, if you know what I mean. Is this real?'

'It's Greek,' Lorimer said, gently taking the helmet out of Torquil's big hands. 'About three thousand years old.'

'Have you got any booze?' Torquil asked. 'I'm gagging for a drink. What a fucking awful day. Have you any idea how much a taxi costs from Monken Hadley down here? Forty-seven pounds. It's outrageous. Scotch, please.'

Lorimer poured Torquil a generous Scotch and himself a slightly less generous vodka. When he turned, glasses in hand, Torquil had lit a cigarette and was sprawled on his sofa, thighs splayed, two inches of shin showing above his left sock.

'What the hell is this crap you're playing?'

Lorimer switched off the music. 'I heard about what happened today,' he said, consolingly. 'Rotten luck.'

Some of Torquil's swagger left him and he looked suddenly deflated and shocked for a moment. He rubbed his face with his hand and took a long pull at his drink.

'It was pretty fucking scary, I can tell you. He's a vicious bastard, that Hogg. He took the car keys off me too, there and then. By the time I got back home after lunch it had been repossessed. Bloody embarrassing.' He exhaled. 'Out. Just like that. I put a call into Simon but I've heard nothing.' He looked plaintively at Lorimer. 'Have you any idea what it's all about?'

'I think,' Lorimer began, wondering whether it were wise to confide in Torquil, 'I think it's something to do with the Fedora Palace.'

'I thought you'd sorted that all out.'

'So did I. But there's something else going on. I can't figure it out.'

Torquil looked aggrieved. 'OK, so I cocked up – and I admit it – and was duly shunted out of Fortress Sure. Now I'm shunted out of GGH. It's not fair. There should be some sort of statute of limitations. I made a wrong calculation, that's all, I can't keep on being punished for the rest of my life.'

'It's more complicated, I think. I just can't put all the pieces together. It's got Hogg worried, though, for some reason. What did he say to you?'

'He came in and said: "You're sacked, get out, now." I asked why and he said: "I don't trust you," and that was it. Well, we called each other a few choice names.'

Torquil frowned and winced, as though the act of recollection were causing him physical pain. 'Bastard,' he said, and tapped ash absent-mindedly on the carpet. Lorimer fetched him an ashtray and a refill.

'How did things go,' Lorimer asked, innocently enough but genuinely curious, 'after Saturday night?' He felt, simultaneously, a vague alarm: here they were, he and Torquil, nattering about problems at work, problems at home. They even had a shared history, now, just like two old friends.

Torquil looked glum and threw his head back to stare at the ceiling. 'It got really bad,' he said. 'Nightmare. She became very quiet, Binns, after she calmed down, icy cold, not like herself at all, sort of drawn in on herself. I apologized, of course, but she refused to speak to me.' He paused. 'This morning she went to a lawyer – while I was getting the sack. Then she chucked me out. Said I could go and live with Irina. She wants a divorce.'

'Hence the suitcase.'

'My worldly goods. It gets worse. I had to speak to this lawyer. He says I've got to start giving Binnie money, regularly, some sort of maintenance while the divorce goes through. I told this lawyer chappie that I'd just got the sack so they could whistle for it. Apparently he and Binnie went over the bank statements, credit cards, building society passbooks, the works. Turns out I'm £54,000 in the red. Thank Christ I don't have a mortgage.'

'How does that line go? When sorrows come they come not as single spies but in battalions.'

'Sorry?'

'Shakespeare.'

'Oh. Right. Thing is, Lorimer, as it turns out, you're the only friend I have.'

'Me? What about Oliver Rollo?'

'Can't stand him. Mindless idiot.'

'What about your family?'

'They've all rather sided with Binnie, say I'm a disgrace. I'm a bit of a pariah, to tell the truth. Shunned all round.'

'I side with Binnie, too.'

'Yeah, but you understand, you were sort of involved.'

'Involved? What're you talking about? You climbed into bed with Irina, not me.'

'But you'd met Irina. And she was meant to be your girlfriend.'

'The key word is "meant". I'd only spoken to her for two minutes.'

'I don't think, Lorimer. That's my trouble in life, I don't think ahead.'

Lorimer knew what was coming next, that premonitory heaviness weighing on him again.

'I was wondering', Torquil said with a weak smile, 'if I could kip down here for a night or two, until it all blows over.'

'Blows over? What do you mean?'

'Binnie'll take me back, once she's calmed down.'

'You sure?'

'Course. She's a forgiving person, old Binns.'

'Well, all right, but just for a night or two,' Lorimer said, telling himself with scant confidence that Torquil knew his wife better than he did. 'I'll get you the duvet.'

211. The Television Set. *You felt cold because you were naked and you pushed yourself up against Joyce's pale, freckly body, your eyes tight shut to keep the colours out. Joyce said, you're wet, you're greasy, keep away from me, don't touch me. When you opened your* *eyes the colour changes had calmed down but your small boxy room pulsed like a beating heart in its socket, contracting and expanding as if the walls were pliable rubber. Noise was a problem now, and you yearned for the perfect silence of the bus ride. All you could hear was the ear-battering yammer of a television set from the floor below and boorish, loutish cheers and shouts. You looked at your watch but your eyes wouldn't focus. Joyce turned into you now, her long breasts falling and squashing into your side and you felt, dully, absurdly, alarmingly, a distinct sexual thrill – although you knew enough to realize that sex under these circumstances could have life-altering side effects. Still, maybe –*

Why are they shouting and screaming, Milo? Joyce said, and you could feel the wiry prickle of her pubic hair pressed against your thigh. Make them stop, Milo, make them stop, my darling.

Joyce had never used endearments before, never articulated affection, you thought, and you liked it, filled with love for her, and an intense desire that fuelled your rage against the television set and its ill-mannered booming voice. You were out of bed, snatching up your shirt and clawing it on.

THIS IS MAKING ME FUCKING ANGRY! you shouted, I'M IN A FURY, I'M FUCKING ENRAGED!

Make them stop, Milo, sweetheart, make them stop, Joyce said, sitting up in bed, tears streaming.

Furious, you opened the door of your boxy little room and strode off down the corridor, your shirt tails flying in the air behind you, heading furiously for the source of the din, the roaring noise, furiously determined to silence the television set for ever.

The Book of Transfiguration

He found it impossible to sleep with another person in the flat, the space shared, another source of unfamiliar noise. He would doze off from time to time but every time Torquil coughed or grunted or shifted on the sofa he was roused instantly, adrenalin-charged, brain working, eyes wide, alarmed – until he remembered his guest's presence in the sitting room.

Torquil slept on, dead to the world, as Lorimer, with deliberate clatter and door-bang, noisily prepared his frugal breakfast in the kitchen. He peered into the dark sitting room and saw Torquil's wide, bare back pale in the gloom, heard the troubled snort and rasp of his breathing, and the unwelcome thought struck him that Torquil might be naked under the spare duvet – but surely no one slept naked on a sofa? Slept naked on someone else's sofa in someone else's house? . . .

He drank his tea and left a note explaining some of the operational idiosyncrasies of the flat and stepped out into the icy greyness of another Pimlico dawn. He carried with him a small grip containing an assortment of clothes and key props for the David Watts adjust, whenever that might arise. He had not found a parking space in Lupus Crescent the night before and consequently had some- thing of a walk to his car, parked outside a Methodist church in Westmoreland Terrace. He could feel the cold biting at his cheeks and forehead and found himself longing vernally for some sunshine, some soft green days. The gusting east wind that had been blowing the night before had not dropped at all and he felt it tugging at the skirts of his coat and heard it thrashing the bare boughs of the sycamore and cherry trees at the corner of the street. Leaves were being whirled along the pavement and flicked into the sky, thick, dark, irregularly shaped leaves – maple, perhaps, or ginko – flung dancing and skittering into the rows of parked cars. The last leaves of last year, he thought elegiacally, suddenly ripped from their branches after a tenacious struggle all winter, to be sent burling along – hang about, he said to himself, there's not a leaf left on a tree in the country that isn't evergreen. What were all these things filling the air? He stooped and picked one up, a jagged rhomboid shape, thick like holly but which snapped in his fingers like shellac or brittle enamel . . .

Lorimer had no affection or nostalgia for the many cars he had owned in his loss adjusting career. A car, as far as he was concerned, was just an efficient device for getting from A to B: he was not interested in cars, in fact he cultivated a deliberate lack of curiosity in them so that Slobodan had no excuse for starting to talk to him about 'motors'. However, it was oddly disturbing to see his Toyota with its top coat burnt off, scorched and blistered, with the occasional patch of racing green still adhering. Flakes of paint were still being snatched from it by the wind but the car was almost wholly paint-free, looking as if it had been specifically camouflaged for some flinty tundra – a grey terrain of rock and lichen with a rare patch of grass. A blowtorch, Lorimer thought, running his fingers over the now cool, roughened steel, of the camping gas variety that painters and decorators use, or chefs to brown the sugar on their *crèmes brûlées*. Quick work too, he assessed, a couple of men, or three, could do the car in ninety seconds. He imagined pale blue flames, a powerful smell, a spit and bubble as the paint ignited. What had Rintoul said? 'It isn't over yet.' There was no choice now: Hogg and his oiling crew had to be called in. If Rintoul and Edmund wanted to play hardball, as Shane Ashgable would have said, they had no idea what lay in store for them.

The Toyota was fine in every other motoring regard and Lorimer drove easily – though a little self-consciously – through the hesitant beginnings of the rush-hour to Silvertown. He was aware, at traffic lights or waiting at junctions, of the curious looks his torched car received. He turned up the volume on his radio and some soothing Dvořák took him most of the way from Westminster to Canning Town while he kept his eyes fixed on the road.

The furniture van arrived with surprising promptness at half past nine and by ten o'clock his house was capable of supporting life. There was a bed and blankets and bed linen, a sofa, a divan for the spare room, a telephone, a portable television, a cherrywood table that could double as a desk and four dining-room chairs. He had bought some modern-looking cantilevered standard lamps so that he did not have to rely exclusively on the central lights in the ceiling and the kitchen was fitted out with a minimum of pots and pans, half a dozen wine glasses, a corkscrew, tin-opener and a young-married's start-up set of cutlery and crockery. Now all he needed was a supply of lavatory paper and provisions and the place would be ready.

He stepped outside his front door and walked down the flagged concrete path that bisected the levelled square of mud which one day would be his front lawn and contemplated his new neighbourhood. He seemed to be quite alone in Albion Village this morning. A brindled cat flowed up and over a wooden fence, there was a car parked outside number 2 and some damp washing flapped and cracked on a whirligig behind number 7, but he was the only sign of bipedal life. Then there was the sudden blaring, ripping noise of a motorbike starting and one duly emerged, carrying a pillion passenger, and as it accelerated past him two bug-eyed heads turned to stare briefly at him. Hello there, Lorimer said to himself, half raising his hand, I'm your new neighbour. Then they were gone and the noise died away and he was left alone in Albion Village and the near-silence again.

That was fine by him: everything was new here, and he felt new also, a new species of man, as if he were in a newer city, different altogether, more anonymously European, somehow. He turned to the east towards this more proximate Europe and filled his lungs: that keen wind in his face had rushed and buffeted its way across France or Belgium or the Netherlands – he felt a little bowel-shift of excitement now he was established here in his new domain. He did not know a soul and, better still, not a soul knew him.

He squared his shoulders. Time for some phone calls on his new white telephone: first, summon the cod-liver oil brigade to deal with Rintoul then, second, set up the meet with rock 'n' roll legend David Watts.

206. Alan told me that there is a tribe in a remote part of the Philippines where you are severely punished if you wake a sleeping person. Sleep is the most precious gift, these tribespeople think, and to wake someone is effectively to steal something precious from him or her.

I was worried about being such an overloaded REM sleeper. Well, you're a classic light sleeper, Alan said, and REM sleep is light sleep. But it doesn't feel light, I said, it feels deep, when it happens. Ah, Alan said, that's because it is only in REM sleep that you dream.

The Book of Transfiguration

David Watts lived in a vast, detached, white stuccoed house – in a quiet street off Holland Park Avenue – of the sort normally described as 'ambassadorial'. It had its own high wall with a gate and security cameras positioned here and there covering all possible angles of approach.

Lorimer had thought hard about how to present himself for this encounter and was quietly pleased with the results. He had not shaved since his meeting with Flavia and his jaw had been dark with stubble. So when he did shave he left a postage stamp-sized rectangle of bristle immediately below his bottom lip. He chose an old suit, off the peg, mouse-grey, and to it added a royal blue V-neck sweater, a white nylon shirt and a thin tie, olive green with a narrow, diagonal, pistachio band. Shoes were rubber-soled ankle boots, highly polished, with yellow stitching on the seams. He had decided to wear spectacles, square, silver-framed with clear lenses, and he added – a nice touch this, he thought – a binding of Sellotape to the right hinge. The look, he hoped, said striven-for unexceptionalness; the pretensions of the figure he wanted to cut had to be *almost* imperceptible.

He was sitting in his car a hundred yards up the road from the Watts mansion, contemplating his reflection in the rear-view mirror, when he realized suddenly that the underlip patch was wrong. He reached into his glove compartment for his electric razor (always carried) and he immediately shaved it off. He sloshed some mineral water over a comb and dragged it through his hair to remove any shine as a final touch. Now he was ready.

It took two minutes to gain access through the gate in the wall and another three before the front door was opened. While he waited he paced around the paved courtyard with its terracotta urns of bay and box aware, as he did so, of the minute adjustments of the cameras tracking his every move.

The man who opened the door eventually was over-weight and baby-faced, his gut covered by a 'The Angziertie Tour' sweat shirt (Lorimer wondered if this were pointedly for his benefit). He introduced himself as Terry and led him across an empty hall, newly parqueted and smelling of varnish, to a small sitting room, furnished with various uncomfortable black leather and chrome chairs. A huge primeval fern sprouted and sprawled in one corner and on the walls were classic posters behind perspex – Campari, SNCF, Esso, Aristide Bruant in his red scarf. Up in the corner of a wall beside the winking red eye of the movement detector was another camera the size of a household box of matches. Lorimer sat himself down on two or three chairs, found one his spine could tolerate, took his glasses off, polished them, replaced them and then sat still, his hands in his lap, and waited, inert and uninterested.

Twenty-five minutes later David Watts came in with Terry and was introduced. Watts was tall but seemed almost anorexically thin, Lorimer thought, with the concave chest and the tapered hips of a prepubescent boy. He was wearing leather trousers and a crew-neck Shetland sweater with a hole in one elbow. The long, buttery hair that had featured in the CD liner-notes photo had gone, replaced by a US marine buzz-cut, and, curiously, his left cheek was unshaved – it looked like a small square of carpet tile stuck to the side of his face. Watts' long, bony fingers stroked and touched this partial beard constantly, and rather repellently, Lorimer thought – as if it were a comfort blanket. Lorimer was glad of his last-minute, prescient shave: two beard patches in the same room would have looked suspiciously mannered.

'Hi,' Lorimer said, not smiling, 'Lorimer Black.'

'Yeah,' said Watts.

Terry offered drinks and Watts finally settled on Italian beer. Lorimer asked for Pepsi and when this was not forthcoming said he would accept no substitute – he was fine, thanks.

'We got Coca, don't we, Terry?'

'Coke, Diet Coke, Caffeine-free Diet Coke, Caffeine-free Regular Coke, Diet-free Caffeine Coke, you name it.'

'I don't drink Coke,' Lorimer said. 'I'm fine, thanks.'

Terry left to fetch the Italian beer and Watts lit a cigarette. He had small, even features, his eyes were pale greyish brown and a spatter of tiny moles was splashed under his jaw and down the side of his neck, disappearing beneath his jumper collar.

'You with the insurance?' Watts asked. 'You the sods been jerking us around all these months?'

Lorimer briefly explained the functions and duties of a loss adjuster: not independent but impartial.

Watts frowned at him and drew on his cigarette.

'Let me get this straight,' he said, there was the faintest hint of the near-west in his glottal urban-speak, of Slough and Swindon and Oxford, 'we draw up a contract with you maggot-farmers, right? We pay the gi-fucking-gantic premium, then when I get ill and cancel they call you guys in to argue the toss?'

'Not all the time.'

'Hang about. They call you in to advise them, professionally, on whether to pay me what they have already agreed they'll pay me if something goes wrong, right?

When we drew up the policy I didn't see anything saying these loss adjuster geezers will be all over your face saying, no way, José.'

Lorimer shrugged, it was absolutely vital to remain calm and unmoved. 'It'll be there in the small print,' he said. 'I didn't invent the way they do business,' he added, 'I just work here.'

'As the concentration camp guard said when he turned on the showers.'

Lorimer sniffed, wiped his nose. 'I resent that,' he said, evenly.

'And I resent you, you maggot-farmer,' Watts said. 'What was the last music you bought, eh?' He listed several well-known rock groups with scathing, harsh contempt, as if he had a fishbone in his throat. 'No,' he said, 'I bet you like Three Bodies Minimum. Just looking at you I bet you're a Three Bodies Minimum type. Bet you.'

'Actually, it was', Lorimer paused, 'Kwame Akinlaye and his Achimota Rhythm Boys. An album called *Sheer Achimota.*'

'*Sheer* what?'

'*Sheer Achimota.*'

'What's that, then, "*Achimota*"?'

'I don't know.'

'"*Sheer Achimota*" . . . You like African music, then?'

'Yeah. I don't listen to European or American rock music post-1960.'

'Oh, yeah? Why's that, then?'

'It has no authenticity.'

'What about my stuff? Can't get more fucking authentic, man.'

'Not familiar with your work, I'm afraid.'

Lorimer could see that this gave Watts genuine pause,

disturbed him in some quite profound but ill-defined way.

'Terry,' Watts shouted, 'where's the fucking beer, man?' He turned back to Lorimer, his fingers caressing the hair on his cheek. 'You don't think I was ill then, that it?'

Lorimer sighed and took a notebook from his briefcase. 'Two weeks after the Angziertie Tour was cancelled you were on stage at the Albert Hall –'

'Aw, come on. That was for fucking charity – Sick Kids in Music, or something. Jesus Christ. TERRY I'M DYING OF THIRST HERE. Where is that fat bastard? Look, I can get you an army of doctors.'

'It doesn't make any difference.'

Watts looked flabbergasted. 'I'll sue,' he said, weakly.

'You're free to take any legal action you want. In fact we prefer these matters to go through the courts.'

'I mean, what's going on here exactly?' Watts said. 'Talk about changing the rules half way through the game. Talk about moving the goalposts. Everybody takes out insurance, *everybody*, it's the most common thing in the world. Even people who don't have a mortgage have insurance. Even people on the dole have insurance. But nobody would do it if you wankers kept popping up moving the goalposts like this. I mean, you maggot-farmers are just saying, "Tough, we won't pay. Fuck off," aren't you? I mean, if people knew this sort of thing went on . . .'

'It's a question of good faith or bad faith.'

'Meaning what? TERRY!'

'Meaning we don't think you are submitting the claim in good faith.'

Watts looked at him curiously, almost fascinated. 'What did you say your name was?'

'Black, Lorimer Black.'

'Just do this one thing for me, Lorimer Black. Keep your head still and look as far to the left as you can, as far round as your eyeballs will go.'

Lorimer followed his instructions: his vision blurred, the transparent profile of his nose hovered in his left-side field of vision.

'See anything?' Watts asked. 'Anything unusual?'

'No.'

'Well, I do, mate.' Watts looked to his left, swivelled his eyeballs as far as they would go. 'I can see a black shape,' he said. 'The very furthest left side of my vision I can see a dark shape. Know what that is?'

'No.'

'It's the devil. It's the devil sitting on my left shoulder. He's been there for six months now. That's why I don't shave my cheek.'

'Right.'

'Now you tell me, Mr maggot-farmer loss adjuster, how the hell is a musician meant to go on an eighteen-month, thirty-five-nation tour with the devil sitting on his shoulder?'

Terry brought him his coat as Lorimer waited in the hall.

'I'll make sure we've got some Pepsi in, next time,' he said cheerily.

'I don't think there'll be a next time.'

'Oh yeah, definitely,' Terry said. 'You made a big impression. I've never seen him talk to anybody – apart from Danielle – for more than two minutes. You got a card? He liked you, mate. You're his kinda guy.'

Lorimer handed him a card, not sure whether to feel flattered or alarmed.

'Why does he keep calling me a maggot-farmer?'

'He calls everyone that,' Terry explained. 'You know on telly when they run a film with swearing and cursing, effing and blinding? And they re-record it, you know "fucking" becomes "frigging", "shit" becomes "shoot", that sort of thing?'

'Yeah.'

'Well, if a character in a film says "mother-fucker" they re-dub it on telly as "maggot-farmer". Honest, you listen the next time. He was well taken with that, was David,' Terry said with a smile. 'The little maggot-farmer.'

He drove straight up Holland Park Avenue through Notting Hill Gate and the Bayswater Road to Marble Arch, then down Park Lane, Constitution Hill, left at Westminster Bridge and on to the Victoria Embankment. Lorimer could not explain why he decided to turn off the Embankment, but the idea came to him suddenly and he followed it at once.

The Fedora Palace was half gone, down to three storeys, lorries carting rubble away, the stiff claws of JCBs scratching at the outer walls, the stour of cement dust thickening the air. Lorimer spoke to a foreman in a hard hat who informed him that the site was to be levelled and the hoardings left up. Lorimer paced about, trying to make sense of this new development, trying to play all the angles, but with little success. He called up Torquil on the mobile.

'Thank God you called,' Torquil said. 'I can't find your washing machine.'

'I don't have one. You have to go to the launderette.'

'You must be joking. Oh yeah, and something's gone wrong with your bog. It won't flush.'

'I'll deal with it,' he said. 'Listen, the Fedora Palace is being demolished, make any sense to you?'

'Ah . . .' Torquil thought. Lorimer could practically hear him thinking. 'No,' Torquil said, finally.

'Hell of a write-off, don't you think? The thing was practically finished. Why knock it down, even with the fire damage?'

'Beats me. Where can you get a decent fry-up around here?'

Lorimer directed him to the Matisse and then switched off the phone. He decided to consider the Fedora Palace case closed: he had his bonus, it was pointless stirring matters up any further, and, in any event, he was more worried about what was going on in his flat.

Chapter 11

Flavia Malinverno was kissing him in a way he had never been kissed before. Somehow she had inserted her top lip between his top lip and his teeth behind. Otherwise it was an orthodox, full-blooded kiss but overriding everything was this strange pressure on his upper mouth. It was an exciting first. Flavia broke off. 'Mmmm,' she said. 'Nice.'

'Kiss me again,' he said, and she did, palms flat on his cheeks, sucking on his bottom lip this time, then on his tongue with a grip like a nursing calf –

It was a lucid dream, definitely and unmistakably, he thought, as he wrote an expurgated version of it down in the dream diary beside his bed. He had wanted to be kissed again and had arranged in his dream for that to come about – Alan would be pleased. He sat upright in his narrow bed in the Institute's cell, a little breathless and shaken at the vividness of the experience, at the irrefutable evidence of his erection, marvelling once again at the ability of mental phenomena to replicate the most complex physical sensations – better than replicate, *invent* whole new sets of physical sensations. The way her lip . . . A kiss of maximum palpability . . . and yet here he was alone on a high floor of a university building in Greenwich at, he checked the time, 4.30 in the morning. The dream was easily explained, causally. He was due to see Flavia again in a matter of hours, she was practically omnipresent in his thoughts, crowding out all other matters – Torquil, Hogg, Rintoul, the Silvertown house . . . He shook his head and exhaled noisily, like an athlete after a work-out, then remembered there were two other guinea pigs also sleeping lightly in the Institute that night. He lay back on his cot, fingers laced behind his head, and realized there was no point in trying to go back to sleep, trying to restart his lucid dream. He smiled at the memory of it: the dream had been a bonus, he had not intended coming to the Institute that night but it had seemed a welcome, not to say a necessary, escape.

When he had returned to his flat the evening before, traces of Torquil were everywhere, like elephant spoor. The crumpled duvet was sprawled over the sofa like a Dali watch, the pummelled pillows sat on an adjacent chair, Torquil's suitcase lay open in the middle of the carpet, its soiled contents exposed like a particularly rebarbative pop-up book, three used ashtrays were perched on various surfaces and the kitchen required a ten-minute wipe-down. Some juggling with the ballcock in the lavatory cistern had finally permitted the flushing away of assorted Helvoir-Jayne turds. He decided to have a lock fitted to his bedroom door: Torquil appeared to have been through his cupboards and chest of drawers and there was a shirt missing. A swift bout of tidying and a whizz round with the hoover restored the place to something close to its normal state.

Then Torquil returned.

'Disaster,' he announced as he came through the door, striding towards the drinks table, where he poured himself three fingers of Scotch. 'I've had it, Lorimer. I could have killed today, I had evil in my soul. If I could've got my fingers round that weasel lawyer's throat.'

He had a cigarette going now and switched on the television. 'Murder one, I tell you. I borrowed a shirt, hope you don't mind. I've got to get my hands on some money. £1,500 this month, school fees due in two weeks. I'm totally fucked. What's for supper?'

'I'm going out,' Lorimer invented, spontaneously.

'Who's that old bag downstairs? I could see her peering through the door at me.'

'She's called Lady Haigh. Extremely nice. Did you speak to her?'

'I just said "Boo!" and she slammed the door pretty smartish, I tell you. I've got to get a job, Lorimer, a well-paid job, a.s.a.p. Where are you going?'

'It's a sleep therapy thing I go to. I'll be out all night.'

'Oh, yeah?' he half-leered, then his own troubles crowded in on him again. 'Think I'll hit the phone tonight, call a few chums, get networking, yeah . . . Is there a decent Chinese in this neck of the woods?'

Lorimer frowned, shifting in his bed, wondering now what the effect of a Chinese takeaway would be in his neat and ordered kitchen. Yet Torquil was the least of his problems . . . He had taken the Toyota round to the rear of G G H where there were two parking spaces (one for Hogg and one for Rajiv) and a small loading bay. Rajiv had tut-tutted sympathetically at the state of the paintwork.

'Nasty customers, eh, Lorimer? Leave this to me, we'll get you a nice shiny new one.'

He went to see Hogg, who was wearing a black tie and sombre suit as if he had just come from a funeral, and told him about the blowtorching of his car.

'How do you know it was Rintoul?' Hogg said, bluntly. 'Could have been vandals.'

'He left a message on my answer machine threatening me, said "It wasn't over yet." '

'Doesn't sound much of threat to me. Anyone see anything, any witnesses?'

'The car wasn't parked in my street, no one would know it was mine.'

'Out of the question,' Hogg said, his hands searching his deep pockets.

'What do you mean?'

'I can't order an oiling on a vague hunch like that,' Hogg said with unconvincing bluffness, slipping a pepper-mint retrieved from his pocket into his mouth. He rattled it around on his teeth, making a noise like a stick against railings. 'Do you know what's involved with an oiling? It's a serious, not to say nefarious, business. We have to be absolutely certain it's called for. And in this case, Sunny Jim, I'm not.'

'You won't oil Rintoul?' Lorimer said, not able to conceal his incredulity.

'You catch on fast, Lorimer. If you're so worried, do your own, that's my suggestion. Take responsibility: chop onions, fry onions.'

It had not ended there: later in the afternoon Rajiv called him.

'Sorry, laddie, he won't replace your car.'

'Why not, for Christ's sake? It's insured, isn't it?'

'Ours not to reason why, Lorimer. Bye.'

So Lorimer had driven home in his toasted Toyota, his brain furious with activity, trying to pin down the cause of Hogg's now overt and provocative hostility. He wondered if Hogg knew that Torquil was staying in his flat – and concluded he quite probably did, for Hogg seemed to know just about everything and he could see how, from Hogg's point of view, Torquil's proximity was a little compromising.

226. *Lucid Dreams*. *Lucid dreams are dreams that the dreamer can control and influence. They are a phenomenon of the deeper levels of REM sleep and take place in what is called the D-state. D-state sleep occupies about twenty-five per cent of REM sleep and occurs in short intense bursts.*

'The fascinating thing about you,' Alan said, 'and what makes you my prize guinea pig, is that your D-state appears to take up forty per cent of your REM sleep.'

'Should I be worried?'

'I don't know. But it does mean you're likely to have more lucid dreams than the average person.'

'Thanks.'

'I think that may be another reason why you don't sleep as much. For someone like you your sleep is too exciting, too exhausting.'

The Book of Transfiguration

The snow came as a surprise, people volubly aired their astonishment in shops and bus queues, testified to their sartorial lack of preparation for it, and lambasted the shamefully inaccurate warnings of the meteorologists. The gusting east wind had turned suddenly northerly and the new currents of air were now surging down Europe from the frozen fjords of Scandinavia, the Baltic Sea, from the icy fringes of the Arctic shelf. By the time Lorimer reached Chalk Farm an inch was lying on the pavements and the roads were a marzipan mush of criss-crossing tyre-tracks. The flakes were big, like styrofoam coins, floating lazily but steadily down from a low, sulphurous-grey sky.

In marked contrast to the day, Sole di Napoli, the restaurant that Flavia Malinverno had chosen, was – unsurprisingly – Neapolitan in origin, painted in tones of pink and lambent yellow, full of images and symbols of the warm south – jugs of dried flowers, sheaves of corn stuffed behind mirror frames, an ill-executed mural above the pizza oven showing the ultramarine bay of Naples and a fuming Vesuvius and a shelfful of straw hats piled carefully above the bar. Each table was graced with a small spiky agave in a pot and the waiters sported blue T-shirts printed with a golden flaming sun above their left breast.

Lorimer stamped the snow off his shoes, dusted flakes from his hair and was shown to his table. Perhaps customers should be presented with a complimentary pair of sunglasses, he thought, just to sustain the mood, and he ordered, despite the weather, a summery Campari-soda – big brother Slobodan's drink of choice, he recalled. He was absurdly early, of course, and Flavia turned out to be twenty minutes late. He sat and waited patiently, his brain in a form of unthinking neutral, watching the snowflakes accumulate and drinking his first and then a second Campari-soda. He was refusing to allow any speculation as to why this invitation had been forthcoming – he recognized it simply as a blessing, as astonishing good fortune – and he vainly tried to banish images of his lucid dream from his mind. There was no getting away from it, he realized with quickening pleasure, he was in way over his head here, absolutely gone, a case study to be filed under 'smitten'. The fact that she was married, the fact there was a saturnine brute of a husband in the frame made no difference. Equally irrelevant, he realized, with a small gnaw of guilt, was the additional fact that he had been having a long-established affair with Stella Bull for over four years . . . No, now was not the time for moral debate, he told himself, these moments were designed for absurdly hopeful dreams, sweet prognostications, reveries so preposterous, so impossible that –

Flavia Malinverno came into the restaurant.

The waiters fell upon her: *'Bellissima!'*, *'Flavia, mia cara!'*, *'La più bella del mondo!'* and so on – she was clearly well known. The manager took her coat and bowed her to the table like an Elizabethan courtier, where Lorimer sat, his sphincter clenched, some sort of asthma attack going on in his pulmonary system and some sort of potent imbecile virus neutralizing his brain cells. The hair was different again, some variation of reddish umber somehow layered with dark gold, the shine on it, in the iridescent sun-tones of Sole di Napoli, making you want to blink. Her lips were browner, not so red. He had not really noticed what she was wearing – suede jacket, scarf, ribbed baggy sweater thing.

She ignored his proffered trembling hand and slid quickly into her seat.

'Brought the snow with you, I see.'

'Mnwhng?'

'Snow, darling. White stuff him fall from sky. Pimlico snow. It was nice and sunny here this morning.'

'Oh.'

'Did you see that car outside? Champagne please, *una bottiglia*, Gianfranco, *grazie mille*. Someone must have set fire to it. Almost a work of art.'

'It's mine.'

She stopped and gave him her head-cocked, narrow-eyed frown. He felt a silly, neighing sort of laugh rumbling behind his teeth and managed to turn it into a bad cough.

'Steady on,' she said. 'Have some water. What happened?'

Lorimer glugged water: perhaps he should tip the rest of the glass over his head just to complete the picture of total arsehole? He gently pounded his chest and tried to compose himself.

'Somebody did set it on fire. Took a blowtorch to it. It's just the paint that's gone. Everything else works fine.'

'Do you mind if I smoke? Why would somebody do that?'

'Not at all. Occupational hazard,' he said. Then, correcting himself, 'Probably vandals.'

'Dangerous job, yours,' she said, taking a puff at her cigarette and stubbing it out. The champagne had arrived and two glasses were poured. 'Cheers, Lorimer Black, we're celebrating.'

'We are?'

'I'm gonna be inna movies,' she drawled. 'Two days' work, one thousand pounds.' She put on an expression of pop-eyed astonishment. 'But Tyimotheh, Mummy told me you wah a stockbrokah!' Then she burst into sniffling tears for a second. 'See, I've even learnt my line.'

They touched champagne glasses, Lorimer noticed his hand was still trembling.

'Here's to the job.'

'Here's to your car. Poor thing. What's it called?'

'A Toyota.'

'No, I mean its name.'

'It doesn't have a name.'

'How boring. You've got to name things. Adam's task and all that. Name things in your life from now on,

Lorimer Black, I insist. It makes everything more ...
more real.'

'I'm not really interested in cars.'

'But imagine taking a blowtorch to it. Is that the worst
thing that's happened to you in your job?'

'I've had death threats. Pretty alarming.'

'I'll say. Je-sus, imagine. This while you're out adjusting
loss?'

'People can get pretty angry.' He must stop saying
'pretty'.

'But no one really gets killed, I hope.'

'Well, there's the odd sad case checks out.'

'Checks out?'

'Adios, planet earth.'

'Got you. Have some more.' She poured and held up
her glass. 'Sham pain to our real friends, real pain to our
sham friends. Where're you from, Mr Lorimer Black?'

As they ate lunch (gazpacho, spaghetti primavera,
sorbet) Lorimer gave her the short amended autobiography: born and raised in Fulham, university in Scotland,
some years 'drifting' before the need for a steady income
(aged parents to support) ended him up in the loss
adjusting wing of the insurance business. He let it be
known that this profession was temporary, that wander-
lust was still part of his soul. How fascinating, she said.
For her part she told him of some of the acting and
modelling jobs she had done, the new movie she had just
auditioned for, but the dominant theme in her discourse
to which they regularly returned was 'Gilbert', who was
being 'impossible, selfish and revolting, not necessarily
in that order'.

'Who is Gilbert?' Lorimer said carefully.

'You met him the other night.'

'I thought he was called Noon.'

'That's his stage name. His real name is Gilbert, Gilbert Malinverno.'

'Not quite the same ring to it.'

'Exactly. So I call him Gilbert when I'm cross with him. It's such a feeble name.'

'What, ah, does he do?'

'He's a juggler. Quite a brilliant one actually.'

'A juggler?'

'But he's given up juggling to write a musical.'

'He's a musician?'

'Fabulous guitar player. But consequently he hasn't made any money for months, which is why I'm calling him Gilbert. He's multi-talented, but obtuse.'

Lorimer's loathing of Gilbert Malinverno was profound.

'Been married long?' he asked, as if the question had just occurred to him.

'About four years. I think I married him for his name, really.'

I changed my name too, Lorimer wanted to say. You don't need to marry someone.

'Flavia Malinverno,' he said. 'What was it before?'

'Not nearly so nice. You know it means "Bad Winter" in Italian? *Mal'inverno.* Talking of which,' she said, looking out at the snow and actually reaching across and squeezing his arm, 'let's have a grappa.'

They did, and watched the afternoon outside gathering into bluey darkness, the snow growing less insistent until there was only the odd flake helixing down. A couple of inches had settled and the roads were furrowed chocolate.

They tussled amiably over the bill and negotiated a split: Flavia the champagne, Lorimer the food and the wine. Outside she rewrapped her scarf around her neck and pulled her suede blouson tight about her.

'Cold,' she said, 'God, this Pimlico snow's cold. God, I'm pissed.'

She took a half step and seemed to hunch into his side as if in search of body heat and Lorimer found, quite naturally, that his arm went around her, feeling her shiver and, quite naturally, they seemed to turn towards each other and they were kissing, not like the kiss in his lucid dream, but her tongue was deep in his mouth and he was about to explode.

The applause of Sole di Napoli's serving staff standing, to a man, in the window whooping and clapping broke them apart. Flavia pirouetted, gave a deep cavalier's bow and ran away.

'Bye, Lorimer Black,' she shouted, 'I'll call you.'

She was round the corner and out of sight before her name had formed on his lips. He crunched softly over the snow towards his seared and scarified motor, wondering why there was a sudden heaviness in the area around his heart.

Chapter 12

'He's a bit peaky,' Monika said. 'He wouldn't get out of his bed, Monday, wouldn't budge. So I knew he wasn't feeling so sunny.'

She and Lorimer were standing in the corridor just outside his father's room, their voices low, like consultants in a ward. Lorimer shivered: the house felt cold. Outside, the day was raw and freezing, the snow still lying, hard and blue with ice.

'Place is freezing, Monika,' he said. 'Something wrong with the central heating?'

'It comes on about six. It's on a timer.'

'Change the timer. It's ridiculous to be this cold. Think of Dad.'

'Can't change the timer, Milo. Anyway, Dad's nice and warm in bed with an electric blanket.'

'Fine,' Lorimer said. 'Can I see him?'

Monika swung the door open to let him in. 'Don't be too long,' she said. 'I want to go shopping.'

Lorimer closed the door softly behind him. The room was small and narrow, large enough for a single bed, a bedside table, a television set and a small armchair. Opposite the bed on the wall was a cluster of cheaply framed portraits of the Blocj family – grandmother, mother, the children at various ages, Slobodan, Monika, Komelia, Drava. And baby Milomre, last born.

His father's blue eyes swivelled towards him as he edged up to the bed and drew up the armchair.

'Hi, Dad, it's me,' he said. 'Not feeling so good, eh? What's wrong, then? Bit of a virus, maybe. Miserable weather out there. Nice warm bed's the place to be. You get yourself well . . .' he went on in this vein of banal prattle for a while as his mother and sisters had instructed him, insisting everything was understood. But it was not evident: his father's faint smile remained his constant, unvarying response to the world, but at least his eyes were on him today, blinking regularly. He reached over and took his right hand, which was resting on the coverlet over his chest, placed there, doubtless, by Monika, always neat, always wanting things 'just so', including the invalid's posture. He could not understand his father's condition: he was not paralysed, he was simply very still. He could walk, he could move his limbs with gentle encouragement, but if not encouraged he would remain almost perfectly inert. On the surface anyway: inside all worked as normal, he supposed, pumping, oxygenating, sluicing, filtering, excreting, and so on. But the exterior man made a sloth look agitated and nervy. Maybe he was in a state of permanent hibernation, like a python coiled in a rock fissure or a polar bear in its ice cave? He assumed there was a medical term for it, some kind of 'vegetative state'. He would rather compare his father to a sleeping bear than a vegetable.

'That's it, Dad, isn't it?' he said. 'You've just had enough so you've switched everything off. You're not a carrot or a potato.' He squeezed his father's hand and felt, he thought, a small answering squeeze in reply. His father's hand was dry and smooth, callus-free, the nails clipped and polished, the back dappled with liver spots. It was a good hand to hold.

'Got to get well, Dad,' he said, a sudden catch in his voice as the prospect of his father's death confronted him, like a ghost or a wraith materializing in the room, and he felt the tear-sting in his eyes. He realized that he was frightened of being in a world that did not contain Bogdan Bloçj, even a Bogdan Bloçj as reduced as this.

To dispel this melancholy mood he irritated himself by recalling his near-unendurable evenings spent in the company of Torquil Helvoir-Jayne, his new best friend. He seemed to do little else but minister to him in various ways: tidying up his routine messes, replenishing the provisions he consumed (three bottles of whisky, thus far) and listening uncomplainingly to his litany of whinges, moans and expressions of self-pity. He had also become the unwilling auditor of the Helvoir-Jayne life story – a terminally bored Boswell to Torquil's indefatigable Dr Johnson – as Torquil sifted repeatedly through his past looking for the causes of the world's unfairness to him, trying to analyse what had happened and why his life and career were in such appalling shape. Lorimer had heard endlessly about the distant elderly parents, his miserable decade at boarding school, his aborted attempts to become a soldier, two years as a subaltern in an unfashionable regiment, his reluctant entry into the insurance world, his assorted girlfriends, his courtship and marriage of Binnie, her ghastly parents and brothers, her intransigence, his modest, unexceptional failings and his dreams of a new brighter future.

'It's in the East,' he said to Lorimer, meaning his future. 'Hungary, Bulgaria, Romania, the Czech Republic. That's your new frontier.' This was the only advice forthcoming from the many phone calls to his chums, his pals in the City. 'If I could only get some capital together. I could buy an office block in Budapest, a supermarket in Sofia, a motorway service station in Moravia. Dirt cheap. Apparently people – Brits, like you and me – are making a fortune out there. Tons of money, cleaning up.' The ache of his frustration was almost heartrending. Lorimer suggested an immediate reconnaissance. 'But I'm broke, Lorimer, I'm skint, without moolah. I'm in debt up to my eyeballs.' And then the shining aspirations would be replaced by the now familiar plaints: bastard lawyers, bitch-from-hell Binnie, devil incarnate Hogg, venal, selfish so-called friends who didn't come through when you needed them ('present company excepted, of course'). He would list them: the Rorys, the Simons, the Hughies, and some American entrepreneur to whom he had once rendered a crucial service called Sam M. Goodforth and whose name he repeated like a mantra, 'Goodforth, Goodforth, where's Sam bloody Goodforth now?' When the level in the whisky bottle dipped below half way Lorimer usually took himself off to bed, where he would lie awake thinking about Flavia Malinverno and listen to Torquil making telephone calls and endlessly switching channels on the television.

Flavia had not yet phoned, some two days after their unforgettable lunch. 'Bye, Lorimer, I'll call you,' she had shouted back at him through the slackening snow. If he shut his eyes he could hear the pitch of her voice exactly, see her tall figure slipping round the corner –'

'What're you holding his hand for?' Drava said, silently entering the room.

'I thought it might be comforting,' he said. It comforts me, anyway, he thought.

'It's plain morbid, that is,' Drava said with a shudder, retrieving her father's hand and replacing it on the counterpane.

In the hall the pungent smell of cooking meat was suddenly dominant and he could hear his grandmother and mother banging around in the kitchen, laughing and chattering in their language. Little Mercy was watching a boomingly violent video in the sitting room. A semi-audible layer of music issued from somewhere.

'Hey, Milo,' his grandmother shouted lustily at him. 'Stay for lunch. We got pig. Lovely boiled pork.'

That was the smell. He made it as far as the kitchen door and paused there – any further and he would dry-heave. He breathed shallowly through his mouth. His mother was making dumplings, rolling balls of dough between her palms and popping them in a pan of hissing fat.

'When's the doctor coming?' he said.

'Tonight, I think, six o'clock.'

'You think? He must come, insist. Make sure Dad gets the best of everything. All the tests, I'll pay.'

'Oh, he's fine, just a bit poorly.'

'Stay for lunch, Milo,' Komelia said coming up behind him and poking him in the ribs, 'Skinny. You need some lovely boiled pork.'

'And dumplings,' Mercy said, skipping out of the sitting room. 'Dumplings! Dumplings! Dumplings!'

'Isn't she clever?' his mother said. 'Plenty dumplings for you, darling. When you going to give me some more clever grandchildren, Milo?'

He saw Drava emerge from his father's room with a chamber pot and realized it was time to go.

'I've got a meeting,' he said weakly. 'Where's Slobodan?'

'Where d'you think,' Komelia said with a sneer. 'The Clarence.'

The Clarence, the Duke of Clarence, to give the pub its full name, was a couple of hundred yards away down the Dawes Road. Lorimer carefully picked his way through the frozen snow, Clarenceward, his condensing breath snatched from him by the numbing wind, the light threatening and baleful to the north. It was only lunchtime but it seemed night was coming on already.

The problem with the Clarence, Lorimer thought, was its utter absence of charm, its unequivocal charmlessness – which might have done duty as a form of charm, in this the day and age of the themed pub – but not even the most nostalgic drinker, Lorimer thought, could summon up much affection for this sorry watering hole. It boasted every pub minus-point, ancient and modern: a meagre choice of fizzy beers, muzak, no edible food, many clattering, flashing and pinging gaming machines, an adhesive, patterned carpet, satellite TV, a smelly old dog, surly old regulars, drunk young regulars, minimal heating, laboratory-bright lighting – and it was his brother's local, Slobodan's pub of choice.

Lorimer pushed open the swing doors to be assailed by the reek of a million extinguished cigarettes and two decades of spilt beer. An old man seemed to have passed out behind a table in the corner, his mouth wide open, his greasy trilby slipping off his head. Perhaps he'd just decided to die, Lorimer wondered, the Clarence could have that effect on you, as if they dosed their carbonated beer with additional *Weltschmerz*.

Slobodan and Phil Beazley were at the bar, where a young barman with walrus whiskers and a chain collar tattooed round his neck washed glasses in a sink of turbid grey water.

'Milo, my main man,' Beazley said for possibly the thousandth time.

'Here, Kev, this is my little bro. He's a millionaire.'

'G'day, mate,' said Kev, unimpressed and indubitably Australian. Lorimer wondered what had brought him all this way, from his hot, sun-filled country, across hemispheres, oceans and continents to wind up behind the bar of the Clarence, in Fulham. He also realized that the ostentatious mention of his alleged wealth was Slobodan's code for 'Don't ask for your money back.' He had in fact been planning a vague inquiry about the return of his loan as the morning's mail had brought a note from Ivan Algomir, complaining about an 'importunate and untimely demand from the Revenue' and wondering when he could cash Lorimer's cheque. Which reminded him: he would have to chase up that Gale-Harlequin bonus, everything was becoming a little stretched.

'What's your poison, Milo?' Beazley asked.

'Mineral –' He changed his mind, the only water in the Clarence flowed from a tap. 'Pint of Speyhawk.'

Speyhawk Special Strength Lager, designed to make a long afternoon slip by. Lorimer brought the foaming tankard to his lips, gulped and felt his brain yield. Beazley and Slobodan were drinking double gins and Coke. Lorimer insisted on paying for the round.

'Dad's . . . not well,' Lorimer burped. He hicked and coughed. Strong stuff.

'He'll be fine.'

'Constitution of a yak,' Beazley said, and for some reason punched Lorimer in the upper arm, unnecessarily hard. 'Hey, Milo, good to see ya.'

'How's business?' Lorimer asked.

'Diabolical,' Slobodan said, his face going long. 'You know old Nick and young Nick?'

Father and son, drivers at B and B. 'Yeah. What about them?'

'They got nicked.'

'What for?'

'Selling drugs down Earls Court station. 'Parently they got a field of marijuana at their place in Tonbridge. An acre and a half.'

'So,' Beazley said, disgustedly, 'we're two drivers down. I'd like to root my boot up old Nick's tradesman's entrance, I can tell you. We're going mental, aren't we, Lobby?'

Lobby agreed, vehemently, mental wasn't in it.

The glimmerings of an idea, a dangerous idea, a Speyhawk idea, began to take shape in Lorimer's mind.

'Listen, Phil,' he began. 'There's a guy been giving me a bit of bother. If I wanted, you know, to put the frighteners on him, do you think, you know, you could give him a word in the ear?'

'You want him sorted.'

'Warned off.'

'Well, we do owe you a favour, don't we, Lobbs?'

'What's he done?' Slobodan asked, genuinely curious.

'He blowtorched my car.'

'Not seen that in ages,' Beazley said. 'Very time-consuming.'

'What's he drive?' Slobodan asked.

'BMW. Big one, new model.'

'I know what you're thinking, Lobby,' Beazley said with real excitement. 'An eye for an eye, a motor for a motor.' He leaned towards Lorimer, confidentially. 'Lobby and me goes round to this guy, right? We got a couple of scaffolding poles – bash, wallop – we're out of there – one seriously fucked-up Beemer. Doddle.'

'Doddle,' Slobodan agreed. 'You tell us when, chief.'

Lorimer said he would and wrote down Rintoul's particulars, feeling a little nervous at what he might unleash but reassuring himself that his action was purely precautionary and that he was only following Hogg's instructions. 'Arrange your own oiling,' Hogg had said, in so many words. So, if Rintoul started playing silly buggers he'd have to deal with Beazley and Bloçj, the enforcers, with their scaffolding poles.

He took another sip of his effervescing Speyhawk, feeling the alcohol surge almost immediately through his veins. He set the glass down, shook his brother's and Beazley's hands, nodded to Kev and walked carefully out of the terrible pub seeing, as he did so, reflected in a foxed mirror by the door, Phil Beazley avidly lean across the bar to claim his undrunk lager.

Outside the light was purple, like a bruise, and the air stung with ice crystals. He strode off to find his carbonized car, slipping the weight of the Clarence's melancholia from his shoulders like an unwanted rucksack.

Unfortunately Lorimer found a parking space not far from Marlobe's flower shack.

'What kind of car's that, then?' Marlobe asked. His stall was colourfully ablaze with many varieties of carnation.

'Fire damage. Vandals, I think.'

'I'd castrate them,' Marlobe said, reasonably. 'I'd castrate them and then I'd cut their right hands off. Wouldn't do much vandalizing after that. Fancy a nice bunch of carnations?'

Lorimer's loathing of carnations had not abated so he bought a bunch of ten daffodils, their buds tightly closed, breathtakingly overpriced.

'There's two men in a Roller sitting outside your house. Been there for hours.'

It wasn't a Roller, it was a Maserati-Daimler or a Rolls-Bentley or a Bentley-Ferrari – one of the limited edition de-luxe hybrids that set you back somewhere in the region of £200,000 – certainly it was the priciest motor vehicle ever to grace the tarmacadam of Lupus Crescent. Sitting at the wheel was fat Terry, David Watts's factotum/gofer/major domo.

'Hi,' Terry said, ever genial. 'David would like a word with you.'

The smoked glass rear window on his side hummed downwards to reveal David Watts in a Wolverhampton Wanderers track suit sitting on cream calfskin.

'Can I have a word, Mr Black?'

'Do you want to come in?'

Watts stood in Lorimer's flat looking about him as if he were contemplating an exhibit in the Museum of Mankind.

'Sorry about the mess,' Lorimer said, collecting aluminium receptacles, scooping up a shirt and a pair of boxer shorts. 'I've got a friend staying.' He stuffed receptacles, shirt, boxers and the daffodils in the swing bin –

what was the point? Something blackened and crusty had dribbled down the front of his cooker.

'That's nice,' Watts said, pointing. 'Is it real?'

'It's Greek, about three thousand years old. Do you want me to draw the curtains?'

Watts had put on a pair of sunglasses.

'No thanks. You've got a ton of CDs. Not as many as me, but you've got a lot.'

'I'm sorry I haven't got back to you, but there's still a process of consultation to –'

'Don't worry about the insurance. Take your time. No, it was that group you mentioned, Achimota. Sheer Achimota.'

'Kwame Akinlaye and the Achimota Rhythm Boys.'

'That's the one. Do you believe in serendipity, Mr Black?'

'Not really.' He believed in its opposite, whatever that was.

'It's the most powerful force in anyone's life. It is in mine. I have to find that CD you mentioned. *Sheer Achimota*. I know it's going to be very important to me.'

'It's an import. I got the CD mail order. There's a shop in Camden –'

Irina came out of the bedroom wearing one of Lorimer's shirts.

'Hello, Lorimer,' she said and went into the kitchen.

'I'm not interrupting, am I?' Watts asked, politely.

'What? No. Um. I just –'

'That girl's got the whitest legs I've seen. Is there any way at all I could buy that CD off you? Name your price. £200.'

'I can lend it to you.' He could hear cupboards being opened and shut in the kitchen.

'Lend?' Watts said, as if the concept was a new one.

'Could you just give me a second,' Lorimer said. 'Excuse me.'

Torquil was lying in his bed, propped on pillows, naked and reading, as far as Lorimer could see, a soft-porn men's magazine. Happily the sheet was bunched at his groin, between his spread legs.

'Oh, hi, Lorimer, guess who's here.'

'I just saw her. Just what the fuck do you mean by this, Torquil?'

'Jesus Christ, what was I meant to do?'

Irina returned with a bottle of white wine and two glasses. She sat on the edge of the bed, her legs demurely crossed, and poured a drink for Torquil, who was now sprawling across the mattress, bare-arsed, searching his trouser pockets for cigarettes. In an antique display of chivalry he lit two simultaneously and handed one to Irina.

'Lorimer?' Irina said, blowing smoke out of the side of her mouth.

'Yes?'

'Man in room. Is he David Watts?'

'Yes.'

'I don' believe I am in house, same house with David Watts.' She started speaking excitedly in Russian. Her legs were indeed amazingly white, Lorimer noticed, and long and thin, the blue veins in her thighs like . . . He thought for a second, like rivers beneath pack-ice seen from the air.

'Not David Watts the singer?' Torquil said, equally impressed. 'In this flat?'

'Yes. I'm lending him a CD.'

'Fuck off.'

'You fuck off.'

'Lying bastard.'

'Come and see for yourself.'

Lorimer rejoined Watts, who was now crouched in front of the custom-built shelves containing his CD collection, his sunglasses pushed up on his forehead. He had already found Kwame Akinlaye – Lorimer shelved his CDs alphabetically and under country of origin.

'Got a lot of classical,' Watts observed. 'Masses of Brazil.'

'I used only to listen to Central and South American music,' Lorimer told him. 'I moved on to Africa about three years ago. Started at Morocco and worked south, around the bulge, you know.'

Watts frowned at him. 'Interesting. Where are you now?'

'Ghana. Moving on to Benin. Next week probably.'

'This is what you call authentic, is it?'

'Compared to the crap we produce in the West.'

A hastily dressed Irina and Torquil arrived and Lorimer introduced them. Torquil pointed at Watts' track suit and sang, 'Come on, you Woo-oolves'. Irina asked for an autograph and so did Torquil, for a person named 'Amy'. Lorimer realized with something of a shock that this was Torquil's fourteen-year-old daughter (away at boarding school) – he trusted she wouldn't ask her father how he came by David Watts's signature.

'I hope I wasn't interrupting anything,' Watts said, signing his name on two leaves of writing paper. 'Love in the afternoon, sort of thing.'

'No, no, we'd finished,' Torquil said. 'In fact, you've got to be going, haven't you, Irina? Got to go, yes? Go?'

'What? Oh, yes, I must go.' She collected her handbag, said shy goodbyes (Lorimer noticing there was no further physical contact between her and Torquil) and left. Watts accepted one of Torquil's cigarettes.

'I'm amazed she knew who you were,' Torquil said. 'Irina, I mean. She's Russian, you see.'

'Everybody in Russia knows David Watts,' said David Watts. 'Sell millions there. Millions.'

'Really? Tell me, is the Team ever going to get back together?'

'Over my dead body, mate. They're thieves, robbers. I'd rather bite my tongue off. I'd rather rip out my windpipe with my bare hands.'

'Not what you'd call an amicable parting of the ways, then? What's happened to Tony Anthony?'

Watts did not stay much longer, he seemed troubled by Torquil's rehashing of the former band's past history. Lorimer lent him a couple more CDs – a singer from Guinea-Bissau and a predominantly brass band from Sierra Leone. He said he would record them and have Terry drop them back the next day and then asked politely, as if he were a dowager or a maiden aunt, if Lorimer could walk him to his car. Terry saw them coming and heaved himself out of the driver's seat to open the door.

'This insurance hassle,' Watts said, flicking away the butt of his cigarette. 'I've been talking to my people and I think there's going to be the mother of all law suits if it isn't paid. Twenty, thirty million.'

'Fine,' Lorimer said. 'We like these matters aired in court.' That should please Hogg, he was thinking, dolefully.

'Nothing personal,' Watts said, 'but it just doesn't look

good, David Watts being jerked off by a bunch of suits. It doesn't look cool.'

'Whatever.'

'I'll get these discs back to you tomorrow, mate,' Watts said stooping into his car. 'Much obliged, Lorimer – can I call you Lorimer? Could be fruitful. Serendipity. Be in touch.'

The car moved off soundlessly, it seemed, on its wide tyres. People in the street stopped to marvel at it. Lorimer remembered from a recent survey in a Sunday newspaper that David Watts was the 349th richest person in the country.

Lady Haigh was waiting for him in the hall. She was smartly dressed in a green tweed suit, wearing a turban skewered with a ruby-tipped hat pin. Jupiter peered out at him, panting evenly, from behind her legs.

'Your friend brought a girl back with him this morning.'

'I can only apologize, Lady Haigh.'

'He makes a terrible din, clumping around all hours of the day and night.'

'I'll tell him to keep quiet.'

'I find him very uncouth, Lorimer.'

'So do I, Lady Haigh, so do I.'

389. Serendipity. From Serendip, *a former name of Ceylon, now Sri Lanka. A word coined by Horace Walpole, who had invented it based on a folktale, whose heroes were always making discoveries of things they were not in quest of. Ergo: serendipity, the faculty of making happy and unexpected discoveries by accident.*

So what is the opposite of Serendip, a southern land of spice and warmth, lush greenery and humming birds, sea-washed, sun-basted? Think of another world in the far north, barren, ice-bound, cold, a world of flint and stone. Call it Zembla. *Ergo: zemblanity, the*

opposite of serendipity, the faculty of making unhappy, unlucky and
expected discoveries by design. Serendipity and zemblanity: the twin
poles of the axis around which we revolve.

The Book of Transfiguration

That evening Torquil told him eagerly and in some detail
what he and Irina had done in Lorimer's bed (sheets
already off to the launderette). They watched a violent
sci-fi thriller on a cable channel (Torquil's choice) before
Torquil called out for pizza and chips. Torquil smoked
a pack of cigarettes and finished the whisky before he
became maudlin – 'Oh Binnie, Binnie, Binnie' – and
then angry, inveighing against Oliver Rollo in particular.
Binnie had been invited to Oliver and Potts's wedding
but not Torquil – it was a vivid indication of his pariah
status and Lorimer could see that it hurt. He started
talking fondly of South Africa, Eastern Europe seemingly
no longer on the fortune-making agenda. 'If I could just
get some capital together, Lorimer,' he moaned frus-
tratedly. 'It's like the old days out there, Happy Valley,
Pioneer Spirit, gin and polo . . . All you need to do is buy
a golf course or a vineyard. Money's pouring in. But
you've got to have something to sell – a game reserve, a
marina. Brits – people like you and me – are making
staggering sums of money in South Africa. Obscene
amounts.'

'Why don't you have a snoop around? Fly out. Pick
up a bargain?' Lorimer encouraged.

'Oh sure. I've got to pay that hard-hearted bitch fifteen
hundred quid tomorrow and I possess exactly –' he
emptied his pockets on the table – 'seventeen pounds
and some change. This isn't a pound coin, it's a hundred

fucking pesetas. Sixteen pounds, some change and a hundred pesetas.'

Lorimer felt despair grip him as Torquil ran through all the possible retail outlets he had visited and that could have perpetrated this pound/peseta subterfuge. This could go on no longer, Lorimer realized; his own life – its careful security, its deliberate order – was being so undermined that he could foresee a serious collapse. He had to find a way of expelling this interloper. The cuckoo was in the nest and growing more comfortable daily; there was only limited time before the fledgling Lorimer would no longer be able to cope.

'The trouble is I can't get on top of things,' Torquil said, the self-pity immense. 'I've got no time. Everything's piling up. I have to find a way of being paid in cash – in advance or at once.' He set his jaw. 'I know it's immoral, but I don't think there's any choice, Lorimer. I have to do it.'

'What?'

'Sell drugs – ecstasy, heroin, crack. I don't care any more, I'm at the end of my tether. Society is forcing me into this. It's society's fault, and Binnie's, not mine.'

Of course. Lorimer suddenly saw the answer with absolute clarity, marvelling at how the mind worked independently of instructions, sometimes.

'Listen, Torquil, if I could get you a well-paid job, cash, that would solve your immediate financial problems, but that involved an eighteen- to twenty-hour day, would you take it?'

'Would I take it? I'd work a twenty-four-hour day if necessary. Tell me where and when.'

'I just have to make one phone call.'

Lorimer punched out the numbers on the phone in

the kitchen, feeling his heart lighten at the prospect of the cuckoo, if not expelled, at least absent for most of the time.

'Yeah?' said the voice at the end of the line.

'It's Milo. Is your Cortina still in running order? Good. I've got a driver for you.'

390. *Origin of the Name 'David Watts'*. *Torquil told me this. One of the few interesting facts Torquil ever told me.*

'Know why he calls himself David Watts?' No, why? 'It's that song by the Kinks.' Never heard of them. 'Jesus Christ, you must have, one of the legendary rock bands of the 1960s.' Rings a bell, I said, now you mention it.

Torquil stood up as if he was performing and sang in a throaty tenor and cod-cockney accent: 'FAH-fuh-fuh-FAH-FAH, FAH-FAH-FAH.' He sang the whole song, word-perfect, which is narrated by 'a dull and simple lad, who cannot tell water from champagne' and who fantasizes about David Watts, a truly heroic schoolboy, epic scrapper, rich, captain of the team, head boy, whom all the girls in the neighbourhood fancy something rotten. The chorus, the refrain, repeated wistfully, 'I wish I could be like David Watts, I wish I could be like David Watts, I wish I could be like David Watts.' It was a song about someone who could do no wrong, someone who was revered and worshipped by his peers, someone who, to all intents and purposes, was perfect. I began to understand a little more clearly: this was how Martin Foster became David Watts.

The Book of Transfiguration

Chapter 13

Hogg sauntered into Lorimer's office without knocking. He was wearing a short sheepskin car-coat and a flat tweed cap and looked like a bookie, or a farmer on a day trip up to town for the agricultural fair.

Lorimer pushed his chair back and put on his most winning smile.

'Morning, Mr Hogg.'

Hogg pointed at him. 'Bite of lunch, me old china?'

They taxied west, to Lorimer's surprise, to Tottenham Court Road, then walked a few blocks with the Telecom tower looming ever nearer until they reached a restaurant called O'Riley's, a low-ceilinged establishment with velveteen banquettes in darkwood booths and William Morris wallpaper. The owner, a Moroccan called Pedro, greeted Hogg effusively and led the two of them through the entirely empty restaurant to a booth at the rear.

'The usual, señor Hogg?'

'Grassyarse, Pedro. And bring one for señor Black, here.' Hogg leant forward. 'Best Welsh rarebit in town. I highly recommend it, Lorimer. Apple pie's not half bad either.'

Pedro brought them two large schooners of amontillado and they scrutinized the menu. 'Eclectic' was the word that came to mind and Lorimer realized he was in a form of classic English restaurant that was fast disappearing – it had been many years since he'd seen the choice of 'tomato juice, orange juice or grapefruit juice' offered as an *entrée*. Hogg ordered the Welsh rarebit and lamb souvlaki while Lorimer opted for stuffed vine-leaves and a breaded veal cutlet with a selection of vegetables. The wine of the day was a Hungarian Bull's Blood and Lorimer's request for a large Perrier was rebuffed at once. 'Nonsense. Bring him a glass of honest-to-goodness Thames water, Pedro.'

Lorimer needed water badly because the amontillado had given him an instant headache above the eyes. Sherry had this effect on him, as well as inducing a general sense of melancholy. But he was also tense, he realized, he could feel the muscles knotting in the nape of his neck and braiding tightly across his shoulders.

Hogg talked with enthusiasm about the good year G G H Ltd was enjoying. Last quarter had been a cracker, he said, but this one was shaping up to beat all records.

'No small thanks to you, Lorimer,' he said, emptying his schooner and calling for another. 'I'm thinking of expanding, adding another member or two to our little family, take some of the load off your shoulders.'

'I'm not complaining, Mr Hogg.'

'I know, Lorimer. But you're not the complaining type.'

Lorimer was uneasy: Hogg's tone of voice seemed to imply that he should have been complaining. He tackled his stuffed vine-leaves (what in God's name had made him order those?) with only half his mind on the job, the other half searching for reasons to explain this invitation to lunch.

'So,' Hogg said, sawing a chunk off his lifejacket-orange Welsh rarebit. 'How goes the David Watts adjust?'

'Very tricky,' Lorimer said. 'As tricky as I've ever encountered.'

'And why's that, Lorimer?'

'Because the guy is an off-his-trolley, barking, out-of-his-tiny-Chinese, grade-A nutter, Mr Hogg.'

'You made him an offer?'

'It won't work. He's not interested in the money. If his manager had still been around it would have been a straightforward deal, I'm sure. But Watts is controlling everything, now, doing his own management, and, I tell you, it follows absolutely no logic. He threatened, or rather, he mentioned a £30 million law suit if we didn't settle.'

'We'd take him to the cleaners.' Hogg looked at Lorimer's sceptical expression. 'What's your professional advice, Lorimer?'

'Pay. This one's a ticker if I ever saw one.'

'Going to blow up in our face?' Hogg was stabbing the cheesy skin on his rarebit, making crude patterns with the tines of his fork. He looked up, his face drained of all his previous false bonhomie.

'I see they've pulled down the Fedora Palace.'

'I passed by the other day.'

'What's the game, Lorimer? That was an expensive building. Damaged, but still very expensive.'

'I haven't the faintest.'

Hogg filled their glasses to the brim with Bull's Blood. The wine was so darkly red it was almost black. Lorimer raised it carefully to his lips, inhaling, expecting a reeking pong of abattoirs, offal, lights, organs, sawdust and faeces, but it was resolutely neutral – offering no more to the nose than a faint smell of grapes. He drank avidly as Pedro whisked their starters away and replaced them with their main courses. Service was impressively speedy, Lorimer thought, until he recalled they were O'Riley's only customers. His breaded veal sat in a small lake of gravy contesting the plate space with roast and boiled potatoes, cauliflower, carrots and some olive green peas – fresh from the can.

'This stinks,' Hogg said, stuffing his mouth full of lamb – he was not referring to the cooking. 'The whole rancid bollocks stinks to high heaven. And I think you know why.'

'I don't, Mr Hogg.'

Hogg pointed his knife at him, chewing vigorously. 'Then you'd better find out, my blue-eyed boy. Everything's on hold until you do.'

'Meaning what?'

'Meaning you, your job, your future, your bonus.'

'That's not fair.'

'You're sucking on hind tit here, Lorimer. Life's not fair. You should know that, you work in insurance.'

Lorimer felt no hunger for his meal; in fact he felt the opposite of hunger – not replete, not nauseous, but suddenly food-phobic, in a curious way, as if he wanted nothing more to do with nutrition, ever. He was still very pro-alcohol, though, decidedly keen on the idea of getting drunk. He gulped Bull's Blood – give me strength, he prayed, give me the strength of a Hungarian bull. Hogg was tearing into his lamb, knife and fork flashing, as if the beast had once done him personal injury. Lorimer covertly topped up their glasses.

'What have we got exactly?' Hogg said. 'A serious fire, deliberately started in a new, nearly complete luxury hotel. A disgusting bit of insurance work that leads to a £27 million claim. Then a loss adjustment to kill for, of positively dreamlike beauty. A week later said hotel is being levelled to the ground. A massive write-off in investment terms – where's the sense?'

Lorimer admitted there appeared to be none but something Hogg had said had inadvertently set an alarm bell ringing, some flaw in his reasoning somewhere. He would have to think it over later, Hogg was in full stride.

'And worse,' he continued, 'the tenth-rate prat who wrote the insurance is foisted on me days before the whole caboodle goes down the toilet at the personal request of Sir Simon Sherriffmuir himself. I fire this useless wanker as soon as is decent and what does he do? He ends up staying in my favourite loss adjuster's flat, the very loss adjuster who did the diamond job on Gale-Harlequin. How do you think that looks to me?' Hogg pushed his plate aside. 'It looks to me, Lorimer, that someone's trying to ream George Hogg up his arse and George Hogg doesn't like it one little bit.'

'It's pure coincidence – pure malevolent coincidence – that Helvoir-Jayne's staying with me, Mr Hogg.' He wanted to tell him about zemblanity, how this was a perfect example of its sinister influence on one's life, but Hogg was still analysing recent events.

'How well do you know Sherriffmuir?'

'I've only met him once. You don't think he's –'

'He wanted shot of Helvoir-Jayne, pronto. Why land him on me, though? Because *you* worked for me and you were going to do the Gale-Harlequin adjust –'

'It makes no sense, Mr Hogg. This is wild speculation.'

Hogg took out and lit a knobbly panatella.

'Be that as it may,' he said cryptically, through wreaths of bluey smoke. 'I hear the sound of roof tiles falling.'

'There has to be an explanation. Who's being

exploited? Ripped off? The only ones entitled to complain are Gale-Harlequin.'

'Somebody got ten mil.'

'Only forty per cent of what they were due.'

'But why tear down their hotel?'

'Beats me.'

'Somebody, somewhere, has used or is using us and is making a dirty deal.'

'But what? Who?'

'That's your job, Lorimer. You make sense of it and come and explain it to me in words of one syllable. Everything's off till you tell me what this has been about.'

'I really need that bonus, Mr Hogg, I'm over-extended, financially.'

'Tough shit. Now, try some of this apple pie.'

392. Hogg, once, in his convivial days, in a pub after work, over a schooner of Bristol Cream and a pint of lager chaser, said, 'Know how you got this job, Lorimer?'

ME: Because I was a good loss adjuster for Fortress Sure.
HOGG: No.
ME: Because I was well-qualified.
HOGG: The world is full to the gunwales of well-qualified people.
ME: Because I've got a sunny demeanour?
HOGG: Think back to the interview. One answer you gave swung it.
ME: I can't remember.
HOGG: I remember. It was like an ice-water enema. I thought, this boy's got what it takes, he's got co-johns.
ME: Cojones. It's Spanish.
HOGG: Nonsense, it's Belgian. It's a Belgian expression. Flemish for 'guts'.

ME: It's not pronounced 'co-johns', Mr Hogg.

HOGG: I don't give a gerbil's dick how it's pronounced. I'm trying to tell you, matey, how you wound up in this public house sharing a libation with me. I asked you a question right at the end of the interview, remember?

ME: Oh, yes. Remind me, Mr Hogg.

HOGG: I said: what's your biggest fault? And what did you say?

ME: I don't recall. I made it up, probably.

HOGG: You said – and I'll never forget this – you said, 'I've got a violent temper.'

ME: Did I?

HOGG: (musing) That impressed me, that did. That's why I brought you into the family, into GGH. We all have faults, Lorimer – even I have faults – but not many of us will own up to them.

The Book of Transfiguration

'Slobodan, this is Torquil. Torquil, Slobodan.'

'Call me Lobby. Everyone else does, 'cept for Milo here.'

'Milo?' Torquil looked at Lorimer curiously.

'Family nickname,' Lorimer said, keeping his voice low. Slobodan couldn't hear, anyway, he was round the other side of the Cortina, kicking the tyres.

'Welcome aboard, Torquil,' Slobodan said. 'You're insured, completely covered. Clean driving licence, willing to work all hours. You've saved our bacon in our eleventh hour of need.'

'Likewise, ah, Lobby,' Torquil said, shaking his proffered hand. They were standing outside Slobodan's house, a faint sun spangling off the Cortina's chrome, a gentle burbling noise of melting snow in the gutters.

'I believe I owe you a fee,' Torquil said, offering Slobodan a cigarette. The two men lit up.

'Forty quid a week for the radio. In advance.'

Torquil turned to Lorimer, who gave him forty pounds, which he handed to Slobodan.

'Ta very much, Torquil.'

'I'll probably need extra for petrol,' Torquil said, 'and meals.'

Lorimer gave him another forty. He didn't care, he was happy.

'Come and meet my associate, Mr Beazley,' Slobodan said. 'We'll get your first job set up.'

'I've got my *A to Z,*' Torquil said, hauling Lorimer's street map out of his pocket.

'That's all you need for this job. And a car. What do you normally drive?'

'I had a Volvo. Estate.'

'Nice motor.'

'But it was repossessed.'

'Shit happens, Tork. It happens to the best of us.'

'I'll see you two later,' Lorimer said. 'Good luck.'

He looked back at the two men as they headed for the office, cigarettes on the go, both of an age, both solidly built, both overweight, one with short hair wearing a pin-stripe suit, one with a grey ponytail wearing an ex-*Wehrmacht* combat jacket. For some reason Lorimer had an odd premonition that they would get along. He had been uneasy about bringing Torquil so close to his family but the absolute need to terminate the continued presence and pressure of the man in his life had demanded swift action and this was the only feasible solution available. All he had said to Slobodan was that people called him 'Lorimer' at work, Milomre being hard to pronounce. Slobodan had barely paid attention. In the event, Lorimer thought, the less said the better – they were both resolutely incurious types, nothing much seemed to surprise them at all. Anyway, he had more complex problems on his hands, such as impending insolvency. He was still rattled from his lunch with Hogg, the man's suspicions fuelling his paranoia, deepening, if that were possible, his utter ruthlessness. But how was he meant to solve the Gale-Harlequin conundrum quickly? He might have a better chance now his life was comparatively Torquil-free.

He was on the point of ringing the bell to the family flat when the door opened and Drava appeared, her arms full of folders.

'How's Dad?' Lorimer asked. 'Did the doctor come?'

'He's fine. Fast asleep. The doctor couldn't tell what was wrong. Gave him some antibiotics and something to help him sleep.'

'Sleep? Surely that's the last thing Dad needs.'

'Sometimes he doesn't sleep for days. You go into his room at night and there he is laying there, eyes wide open. Excuse me, Milo, can't stand here talking all day.'

So it runs in the family, Lorimer thought, as he drove back to the City. In my father's genes, this light-sleeper business. He wondered if he should put another night in at the Institute – because it was so sleep-orientated he always managed a good couple of hours there, even wired up to Alan's machines. He wondered what the data was showing – they must have enough of it by now – wondered if Alan was going to be able to help. Where was Alan these days, anyway? He hadn't seen him for ages.

The Fedora Palace was down to one storey, the jagged

concrete of its remaining walls just visible above the hoardings which, he noticed, were now embellished with a new name and logo: BOOMSLANG PROPER-TIES LTD, the sanserif type encircled by a stylized drawing of an acid green snake. Boomslang – who the hell were they?

'No idea,' the site manager told him. Everything had been sold to this new company a matter of days ago, he said, and some young bloke had come along with these plastic signs and had stuck them up.

Lorimer telephoned Boomslang Properties at an address in Battersea and arranged an appointment for six o'clock that evening. He had told the girl who answered the phone that it was an insurance matter and mentioned he was investigating the prospect of a rebate. The thought of receiving money always made people fix appointments promptly.

Boomslang Properties was to be found above a shop selling expensive crockery and kitchenware in a prettified parade not far from Albert Bridge. A young girl in jeans and a large sweater printed with cartoon characters put her cigarette and magazine down and stared at him uncomprehendingly.

'We spoke earlier this afternoon.' Lorimer repeated his business patiently, 'I've come about the Fedora Palace site.' He could see it was still ringing no bells.

'Oh, God, yah . . .' She shouted: 'Marius? Mr Fedora, insurance?' There was no reply. 'He must be on the phone.'

A giant of a young man, in his twenties, six foot four or five, blond and ski-tanned, stooped out of a door down the passageway, the sound of a flushing toilet in his wake. His sleeves were rolled up and he was wearing braces.

He wiped his hands on his trouser seat before offering the right one in greeting.

'Hi,' he said, 'I'm Marius van Meer.' The accent was South African, Lorimer thought, as he followed van Meer – his back the size of a coffee table – into his office, where he spun him some vague guff about a possible mis-estimate of the claim settlement and the possibility of a further tranche being forthcoming if, etcetera, etcetera. Marius van Meer smiled at him amiably – it was very quickly clear he had no idea what Lorimer was talking about. So much the better: Lorimer quietly dropped his cover story.

'You do know there was a fire in that hotel?'

'Ah, yeah, I did hear something about it. I've been in Colorado skiing these last few weeks.'

'But you bought the site off Gale-Harlequin?'

'This is really my dad's business. I'm just learning the ropes, sort of.'

'And your father is?'

'Dirk van Meer. He's in Jo'burg.'

This name sounded familiar, one of the southern hemisphere moguls, he thought. Diamonds, coal, resorts, TV stations, something of that order.

'Would it be possible to speak to him?'

'He's a bit hard to get hold of at the moment. He's the one tends to call me, you see.'

Lorimer looked round the small office: everything was new – carpet, chairs, blind, desk, even the giant bag of golf clubs parked in the corner. He could hear the girl on the phone outside talking to a friend, arranging a dinner party. He was wasting his time.

He stood up. 'What does Boomslang mean, by the way?'

'That was my idea,' Marius said proudly. 'A boomslang is an African tree snake, beautiful but harmless. Unless you're an ig.'

'An ig?'

'Yah. It eats igs. Robs birds' nests. Beautiful lime green snake.'

Lorimer cruised down Lupus Crescent looking vainly for a parking spot and patrolled the adjacent streets for five minutes until Turpentine Lane yielded a few yards of vacant kerb. He trudged back towards the house, further bemused by this Gale-Harlequin/Boomslang development and further frustrated: what did Hogg expect of him? Should he jump on a plane and fly to Johannesburg? He peered down at Lady Haigh's basement window. The lights were on, she must –

The blow glanced off the side of his head (it was that minute inclination of his head to the right that saved him, he later analysed) and his left shoulder took the full brunt of the club-swing. He bellowed his pain and shock, his left arm fizzing in agony, pricked by ten thousand hot needles, and, quite reflexively – he was staggering round from the force of the blow as it was – he wheeled his briefcase in a self-protective arc. He heard a crunching noise as its edge went into his assailant's face, a noise not violent so much as quietly and domestically satisfying, like a splash of milk falling on crisp cornflakes. His attacker screamed in his turn and staggered away, falling to the ground. Lights were flashing in Lorimer's face – anti-aircraft fire over Baghdad – and he aimed a couple of kicks in the squirming, scrabbling body's direction, the second of which connected with an ankle. The figure, wearing dark clothes, a hood over its head, clambered to its feet and limp-ran away, surprisingly fast, club or bat or two-by-four in its hand, and Lorimer fell over, himself, his head suddenly speared with a new form of nerve-end trauma. Gently he touched the hair above his left ear – wet, horrifically tender, a lump rising under his fingertips. Blood.

No one came out and no one seemed to have heard anything – the whole 'fight' must have lasted three seconds. Inside, peering into the bathroom mirror, he discovered he had an oozing one-inch cut above his ear and a lump the size of a halved ping-pong ball. The big muscle on the back of his shoulder was dark red and badly contused but no bones seemed to have been broken. He wondered if he would be able to move his left arm in the morning. He stumbled out of the bathroom and filled a glass with medicinal Scotch. He was very pleased Torquil was not at home. He jammed the telephone receiver under his chin and punched out a number.

'Yeah?'

'Phil?'

'Who wants to know?'

'It's Lor – it's Milo.'

'Hey, Milo, my main man. Lobby's not here. How you doing?'

'Not so good. Somebody just took a swing at my head with a baseball bat.'

'That scumbag who's been bugging you?'

'Rintoul.'

'Do you, like, want me to sort him instead of his motor? Break all his fingers or something? It proper fucks you up, eight broken fingers, I tell you. Can't even take a piss.'

'No, just do the motor. He'll get the message.'

'Consider it done, Milo. My pleasure.'

He drank his whisky and took four aspirin and managed to shrug off his jacket and kick away his shoes before sliding himself into bed beneath the duvet. He felt his shoulder and arm stiffening, as if being subjected to some localized freezing device. He felt too an immense weariness descend on him as the adrenalin flood seeped away or wore off or whatever happened to adrenalin when it was no longer needed. He felt himself start to shiver and for the first time the delayed shock made tears prick his eyes. What a vicious . . . What kind of desperate coward would . . . If he had not moved his head that fraction what damage might have been done to him? The only consolation was that he knew that, for the first time in years, he was about to sleep a whole night through.

Torquil woke him at 2.15 a.m. Shook him awake, his big clumsy paw gripping his ruined shoulder.

'God, sorry,' Torquil stepped back in alarm. 'What happened to you? Look like shit.'

'Someone tried to mug me. Got hit on the head.'

'Bastard. Guess how much I made?'

'Torquil, I've been attacked, brutalized, I have to sleep.'

'I worked nine hours non-stop. Guess.'

'I need sleep.'

'£285. Lobby said the work's there for me. Nights are even better. There's a surcharge after ten.'

'Congratulations.' Lorimer hunched into the pillow.

'I thought you'd be pleased for me,' Torquil said, petulantly.

'I am,' Lorimer mumbled. 'I'm very pleased. Now go away and leave me alone, there's a good boy.'

234. 1953. *It is one of the most astonishing facts in scientific history, Alan said, one of the most inexplicable occurrences in* *the history of the study of the human body. What? Consider this, Alan said, after millennia of sleep and sleeping, REM sleep was only discovered in 1953. 1953! Did no one ever look at another person sleeping and wonder why their eyeballs were moving? Well, did it exist before 1953? I said. Perhaps REM sleep is a late evolutionary refinement amongst human beings. Of course it did, Alan said. How do you know? Because we only dream in REM sleep, and people have dreamed since the beginning of time.*

The Book of Transfiguration

'– and this is Adrian Bolt,' Hogg was saying, 'Dymphna Macfarlane, Shane Ashgable, Ian Fetter, and, last but by no means least, Lorimer Black.'

'How do you do?' Lorimer said, coaxing his features into what he hoped was a smile of welcome. He was now familiar with the full meaning of the expression 'etched with pain'. He felt like Gérard de Nerval in the photograph by Nadar. A very sharp burin had been at work on his head but the ache in his shoulder had shown ambitious powers of improvisation in the hours since the attack. His whole left side was experiencing collateral damage, even his left foot seemed to be throbbing dully in sympathy. Hogg was introducing the GGH loss adjusters to their newest colleague, Felicia Pickersgill, a tough-looking woman in her forties with thick, badgery grey hair and a shrewd, unimpressed look in her eye. He had not really concentrated on Hogg's preamble but he thought he recalled that she had held some senior rank in the WRENS or the army, something in the services anyway, before she had joined a bank and then an insurance company, probably Military Police, Lorimer thought, Hogg would respond well to that in a curriculum vitae. However, all Lorimer wanted to focus on was the wine in the bottles standing behind the plates of canapés on Hogg's desk. He had vomited twice on waking this morning and had generously brandied his tea as a result. The pain had dimmed for a while but now he needed more analgesic alcohol.

'– extremely pleased to welcome Felicia to GGH and look forward to her special expertise contributing to the success and reputation of the firm.'

'Hear, hear,' Rajiv and Yang Zhi said in unison and Janice began to clap, but Hogg held up a palm for silence.

'Felicia knows, as indeed you all know, that you represent the hand-picked élite of our profession. We are few in number but our power and influence is out of all proportion to our size. GGH has established itself as pre-eminent in the highly competitive world of specialist loss adjusters. Much of this success is down to you and your efforts. I know I can be a bit stern and severe (dutiful chuckles) but it's because only the highest standards allow us to thrive. To thrive and flourish in a difficult, nay, harsh world. When things get tough, as an American cinema artiste once said –'

(Oh get on with it, Lorimer thought.)

'– the tough get going. Only the toughest survive here and Felicia, I know, is going to make a valuable contribution to our "special forces". We look forward to working with her.'

Hogg led the applause, Lorimer led the advance on the food and drink. He was on his second Chardonnay when Hogg pushed his big face up to his.

'I hope you were listening, Lorimer, cleaned out the ear wax. Words of wisdom. What's the matter with you? Look like death warmed up.'

'Someone tried to mug me last night. Severe blow on the shoulder.'

'Oh. Any advance on Gale-Harlequin?'

'I think I may have a new lead.'

'I thought I might put Felicia on the case. Bit of back-up for you.'

Lorimer did not like the sound of this. 'I'm better on my own, I think.'

'We only judge by results here, Lorimer.' Hogg turned away.

Lorimer smiled weakly and popped a vol-au-vent into his mouth, drained his glass and refilled it and went in search of Dymphna.

'Why are you walking in that canted-over way?' she asked. 'You look awful.'

'Random urban violence. But you should see the other guy.'

'I don't like the look of this Felicia. Do you think she and Hogg are lovers?'

'I refuse to contemplate that possibility.'

'Shane thinks she's been sent to spy on us.'

'Could be. Hogg's got a terminal dose of bunker mentality at the moment. Listen, Dymphna, you know lots of journalists. Could you introduce me to one who understands property deals?'

'I can always ask Frank.' Frank was her ex-boyfriend who had worked on the financial pages of *The Times*.

'I just need someone who knows the ropes. I'll give him the information, he can supply the analysis.'

Dymphna lit a cigarette and looked interested. 'What's all this about? Gale-Harlequin?'

'Yes. No. Possibly.'

'That just about covers everything,' she said, sardonically. 'I hear Hogg won't pay your bonus.'

'Who told you that, for God's sake?'

'Rajiv. Don't worry, I'll find you your journalist.' She looked at him meaningfully. 'What's my reward?'

'My undying gratitude.'

'Oh, you'll have to do better than that, Lorimer Black.'

Chapter 14

The day of the Dupree inquest dawned bright and cloud-free, with a blue sky of near alpine clarity and a low blazing sun that cast sharp shadows and burned blindingly off the rows of car windows parked outside the coroner's court in Hornsey.

Lorimer walked slowly down the steps to the innocuous brick building – like a science lab in a new comprehensive school, he thought – not looking forward to his first appearance as a key witness and wincing as he inadvertently flexed the fingers of his left hand. Any movement seemed to affect adversely the big shoulder muscle (the trapezius, as he now knew it was called, having looked it up in an encyclopaedia), transforming itself into a pain-trigger, tracing itself back to the crushed fibres. His shoulder had now turned a lurid damson-brown, like some horrible algae infesting his epidermis.

'Morning, Mr Black.' Detective Sergeant Rappaport stood in the lee provided by the concrete columns of the main door, a small cigar in his hand. 'Lovely day for it.'

Lorimer noticed that the coroner's court was adjacent to an anonymous-looking building signed 'Public Mortuary'. The disturbing thought arrived in his head that it might contain the body of Mr Dupree, awaiting the verdict on his passing. It was better not to know.

'What exactly will I have to do?' Lorimer asked.

'A formality, Mr Black. Just tell them how you found Mr Dupree. Then I give my spiel. There's a member of the family with a few observations on Mr D's state of mind at the time of the incident. Should wrap things up inside of an hour. By the way, what's happened to your car?'

Lorimer told him and they went inside and upstairs, where, in a dim hall, small groups of people stood around, hushed and nervous as if at a funeral, talking in low voices. Juvenile delinquents, washed, smart and contrite, squired by their parents, glum no-hopers, petty thieves, self-righteous merchants pursuing creditors through small-claims courts, traffic code violators, ashamed drunken drivers swearing sobriety. Lorimer felt cast down being amongst their number: 'witness to a suicide', that was his tag, his category, and somehow it reduced him to their level. Here were life's niggles and gripes, not real problems – the snagged nail syndrome, the minor tooth-ache disturbance, the sprained ankle effect. There was no drama or tragedy or big emotion about what happened here; instead there were misdemeanours, cautions, tick-ings-off, wrist-slappings, minor fines, licences endorsed, bans administered, debts verified, injunctions granted . . . It was all too tawdry.

Yet he still felt dry-mouthed and insecure when he took the stand and swore his oath and the coroner, a stout woman with a rigid ash-blonde perm, asked him to describe his discovery of Mr Dupree. He did so, recalling the day, the hour of the appointment.

'You had no inkling such a likelihood – Mr Dupree's suicide – was, ah . . . likely?'

'It was a completely routine meeting as far as I was concerned.'

'Could he have been suffering from depression?'

'I don't know. I suppose so. It had been a serious fire, his factory was completely ruined. Anyone would have been entitled to feel depressed in those circumstances.'

She consulted her notes. 'You are a loss adjuster, I see. In what way were you involved with the deceased?'

'Our job is to ascertain the validity of an insurance claim. We are employed by the insurance company – to see if it's fair.'

'And in this case it seemed fair.'

'As far as I know,' Lorimer said evasively. 'There were some figures that had to be confirmed – the exact value of an order from the USA. I know our investigation was effectively over.'

Rappaport took the stand after him and read off the relevant facts: Mr Dupree's age, the time of Lorimer's phone call, the time of death, the cause of death, the authenticity of the death certificate, the absence of indications of foul play. His voice was strong, his pleasure in his role evident, so evident he seemed constantly to be repressing a self-satisfied smile.

Through the window to his right Lorimer could see a square of blue sky being invaded by some serious-looking grey clouds . . . His mind wandered, as he realized for the first time in his adult life he was going to have to ask his bank manager for an overdraft – a bad sign that, an evil omen. Damn Hogg. He did not hear Rappaport come down from the stand and was only half aware of the conversation between the clerk and the coroner. But he could have sworn that when they called the next witness the clerk uttered a name very similar to 'Mrs Malinverno'. It just showed how she dominated his –

He looked around to see a thin, pale-faced woman

with a weak chin and sharp nose, wearing a black suit, step nervously into the room and fussily take her place – much smoothing of skirts, dusting and hitching of sleeves – across from the coroner. She had an amber brooch on her lapel which she kept touching as if it were a talisman of some kind. She pointedly avoided looking at him, Lorimer noticed, even her shoulders were canted around, suggesting that some physical effort was being employed to prevent her turning to face him. The family member, he supposed, looking over at Rappaport, who grinned, gave him an A-OK sign and mouthed 'well done'.

The coroner was speaking: 'Mrs Mary Vernon, you were the late Mr Dupree's sister?'

'That's correct.'

Hence the black, Lorimer thought. Dupree had been unmarried, Rappaport had told him, 'wedded to his work', as the expression went. Must be an awful shock, a suicide in the family, Lorimer thought sympathetically, so many questions unanswered.

'I had been abroad on a Mediterranean holiday,' Mrs Vernon, née Dupree, was saying, with a slight tremble in her voice. 'I had spoken to my brother on the phone twice in the week before he died.'

'How would you describe his mood?'

'Very worried and depressed, which is why I came straight from the airport to see him. He was very upset at the way the insurance company was behaving – the delays, the questions, the refusal to pay.'

'This company was Fortress Sure?'

'He kept talking about the loss adjuster they had sent round.'

'Mr Black?'

Finally her eyes moved to him. The inhumane coldness of her gaze flayed him. Jesus Christ, she thinks it was me who –

'It must have been,' she said. 'My brother, Osmond, never mentioned his name, he kept talking about the loss adjuster.'

'Mr Black said that the appointment with your brother was completely routine.'

'Why was my brother so upset, then? He dreaded the visit of the loss adjuster, dreaded it.' Her voice was rising. 'Even when I called the last time he kept saying, "The loss adjuster is coming, the loss adjuster's coming." ' She was pointing at him now. 'These people were tormenting and terrifying an emotionally disturbed elderly man whose whole life had been destroyed.' She rose to her feet. 'I believe that this man sitting here, Mr Lorimer Black, drove my brother to his death!'

At which point the clerk shouted, 'Order! Order!', the coroner started thumping her gavel on the desk and Mrs Vernon burst into tears. Lorimer was thinking: Hogg, what had Hogg done to terrorize Mr Dupree? Some people were never meant to cope with Hogg. He was too much, too powerfully malevolent, too strong a force, Hogg . . . Business was adjourned for ten minutes as Mrs Vernon was helped from the room, then the coroner duly returned a verdict of death by suicide.

'There you go,' Rappaport said, handing over the slip of paper upon which was written Mrs Vernon's address and telephone number. Lorimer felt he had to call or write to explain to clear his name, rid his reputation of this appalling slur or, even, better, arrange somehow for Hogg to tell her the truth, which would be far more effective.

Rappaport had advised against trying to make contact, but had been happy to procure the address.

'Clearly overcome with grief,' Rappaport analysed, confidently. 'They don't want to hear it, Mr Black. I wouldn't give it a thought. Happens all the time. Wild, wild accusations are made all the time. Totally out of order. Strangely attractive woman, though.' They were standing by the coffee machine in the lobby drinking the hot fluid it provided.

'No,' Rappaport went on, philosophically, 'they want to blame someone, you see, they need to, anyone – usually because of their own guilt, somewhere along the line, and usually it's us, the police, they go for with their wild accusations. Lucky for me you was in the frame.' He chuckled.

'Lucky for you?' Lorimer said bitterly. 'She practically accused me of murder.'

'Got to develop a thicker skin, Mr Black.'

'My professional reputation's at stake, if this gets out.'

'Ah, seeking the bubble reputation, Mr Black. Don't worry about it. Anyway, nice to see you again. Cheers.'

Rappaport sashayed off, body swaying like a gun-slinger, through the crowds of yobbos, petty criminals and pinched-faced litigants. Perhaps he isn't so dim after all, Lorimer thought, troubled, resenting Rappaport's cockiness, his breezy insouciance, and realizing that at this particular moment his hatred extended to every human being on the planet. But I'm an innocent man, he wanted to yell out to these furtive people, I'm not like you. Hogg has landed me in it again.

100. George Hogg's Philosophy of Insurance. *Hogg spoke frequently about this theory, it was close to his heart. 'To the*

Savage in the jungle,' he would say, 'to our Savage Precursors, all
life was a lottery. All his endeavours were hazardous in the extreme.
His life was literally one big continuous gamble. But times have
changed, civilization has arrived and society has developed, and as
society develops and civilization marches forward this element of
chance, of hazard, is steadily eliminated from the human condition.'
At this point he would pause, look around, and say, 'Anyone here
foolish enough to believe that? . . . No, my friends, life is not made
that way, life does not run smoothly along tracks that we have laid
down. We all know, deep in the secret places of our souls, that our
Savage Precursors had got it right. However much we seem to have
it under control, to have every eventuality covered, all risks taken
into account, life will come up with something that, as the good
book says, "disturbs all anticipations". And this is what we,
the loss adjusters, embody. This is our vocation, our métier, *our*
calling: we exist for one reason alone – to "disturb all antici-
pations".'

The Book of Transfiguration

Lorimer's mood was still dark and unsettled as he drove
to Chalk Farm and parked his car not far from Flavia's
house. He felt a profound need to see her again, even
clandestinely, the whole Dupree business reminding him
of that first day, that first magical, dream-like glimpse. It
was as if the sight of the flesh and blood Flavia would
confirm his sanity somehow, reassure him that all was not
skewed and awry in his increasingly demented existence.

He parked thirty yards down the street from her front
door and settled down, with thudding heart, to wait.
The street was avenued with lime trees and the ageing,
flaking, psoriasistic stucco houses on either side were built
on a grand scale, with large bow windows, porches and

balustraded flights of steps up from the street, but were now all sub-divided into bedsits, flats or maisonettes, judging from the crowded ladders of bell-pushes ranked beside the doors.

The clouds had obliterated the morning's fresh blue sky and now spots of rain began to tap against the windscreen as he hunched down in his seat, arms folded, and concentrated on feeling sorry for himself for a while. It was all getting out of hand: Torquil, the Rintoul attack, Hogg's suspicions and now this hellish accusation from Mrs Vernon. Even when the coroner had returned her verdict, Lorimer thought he could detect a look of unpleasant doubt in her eye . . . And Flavia, what was going on – meeting him, flirting, kissing him? But that kiss outside the restaurant was different, of a different order, suggesting profounder change.

He saw her, an hour and a half later, coming up the hill from the tube station, an umbrella up, wearing a chocolate-brown fun fur, a plastic shopping bag in one hand. He let her pass by the car before stepping out and calling her name.

'Flavia.'

She turned, surprised. 'Lorimer, what're you doing here?'

'Sorry, I just had to see you. I've had the most shocking –'

'You've got to go, you've got to go,' she said in a panicky voice, glancing over her shoulder at the house. 'He's in there.'

'Who?'

'Gilbert, of course. If he sees you he'll go berserk.'

'Why? He seemed fine in the café.'

Flavia stepped behind a lime tree so she couldn't be

seen from the windows of her house. She made an apologetic face.

'Because I told him something which, on sober reflection, I probably shouldn't have.'

'Like what?'

'That we were having an affair.'

'Jesus Christ.'

'He found your number, on the scrap of paper. Rang it and got your answering machine. He's a manically jealous sort of person.'

'Why did you tell him, then? For God's sake –'

'Because I wanted to hurt him. He was being vile, cruel, and I just sort of blurted it out.'

She paused, her face shadowed, as if she'd never considered the full consequences of her daring lie.

'I suppose it was a bit risky.' Then she smiled at him, radiantly. 'Do you suppose it's because I really do want to have an affair with you, Lorimer?'

He swallowed. He was breathing faster. He clenched and unclenched his fists – what did one say in response to that sort of remark?

'Flavia – I love you.' He did not know what made him utter the fateful words, make that timeless declaration – sheer fatigue, probably. The fact that he was getting soaked by the rain.

'No. No, you've got to go,' she said, her voice suddenly nervous, almost hostile. 'You'd better keep away from me.'

'Why did you kiss me?'

'I was drunk. It was the grappa.'

'That wasn't a drunken kiss.'

'Well, you'd better forget it, Lorimer Black. And you'd better stay away, I mean if Gilbert saw you –'

'Fuck Gilbert. It's you I'm thinking about.'

'Go away!' she hissed at him, and stepped out of the shelter of her tree and strode across the road to her house, not looking back.

Cursing, Lorimer clambered back into his car and drove away. Anger, frustration, lust, bitterness, helplessness jostled for preeminence in his mind until a newer, more sombre note overshadowed them all: what he was feeling was close to despair. Flavia Malinverno had come into his life and had transformed it – she could not be lost to him.

'Totally out of the question,' Hogg said, his voice reasonable, brooking no dissent. 'Who do you think I am? Your mother? Sort out your own problems, for God's sake.'

'She thinks I'm *you*. She thinks it was me who did the Dupree adjust. You just have to tell her I wasn't involved.'

'You can whistle for it, Lorimer. We never, we never go back after an adjust, never deal with the client again, you know that. It can jeopardize everything, ours is a very delicate business. Now, what's new with Gale-Harlequin?'

Lorimer blinked, shook his head, he was wordless.

'Spit it out, lad.'

'Some developments. I'll get back to you.'

He switched off the phone and accelerated away from the traffic lights at Fulham Broadway. There had to be some way of getting at Hogg, some way of making him go to Mrs Vernon and explain. But whatever that strategy might be it did not bear thinking of at the moment. His utter lack of any ideas brought the despair seeping back.

Slobodan was standing on the pavement outside the

office, smoking, enjoying a breath of fresh air, rocking to and fro on his heels, as Lorimer pulled up.

'You know, I could weep to see a car in that state. It'll be pure rust in a week. Look at that.'

True enough, rust flowers were beginning to bloom on the Toyota's broiled bodywork.

'Is Torquil back?'

'Yeah. Boy, is he putting in the hours. I reckon he'll pull in two and a half grand this week. He's in shock at all this dosh he's making. You see, the trouble with Torquil was that he never realized just how much money working-class people can earn. He thought we were all poor and miserable, scraping a living, looking for handouts.'

Lorimer thought that this was as profound a statement as Slobodan had ever uttered. He agreed and they went inside where they found Torquil in noisy debate with the other drivers, stretched out on the two sofas, mugs of tea and cigarettes on the go.

'If you do A3, M25 you're done for. Talking two and a half hours to Gatwick.'

'Trevor two-nine was forty minutes getting through Wandsworth High Street yesterday.'

'Murder.'

'Nightmare.'

'OK. What if you went Battersea, Southfields –' Torquil suggested.

'Trevor one-five can get you in the back of Gatwick from the Reigate end.'

'– No, listen, then New Malden, but miss out Chessington and cut down through –' Torquil looked round and saw Lorimer. 'Oh hi. Lobby told me you were dropping by. Shall we have a bite?'

Phil Beazley popped his head out of the control room and beckoned Lorimer over.

Beazley lowered his voice. 'We done it.'

'Done what?'

'Last night. Me and a couple of mates. Gave that motor a right dusting.'

Lorimer felt a tremor of alarm, of almost shock at what he had done. He had never before ordered violence done on anyone or anything and felt a corresponding loss of innocence. But Rintoul could have killed him, he should not forget that.

'Got a present for you,' Beazley said, reaching into a pocket and pressing something into Lorimer's hand. 'Little souvenir.'

Lorimer opened his hand to reveal a chrome three-pointed star set in a circle. The logo of the Mercedes-Benz company.

'I snapped it off the bonnet before we went to work with the sledgehammers and the rivet gun.'

Lorimer swallowed. 'Rintoul drives a BMW. I told you.'

'No. You said a Merc. Definite. I remember. Anyway we never saw no BMW.'

Lorimer nodded slowly, taking this in. 'Never mind, Phil. Good work. We'll say that takes care of the loan.'

'You're a gent, Milo. Lobby'll be pleased.'

'You all right?' Torquil asked as they walked along the road to the Filmer Café. 'You look a bit out of it. Knackered. Still not sleeping?'

'Sleep is the least of my problems,' he said.

The Filmer (Classic British Caffs no. 11) was busy and stiflingly warm, condensation beading and dripping from all its windows, steam and fumes coiling from shuddering pots and pans on the big cooker at the rear, a blurry fug of cigarette smoke adding to the generally cloudy smudged feel of the place. It was run by a couple from Gibraltar and the Union Jack was much in evidence. Union Jack bunting looped across the windows and draped the portrait of Winston Churchill on the rear wall, little Union Jacks fluttered amidst the condiments and sauce bottles in the centre of the tables, the staff sported shiny PVC Union Jack aprons. Torquil removed his jacket and slung it over the back of the chair. Lorimer saw he was wearing a sweater and corduroys, no tie, and he needed a shave. He ordered bacon, sausage, egg, beans and chips with sliced white bread on the side. Lorimer asked for a glass of milk – he seemed to have lost his appetite, these days.

'What do you make of this?' Lorimer asked, handing over an invitation which had arrived in the morning's mail.

'Lady Sherriffmuir.' Torquil read, '"At Home for Toby and Amabel"' . . . Are you sure this is meant for you?'

'It has my name on the top, Torquil.'

'I suppose mine'll have gone to bloody Binnie. Damn. Hell! Why's he asking you? Have you met him?'

'Just the once.'

'Must have made quite an impression. Very honoured.'

'I can't quite understand why, either.'

'He's got a lovely place in Kensington . . .' Torquil frowned as if the concept of 'home' troubled him. He pouted, then pursed his lips, poured some salt on the table top and dabbed at it with a forefinger.

'Anything on your mind?' Lorimer prompted.

Torquil licked his salted forefinger. 'I hope you don't

take this the wrong way, Lorimer, but I'm going to move in with Lobby.'

'Absolutely, fine with me. No problem. When?'

'It's easier for me working nights, you see. It's just more practical. I just don't want you to feel –'

'Excellent idea.'

'I mean if you want me to stay on, I wouldn't dream of moving. I would hate to –'

'No, makes much more sense.'

'Very good of you.' Torquil beamed, hugely relieved. 'Have you any idea how much money I'm going to make this week? I mean if I get a few more airport jobs and good night work I could be talking over two grand. Phil Beazley's going to get me some pills to keep me awake.'

He talked on in tones of astonishment about his good fortune, and how he owed it all to Lorimer. Binnie would get her money, he said, and taking account of running costs at this rate he could have, cash in hand, maybe a thousand pounds a week, easy.

'Apparently you pay hardly any tax,' he said. 'You declare about one-tenth of what you earn, and write off all your expenses – fuel, insurance – against it. And I've got no time to spend anything, anyway. Never been so flush. Never had so much folding money in my life.'

Lorimer thought Torquil and Slobodan would co-exist perfectly: they both smoked too much, drank to excess, they ate the same food, enjoyed the same middle-of-the-road rock music, shared the same defiantly sexist attitude to women, were not readers, indifferent to things cultural, were mildly racist, uninterested in current affairs and both unreflectingly voted Conservative. Apart from their accents, and the strata separating them socially, they could have been cut from the same cloth.

Torquil pushed away his empty plate, popped the folded square of bread that had polished it greaseless into his mouth, and reached for his cigarettes.

'You know,' he said, chewing ruminatively, 'if I mini-cabbed hard for six months I could take the rest of the year off. Never need to sell a line of insurance again.'

'Talking of which,' Lorimer said, 'can you cast your mind back to the Fedora Palace deal?'

Torquil winced. 'You see, the trouble was I never asked any advice. I'd just had a bit of a shameful bollocking from Simon about my attitude, not pulling my weight, lack of initiative and all that, so when what's-his-name – Gale – suddenly said he would pay that huge premium in the interests of speeding things up, I jumped at it.'

'You and Gale cooked it up between you.'

'I mentioned a figure and he mentioned a higher one. I mean, it's plain business sense, isn't it. You don't take less,' he frowned, 'do you? I mean it was a hotel, for God's sake. Bricks and mortar, state of the art. What could go wrong?'

'What was Gale's hurry?'

'I don't know. He just wanted it done quickly. Seemed reasonable to me. I thought I'd done everyone a favour and earned a nice sum of money for the Fort. Nobody said anything at the time, not a word of caution. Rubber-stamped all round.' He looked at his watch. 'I'm well out of that business, I tell you. I'd better go. Got a wait and return to Bexley this after.'

He had dreamt about tennis, his only sport, looking down at himself as he served, as if from a specially positioned video camera, watching the fluffy yellow ball fly up to meet him and then hearing – very clearly – the swish and bite of the racquet strings as they cut over the ball with brutal severity, sending it arcing away with its devilish spin, one of his rarely achieved unplayable second serves, not fast, but deep and with a bend on it like a banana, hitting the court surface (red clay) and kicking off at a different angle, and with somehow greater speed and height, as if some kind of booster spring mechanism had been released in the ball itself, importing that physics-defying extra few m.p.h. of velocity. His partner in this dream game had not been Alan, his usual opponent, but Shane Ashgable – whom he had not played before because Shane fancied himself as a tennis player. But Shane could not cope with these serves at all, as they came looping deceptively over the net at him, his timing and positioning hopelessly, laughably, wrong.

Lorimer rubbed his eyes and duly jotted the dream down in his diary. Was it lucid? Borderline – certainly his serves were surreally consistent and on target but he could not recall actually willing them to bend and kick like that. And it was not strictly true that tennis was his only sport, he liked athletics too – more precisely, he liked watching athletics on television. But he had been good at the javelin while at school, on distant sports days, hurling it further than stronger, beefier boys. Like a golf swing a javelin throw relied more on timing and positioning rather than brute strength. In the same way that diminutive golfers effortlessly drove the ball fifty yards further than burlier players so the javelin-thrower knew it was not about gritted teeth and testosterone. When the throw was correct you saw it in the way the spear behaved, almost vibrating with pleasure, as all the power in the arm and shoulders was transferred precisely – in a complex equation, a mysterious combination of torque, moment of release, angle of delivery – to two metres of sharpened aluminium pole soaring through the air.

The tennis dream, he knew, was always a harbinger of summer – still months away, he realized – but perhaps it was a good omen, now, a crack in the permafrost. For him the first tennis dream of winter was like the first swallow or first cuckoo, a sign that sap was somewhere rising. Perhaps it was because he had learned and played his best tennis in summer in Scotland when he had been at college. Here was the source of its seasonal associations: the mixed double tennis league matches played on long summer evenings against the local tennis clubs – Fochabers, Forres, Elgin and Rothes – against solicitors and their elegant, thin-wristed wives, young farmers and their strapping girlfriends. Ginger beer shandy on clubhouse verandahs as the Scottish dusk struggled feebly to establish itself against a northern sun unwilling to dip below the horizon. Patches of sweat on the embroidered bodices of dental nurses, the dark damp fringes of hotel receptionists, a bloom of clay dust on the shiny shaved calves of ruthless schoolgirl aces, the residue that washed off later in the shower tray like red gold, panned. Tennis was summer, civility, sweat and sex, and the memories of the occasional stroke perfectly executed – weight on the right leg, racquet prepared for an age, leaning into the backhand, head down, the stiff-armed follow-through, the wrong-footing, the gentle applause, the incredulous cries of 'Shot!' That was all you needed, really, those tennis court epiphanies were what you really sought . . .

He felt his bladder distended, switched on the light and unplugged himself, reaching for his dressing gown. On the way back from the dazzling lavatory he thought he made out someone sitting among the winking lights of the monitor banks.

'Hey, Alan,' he said, wandering over, pleased to see him. 'Up late.'

'Sometimes I pop in while you're all sleeping, just to check up on my guinea pigs. That was some dream you were having.' He pointed to the jagged line of a printout.

'I was playing tennis.'

'Against Miss Whatshername? Zuleika Dobson, isn't it? Coffee?'

'Flavia Malinverno. Most amusing. Yes please.'

Alan poured him a papercupful from a flask. He was wearing, Lorimer noticed, black leather trousers and a satiny Hawaiian shirt, gold chains glittered at his neck.

'Busy night?'

'Darling, I could have danced till dawn. That was a peach of a lucid dream last time.'

'Which did feature Miss Flavia Malinverno,' Lorimer said with some bitter longing. Then suddenly, for no particular reason, he told Alan about Flavia, the meetings, the kiss, the news about the 'affair', Gilbert's mad jealousy, Flavia's sudden reticence.

'Married women, Lorimer, you should know better.'

'She's not happy with him, I know. He's a fraud, completely vain, I could tell. There was something between us, something real, in spite of the duplicity. But she's denying it. Sorry, I'm boring you.'

Alan covered his yawn with four fingers. 'It is very early in the morning.'

Lorimer felt he might never sleep again.

'What do I do, Alan? You are my best friend. You're meant to solve these problems for me.'

Alan patted his knee. 'Well, they do tell me faint heart never won fair maid.'

212. The Television Set. *All that was in your head was the deafening noise of the television set and the constant bellowing, cheering, whistling and catcalling that accompanied it. The whole college seemed to have assembled in the common room to watch – what? A football match? Miss World? The Eurovision Song Contest? Formula 1? You could hear the slap of your bare feet on the lino as you drew near, could hear the noise levels increase and the rays of white light shining down from the fluorescent strips seemed to spear into your brain like elongated acupuncture needles. Joyce was terrified, crying; you were sick, sick with your rage and fury, and all you knew was that the noise of the television set had to stop. You halted at the door and your right hand reached out for the door knob. You saw your hand grip the doorknob, turn it and push the door open and suddenly you were walking into the common room, shouting for silence, striding into the centre of the crowded room, a hundred pairs of eyes turning towards you.*

The Book of Transfiguration

Chapter 15

'Hello? Milo? Milo? Hello, Milo?'

'Hello, Mum. I can hear you.' She had called him on the mobile, the only number of his that the family possessed. He felt as if the air were being slowly sucked out of his lungs – it had to be bad news. He was driving along the Embankment heading west, the river on his left, the morning blowy, grey and heavily overcast, if marginally milder.

'Everything OK, Mum?'

'Yes, everything's fine.'

'Good.'

'Did Lobby call you?'

'No.'

'Oh . . . Bit of sad news.'

Something to do with Slobodan, then, that was less worrying. 'What is it?'

'Your dad passed away last night.'

'Oh God. Jesus.' He began to brake.

'Yes. Very quiet, very peaceful. It's a blessing, Milo.'

'Yes, Mum. You all right?'

'Oh, I'm fine, me. Everyone's here. Well, the girls are.'

'Should . . . Ah, should I come round?'

'No point. He's not here any more. They took him.'

He felt his face tighten. 'I'll call later, Mum. I'm in traffic.'

'Sorry to bother you, darling. Bye.'

Lorimer slowed down and bumped up on to the pavement, switching on his hazard lights. He walked to the stone balustrade, leant upon it and looked down at the wide brown river. The tide was high but, aptly, on the turn, the water now flowing vigorously east, to the sea. He urged tears to come, but they would not. Well, he thought, that's it: Bogdan Blocj, RIP. He stared at the Thames and tried to think of something profound, some line of poetry, but all that came into his head were facts about Chelsea Embankment (built in 1871–4, cost a quarter of a million pounds, designed by someone called Bazalgette) that had lodged in his brain from some book he had read ages ago. Poor Dad, he thought, poor old fellow – it hadn't been any kind of life at all, he considered, the last decade. Maybe it was a blessing, a blessing to the five women who had looked after him all those years, feeding him, dressing him, cleaning him, moving him about the house like a potted plant. There was a little consolation, however, Lorimer thought, in the time they had spent together the other day, when he had held his father's hand, just the two of them alone, feeling his dry, clean hand in his and sensing the slight responsive squeeze. Some comfort in that.

A wooden box bumped up against one of the supports of Albert Bridge and then the current rushed it speedily downstream. Lorimer's eye seized hungrily on it and freighted it with sententious symbolism: that's us, he thought, flotsam and jetsam on the tide, hurried along to our ultimate destination, held up here, whooshed along there, stalled in an eddy for a while then flipped over a weir, unable to control our progress until we wind up in the calm estuary heading for the open sea, which is boundless and endless . . .

The wooden box banged against a pier and was caught and scraped along the wall beneath him. He read the letters branded on to the box's side, 'Château Cheval Blanc 1982'. Only in Chelsea, he thought; there was clearly flotsam and flotsam.

280. Lysergic acid diethylamide. *I once asked Alan if my light-sleeping problem, my REM sleep overload and imbalance, could be a sign of neurosis, of some deep, unacknowledged mental crisis, of impending mental breakdown, say.*

'Not in your case, I think,' Alan said, frowning hard. 'No, I think we have to look elsewhere. It is true that depressed people sleep less but then they experience little REM sleep – which is often taken as an indication that REM sleep is absolutely vital for our well-being in some mysterious way, as if we need to dream, in a fundamental physiological sense.' He paused. 'There's only one drug that's been discovered that seems to promote REM sleep and that's lysergic acid diethylamide, or LSD as it is more commonly known. Have you ever taken LSD?'

'Only once.'

'How was it?'

'It changed my life.'

The Book of Transfiguration

According to Flavia Malinverno the film she was working on – *Malign Fiesta* – was a 'very loose adaptation' of a novel by Percy Wyndham Lewis, a writer with whom Lorimer was not familiar. As he found a parking spot not far from the empty hospital in Chiswick where much of the shooting was taking place, and duly parked the rapidly rusting Toyota, Lorimer considered he might appropriate the title for his own autobiography, should he ever write one – it seemed to capture the spirit of recent weeks. He wandered towards the hospital past the straggling row of trucks, clapped-out buses, campervans and groups of people in anoraks and windcheaters chatting to each other and drinking from plastic cups – all the signs that announced that a motion picture was being filmed in your neighbourhood. Their lack of purpose, the lethargy, the air of resigned inertia reminded him of a disbanded circus awaiting news of its next destination, or a column of reasonably well-to-do refugees halted at a roadblock for days as officials and militia haggled over whether the motley crew should be allowed across the frontier.

A shivering young guy, ill-dressed against the weather, in just a sweater and a baseball cap, with dripping nose and walkie-talkie, asked if he could help Lorimer in any way. Lorimer had once done an adjust on a film company and had mooched around several film sets in the course of it and so knew what the magic password was, the one that opened every door.

'Equity,' he said.

'The actors are in the main building,' said the young guy, sniffing robustly and swallowing. 'You'll see the signs.'

He followed meandering black cables as thick as his arm into the semi-circular drive, under the grandly columned entrance and in through the main doors. The hall was brilliant with huge arc lights all pointing at an impressive central staircase that swept up and divided against the rear wall, decked with flowers as if for a ball or wedding. Many dozens of people stood around looking at a woman who was fiddling with the flowers and a man with a hand-held vacuum cleaner who was hoovering up every trace of dust and lint from the carpet. From somewhere came a busy sound of energetic hammering. He was the only person in a suit and stood out markedly amongst so much leather and suede, foul-weather gear and leisure wear.

A brisk young woman wearing a headset and carrying a styrofoam cup approached.

'Can I help?'

'Equity,' he said.

'Actors that way,' she said, pointing through an ornate doorway.

Lorimer obediently headed off, passing thirty feet of trestle table with many urns and plates, trays and baskets of high-calorie food. People stood in front of it, sampling, munching, sipping, slurping, waiting. He heard a man shout, 'Kill that blonde, Jim!' but no one paid any attention.

Flavia had told him that the film was a romantic comedy and the next room, he guessed, contained the set that would concern her and where she would utter her immortal line about Tyimotheh's subterfuge. There was a glossy dining table with sixteen chairs and laid for a substantial meal, if the ranked silverware was anything to go by. More people were polishing crystal glasses and touching up and adjusting the floral table centres. Beyond this set was a long, high-ceilinged room that must have been an old hospital ward, divided down the middle by a row of bulb-ringed dressing tables and racks of clothes. Here he encountered his first actors – men and women in evening clothes of the 1920s, having their hair combed, lipstick retouched, jewellery fastened and checked against the evidence contained in many polaroid photographs.

A woman with wild, backcombed blue-black hair and

holding a small sponge asked if she could help. Now that he was amongst actors he fell back on the truth. 'I'm with the insurance company,' he said.

'Oh. You'll want, um, Fred Gladden. If you don't mind waiting I'll get someone to find him for you.'

'Thanks.' Lorimer knew from experience that this could take a minute, an hour or might never actually come about, so he moved away and leant against a wall, safe for a while. The minute came and went as he stood there discreetly, arms folded, watching the comings and goings, as meaningful to him as the busy scurryings of an ant colony. Then he suddenly remembered, unprompted, that his father had died a few hours previously and realized that already time had passed when he had not been thinking about him, indeed had completely forgotten about him and his death and this made him unbearably sad. Sad to think how easy it was not to think about Bogdan Blocj, how easy it was to find yourself in a state where you were not regretting that you would never hold his hand again.

His vision shimmered and all the bright lights acquired blurry coronas. He exhaled and inhaled, filling his lungs with air and asked himself what he was doing here, standing around on this film set under false pretences, engaged on this foolish forlorn quest. His father had been dead for a matter of hours, shouldn't he be doing something respectful, sober, suitably mournful? Such as what? His father wouldn't care, in fact the old Bogdan Blocj might have approved of something so sexily inopportune, trying to win back his girl . . . He made another dutiful filial effort, trying to conjure up some idea of the man beyond the idea of 'Dad', a man he remembered most readily standing in his brown overall, clipboard in hand, spectacles on the end of his nose, amongst his shelves of well-wrapped cardboard boxes . . . But nothing else came. The man he knew best had been the smiling, mute invalid, a dapper, silent figure in his blazer and flannels and neat white beard whose twinkling eyes seemed to see everything and nothing at all . . . Jesus Christ, he roused himself, get a grip: he had his own life to live and it was a life that was going downhill fast. Some sort of brakes had to be applied before the whole thing came apart –

Flavia Malinverno entered the room at the far end, carrying a book, and sat down on a wooden form.

He edged closer, circling round and approaching from the side, unchallenged and unquestioned, realizing that in his classically cut suit people might take him for an extra. Flavia was wearing a black wig, bobbed, with a low fringe that seemed to be resting on her improbably long, false eyelashes. She was reading *Malign Fiesta* by Wyndham Lewis – good for you, girl, he thought, professional, diligent actor – and his heart bulged and sagged with pathetic, humiliating longing for her. But what has anyone in the history of humankind ever been able to do about that sort of thing, he thought as he slid on to the bench beside her – without her looking up – and inched along stealthily, who has ever been able to control that category of pure feeling?

'Any good?'

'Well, it's got bugger all to do with this film, I can tell –'

She looked up at this point and saw him, her mouth tightening at once, her jaw set. Her face was opaque with white panstick make-up, her lipstick was the cherriest of reds and she had a beauty spot in the middle of her left cheek. She wore a dress of taupe *crêpe de chine* and great loops of pearls dangled to her lap.

'Flavia –'

'Lorimer, I told you to stay away from me.'

'No. You have to hear me out.'

'Look, I'm going to call security, I mean it –'

'My father died this morning.'

She sat down slowly. The mention of his father's death had made tears fill his eyes and he could see that for once, perhaps for the first time ever, she believed him.

'Look, I'm sorry . . . But that has nothing to do –'

'You're the one responsible. If you hadn't told Gilbert nothing would have advanced this far, this fast. You provoked everything.'

She reached into a beaded bag and brought out her cigarettes, lit one and blew a jet of smoke straight out in front of her.

'OK, I shouldn't have, and I regret it, and I'm sorry if it seemed I was using you. Now you must go away.'

'No. I want to see you again.'

Her jaw dropped in a mock gasp of incredulity. She shook her head as if to dispel a buzzing fly.

'For Christ's sake, I'm a married woman.'

'But you're not happy, I know you're not.'

'Don't you lecture me on the state of my marriage, chum.'

'Hi. Are you with the Bond Company?' Lorimer looked up to see a young man with thinning blond hair in a leather jacket and jeans standing there with his hand extended. 'I'm Fred Gladden,' he said, 'Co-producer.'

'I think he went that way,' Lorimer said, pointing. 'I'm with Equity.' He indicated Flavia. 'Some mix-up with her union dues.'

'Oh, right, sorry,' Fred Gladden apologized, needlessly. 'They just told me a man in a suit. That way?'

'Yes,' Lorimer said. 'He's carrying a briefcase.'

Fred Gladden strolled off to look for a suited man with a briefcase.

'Look at you,' Flavia said, trying not to smile. 'Look how you lie. It's unbelievable, like a reflex, so fluent.'

'I'm a desperate man,' Lorimer said. 'And I think when it comes to duplicity you could teach me a few lessons.'

The brisk young woman in the head set shouted, 'Scene 44. Dinner party. Rehearsal.'

Flavia rose to her feet and said. 'That's me. Look, I can't see you any more, it's too difficult. There are things I haven't told . . . Goodbye.'

'What things you haven't told?'

Lorimer followed her through to the set. Her dress had a low waist which was fringed and the fringe swayed to and fro with the swing of her hips. He felt a surge of desire for her so palpable that saliva squirted into his mouth.

'Flavia, we must —'

'Go away, Lorimer.'

'I'll call you.'

'No. It's finished. It's too difficult, too dangerous.'

They had reached the set where an elderly, red-faced man was simultaneously talking into a mobile phone and pointing the actors to their allotted seats around the dining table.

'Flavia Malinverno,' he said, 'you're over there, darling. Just tell the lazy bastard to get his arse down here, he's got a film to direct.'

Flavia glanced round at Lorimer, still behind her.

'Charlie,' she said to the red-faced man, 'I think this bloke's stalking me.'

Red-faced Charlie stepped in front of Lorimer and clicked his phone shut. Lorimer's eyes followed Flavia, watching her take her place at the dinner party.

'What's going on, pal?' The suspicion in Charlie's voice was menacing, clearly a man used to having his orders obeyed.

'What? I'm with the Bond Company, looking for Fred Gladden.'

Lorimer was duly told where he might find Fred Gladden and was obliged to move away. He glanced back only to see Flavia in laughing conversation with the actor sitting beside her and felt a satisfying pang of jealousy. He had achieved a little but it was not enough, a paltry thing, compared with what he dreamed of.

He stepped out of the electric warmth and unreal luminescence of the hospital into the dull and pearly gloom of a Chiswick morning, the low-packed clouds filtering the light shadow-free and he sensed his depression settle weightily on him again as if his pockets were filled with stones. He felt an unreasoning anger build in him against Hogg, realizing, with some degree of shock, that in the end it was only the news of his father's death that had made Flavia talk to him at all. A final service rendered his son by Bogdan Blocj, from beyond the grave too. It was both sobering and shaming: he had blurted out the news unthinkingly, but it was something that should have been stated to the woman he loved, surely? He felt confident that the shade of Bogdan Blocj, wherever it might lurk, would not condemn him.

'Thanks, Dad,' he said, looking up, out loud, attracting a few curious glances, 'I owe you one.' And he wandered back to his chargrilled Toyota with something of a spring in his step, thinking, wondering what she meant by 'too difficult, too dangerous'. Difficulties could be overcome and, as for danger, why, danger was a constant in his life.

132. Brown Shoes. *I remember the day I thought I had caught Ivan out. He was wearing a hairy, snot-green tweed suit with black brogues. I pointed at them and said, 'Ivan, the ultimate sin – black shoes with tweed.'*

'Oh, you're completely wrong, Lorimer, this is very acceptable. I'm glad you noticed it, however. It's a sign of a deeper malaise, something that's been worrying me for years.'

'What's that.'

'It's been difficult, but I've decided that the brown shoe must be condemned. Suede yes, a brown boot – just. But I think the brown shoe is fundamentally below the salt. Something irretrievably petit bourgeois about a brown shoe, quintessentially suburban and infradig. I threw all mine out last week, fourteen pairs, some I've had for decades. Threw them in the dustbin. I can't tell you how relieved I am, the weight off my mind.'

'All brown shoes?'

'Yes. No gentleman should wear a brown shoe, ever. The brown shoe is finished. The brown shoe, Lorimer, has got to go.'

The Book of Transfiguration

Lorimer wrote out a cheque for £3,000 and handed it apologetically to Ivan Algomir.

'Charge me interest on the balance, Ivan, please. I'll pay you the rest as soon as I can – some sort of administrative snarl-up in the office.'

Ivan folded the cheque and put it in his pocket, ruefully. 'I'd appreciate it, old chap. This will help, though.

They're like starving wolves following a stagecoach, the Revenue, if you throw them a scrap from time to time you might just escape.'

Another ghastly embarrassment down to Hogg, Lorimer thought. First he destroys my love life, now he's jeopardizing my friendships.

'I feel terrible about this, Ivan. What if I returned the helmet?'

'Good God, it's only money, Lorimer. I'll elude them. I must say you look smart.'

Lorimer told him where he was going: Lady Sher-riffmuir's 'At Home'.

'In Kensington,' he said. 'Look, I've had the cuffs altered.'

Lorimer held up the sleeves of his suit coat to show single-button cuffs that actually unbuttoned. Ivan had told him how he abominated the two-, three- or four-button cuff as pretentious and *arriviste*. A cuff was a cuff: it was there to allow you to fold up your sleeve, not as decoration.

'The shirt is first rate,' Ivan said. Lorimer had had them made to Ivan's design also, the collar deliberately miscut so that the point on one side rode over the revere a little awkwardly and untidily but, as Ivan pointed out, it was a defect that only arose with hand-made shirts, and what was the purpose of having hand-made shirts if they could not be recognized as such. 'Only people who have hand-made shirts themselves will recognize the problem,' Ivan assured him, 'but they're the only people you want to notice.'

Lorimer lifted his trouser leg to show off his midnight blue socks.

'Shoes are only just passable,' Ivan said. 'Thank God

you've got no tassles but I don't know if I like these American loafers. Very *nouveau*. Still.'

'I think they're right for this City crowd.'

'Just. Good God, what's that tie?'

'My school. Balcairn.' Actually it was a tie he had had his tailor make up for him. Navy blue with thin bands of mauve and an unidentifiable crest.

'Take it off at once. I'll lend you another. School ties are for schoolboys and schoolmasters. No grown man should be seen dead in a school tie. Same goes for regimental and club ties. Appalling bad taste.'

Ivan came back with a tie in lime green silk covered in a motif of tiny blue spiders. 'Bit of fun. It is an "At Home", after all.' Ivan looked him up and down in a kindly, almost proprietorial way, the old knight sending out his squire to joust in the lists of High Society.

'Very good, Lorimer. Even I can't find much fault.'

Chapter 16

For Lorimer, the notion of an 'At Home' summoned up images of half a dozen bottles of Chardonnay chilling in the fridge, perhaps a bowl of punch, peanuts and crisps, a few olives, a couple of baguettes sliced into roundels and a demilune of brie. The moment the bearskinned guardsman pushed open the door to the front courtyard of the Sherriffmuir mansion Lorimer knew that he and Lady Fiona might as well be talking a different language. On either side of the flagged path to the columned entry porch were, immediately to his left, a fakir on a bed of nails, opposite him a troupe of dusky tumblers leaping off shoulders or hurling each other into triple somersaults. Beyond them was a fire-eater blasting his gasoline breath into the night sky, a snake charmer tootling his flute at a swaying cobra and a Cossack with a small bear on the end of a chain tottering around on its hind legs as a fellow Cossack played a squeezebox accordion.

In the hall a team of girls in dominoes and black cat suits relieved guests of their coats and handed out numbered tokens, before inviting them to stroll a gauntlet of tuxedoed, smiling waiters holding out trays of champagne, bellinis, bucks fizz, mineral water or fuming pewter mugs of mulled wine.

Lady Fiona Sherriffmuir, her son Toby and her daughter Amabel waited beyond the libation-bearers

288

in front of a set of mahogany double doors. Lorimer advanced towards them across the shiny checkerboard marble, champagne in hand, his steps ringing out, worrying that the steels in his shoes might be carving out fine chips from the polished, gleaming squares.

'I'm Lorimer Black,' he managed to say to Lady Fiona, a bosomy, statuesque woman in a sheath of petrol-blue shot-silk. She had a tiny, perfect nose with highly flared nostrils and one of the best sets of teeth Lorimer had seen outside a Hollywood movie. Her grey-blonde hair was swept back from her high, smooth brow and two waves curled behind her ears, the better to set off the starbursts of emerald clipped to her lobes.

'How is Angus, the old rascal?' she asked, leaning forward to kiss Lorimer lightly on both cheeks. 'So sorry he hasn't come. Goodness I haven't seen you since Mustique, you must have been thirteen or fourteen.'

'Oh, Mustique,' Lorimer said. 'Great.'

'You probably won't remember Toby or Amabel, they were just babies.'

'Just babies, probably,' Lorimer muttered.

Toby was a gangly, loose-lipped eighteen-year-old with baddish acne. Amabel was a haunted-looking, hard-faced drug addict in a white trouser suit, chewing her lip and fiddling with the bracelets on her wrists. She could have been a decade older than her brother, as far as Lorimer could judge, her young face full of bitter worldliness.

'Hi,' Toby said. 'Good to see you again.'

'Yeah, hi,' Amabel said and, like her mother, kissed him on both cheeks. 'How's Lulu? Is she coming?'

'Lulu? Great,' Lorimer said, thankfully hearing others on his heels, Lady Fiona crying behind him, 'Giovanni! Silvana!'

'Tell Lulu to call me,' Amabel said, lowering her voice. 'I've got something for her.'

'Super,' Lorimer said, nodded vigorously and then moved through into the first of a series of reception rooms – a drawing room, a library and a ballroom – which in turn gave on to a tented marquee pitched over the lawn of the rear garden, where food of all types could be obtained and there were fifty or so round tables with gold chairs for those who wanted to sit and eat. Not to say that food was unavailable in every other room, patrolled as they were by more waiters with trays of miniature crab cakes, miniature cheese burgers, miniature pizzas. There were also quails' eggs, plovers' eggs and gulls' eggs, cocktail sausages, vegetarian cocktail sausages, goujons of sole, haddock and monkfish with assorted dips, chicken satay and doubtless many other nibbles that Lorimer did not spot and either sample or hungrily note.

The rooms were already comfortably full; Lorimer calculating quickly as he passed through them that at least three hundred people must have been in the house, not counting staff. In the drawing room some red-sashed Aztecs strummed guitars and snorted into nose flutes. In the library there was non-stop cabaret, currently a magician performing tricks with a length of washing line and scissors, and in the ballroom a jazz pianist picked out easy-listening standards on a grand piano in the middle of the sprung floor.

Lorimer wandered curiously amongst the throng – men in dark suits, women in elaborate finery – unnoticed, unrecognized and unspoken-to. By the time he reached the marquee – where half a dozen chefs stood behind hot plates serving everything from *penne arrabiata* to Lancashire hotpot – he had drunk three glasses of champagne and was wondering if he could decently leave. He retraced his steps – in the library there was another man doing astonishing balloon sculptures, squeakily producing a giraffe, an Eiffel Tower and an octopus in about ten seconds – but he saw that the Sherriffmuirs were still at their station and guests were still arriving. So he drank another glass of champagne and ate some mini-hamburgers to neutralize the alcohol.

He was staring at a picture, trying to decide if it was a Canaletto or a Guardi, when he felt a hand squeeze his left buttock and turned round to find Potts standing there with a look of *faux* innocence on her face and a cigarette in her hand.

'I thought I recognized that bum,' she said. 'What a treat.'

'Hello – or rather, congratulations. Is Oliver here?'

'God, wash your mouth out. I couldn't go through with the wedding. I sort of freaked out at the last minute and Mummy was furious but I couldn't imagine wedded bliss as Mrs Oliver Rollo. Sorry, not for the Potts.'

'What drama.'

'It was. And it means I'm footloose and fancy free, Mr Black.'

Sir Simon Sherriffmuir appeared from nowhere and put his arms around Potts, hugging her fiercely.

'How's my favourite wicked lady?' Sir Simon said. 'That dress is a little dowdy, isn't it?'

Potts's dress, as well as being very short, had a transparent bodice that allowed everyone to see the semi-transparent, embroidered brassière beneath.

'Dirty old man,' Potts said. 'Do you know Lorimer Black?'

'Indeed I do. One of my superstars.' Sir Simon briefly

rested his hand, pontiff-like, on Lorimer's shoulder, squeezed and said with apparent sincerity, 'So glad you could come, Lorimer. Where's that idle old father of yours?'

Sir Simon was wearing a silk suit that managed to appear both light and dark grey simultaneously, a cream silk shirt and a maroon, flecked tie. Lorimer made a mental note to check with Ivan about silk suits.

'Very happy to be –'

'Plenty to drink, you two lovebirds?' Sir Simon carried on, heedless. 'Don't miss the cabaret, some amusing stuff going on.' He blew a kiss at Potts and seemed to lean away, rather than walk, saying to Lorimer as he left. 'We must have our little chat, later.'

What little chat? Lorimer asked himself. Was this the reason for the invitation?

'I'm just going to powder my nose,' Potts said, slyly. 'Coming?'

'Not for me, thanks,' Lorimer said.

'Don't go away, then,' she said. 'I'll be right back.'

She sidled off and Lorimer headed for the marquee at once. Progress was tricky now, the crowd seemed to have doubled. What did Sir Simon mean by 'lovebirds'? Perhaps he'd seen Potts grab his ass. He decided that if he hid in the marquee for half an hour he should be able to make his escape unnoticed.

The noise level was reaching 'uncomfortable', with people beginning to shout at each other, and in the library a semi-circle of about sixty onlookers had formed around a man who was balancing four plates on their edges, one on top of the other, and about to add a fifth.

In the marquee he found a table behind a rose-entwined pillar and ate some cold salmon and new potatoes. He was alone for ten minutes, during which time he spotted three cabinet ministers, a news anchorwoman, a knighted actor, an ageing rock singer and a couple of flamboyant billionaire entrepreneurs, until he was joined by a middle-aged Brazilian couple, who formally introduced themselves and asked if they could share his table. The names of their host and hostess seemed to mean nothing to them, so Lorimer told them a little about Sir Simon and Fortress Sure just to be sociable and then excused himself, saying he was going for seconds. As he stood up they began signalling energetically to someone beyond and Lorimer turned to see a face he recognized approaching their table. Francis Home was wearing a white dinner jacket, a red stock and billowy black trousers.

'Mister Black,' he said. 'Francisco Homé.'

They shook hands and cogs began to turn in Lorimer's brain, but to little effect. Home said a few words in Portuguese to the couple and then said confidentially to Lorimer, 'By the way, I am no longer with Gale-Harlequin.'

'I know,' Lorimer lied, and then tried an inspired guess. 'I hear you're with Dirk van Meer.'

Home shrugged. 'On a consultation basis. Do you know Dirk?'

'His son, Marius.'

Home looked around. 'Is Dirk here yet? Simon told me he was coming.'

'I haven't seen him.' Lorimer indicated his empty plate. 'I'm starving, can't think why. See you later.'

'I'll tell Dirk we met.'

Christ almighty, Lorimer thought, dumping his plate, what is going on here? Sir Simon Sherriffmuir, Francis Home and now Dirk van Meer . . . He pushed his way through to the ballroom and headed for the front door. Surely he could leave safely now?

Gilbert 'Noon' Malinverno was juggling in the library. More precisely, he was sitting pedalling his unicycle in a wobbling to-and-fro motion while juggling with five yellow Indian clubs. Against his better nature, Lorimer had to admit this was impressive stuff, an opinion shared by the large crowd which had gathered, yelping and applauding as the clubs went higher and faster. Lorimer discovered he was standing beside the plate-balancer and the magician.

'Five clubs in a cascade pattern,' the plate-balancer said to the magician, 'never seen anyone do it before, outside Russia.'

'And on a unicycle,' the magician said bitterly. 'Flash bastard.'

Lorimer began to edge towards the drawing room. Glancing at Malinverno as he did so, he saw that there seemed to be something wrong with his face. He had sticking plaster on his ear, a black eye and he noticed that when Malinverno grimaced upwards, calculating the tumbling arcs of his spinning yellow clubs, a wide black gap was revealed in his upper row of teeth, as if two were missing. To Lorimer it looked very much as if Malinverno had been struck across the side of his face with some force, with a hard, long and unyielding object – say the edge of a briefcase swung round in self-defence.

'Bloody hell,' Lorimer said out loud.

'Pretty amazing, isn't it?' the person next to him agreed.

So it was Malinverno, Lorimer was thinking, incredulously, not Rintoul. It had been Malinverno who had jumped him – genuinely insane with jealousy. But to go that far – what had she told him about their 'affair'? It must have been steamy triple-X stuff to arouse Gilbert's passions so, to make him storm down to Lupus Crescent at dead of night with a juggling club in his hand and vengeance in his heart? . . . Jesus, Lorimer thought, with some excitement, this woman is dangerous.

Malinverno caught all his clubs and leapt off his unicycle and acknowledged the roaring crowd with a stiff, lopsided smile, from which Lorimer derived some satisfaction. Still hurting – good. He realized he owed Rintoul an apology.

A powerful grip fastened itself above his left elbow and he was drawn backward from the fringe of the crowd with some urgency.

'What in the name of fuck are you doing here?' Hogg's harsh voice enveloped him, hot in his ear, edged with a whiff of cinnamon and spices. Mulled wine. He turned: Hogg was red-faced, from the warm wine, Lorimer hoped, though he did look angry.

'Mr Hogg, nice to –'

'You heard me, boy.'

'I was invited.'

'Bullshite.'

'I think Sir Simon thinks I'm the son of an old friend of his.'

'Stinking bollocks. What kind of cretin do you take me for, Lorimer?'

'It's true. He thinks I'm the youngest son of someone called Angus Black.'

For a moment he thought Hogg might actually strike him. His eyes bulged and Lorimer realized that the man was sweating horribly, a dark, damp rim where his collar bit into his thick neck.

'I'll see you in my office, Monday morning, 9 a.m.,' Hogg said. 'And I want the truth, you bastard.'

He glared at him again and then left, his wide shoulders bumping people out of the way as he strode out of the room. Lorimer felt weak, suddenly exhausted and strangely frightened as if he had woken up in a circle of hell and realized only deeper and more sinister ones awaited him.

His eyes met Gilbert Malinverno's.

'Hoi! You, Black! Wait!'

Lorimer was off at once, though he would actually have welcomed a punch-up with Malinverno, knock a few more teeth out of that proud jaw, blacken the other eye, but he knew that Lady Sherriffmuir's 'At Home' was not the venue for that particular showdown. He scampered out of the ballroom and down the stairs to the marquee, following a waiter into the screened service area behind the buffet. He picked up a case of empty wine bottles.

'Get rid of these for you,' he said to no one in particular and lugged them through a flap in the tent outside.

He dumped them beside some canisters of Calor gas and, glancing back over his shoulder, crept down terraced gravel paths with dark, shrubby borders on either side towards the rear wall which, as he knew it would, contained a firmly locked and bolted door. Along the top of the wall was some sort of vicious revolving spike device designed to repel intruders and on an iron post a swivelling camera.

He felt like a POW who'd just tunnelled out of his Stalag to find himself still short of the perimeter fence. He looked back at the blazing rear windows of the enormous house. He couldn't go back in there – too many people looking for him: Potts, Sir Simon, Home, Hogg and Malinverno in ascending degrees of threat and malignancy. 'Malign Fiesta' wasn't in it, he thought, and a bowel-loosening, unmanning image of Flavia came suddenly into his head, unbidden. That girl ... What was she doing to his life?

He heard footsteps coming down the gravel path towards him, a light tread, not Malinverno, he deduced. Perhaps a waiter sent to investigate the theft of empty wine bottles? Lorimer put his hands in his pockets and whistled tunelessly, kicking at pebbles as if it were the most normal thing in the world to leave a glamorous party and seek some quality time by the rear gate and the dustbins.

'Hi,' Lorimer said, breezily. 'Getting a breath of –'

'Do you want to get out?' Amabel Sherriffmuir asked him. 'I brought a key.'

'Yes please,' Lorimer said. 'There's someone I'm trying to avoid in there.'

'Same here,' she said. 'My mother.'

'Right.'

'That's why I was sitting in the security room watching the televisions. I saw you.'

She unlocked the door.

'It fucking makes you want to puke, doesn't it,' she said with feeling, gesturing back at the glowing lit mansion, her home. 'All this crap.'

'I'm very grateful to you,' Lorimer said.

She handed him a small cardboard tube – a 'Smarties' tube, Lorimer saw – it felt heavy and rattled, as if full of shot or seed.

'Could you give that to Lulu?' she said. 'It's a present. And tell her to call me.'

She kissed him on each cheek once again, Lorimer thinking that perhaps it did not seem the moment to disabuse her of the fact that he was neither the son of Angus Black nor, he assumed, the brother of Lulu.

'Of course,' he said. 'Thanks again.' He slipped out into the mews. Some rain had fallen and had made the cobbles shine. He was not the son of Angus Black but he was the son of the recently deceased Bogdan Blocj and so, as he walked briskly out of the mews and on up to Kensington High Street, he discreetly sprinkled the contents of the tube of Smarties behind him as he went, hearing the tick and rattle of the ecstacy or the crack rocks or the LSD tablets bounce off the pavement like small hail in his wake. Bogdan Blocj would have approved, he thought. He found a cab at a rank and was home before midnight.

Lady Haigh peered through the gap in her door as he crossed the hall. He could see she was wearing a hairy old dressing gown and a kind of night cap.

'Evening, Lady Haigh,' he said. 'Cold night out.'

She opened the door a further inch or two.

'Lorimer, I've been worrying about dog food. I give Jupiter the very best and he's become accustomed to it. It seems most unfair to you.'

'I don't understand –'

'To ask you to bear this extra expense, just because I've been spoiling him.'

'Oh, don't give it a thought.'

'I tried him on a cheaper tin the other day and he didn't even sniff at it.'

'I'm sure it won't be a problem.'

'I'm so glad your friend has gone. I thought he was most uncivil.'

'More of a colleague than a friend. He's been having a difficult time. He lost his job and his wife threw him out.'

'Sensible woman. He did seem to like rabbit, I remember.'

'Torquil?'

'Jupiter. I cooked him a rabbit once and he ate it. That can't be very expensive, can it? Rabbit.'

'I shouldn't think so.'

She smiled at him, a wide smile of relief. 'That's put my mind at some ease. Good night, Lorimer.'

'Good night, Lady Haigh.'

Upstairs Lorimer made himself a cup of milky coffee and fortified it with a splash of brandy. He had two messages on his answer machine. One from Dymphna giving him the name and telephone number of a financial journalist who would be happy to assist him, the other was from Stella. 'Hello, stranger,' the message said. 'Hope everything's hunky-dory, dory-hunky. Don't forget Sunday. See you about twelve. Big kiss.'

He had forgotten: a long-mooted Sunday lunch and he had a horrible feeling it coincided with Barbuda's half-term or similar exeat. He had noticed a distinct increase of the Barbuda element in his dates with Stella and suspected she was trying to improve lover–daughter relationships. The lowering of spirit he experienced on hearing her voice told him something else too: it was time to bring the affair with Stella Bull to a decent and humane end.

Chapter 17

Dymphna's journalist friend was called Bram Wiles and he had said he was more than happy to have his brains picked. Consequently, Lorimer had arranged to meet him in the Matisse at midday, where and when Lorimer was duly present, his habitual fifteen minutes early, in a booth at the rear reading the *Guardian*, when he felt the shudder of someone sitting down on the bench opposite.

'Shite of a day,' Marlobe said, filling his pipe with a blunt finger. 'Your motor looks desperate.' Lorimer agreed: there had been a thick frost and the harsh wind had risen again. Moreover, the previous night's combination of rain and freeze seemed to have encouraged the rust to spread on his Toyota, exponentially, like bacteria multiplying in a petri dish, and it was now almost completely orange.

Marlobe lit his pipe with great spittley suckings and blowings, turning the immediate area a blurry bluey grey. He inhaled his pungent pipe smoke deep into his lungs, Lorimer noticed, as if he were smoking a cigarette.

'Your Kentish daffodil grower doesn't stand a monkey's in this weather.'

'I'm afraid I'm expecting someone,' Lorimer said.

'What's that got to do with me?'

'I'm having a sort of meeting. He'll need to sit where you are.'

The sullen Romanian waitress slid his cappuccino across the table at him, making sure some of the foam lapped over the side and pooled in the saucer.

'What you want?' she asked Marlobe.

'Sorry, darling.' Marlobe bared his teeth at her. 'I'm not stopping long.' He turned back to Lorimer. 'Whereas . . . Whereas your Dutchman is sitting pretty.'

'Really?'

'State subsidies. Three guilder per bloom. Your Kent-man and your Dutchman are not on a level playing field in the world of daffs.'

This was clearly nonsense but Lorimer did not feel like arguing with Marlobe so he said, vaguely, 'The weather's bound to improve.'

Marlobe gave a high screeching laugh at this and banged the tabletop fiercely with his palm.

'That's what they said at Dunkirk in 1940. And where did it get them? Tell me this, do you think von Rundstedt stood in the turret of his *Panzerkampfwagen* and wondered if perhaps it would be a bit milder tomorrow? Eh? Eh?'

'I don't understand what you're talking about.'

'That's the problem with this country. Looking on the bright side. Always looking on the stinking bright side. It's an illness, a sickness. That's why this nation is on its knees. On its knees in the gutter looking for scraps.'

A boyish-looking young man approached their booth and said to Marlobe, 'Are you Lorimer Black? I'm Bram Wiles.'

'No, I'm Lorimer Black,' Lorimer said quickly. He had asked the Spanish duenna waitress to direct anyone asking for him to the booth.

Marlobe stood up slowly and glared at Bram Wiles with overt hostility.

'All fucking right, mate. No hurry. We got all fucking day.'

Wiles visibly flinched and backed off. He had a long blond fringe brushed straight down over his forehead to meet the rims of his round black spectacles. He looked about fourteen.

Marlobe, with even more deliberate, challenging slowness, edged out of the booth and then stood blocking entry for a while as he relit his pipe, matchbox clamped over the bowl, huffing and puffing, and then moved off in a vortexing whirl of smoke, like some warlock in a movie, giving Lorimer the thumbs-up sign.

'Nice talking to you. Cheers, pal.'

Wiles sat down, coughing, and flapped his hands.

'Local character,' Lorimer explained, managing to attract the attention of the sullen Romanian and order another coffee. Bram Wiles had a small goatee but his facial hair was so fine and white-blond that it was only visible at a range of two to three feet. Lorimer often wondered about grown men with long fringes – what did they think was the effect as they ran the comb down their foreheads, spreading their hair flat across their brow? Did they think they looked good, he wondered, did they think it made them more attractive and appealing?

Wiles may have looked like a fourth-former but his mind was sharp and acute enough. Lorimer simply laid all the facts out before him, Wiles asking all the right questions. Lorimer did not speculate or air his own hunches or suspicions, merely told the story of the Fedora Palace affair as it had unfolded. At one stage Wiles took out a notebook and jotted down the relevant names.

'It doesn't make much sense to me, I must say,' Wiles considered. 'I'll make a few calls, check a few records.

We may stumble across a clue.' He put away his pen. 'If there is something hot then I can write about it, yeah? That's understood. It would be my story, to place where I wanted.'

'In principle,' Lorimer said cautiously, in the face of this freelance zeal. 'Let's see what we get first. My job may be at stake.'

'Don't worry,' Wiles said cheerfully. 'I wouldn't implicate you in any way. I always protect my sources.' He looked at his notes. 'What about this Rintoul fellow?'

'I think Gale-Harlequin are suing him. I'd go easy with him, if I were you. Bit of a wide boy.'

'Right. Point taken.' He looked up and smiled. 'So, how was Tenerife?'

'Sorry?'

'Dymphna told me you and she had a few days there.'

'Did she? Oh. Yeah, it was . . . you know, nice.'

'Lucky bastard,' Wiles said, ruefully. 'I always rather fancied Dymphna.'

Maybe if you changed your hairstyle you might stand more of a chance, Lorimer thought, and then felt a little ashamed at his lack of charity – Wiles was doing him a favour after all, and only because of his unrequited love for Dymphna.

'We're just, you know, good friends,' Lorimer said, not wanting to close any doors in Wiles's amatory life. 'Nothing special.'

'That's what they all say.' Wiles shrugged, his eyes sad behind his round frames. 'I'll get back to you. Thanks for the coffee.'

77. *The World's First Loss Adjuster.* *The very first policy of life insurance was written in England on the 18th June 1853. A* man, one William Gibbons, insured his life for the sum of 383 pounds, 6 shillings and 8 pence for one year. He paid a premium of eight per cent and sixteen underwriters signed the contract. Gibbons died on the 20th May the following year, some four weeks short of the period covered in the insurance policy, and his bereaved family duly submitted a claim. What happened?

The underwriters refused to pay up. They did this on the grounds that a year – strictly defined – is twelve times four weeks – twelve times twenty-eight days – and therefore on the basis of this calculation William Gibbons had in fact lived longer than the 'strictly defined' year he had insured his life for, and had thus 'survived the term'.

What I want to know, Hogg used to say, is the name of the man who came up with that calculation to define a year. Who was the clever devil who decided that the way out of this mess was to strictly define a year? Because whoever it was who decided that a 'year' was twelve times twenty-eight days was, in fact, the world's first loss adjuster. Such a person must have existed and, Hogg would insist, this person is the patron saint of our profession. He certainly disturbed the anticipations of the Gibbons family when they turned up to claim their 383 pounds, 6 shillings and 8 pence.

The Book of Transfiguration

Lorimer turned down Lupus Crescent and angled his body into the wind – a snell and scowthering one as they used to say in Inverness – and hauled his coat close about him. Marlobe was right, it was a shite of a day, with dense, rushing clouds showing strong contrasts of luminous white and dark slatey grey. What was happening to the weather? Where was bloody spring? He felt the wind, or the tiny grains of brick and street dust in the wind, make tears smart in his eyes and he turned his face to one side – to see David Watts's Rolls-Lamborghini or whatever it was silently keeping pace with him, like a limo behind a mafia don out for a stroll. He stopped and the car stopped.

Terry smiled genially as he crossed the street towards him.

'Mr Black. What a day, eh? David would like a word, if that's all right.'

Lorimer slid into the calfskin interior and smelt and touched the money implicit in every fixture and fitting. He sat back and let Terry cruise him from Pimlico to the south bank of the river. What in God's name was going on now? On a Saturday, no less. They crossed Vauxhall Bridge and turned on to the Albert Embankment, straight on through Stamford Street and Southwark Street, down Tooley Street, passing Tower Bridge to the left.

The car pulled up in front of a warehouse conversion a few hundred yards downstream from Tower Bridge. Tasteful gilt lettering affixed to the sooty brick told him they were at Kendrick Quay. The streets around were deserted of people but, curiously, were full of parked cars. There were many new traffic indicators and signs, islands of neat landscaping, grouped laurels and phormiums, securely staked leafless saplings, newly cast bollards set in newly laid cobbles. And, on every angle of wall, a camera sat, high and out of reach.

Terry pressed a code into a keyboard mounted on a stainless steel plinth and glass doors slid open. They rode up in a lift smelling of glue and glazier's putty to the fifth floor. Exiting the lift, Lorimer saw a printed sign with an arrow saying 'Sheer Achimota' and a weary, zemblan premonition took root in his head.

The 'Sheer Achimota' offices were empty apart from some unpacked computer hardware and an ebony desk with a slim, flat phone. The floor-to-ceiling plate-glass curtain wall on the river side looked out on the turbulent and ebbing Thames, the sky still wrought with its billowy juxtapositions of brightness and dark and, square in the middle of the view, was Tower Bridge's silhouette, irritatingly too familiar an outline, Lorimer thought, and irritatingly too omnipresent. Working in this office for any length of time you would come to hate it: a cliché in your face all day.

Watts stood in a corner, jogging and swaying, head-phones plugged in his ears, eyes tightly closed. Terry coughed several times to interrupt the reverie and left them alone. Watts fiddled with his boogie-pack and even-tually managed to switch it off. He removed the left earphone and let it dangle on his chest. Lorimer noticed that his hairy cheek patch had gone.

'Lorimer,' Watts greeted him with some enthusiasm. 'What do you think, man?'

'Very panoramic.'

'No. "Sheer Achimota". That's the name of the man-agement company, the record label, the new band and probably the new album.'

'Catchy.'

Watts roamed the room towards him. 'Fucking amazing, man. I sent Terry up to that place in Camden you told me about. He came back with eight carrier bags of CDs. I listened to African music non-stop for . . . for seventy-eight hours. And, this'll finish you, guess what?'

'You're going to Africa?'

'He's gone.'

'Who?'

'Lucifer.' He tapped his left shoulder, tapped his left cheek. 'Old Satan got pissed off and left.' Watts was close to him now and Lorimer could see his eyes were bright.

Lorimer wondered if he was on anything or if it was simply the relief of the recently exorcized.

'Thanks to you, Lorimer.'

'No, I can't take –'

'– Without you, I'd never have heard *Sheer Achimota*. Without you I wouldn't have got that ju-ju working for me. Strong African ju-ju scared the shit out of Satan. Thanks to you, *Sheer Achimota* did it.'

Lorimer checked the room's exits. 'Whatever it takes, Mr Watts.'

'Oi. Call me David. Now, I want you to come and work for me, run Sheer Achimota, sort of chief executive type kind of thing.'

'I've already got a job, um, David. But thanks very much.'

'Quit it. I'll pay you whatever you want. Hundred grand a year.'

'It's very kind. But –' But I have a life to live.

'Of course I'm still suing bastard Fortress Sure. But that's nothing against you. I've told them to say nothing against Lorimer Black.'

'I recommended they pay you.'

'Sod the money. It's the mental wear and tear. I was out of my mind with worry, what with the devil on my shoulder, and all. Someone's got to pay for that stress-load.'

Lorimer thought it best to break things to him easily. 'I could hardly leave my job and come and work for you if you are suing the company I was representing in the case.'

'Why not?'

'Well . . . Not ethical?'

'Where's your home planet, Lorimer? Anyway, no

hurry, think about it. It'll be cool. I'll pop in from time to time. We could hang out.' He refitted the left earplug. 'Could you send Terry in? You can find your own way home, can't you? Looking forward to our association, as they say.'

In a pig's ear, Lorimer thought, as he trudged the deserted streets looking for a taxi, and wondering vaguely if 'Sheer Achimota' might exorcize his own set of demons and set some powerful African ju-ju to work on his behalf for a change.

397. De Nerval's Tray. *There is no doubt that de Nerval's love for Jenny Colon was overwrought and obsessive. Jenny Colon was an actress, and Gérard used to go to the theatre night after night to see her. She had been married, in Gretna Green of all places, to another actor called Lafont. That marriage ended and she had a protracted liaison with a Dutch banker called Hoppe and many other men before de Nerval arrived in her life. Jenny Colon was described as a 'type rond et lunaire'. Lunaire? My dictionary only supplies 'lunar' and the name of a flower, moonwort. Lunar . . . That speaks to me, naturally enough, of madness. Enough to drive a man mad.*

De Nerval and Jenny Colon started a love affair but it was not long-lived. It ended, according to my biography, when de Nerval, surprising her one day, lunged at her trying to kiss her lips, her lunary lips. Startled, Jenny reflexively pushed him away and Gérard, trying to stay on his feet, clumsily reached out for support and accidentally broke a tray she owned, a precious tray. The relationship never recovered after the silly incident of the broken tray. A few weeks later Jenny left him and married her flautist. But a tray? To let a tray be the final straw, the breaking point. Who knows what deeper motives existed, but I can't help feeling that more could have been done, that de Nerval could have done more to bring about a

reconciliation. It seems to me that Gérard de Nerval didn't try hard
enough – no lovers should let a tray, however precious, come between
them.

The Book of Transfiguration

He filled the afternoon with the mundane business of
modern life: paying bills, cleaning his home, shopping
for food, tidying things away, visiting launderette and dry-
cleaner, retrieving money from automated teller machine,
eating a sandwich – banal activities that had the curious
property of being immensely satisfying and reassuring,
but only *after* they were over, Lorimer realized. He telephoned his mother and learned that his father was to be
cremated on Monday afternoon at Putney Vale crematorium. His mother said there was no need for him to
attend if he was too busy and he had felt hurt and almost
insulted at her needless consideration. He told her he
would be there.

It grew dark early and the wind angrily rattled the
window frames of the front room. He opened a Califor-
nian Cabernet, put some meditative Monteverdi on the
CD player, then changed it for Bola Folarin and Accra
57. Bola was renowned for his excessive use of drummers,
utilizing every combination known to Western groups
but supplementing them with the dry bass of the talking
drums of the West African hinterland and the staccato
contralto of the tom-toms. Something in those atavistic
rhythms combined with the wine made him restless,
made him indulge in a fit, a seizure of pure painful
longing – 'Sheer Achimota' at work, he wondered? –
and, spontaneously, he hauled on his coat and scarf,
corked the wine bottle and jammed it in a pocket, and

headed out into the wild night to find his rust-boltered Toyota.

In Chalk Farm the wind seemed even stronger, explained by Chalk Farm being higher, he supposed, and the lime tree branches above his parked car creaked and thrashed in the gale-force gusts. He swigged Cabernet and stared at the large bay windows of what he took to be the Malinverno flat. There was a kind of fretted oriental screen that obscured the bottom third of the window pane, but the head and shoulders were visible of anyone who stood up. He could see Gilbert Malinverno pacing about – indeed, he had been watching him for the last half hour as he practised his juggling (perhaps the musical had been abandoned?), flinging handfuls of multi-coloured balls up into the air and changing effortlessly the patterns and directions of their flow. It was a real talent, he grudgingly conceded. Then Malinverno had stopped practising and from the focus of his gaze Lorimer assumed someone else had entered the room. He had been pacing to and fro gesticulating wildly for ten minutes now and at first Lorimer had imagined this was some form of juggler's exercise, but then had concluded, after a series of angry jabbing pointings, that Malinverno was in fact shouting at someone, and that someone was, doubtless, Flavia.

Lorimer wanted to hurl his wine bottle through the window and take the brute on and break his bones . . . He gulped at his Cabernet and was wondering how much longer he could realistically spend out here in his car when he saw the front door of the house open and Flavia run down the steps and go striding off down the hill. In a second Lorimer was out of his car and closing on her.

She turned a corner before he could reach her and entered a small parade of shops, going into a brightly lit 24-hour supermarket called Emporio Mondiale. Lorimer followed her in, after only the briefest of hesitations, but she was nowhere to be seen. Blinking in the brilliant white light, he carefully checked a few of the labyrinth of tall aisles – teetering battlements of sanitary napkins and toilet rolls, kitchen towels, disposable nappies and dog biscuits. Then he saw her bent over an ice-cream freezer, rummaging in its lower depths, and backed off, a little breathless, then composed himself, but when he advanced forward again she had gone.

He headed straight to the checkout, where a solitary Ethiopian girl was patiently counting through a mass of brown coins that an old lady was unearthing from a cavernous handbag – but no Flavia. Christ, where was she? Perhaps she'd gone back out the entrance? And he raced back the way he had come. Then he saw her: vanishing down a side alley that led to the newspapers. He decided that a flanking move was the correct choice here and so ducked down breads and breakfast cereals, heading for the spice jar whirligig and the cabinet of dreadful salads.

He turned the corner at the bottom and she fired a blast of air freshener at him. *Pffft.* He caught a farinaceous gust of sweet-smelling violets full in the face and sneezed several times.

'I don't like being followed,' she said, replacing the aerosol. She was wearing sunglasses and a bulky old leather jacket with a hood and many zips. He was sure her eyes would be red and weepy beneath the opaque green glass.

'What's he done to you?' Lorimer blurted out. 'If he's hit you – I'll –'

'He's actually been talking about you, or rather shouting about you, for the last half hour. That's why I had to get out. He claims he saw you at some smart party.'

'You do know that he attacked me. Tried to club me on the head.' All his old outrage returned. 'After you had told him about our so-called affair.'

'What are you talking about?'

'Your husband tried to hit me over the head with a club.'

'Gilbert? —'

'What did you tell him we'd been up to?'

'He was in a terrible rage and I was frightened. And angry – so, well, I made all sorts of things up, said it had been going on for over a year. Maybe that's what set him off? He did go thundering out of the house. Was it you who knocked his teeth out? He said he'd been mugged.'

'It was self-defence. He tried to hit me with one of his fucking juggling clubs.'

'There's a lot of pent-up rage in you, isn't there, Lorimer?' She took down another aerosol spray from the shelf and enveloped him in a cloud of something piney.

'Don't! For God's sake!'

'We can't see each other.' She glanced nervously over her shoulder. 'God knows what would happen if he came into the shop now.'

'Does he hit you?'

'He's incredibly fit and strong. Sometimes he gets me in these grips. Shakes me about, twists my arms.'

'Animal.' Lorimer felt a form of pure rage sluice through him, of the sort crusaders might have experienced at the sight of a holy shrine desecrated, he imagined. He rummaged in his pockets and took out his bunch of keys, threading two off and holding them out to her.

'Take them, please. If you ever need a place to be safe, to get away from him where he can't find you. You can go here.'

She did not take them. 'What is this?'

'It's a house I've bought. Pretty much empty. In Silvertown, a place called Albion Village, number 3. You can go there, escape him if he gets violent again.'

'Silvertown? Albion Village? What kind of a place is that? Sounds like a children's book.'

'Sort of development near Albert Dock, by the City airport.'

'One of those modern developments? Little boxes?'

'Well . . . yes. Sort of.'

'Why do you want to buy a little cardboard house like that, miles from anywhere, when you've got a perfectly good place in Pimlico? I don't get it.'

He sighed. He felt a sudden urge to tell her, especially as she now reached out and took his keys.

'It's . . . It's something to do with me. It makes me feel – I don't know – safe. Safer, I suppose. It's my insurance. There's always somewhere I can go and start again.'

'Sounds more like a place to go and hide. What are you hiding from, Lorimer Black?'

'My name's not Lorimer Black. I mean it is, I changed it, but I wasn't born Lorimer Black.' He knew he was going to tell her. 'My real name is Milomre Blocj. I was born here but in fact I'm a Transnistrian. I come from a family of Transnistrian Gypsies.'

'And I come from a planet called Zog in a far-flung galaxy,' she said.

'It's true.'

313

'Piss off out of it.'

'IT'S TRUE!'

A few puzzled shoppers looked round. A lanky Pakistani with his name on a plastic badge came to investigate. He gestured at the shelves.

'All these items are for sale, you know.'

'Still making up our mind, thank you,' Flavia said, with a winning smile.

'Milomre?' She pronounced it carefully.

'Yes.'

'Transnistria.'

'Transnistria. It's a real place, or was. On the west shore of the Black Sea. My family call me Milo.'

'Milo . . . I prefer that. How fascinating. Why are you telling me this, Milo?'

'I don't know. It's always been a secret. I've never told anyone before. I suppose I must want you to know.'

'Think it'll win me over? Well, you're wrong.'

'Take your sunglasses off for a second, please.'

'No.' She reached for a can of spray starch and Lorimer backed off.

She bought some spaghetti, a jar of sauce and a bottle of Valpolicella. Lorimer walked back up the road with her. A few heavy drops of rain began to smack on to the pavement.

'You're not going to cook supper for him, are you?' Lorimer asked scornfully. 'After what he's done to you? How pathetic.'

'No, he's going out, thank God. I've got a friend coming over.'

'Male or female?'

'Mind your own business. Male . . . Gay.'

'Could I join you?'

314

'Are you mad? What if Gilbert came back? "Oh, Gilbert, Lorimer's popped in for a bite of supper." Crazy fool.'

They had reached his car, which now looked as if it were suffering from a terrible rash, pocked with dark dots where the raindrops had spattered on the light dusty orange of the rust. With the dampness in the air the Toyota seemed to exude a crude smell of metal, or worked iron, as if they were standing in a smithy.

'Good lord, look at your car,' Flavia said. 'It looks worse.'

'It rusted up almost overnight.'

'They were cross with you, weren't they?'

'It was a job I was on –' He paused, something suddenly occurring to him. 'They blamed me for their troubles.'

'While you were adjusting loss.'

'Yes, I was adjusting loss.'

'I'm not sure if you're cut out for this life of loss adjusting, Lorimer. Very hazardous.'

'Hazardous in the extreme,' he said, suddenly feeling very tired. 'Can I see you next week, Flavia?'

'I don't think that would be a good idea.'

'You do know, you must be aware, that I'm passionately in love with you. I'll never take no for an answer.'

'Suit yourself.' She shrugged as she walked backwards a few paces. 'Goodnight, Milo whatever-your-name-is.'

'Use the house,' he called after her. 'Any time, it's all set up. Number 3, Albion Village.'

She turned and trotted across the road to her house and scampered up the steps. He felt like weeping: something important had happened – tonight he had told someone else about the existence of Milomre Blocj. And she had kept his keys.

*

He went to sleep at the Institute, hoping he would dream lucidly and lustily of Flavia, that in his dream she would be naked and he would be able to take her in his arms. Instead he dreamt of his father, lying in bed, ill. They held hands, interlacing their fingers, exactly as they had done the final time they had seen each other, except that on this occasion Bogdan Blocj raised himself on one elbow and kissed him on the cheek, several times. Lorimer could feel the neat white bristles of his beard sharp against his skin. Then he spoke to him and said, 'You did well, Milo.'

Lorimer woke, drained and vulnerable, and wrote the dream down in the diary with a trembling hand. It was a lucid dream because something had happened in the dream that he had wished for but had never happened in his life, and for the duration of that dream it had seemed real.

As he dressed later, preparing himself for Sunday lunch with Stella and Barbuda, he reflected that this was one reason why dreams were so important in our lives: something good had happened in the night while he was unconscious – he had achieved and expressed an intensity of relationship with his father that he had never experienced while the man had been alive. He was grateful to his extra dose of REM sleep. This, surely, was the consolation of dreams.

Barbuda looked at her mother pleadingly and said, 'Please may I leave the table, Mummy.'

'Oh, all right,' Stella said and Barbuda left with alacrity. Stella reached over and poured the rest of the Rioja into Lorimer's empty glass. She had had a lighter blonde rinse put through her hair, Lorimer thought, that's the difference; she looked healthier and she was wearing all white, white jeans and a white sweat shirt with an appliquéd satin bird on the front. And did he detect a sheen of sunbed bronze?

Barbuda had left the room without a backward glance, a further sign that she had returned to her familiar mood of sour hostility. The Angelica name-change had finally been vetoed and the moment of solidarity that had existed between daughter and her mother's lover appeared forgotten. As far as Lorimer could recall she had not addressed one word to him throughout the three courses of Sunday lunch – smoked salmon, roast chicken and all the trimmings and a bought-in lemon meringue pie.

Stella recharged her coffee cup, reached over and took his hand.

'We've got to have a serious talk, Lorimer.'

'I know,' he said, telling himself there was nothing to be gained by further procrastination. He liked Stella, and in a way the mutually beneficial, respectful nature of their relationship suited him ideally. But its continuance presupposed a world without Flavia Malinverno in it, and thus it was impossible and would be best concluded in as decent and hurt-free a way as possible.

'I've sold the business,' Stella said.

'Good God.'

'And I've bought a fish farm.'

'A fish farm.'

'Near Guildford. We're moving.'

'A fish farm near Guildford,' Lorimer repeated gormlessly, as if he were learning a new phrase in the language.

'It's a going concern, guaranteed income. Mainly trout and salmon. Fair amount of prawns and shrimps.'

'But, Stella, a fish farm. You?'

'Why should that be any worse than running a scaffolding firm?'

'Fair point. You'll be closer to Barbuda's school, as well.'

'Exactly.' Stella was running her thumb over his knuckles. 'Lorimer,' she began slowly, 'I want you to come with me, be my partner, and my business partner. I don't want to get married but I like having you in my life and I want to share it with you. I know you've got a good job, which is why we should set it up properly, as a business venture. Bull and Black, fish farmers.'

Lorimer leant over and kissed her, hoping the smile on his face concealed the despair in his heart.

'Don't say anything yet,' Stella said. 'Just listen.' She began to go over the figures, turnover and profit margins, the kind of salary they could pay themselves, the prospects for major expansion if they could break into certain markets.

'Don't say yes, no or maybe,' Stella went on. 'Give yourself a few days to mull it over. And everything it implies.' She grabbed his head and gave him a serious kiss, her lithe tongue flicking in and out of his mouth like . . . like a fish, Lorimer balefully noted.

'I'm excited, Lorimer, it really excites me. Out of the city, in the country . . .'

'Does Barbuda know anything about these plans?' Lorimer said, gladly accepting the offer of a celebratory post-prandial brandy.

'Not yet. She knows I've sold Bull scaffolding. She's pleased about that, she's always been embarrassed by the scaffolding.'

Revolting little snob, Lorimer thought, saying, 'The fish farm will go down better,' without much confidence.

Stella hugged him fiercely at the door as he left. It was only four o'clock but already the streetlamps shone bright in the gathering murk. Lorimer's depression was acute, but there was no way he could burst the bubble of her fishy dreams here and now. He kissed her goodbye.

He stood on the pavement by his car, reflecting a while, looking across at the high, lit cliff faces of the sprawling housing estate a few streets away, thumbtacked with satellite dishes, washing hanging limply on balconies, one of the great ghetto colonies of the city's poor and disenfranchised which arced east, south of the river, through Walworth, Peckham, Rotherhithe and South-wark, small slum-states of deprivation and anarchy where life was lived in a manner that would be familiar to Hogg's Savage Precursors, brutish and nasty, where all endeavours were hazardous in the extreme and life was one gargantuan gamble, a cycle of happenstance and rotten luck.

Was this all there really was, in the end, he wondered? Beneath this veneer of order, probity, governance and civilized behaviour – aren't we just kidding ourselves? The Savage Precursors knew . . . Stop, he told himself, he was depressed enough as it was, and bent to unlock his car. He heard his name softly called and looked round to see Barbuda standing ten feet away, as if restrained by an invisible *cordon sanitaire* around him.

'Hi, Barbuda,' he said, the two words overburdened by all the friendliness, pleasure and genuine good-natured blokiness he could force upon them.

'I was listening,' she said, flatly. 'She was talking about a fish farm. Near Guildford. What's she gone and done?'

'I think your mother should tell you that.'

'She's bought a fish farm, hasn't she?'

'Yes.' There was nothing to be gained by lying, he thought, seeing Barbuda's bottom lip fatten as she pushed it forward.

'A fish farm.' She made it sound vile, horror-filled: a vivisection laboratory, the dankest sweat-shop, a child brothel.

'It sounds like fun,' he said, urging a chuckle into his voice. 'Could be interesting.'

She looked skywards and Lorimer saw the shine as the streetlamp caught her teartracks.

'What am I going to tell my friends? What will my friends think?'

It seemed not to be a rhetorical question so Lorimer answered. 'If they think any the less of you because your mother owns a fish farm, then they're not true friends.'

'A fish farm. My mother's a fish farmer.'

'There's nothing wrong with a fish farm. It could be very successful.'

'I don't want to be the daughter of someone who owns a fish farm,' Barbuda said in a desperate, whining voice. 'I can't be. I won't be.'

Lorimer knew the feeling: he understood the reluctance to have an identity thrust upon you – even though he could not bring himself to sympathize with the brat.

'Look, they know she runs a scaffolding firm, surely they –'

'They don't know. They know nothing about her. But if she moves to Guildford they'll find out.'

'These things seem important, but after a while –'

'It's all your fault.' Barbuda wiped away her tears.

'What do you mean?'

'She's done it for you. If you weren't in her life she would never have bought the fish farm.'

'I think she would. Anyway, look, Barbuda, or Angelica, if you like –'

'It's all your fault,' she repeated in a small hard voice. 'I'll kill you. One day I'll kill you.'

She turned and ran, on light, quick feet, back into the house.

Well, you'll just have to join the queue, Lorimer reflected with some bitterness, exhaling. He was becoming fed up with this role of fall-guy for other people's woes, he was reaching the end of his tether; if life didn't ease up on him he might just possibly break.

There were four fire engines outside the ShoppaSava when Lorimer drove past and a small crowd had gathered. Some fitful wisps of smoke and steam seemed to be issuing from the rear of the building, Lorimer could see, parking the Toyota and wandering along the street to discover what had happened. He peered over the heads of the onlookers at the blackened plate-glass doors. Firemen, draped in breathing apparatus like deep sea divers, were wandering around in a relaxed manner, swigging from two-litre bottles of mineral water, so Lorimer assumed the worst was over. A policeman told him it had been a 'ferociously fierce' fire, with everything pretty much consumed. Lorimer mooched around for a few more minutes and then headed back to his car and realized, after a moment or two, that he was following a figure that was vaguely familiar – a figure in pale blue jeans and an expensive-looking ochre suede jacket. Lorimer ducked into a shop doorway and watched the figure covertly: was this what it was like being a secret agent in the field, he asked himself with some bitterness, a life of eternal vigilance the price demanded? Gone forever that unreflecting amble through your own particular *quartier* of your own particular city, always edgy and alert like –

He watched the man climb into a glossy new-model BMW – Kenneth Rintoul. No doubt he's been sniffing around number 11, trying to catch him off his guard. A little bit of grievous bodily harm of a Sunday afternoon, just the ticket. Lorimer waited until Rintoul had driven off and then loped diffidently to his rust-bucket. The mobile rang as he opened the door. It was Slobodan.

'Hi, Milo, you haven't heard anything from Torkie, have you?'

'No. Why?'

'Well, he went home, Saturday, to sort out some sort of lawyer business but he never came back. I'd cooked him dinner and he's missed a ton of work. I wondered if he'd shown up at your place.'

'No. No sign. Tried his home number?'

'Nothing but answer machine. You don't know if he's turning up Monday morning, do you?'

'I'm not Torquil's keeper, Slobodan.'

'Fair dos, fair dos. Just thought you might be in the loop, is all. See you tomorrow, then. Three.'

Lorimer had forgotten. 'Oh yeah, right.'

'Shame about old Dad, eh? Still he had a good –'

Lorimer interrupted before he could round off the homily. 'See you tomorrow.'

'Cheers, Milo.'

When he reached home, and as he crossed the hall to

the stairs, he heard Jupiter give a brief, gruff bark from behind Lady Haigh's door. He was usually the most silent of dogs and Lorimer chose to interpret this exception as a fond, canine 'hello'.

Chapter 18

Monday, Lorimer reflected, had not started in a promising manner: in the night someone had stolen his car. In the dawn darkness he stood by the empty space where he had parked it and asked himself what inept thief, what desperate fool, would choose to steal a car with such an obvious dose of terminal corrosion? Well, to hell and back with it, he thought, at least it's insured, and strode off into the gloom towards Victoria Station to catch a tube.

He sat in a hot, crammed compartment with his fellow commuters, trying to keep irritation at bay and, also, ignore the thin, keening note of indeterminate worry that nagged at him like tinnitus. Moreover, he was already missing his car, knowing he would have needed it for the funeral, to make the long trajectory across town to Putney. It's just a motor car, he told himself, a mode of transport – and a pretty inauspicious one at that. There were other methods available when it came to the ferrying of his person from point A to point B: by the standards of the world's injustices he was getting off lightly.

The tube network bore him efficiently beneath the city's streets so that he was at the office fifteen minutes before his appointment with Hogg. He was about to clamber up the flight of stairs when he saw Torquil emerge on the landing, suited and tied, and with a pile of files under his arm. Torquil conspiratorially waved him back outside and presently joined him on the pavement. They wandered a way along the street, Torquil regardlessly hailing every occupied taxi that passed as if it would at once disgorge its paying customer at his imperious behest.

'The most amazing thing happened this weekend,' Torquil told him. 'There I was, Saturday evening, arguing the toss with Binnie about getting the kids into cheaper schools, when Simon calls.'

'Sherriffmuir?'

'Yes. There and then he offers me a job. Director of Special Projects at Fortress Sure. My old salary, secretary, car – better car, actually – as if nothing had ever happened. TAXI!'

'Special projects? What does that mean?'

'Well, not so sure . . . Simon said something about feeling our way forward, establishing parameters as we go, sort of thing. For Christ's sake, it's a job. Pension, BUPA, the works. TAXI! I knew Simon would see me right. Just a question of when.'

'Well, congratulations.'

'Thanks. Ah, got one.' A black cab had stopped across the street and was waiting to make its tight turn.

'And,' Torquil added, a little smugly, 'the Binns has forgiven me.'

'Why?'

'Well, you know. The kids, I suppose. Anyway, she's a noble soul. And I promised to be a good boy.'

'What about Irina?'

Torquil looked blank for a moment. 'Oh, I told her I couldn't see her – for a while. She took it pretty well. I think we might let that one just fizzle out, anyway. Plenty more fish in the sea.' Torquil opened the cab door. 'Look, let's have lunch some time.'

'I'll tell Lobby you won't be turning up.'

'Lobby? Oh, God, yeah, would you? Forgot about him in all the excitement. Tell him I'm taking a cut in salary, that'll make him laugh. It's true, actually. Sorry to hear about your pa, by the way.'

Lorimer closed the door on him with a satisfying bang and watched Torquil rummaging in his pockets for a cigarette while telling the taxi driver where he wanted to go. He didn't bother to wave goodbye as Torquil didn't bother to look out of the window.

Lorimer bounded up the pine stairway, heading for Rajiv's counter, about to tell him of the car theft, but Rajiv pre-empted him, tapping his nose and pointing skyward.

'Mr Hogg's asked three times if you've come in.'

So Lorimer went straight up; there was no sign of Janice so he rapped on Hogg's door.

'Who is it?'

'Lorimer, Mr Hogg.'

Hogg threw a rolled-up newspaper at him as he entered and it bounced off his chest and fell to the carpet. It was the *Financial Times*. Lorimer's eye was immediately caught by the second headline: 'Property giant snaps up Gale-Harlequin. Racine Securities pays 380 million.' He scanned through the rest of the article: 'Shares purchased at 435p . . . Investors take large profits.' There followed a list of investors – two fund managers, a famous US property tycoon and arbitrageur and a couple of other names he did not recognize. Hogg stood, hands on hips, legs braced as if on a rolling poop deck, watching him while he read.

'How much did you make?' Hogg said, with quiet venom. 'Stock options or a flat deal?'

'I don't know what you're talking about.'

'You must think I'm like some virgin novice nun from a convent stuck up in the mountains, a hundred miles from the nearest . . .' the simile ran out of steam. 'Don't make me fucking laugh, you tosspot.'

'Mr Hogg –'

'Now I know why the adjust went so smoothly. No one wanted the boat rocked with this one coming up on the rails.'

Lorimer had to admit it made some sense.

'I did a straightforward adjust, pure and simple.'

'And you're fired, pure and simple.'

Lorimer blinked. 'On what grounds?'

'Suspicion.'

'Suspicion of what?'

'How long have you got? I suspect you of every nasty, suppurating, corrupt trick in the book, matey, and I can't afford to suspect a member of my staff for even one second. So you take the prize fucking biscuit, chum. You're out. Now.' He actually smiled. 'Car keys.' He held out a broad palm.

Lorimer handed them over. 'By the way, it was stolen this morning.'

'No. We lifted it. You'll be getting invoiced for the respray. Janice!'

Janice peered nervously round the door.

'Take Mr Black to his office, let him pack up his personal effects and then lock the door. On no account is he to be left alone for one second, or make a phone call.' He offered Lorimer his hand. 'Goodbye, Lorimer, it's been real.'

It was to his credit, so Lorimer told himself later, that he did not shake Hogg's hand. He merely said, trying to keep the tremor out of his voice: 'You are making an enormous mistake. You will live to regret it,' turned sharply on his heel, back muscles already in spasm, and managed to walk out.

201. *An Old Joke*. *Hogg told me this joke more than once, it's a particular favourite. A man goes into a sandwich bar and says, 'Can I have a turkey sandwich?' The guy behind the counter says, 'We've got no turkey.' 'OK,' the man says, 'in that case I'll have chicken.' The guy behind the counter says, 'Listen, mate, if we had chicken you could have had your turkey sandwich.'*

Since Hogg told me this joke it has perturbed me unduly, as if it contains some deep truth about perception, about truth, about the world and our dealings with it. Something about this old joke disturbs me. Hogg, for his part, could hardly get the words out for laughing.

The Book of Transfiguration

Lorimer placed the cardboard box containing his personal effects on the hall table and rested his hand on the crown of his Greek helmet. The metal felt cool and pleasingly rough under his hot palm. Give me strength, he thought. He analysed his feelings and came up with nothing concrete: vague outrage, vague worry about the future and, curiously, vague relief.

There was a message to call Bram Wiles on his answer machine.

'Did you see today's papers?' Wiles asked immediately.

'Yes. What do you make of it?'

'One of the investors in Gale-Harlequin is a company called Ray Von TL – it has just over a fifteen per cent stake. It's registered in Panama. I suspect that if we could find out who was behind Ray Von TL we'd have a few more answers.'

Lorimer had a few guesses: Francis Home? Dirk van Meer? He would not be surprised. Fifteen per cent of Gale-Harlequin was suddenly worth this morning a nice 48 million. A handsome slice of the pie to call your own. But how did such massive profit-taking impinge on the insignificant lives of Torquil Helvoir-Jayne and Lorimer Black?

'You know Gale-Harlequin was only floated on the stock exchange fourteen months ago?' Wiles asked.

'No, I didn't. Could it have a bearing?'

'I should think so, wouldn't you? Somewhere along the line.'

Wiles speculated on possible schemes and plans but they were all guesses. Lorimer asked him to keep on digging, to see if he could find out any more about this Ray Von TL company – it seemed their only lead. Even then, as Wiles reminded him, it might be perfectly legitimate: there were many offshore investors in British companies.

After he hung up Lorimer thought for a while, hard, and with ever-mounting alarm. One of Hogg's regular maxims nagged away at the edge of his brain – 'we set a sprat to catch a rhino' – for the first time in his life he thought it made some kind of perverse sense. He rephrased it along classic Hoggian lines: in difficult times a fool is more use than a wise man.

He found a black tie at the back of a drawer and put it on – it certainly suited his mood. From a position of steady normality – steady job, steady prospects, steady girlfriend – he now found himself adrift in uncertainty and chaos: no job, no car, no girlfriend, insolvent, fatherless, sleepless, loveless . . . Not the ideal set of circumstances to find oneself in, he reflected, given that he was about to go to a funeral at a crematorium.

He walked down Lupus Crescent, wondering whether his bank card would still work, and was beckoned over by Marlobe. He had a copious stock of lilies in today and even in the dull, chilly, wintry air their perfume was cloying and almost nauseating, Lorimer thought, making his sinuses tickle and catching at his throat. Lilies that fester . . . How did the line go? Lilies, daffs, tulips, the omnipresent carnations. He bought a bunch of pale mauve tulips for his father's grave.

'Off to a funeral then?' Marlobe observed cheerily, pointing at his black tie.

'Yes, my father's.'

'Oh yeah? Commiserations. Is it burning or under the ground?'

'Cremation.'

'That's what I want. Burnt to a crisp. Then have my ashes scattered.'

'Over the carnation fields of the Zuider Zee?'

'Come again?'

'Nothing.'

'Talking about fire . . .' Marlobe leaned forward, pushing his pale gingery face close to Lorimer's. 'Did you see what happened over at ShoppaSava? Burnt out. They might even demolish the place.'

'Shame. It was a good supermarket.' Fire, Lorimer thought suddenly, occupied a prominent place in his life. Who was the god of fire? Prometheus? His life recently seemed to be dogged by some malicious Prometheus, showing him his power in all its protean forms.

330

'It's an ill fucking wind . . .' Marlobe said doomily, like some demotic sage, then grinned, showing his fine teeth. 'Won't be selling any more flowers, though, eh? Ha-ha. Eh? Eh?'

As Lorimer walked away he began thinking about the fire: no, surely, not even Marlobe was that ruthless – to destroy an entire supermarket? Surely not? He sighed loudly in the street. But then he resolved that nothing was going to surprise him any more, not after the events of recent weeks, all anticipations had been well and truly disturbed, his mind would be forever open, always a door ajar to the most outlandish possibility. He slipped his card in the machine and, gratifyingly, it poked out a crisp tongue of new notes.

*396. **Prometheus and Pandora**. Prometheus, a titan and a demiurge, also known as 'the great trickster', and a culture-hero. Bringer of fire to earth and man. Stealer of fire from Zeus. Prometheus, firestealer, firebringer.*

Zeus, determined to counterbalance this beneficence, created a woman, Pandora, endowing her with fabulous beauty and instinctive cunning, and sent her to earth with a jar containing all manner of miseries and evils. Pandora duly lifted the lid from the jar and all these torments flew out to punish and distress mankind forever. So, Prometheus brings the blessing of fire, and Zeus sends Pandora with her malign jar. There is too much of Prometheus and Pandora in my life at the moment. But I am consoled by the coda to the legend. Hope was in Pandora's jar, but Pandora closed the lid before Hope could escape. But Hope lurks somewhere, she must have squeezed out of Pandora's jar by now. Prometheus and Pandora, my kind of gods.

The Book of Transfiguration

Once through the gates and away from the the traffic, Putney Vale Crematorium did not resemble, Lorimer saw, all crematoria everywhere. He had assumed that some time in the 1960s one firm of architects had been given the sole contract for the nation. There was no spacious, neatly mown park, no carefully positioned conifers and larches, shrubberies and flower beds, no low brick buildings or featureless waiting rooms with their dusty arrangements of artificial flowers.

Instead, Putney Vale was a gigantic, scruffy, over-populated graveyard, set behind a superstore, dotted with clumps of trees with a dark avenue of shaggy yews leading to a dinky Victorian Gothic church, converted somehow to take the crematorium's furnace. Despite its idiosyncratic appearance the same mood always seemed to accrue around these places – regret, sorrow, dread, all the soul-sapping *mementi mori* – except Putney Vale had them loudly amplified: the acres of the encroaching necropolis, the bottle-green unpruned lugubrious yews seeming almost to suck in light out of the air like black holes (trees of death. Why did they plant the wretched things? Why not something prettier?) – all adding up to this atmosphere of municipal melancholia, of standard-ized, clock-watching obsequies.

But as if to prove him wrong he sensed at once, as he stepped out of his taxi, that his family were in jovial and buoyant mood. As he approached the church he heard a blare of laughter rise above the hum of animated chat. Groups of B and B drivers were gathered on the lawn outside having a smoke, their cigarettes held respectfully out of sight, in cupped hands behind their backs, keeping their distance from the central knot of Bloçj family members. He saw Trevor one-five, Mohammed, Dave,

Winston, Trevor two-nine and some others he did not recognize. They greeted him boisterously. 'Milo! Hi, Milo! Looking good, Milo!'

His family was gathered before the arched doors waiting for their turn: his grandmother and mother, Slobodan, Monika, Komelia, Drava and little Mercedes – all looking smarter than normal in new clothes he had not seen before, hair coiffed and combed, make-up prominent. Slobodan was wearing an orange tie and had reduced his ponytail to a sober bun, and Mercy ran up to show him her new shoes agleam with many silver buckles.

Slobodan actually embraced him, in new head-of-the-family mode, Lorimer assumed, slapped him on the back and squeezed his shoulders repeatedly.

'Phil's on the box,' Slobodan said. 'Just got a skeleton crew on. Dad wouldn't want us to shut down completely.'

'I'm sure he wouldn't.'

'Everything all right, Milo?' Monika asked. 'You look a bit tired.'

'I am. And I find these places incredibly depressing.'

'Hark at him,' Monika said huffily, as if he were somehow lowering the tone. He turned away and kissed his other sisters, his mother, his grandmother.

'I miss him, Milo,' his mother said briskly, clear-eyed. 'Even though he never say a word for ten years. I miss him about the house.'

'We have saying in Transnistria,' his grandmother chipped in. 'We say, "A cat may have nine lives and a man may make nine mistakes." I don't think Bogdan he even make one mistake.'

What an appalling saying, Lorimer thought, instantly computing the big mistakes in his life. Nine? Why only nine? And after the ninth mistake, then what? Death, like a cat? And how did you define the error or misconception or blunder or slip-up that tipped over into mistake-category? He was still pondering this piece of unsettling Transnistrian lore when a man in a dark suit announced that their time had come and they filed into the chapel.

At once Lorimer realized he had left his tulips in the taxi that had brought him here and the thought depressed him unduly. He had not been concentrating on his father's funeral. He had been thinking about himself and his endlessly mounting problems. Perhaps that was mistake number nine? Get a grip, he told himself sternly – this was irrational, panicky stuff.

A young priest who clearly knew nothing about Bogdan Blocj conducted the service and uttered a few weary platitudes. Everyone bowed their heads as the curtains slowly met to obscure the casket – everyone except Lorimer, who kept his eyes fixed on the pale oak hexagon as long as he could. An organist struck up a busy fugue and Lorimer strained his ears to catch the whirr of machinery, of belts moving, of doors opening and closing, of flames igniting.

They filed sheepishly out into the chill of the overcast afternoon, where there followed the ritual lighting of the cigarettes. For the first time the full carnival spirit seemed to have left the mourners and they talked in lower voices, scrutinizing the rows of cellophane-wrapped bouquets with scientific intensity as if they might contain rare species, exotic hybrids, newly discovered orchids.

To Lorimer's intense consternation the mobile phone in his breast pocket began to chirrup like a hungry fledgling. Everyone looked round at him, impressed, as if to say, see, even here Milo has to be on call, as if he were a surgeon waiting for a vital organ to transplant. He fumbled to remove the phone and walked off some distance to answer it, hearing Trevor one-five's admiring comment: 'Look at him, never stops, amazing.'

'Hello?'

'Black?' It was Hogg.

'Yes?'

'Get your arse down to the junction of Pall Mall and St James's. Six o'clock this evening. Good news.'

'What's this all about?'

'Be there.'

He rung off and Lorimer thought: this is most confusing, these are complexities beyond complexities. Hogg just assumed he would be there, he realized, that he would still jump to his command. For a moment he pondered an act of defiance – and decided against it. It was too hard to resist, and Hogg knew he would come, knew in his bones. There was too much shared history for him to refuse – and it was too soon. And Hogg had not merely issued an order: 'good news', he had said, that was the lure, that was the invitation, and this was as close to mollifying as Hogg would ever become. Of course what was 'good news' to George Hogg wouldn't necessarily be perceived as such by anyone else. Lorimer sighed: he sensed again his impotence and ignorance, the bystander who can only see glimpses of the race and cannot tell who's winning or who's being lapped; he felt the buffeting, burly power of forces he did not comprehend or welcome, pushing at and shaping his destiny.

The front door of number 11, Lupus Crescent was open, much to Lorimer's surprise, and in the hall stood a lanky, red-eyed, sniffing Rastafarian whom Lorimer recognized as Nigel, Lady Haigh's mulch- and compost-supplier.

He was about to ask him what the trouble was when the door of Lady Haigh's flat opened and two undertakers appeared, manoeuvring a low gurney upon which lay a thick, rubberized zip-up plastic bag. With sad, professional smiles they swiftly trundled their burden out of the front door.

'Jesus Christ,' Lorimer said. 'Lady Haigh.'

'She wouldn't answer the bell,' Nigel said. 'So I went round the back, through a friend's house, nipped over the fence and saw her lying on the kitchen floor. I broke in, there was a phone number by the phone, and I called this gentleman.' His voice was level but tears shimmered pinkly in his eyes and he sniffed again.

Lorimer turned to see he was referring to a harassed-looking, balding man in his fifties coming through the door, a tuft of his fine thinning hair standing straight up, filaments waving to and fro as he moved. He sensed Lorimer's gaze upon it so he stopped wiping his hands on a handkerchief and palmed his hair flat across his pate.

Lorimer introduced himself.

'What a terrible shock,' Lorimer said, with absolute sincerity. 'I live upstairs. I've just come from my father's funeral. I can't believe it.'

The harassed man seemed not to want to hear any more depressing statements from Lorimer and looked anxiously at his watch.

'I'm Godfrey Durrell,' he said. 'Cecilia's nephew.'

Cecilia? This was news – and a nephew as well. He felt sad that Lady Haigh had died but also he remembered how she longed for this release. A drip of guilt began to intrude on his shock and upset: how long had it been since he had last seen her, or given a thought to her welfare? It had been the dog food conversation, which was – when? Hours, days or weeks ago? His life seemed currently to be defying the segmented orders of diurnal time, hours lasting days, days compressed into minutes. He thought suddenly of Jupiter's untypical solitary bark on – good God – Sunday night and wondered if it were as close as he could come to a pealing howl over his dead mistress's body . . .

'I'm glad you're here,' Durrell said. 'I've got to get back.'

'Where?' Lorimer felt he had a right to know.

'I'm a radiologist at the Demarco-Westminster Clinic. I've got a waiting room full of patients.' He re-entered the flat and emerged moments later in a semi-crouch, his left hand gripping the generous scruff of Jupiter's neck.

'I believe he's yours now,' he said. 'There are about a dozen notes taped up around the house saying he's to be delivered to you, in the event, etcetera.'

'Yes. I did promise –'

He was locking the door. 'I'll be back whenever I can,' he said, opening his wallet and handing Lorimer his card. He shook Nigel's hand, thanked him and, with a nervous smoothing gesture at his hair, quickly left.

Jupiter sat down slowly at Lorimer's feet, his tongue lolling thirstily. He probably needs a drink, Lorimer thought, all those hours of waiting.

'I was worried about the dog,' Nigel said. 'I'm glad you're taking him.'

'He's a nice old dog,' Lorimer said, stooping to give him a possessive pat. 'Poor old Lady Haigh.'

'She was a great lady, Cecilia,' Nigel said with feeling.

'Did you call her Cecilia?' Lorimer asked, thinking

about his own diffidence, feeling obscurely jealous that Nigel should have been so familiar, so easily.

'Sure. I used to sing that song at her, you know: "Cecilia, you're breaking my heart, you're shaking my confidence daily" .' Nigel's rasping baritone carried the tune well. 'She used to laugh.'

'Fine old lady.'

'But she was tired waiting. She wanted to die, man.'

'Don't we all.'

Nigel laughed and raised his hand. Unthinkingly Lorimer gripped it, shoulder-high, thumbs interlocking, like two centurions taking their leave at the frontiers of some distant province, far from Rome.

'It gets to you, man,' Nigel said, shaking his head. 'Go to pay a visit and find a dead body.'

'I know exactly what you mean,' Lorimer said.

'Come on Jupiter,' Lorimer said, after Nigel had sauntered off, and walked upstairs with the old dog obediently following. He gave him a bowl of water and he lapped noisily and splashily at it, heavy drops sprinkling the carpet, so Lorimer fetched a newspaper and put it under the bowl. Life with Jupiter: lesson one. He probably needed food, a walk, a shit . . . He looked at his watch – ten past five. No, he'd better keep this appointment, he did not want to incur the wrath of Hogg any further. Two deaths in as many days: this was adding new and unknown stresses and strains, life was bearing down on him hard, disturbing all anticipations.

213. The Television Set. *You still don't remember what they were watching on the television, you heard only the noise of its imbecile chatter, even louder when the cheering subsided as you strode naked into the middle of the common room. Then the whistles and* *hoots began, screams and gasps, fingers were pointed towards your groin area. And you were shouting yourself, gripped by your rage, your burning, consuming fury, screaming for silence, for some respect, for tolerance of others' needs and reasonable demands.*

So you seized the television set from its tall plinth and effortlessly, it seemed, raised it above your head before dashing it to the ground and turning to those hundred pairs of eyes and yelling – what? The room went quiet and turned red, green, yellow, grey and red again and people were falling on you, some glancing blows were struck as you hit out, defending yourself, but soon you were on the ground, someone's jacket wrapped around your middle, your nose full of the reek of burning dust and scorched plastic from the shattered machine, hearing one word which managed to find a way through to your multicoloured, suffering cortex – 'Police,' 'Police,' 'Police'.

You did the right thing. The only thing. You were right to leave, leave the college, leave Joyce McKimmie (where are they now? Shy Joyce and little Zane?), you were right never to go back to the house at Croy, even though there was murder in your heart and you wished to see Sinbad Fingleton just one more time and visit significant harm upon him.

No one should be asked to live with that kind of shame and humiliation, that kind of hellish notoriety, especially not you. You were right to go south and ask your father to find you the safest and most ordinary of jobs. You were right to leave the shame and the humiliation to Milomre Blocj and to start afresh with Lorimer Black.

The Book of Transfiguration

Chapter 19

Lorimer stood shivering on the corner of Pall Mall and St James's, watching his breath cloud and hang almost motionless in front of him beneath the ochre glow of the streetlamps, as if it were reluctant to be dispersed and wanted to be breathed back into his warm lungs again. It had every sign of being another hard frost tonight but at least he did not have to worry about its effect on the Toyota's bodywork. Small mercies, duly thankful. He blew into his cupped hands and stamped his feet. It was ten past six – he would wait another five minutes and then he'd –

Across the street a large car stopped and a man in a dark blue overcoat climbed out and disappeared up some steps into a building.

'Mr Black?'

Lorimer turned to confront a diminutive, portly man, smiling warmly. He seemed top-heavy, all chest and gut and gave the impression of teetering forward, on the edge of losing his balance. He had thick sandy hair combed back in a rock 'n' roller's tidy quiff. He must have been in his sixties, his face worn and weather-beaten despite his apple cheeks and wobbly jowls. A green loden-coat and brown trilby he'd raised from his head in greeting sat oddly on him, as if he'd borrowed them from some other man.

'Freeze your b-b-balls off,' the little man said, jocularly, replacing his hat and extending his hand. 'Dirk van Meer.'

'How do you do?' Lorimer said, very surprised. Oddly enough, the accent sounded more Irish than South African.

'I wanted to meet you myself,' he said, 'in order to underline the importance of what I'm going to say. Didn't want an intermediary, you see.'

'Oh?'

'My associates have already spoken to your friend Mr Wiles and he's been most co-operative.'

'As I keep saying to people: I simply don't understand what's going on.'

'Ah, but you're an intelligent young fellow and soon you'll be able to add up two and two. I wanted to talk to you before you figured out it was four.'

'Look, Wiles couldn't tell me anything.'

'The trouble is, Mr Black, you know more than you think. Sheer bad luck.'

Sheer Achimota, Lorimer thought, for some reason. Powerful ju-ju.

'It's terribly simple,' van Meer went on, genially. 'All I require of you is your silence and your promise to remain silent.'

'You have my promise,' Lorimer said at once. 'Unequivocally.' He would promise this jolly, smiling gnome anything. Somehow the complete absence of threat in his voice and manner was terrifying, spoke of awesome power.

'Good,' van Meer said, taking his arm and turning him so that he faced up St James's. He pointed at a building. 'You know that club there? Yes, there. Go inside and ask for Sir Simon Sherriffmuir. He'll have some interesting news for you.' He gave Lorimer a little pat on the shoulder. 'I'm so glad we understand each other. Mum's the word.' He theatrically put his finger to his lips, and backed away, adding with no trace of threat in his voice at all, 'I will hold you to your unequivocal promise, Mr Black. Be assured.'

Lorimer found this remark more distressing and gut-churning than a cut-throat razor waved in his face and felt his mouth dry and his gorge contract. Van Meer gave a wheezy chortle, a wave and wandered off along Pall Mall.

The uniformed porter took Lorimer's coat and with an elegant gesture of the arm indicated the bar.

'You'll find Sir Simon in there, sir.'

Lorimer looked about him: early evening and the place was quiet. Through a door he caught a glimpse of a large room with armchairs set around round polished tables and large, undistinguished nineteenth-century portraits. As he moved to the bar he saw green baize noticeboards, staff walking briskly and quietly to and fro. The feel was institutional rather than clubby – as he imagined the officers' mess of a grand regiment might be in time of peace, or the committee rooms of some venerable philanthropic society. His feeling of not belonging was acute and destabilizing.

Sir Simon was standing at the bar, Hogg beside him, darkly and greyly suited, hair oiled back. A smarter Hogg than the one he knew, more menacing somehow, and greeting him with no smile, though Sir Simon was affability itself, asking him what he would drink, recommending a special brand of Scotch – a suggestion backed up with a swift and pointed anecdote – steering him to a corner table where the three of them sat down in scarred leather armchairs. Hogg lit one of his filterless cigarettes, and Sir Simon offered a small black cheroot (politely declined). Smoking material was ignited, smoke soon dominated the atmosphere, and there was some conversation about the severity of the weather and hopelessness of seeking for signs of spring. Lorimer dutifully agreed with everything that was said, and waited.

'You spoke to Dirk,' Sir Simon observed, finally. 'He particularly wanted to meet you.'

'I can't think why.'

'You understood what he – what we – are asking of you?'

'Discretion?'

'Absolutely. Absolute discretion.'

Lorimer could not help but look over at Hogg, who was leaning back in his chair, thighs crossed, puffing serenely at his cigarette. Sir Simon noticed.

'George is completely *au fait*. There is no remaining problem, I think that's fair comment, George, isn't it?'

'Fair as trousers,' Hogg said.

Sir Simon smiled. 'We want you back at GGH, Lorimer. But not now, in a year or so.'

'May I ask why?'

'Because you're in disgrace,' Hogg said, impatiently. 'You had to go.'

'Yes, you should never have gone to Boomslang,' Sir Simon said disapprovingly, yet with sympathy. 'That put you beyond the pale, especially as far as Dirk was concerned.'

Lorimer was baffled. 'Look, I was only trying –'

'Pull the other one, Black,' Hogg said with some of his old aggression. 'You were digging for dirt to save your decomposing hide.'

'For some answers. And on your instructions.'

'That's a pile of bollocks –'

'– Put it this way,' Sir Simon interrupted. 'We have to be seen to have acted. In case. There *were* serious irregularities.'

'Not mine,' Lorimer said, with some force. 'I was just doing my job.'

'Every time I hear that excuse,' Hogg said, vehemently, 'I reach for my guillotine.'

'We know you think you were,' Sir Simon said, more emolliently, 'but that would not be apparent at all to . . . to others, to outsiders. That's why it's better to let you go.'

To become what, Lorimer wondered, cynically? The lone trader, the rogue dealer, the berserk broker? More like the lost loss adjuster. Deniability was heavy in the air along with the blue smoke from Sir Simon's foul cheroot. There had been some serious level of knavery here, Lorimer thought, some particularly devious and particularly profitable malversation, as it was known, to make these powerful men so calmly concerned. He wondered if he would ever discover what had really been at stake in the Fedora Palace affair, what the true rewards were for the participants. He strongly doubted it.

'So – I'm the scapegoat?'

'That's an unnecessarily crude way of putting it.'

'Or you could say I'm your insurance.'

'The analogy is inappropriate.'

'What about Torquil?' Lorimer persisted. 'He was the one that fouled up in the first place.'

'Torquil is Sir Simon's godson,' Hogg said, as if that would put an end to all further conversation.

'It's for the best if Torquil is back at Fortress Sure where I can keep an eye on him,' Sir Simon said, raising a finger to summon the bar steward for another round of drinks. 'I'm sorry it has to be you, Lorimer, but it's better this way, long term.' Drinks were replenished and Sir Simon raised his glass, examining the smoky amber of his whisky against the shaded glow of a nearby lamp.

Better for who, Lorimer thought. For whom?

Sir Simon smelt then sipped his drink – he was clearly in mellow mood.

'Mud doesn't stick in our world,' he said, reflectively, almost with a tone of pleasant surprise. 'That's one of the great advantages about this place. Come back in a year – you'll find everyone has short memories.'

Mud doesn't stick? Suddenly he was mud-plastered. He was being sacked and with it only the compensation of a vague promise to sweeten the pill.

'There is one thing I would ask in return for my . . . discretion,' he said, sensing Hogg coiling up angrily.

'You're in no position to ask for –'

'– Just a phone call.' Lorimer scribbled down the details from the scrap of paper in his pocket on to a paper napkin. 'I'd like Mr Hogg to call this person, Mrs Mary Vernon, or leave a message, and confirm I had nothing to do with the Dupree adjust.'

'Make any sense to you, George?' Sir Simon looked to Hogg for confirmation.

Hogg took the napkin from Lorimer. 'As easy as counting chickens,' he said, standing up, hitching his trousers over his belly and striding off.

Sir Simon Sherriffmuir smiled at Lorimer. 'You know,

I can practically hear your brain working, dear boy. It's not an advantage. Cultivate a certain languor. A certain *ennui*. A sharp brain like yours, rudely exposed – it worries people in our world. Keep your light under a gigantic pile of bushels, that's my advice, and you'll go much further.'

'It's all very well for you to say.'

'Of course it is. Stop thinking, Lorimer, don't worry about the big picture, trying to figure out how it all fits. That was what was bothering George. That was why he was becoming so . . . irate. Now he understands, now he's an even richer man. And he's happy. My advice to you is to go away, take a holiday. Go skiing. Go to Australia, people tell me it's a wonderful place. Have fun. Then come back in a year and give us a call.' He stood slowly up, the meeting was over. Lorimer allowed himself briefly to admire the exact waisting of Sir Simon's jacket, its cut audaciously longer than standard.

'All will be well, Lorimer, all will be well.'

He took Sir Simon's spread-fingered hand, feeling the latent power in his grip, its firmness, its generous pressure, its sure confidence. It was all lies, of course, but beautiful, de luxe lies, the work of a master craftsman.

'See you next year, Lorimer. Expect great things.'

In the hall he met Hogg coming back. They side-stepped each other.

'I left a message,' Hogg said. 'Everything's covered.'

'Many thanks.'

Hogg scratched his cheek. 'Well, here we are, Lorimer.'

'Here we are, Mr Hogg.'

'What do you want, Lorimer, what're you after?'

'Nothing. I've got what I want.'

'Why are you looking at me like that, then?'

'Like what?'

'I want to ask you something: did you tell anyone that I was pursuing an amorous liaison with Felicia Pickersgill?'

'No. Are you?'

'I'll have your tripes for garters, Lorimer, if you're lying to me.'

'I'm not lying.'

'Why did you do it?'

'What?'

'Dig, dig, dig. When the cranes fly south, Lorimer, the farmer rests on his spade.'

'You sound like my grandmother.'

'There's something feminine about your looks, anyone ever told you that? You're a handsome young man, Lorimer.'

'*Et in arcadia ego.*'

'You could go far. In any profession.'

'I've got a chance to start a fish farm.'

'The farming of fish, now there's a fascinating *métier.*'

'Trout and salmon.'

'Halibut and the sea bream.'

'Cod and sole.'

'The John Dory. A wonderful fish.'

'If I start it up I'll invite you down. It's in Guildford.'

'I'm afraid I won't set foot in Surrey. Sussex, though, now there's a decent county.'

'Well, I'd better be going, Mr Hogg.'

Hogg's face froze, his nostrils flared and then, after a moment, he stretched out his hand. Lorimer shook it – Hogg had a grip of iron and Lorimer felt his knuckles grind.

'Send me a Christmas card. I'll send you one. It'll be our signal.'

'Definitely, Mr Hogg.'

Hogg turned, and then immediately turned back.

'Change is in the nature of things, Lorimer.'

'The disturbance of anticipation, Mr Hogg.'

'Good lad.'

'Cheerio, then.'

'I'll keep your seat warm,' Hogg said thoughtfully, then, 'and don't play silly buggers, OK?'

He strode off with his burly bosun's swagger, a steward pausing politely to let him pass. In the bar Lorimer saw Hogg sit grandly down and accept one of Sir Simon's cheroots.

Waiting for him at the bottom of the club steps was Kenneth Rintoul. Kenneth Rintoul in his thin black leather greatcoat and a woollen cap standing at the blurry fan of light cast by the great lamps flanking the door.

'Mr Black.'

Lorimer raised his hands protectively and, he hoped, threateningly, as if they betokened a youth spent in ju-jitsu clubs.

'Watch it, Rintoul. I have friends in there.'

'I know. A Mr Hogg told me to meet you here.'

Lorimer glanced over his shoulder, expecting to see Hogg and Sherriffmuir peering out of the window, noses flattened on the pane – or else some covert *paparazzo* recording this encounter as evidence. Evidence – their insurance.

Lorimer began to walk quickly down the slope towards St James's Palace, Rintoul kept pace with him, easily.

'I want to apologize, Mr Black. I want to thank you.'

'Oh yeah?'

'The law suit's been dropped. Hogg says this is all thanks to you.'

'Don't mention it.' Lorimer was deep in urgent thought.

'And I want to apologize, personally, for my earlier, ah, remarks and actions. The phone calls, etcetera. I was out of order.'

'No problem.'

'I can't tell you what this means to me.' Rintoul had grabbed Lorimer's right hand and was shaking it vigorously. Lorimer gently retrieved it, convinced this gratitude was now captured on film. 'What it means to me and Deano.'

'Could I ask you a couple of questions?'

'Ask away, Mr Black.'

'Simply as a matter of curiosity, tie up some loose ends,' Lorimer said. 'Have there been any instances of, of car vandalism near your office?'

'Funny you should mention it,' Rintoul said. 'You know the big wholesale carpet warehouse underneath the office. The owner had his Merc well trashed the other night. Write-off. It's happening all over, Mr Black. Kids, junkies, eco-warriors. They blame the motor car for all their problems.'

'But it was you who set my car on fire.'

'I have to admit it was Deano – he was a desperate man, hard to restrain.'

'One other thing: did you write BASTA on my car bonnet in letters of sand? BASTA.'

'BASTA . . . Wasn't me, I swear. What's the logic in writing in sand? If you know what I mean?'

'Fair point.'

Destined to remain one of life's mysteries, then,

Lorimer thought. Well, not everything could be explained in life, of course. Hogg would echo that – with his urge to disturb all anticipations. Rintoul bade him a warm goodbye and strolled off up Pall Mall, just like Dirk van Meer before him, his stride jaunty, his head held back. Lorimer saw him pause and then the flare of a match silhouetted his woollen cap. All was well in Kenneth Rintoul's world.

Lorimer walked past Clarence House, heading for the wide boulevard of the Mall, intending to hail a taxi, but then deciding to walk home and think things through, stroll the city streets and try to figure out, despite Sir Simon's good counsel, just exactly what was going on and why his life was being steadily torn apart. He turned right under the leafless plane trees, his feet crunching on the gravel, and headed towards the broad, solid, floodlit façade of the palace. A flag was flying – so, they were home tonight, good, he liked to know that, when they came and went, he liked them to be there in their big, solid palace, fellow citizens – after a fashion – the thought was obscurely comforting.

Turning into Lupus Crescent, Lorimer saw a small group of people gathered around Marlobe's flower trolley. He checked his collar was as high as possible, hunched his head down into his shoulders and crossed the street to the other side.

'Oi,' Marlobe beckoned him over imperiously. Wearily, he went.

'I undercharged you on them tulips,' Marlobe said. 'You owe me two quid.'

Great, wonderful, have a nice day, Lorimer thought, and searched his pockets for change. He finally gave

Marlobe a ten pound note and waited while he fetched out and re-opened his cash box, idly taking in the others gathered under the battery-powered electric light clipped to the awning. There was a young man and young woman whom he did not recognize and Marlobe's regular crony with the slushing voice. To his minor surprise – nothing was ever going to surprise him in a major way again – they were all looking at the pages of a porno-graphic magazine, all sprawling, spatchcocked flesh tones on a double spread, debating some point about one of the models. Marlobe, Lorimer's change in his hand, paused to chip in, jabbing his finger at one particular photograph.

'It's you,' he said to the young woman. 'It's you, plain as day. Look at it.'

The girl – she was eighteen, twenty, forty-five – slapped his arm and laughed.

'Get away,' she said. 'Dirty bastard.'

'Wages not enough for you?' Marlobe leered. 'Taken up a bit of modelling, eh? Have you? Eh?' Lorimer recognized her now as someone who worked in their local post office; she had a thin, lively face spoilt by a small mouth.

'It's you,' Marlobe persisted. 'Spitting image. You're moonlighting.'

'Horrible bush,' Slushing-Voice opined.

'You're terrible,' she said, giggling, administering another weak slap to Marlobe's forearm. 'Come on, Malcolm,' she said to her beau. 'He's terrible, isn't he?' They walked away, laughing, with many an over-the-shoulder rejoinder.

'That's one horrible bush,' said Slushing-Voice.

'Let me see,' Marlobe said, poring over the glossy

pages. 'That's her, or it's her twin sister, or I'm a monkey's arsehole. She's got a sort of mole on her thigh, look.'

'She didn't deny it, eh?' said Slushing-Voice, knowingly. 'Bit of a give-away, that.'

Marlobe finally held out Lorimer's change, still scrutinizing the pictures. 'What I should've done is asked her to drop her knickers so's I could've checked on the mole.'

'If she's got a mole on her thigh . . .' Slushing-Voice deduced.

'Could I have my change please?'

'I should've asked her if she had a mole.'

'Look at the minge on that one.'

'God. What a horrible cunt.'

'You're disgusting,' Lorimer said.

'Say again?'

'You're disgusting, shameful. I'm ashamed to think we're both human beings.'

'Just a bit of fun, mate,' Marlobe said, with his aggressive smile breaking across his face. 'Bit of chat. You fuck off out of it if you don't like it. No one asked you to eavesdrop, did they?'

'Yeah,' said Slushing-Voice. 'Just a bit of fun.'

'You're filth. To talk like that in front of her. To talk like that.'

'She weren't complaining.'

'Yeah. Fuck off. Poncey wanker.'

Lorimer, later, did not know what made him do it, indeed he did not know how he even managed to do it but, strengthened by the cumulative power bestowed on him by the day's trials and humiliations, he stepped forward and took a grip of the lower rim of Marlobe's flower shack and heaved. Whether it was because the rear flaps were still hinged out, making the edifice top-heavy, or whether it was simple good timing, of the sort weightlifters experience when they go for that final jerk and press, Lorimer did not know, nor could ever evaluate, but – in the event – the whole trolley went over with a dull but satisfyingly heavy bang and a great rushing of water as the metal vases and buckets voided themselves.

Marlobe and Slushing-Voice looked on in shock and some fear.

'Fuck me,' said Slushing-Voice.

Marlobe looked suddenly unmanned at this display of strength, all his confidence gone. He took half a step towards Lorimer, then stepped back. Lorimer realized he had his fists raised, his face locked in a grimace, full of hate.

'There was no call for that,' Marlobe said in a small voice. 'No call at all. Bloody hell. Bastard.' He bent down and began to pick up scattered flowers. 'Look at my flowers.'

'The next time you see her,' Lorimer said, 'apologize.'

'We'll get you, wanker! We'll sort you, wanker!' Lorimer heard Slushing-Voice bravely shout after him as he walked down Lupus Crescent. He could feel the adrenalin tremors and shiverings still firing in his body, not sure if it were the residue of his anger or merely the after-effect of his astonishing physical exertion. He opened the door, crossed the dark hall (thinking suddenly of Lady Haigh) and plodded up his stairs, feeling gloom and remorse, self-pity and depression struggling to take possession of his soul.

He stood in his hallway trying to calm himself, trying to bring his ragged breathing under control, and rested his palm talismanically on the crown of his Greek helmet.

An unfamiliar scratching noise on his carpet made

him look round and he saw Jupiter nose open the door that led into the sitting room.

'Hello, boy,' he said, his voice brimming with pleasure and welcome, suddenly understanding why people kept dogs as pets, as if it were a revelation. He crouched to scratch Jupiter's neck, pound his ribs, play with his flapping ears. 'I've had a stinking, rotten, vile, depressing, stinking, shitty, vile, rotten day,' he said, suddenly realizing also why people talked to their dogs as if they could be understood. He needed some comfort, some reassurance, some notion of protection, somewhere safe.

He stood up, closed his eyes, opened them, saw his helmet there, picked it up, turned it in his hands and put it on.

It fitted him perfectly, or rather fitted him too perfectly, slipping on as if it had been made for him; and the moment he slid it on, round the back of his head over the bump of his prominent occipital bone, and felt it fit snugly under, almost with an audible click, he knew, he knew at once, that it would not come off.

He tried to take it off, of course, but it was the perfect curve round the back of the helmet, offsetting the small flare of the nape-guard, an elongated, inverted S-shape, a line he had often admired, that made removal impossible. It seemed as if the form of the helmet was designed for a head of exactly his phrenological configuration (perhaps, he suddenly thought, that was what he had subconsciously realized when he saw it? Sensed that recognition and so felt compelled to buy it?). His exact configuration but slightly smaller all round. The nose-guard lay parallel to the bridge of his nose, but not touching, ending the ideal one centimetre beyond his nose's tip. The oval eye cutouts followed exactly the margin of the bones around the orbital cavity, the jut of the cheek-plates mimicked precisely the forward thrust of his jaw-bone.

He studied his reflection in the sitting-room mirror and liked what he saw. He looked good, he looked tremendous, in fact, exactly like a warrior, a Greek warrior, eyes gleaming behind the rigid metal features of the helmet, mouth firm between the corroded jade-coloured blades of the cheek-plates. The suit, the shirt and the tie looked incongruous but from the neck up he could have passed, he thought, for a minor classical deity.

A minor classical deity with a major problem, he concluded, as he refilled Jupiter's water bowl and, for want of anything else, provided him with some sustenance in the form of squares of bread soaked in milk which, he was glad to see, Jupiter ate with tongue-smacking gusto.

He spent another ten fruitless minutes trying to ease the helmet off, but in vain. What to do? What to do? He paced about his flat – Jupiter dozing, sprawled indelicately on the sofa, cock and balls on show, quite at home – catching the occasional satisfying glimpse of this helmeted figure as it strode past the mirror on the mantelpiece, to and fro, the metal head with its shadowed oval eyes, sternly expressionless.

398. The Proof of Armour. The armed man could not afford to take chances, and so his equipment had to be 'proved', guaranteed that it could withstand the impact of a point blank thrust from a lance or shot from an arrow, and, later, from a pistol, arquebus, caliver and musket. In the Musée d'Artillerie the breastplate of the Duc de Guise is of great thickness and there are three bullet marks on it, none of which has penetrated.

It was, paradoxically, this very fact – that armour was indeed proof against firearms (and not that the arrival of firearms made armour obsolete) – which led to it being abandoned. In the seventeenth century Sir John Ludlow noted that, 'Where there was some reason to fear the violence of muskets and pistols they made their armour thicker than before and have now so far exceeded that, instead of armour, they have laden their bodies with anvils. The armour that they now carry is so heavy that its weight will benumb a gentleman's shoulders of thirty-five years of age.'

The armoured man had proved that his suit of tempered steel could withstand the most powerful weapons in use, but in so doing discovered that the increase in the heaviness of the metal in which he clad his body produced a weight that became burdensome in the extreme and, finally, insupportable.

The Book of Transfiguration

'Hi, Slobodan, it's Milo. Got a bit of a problem here.'

'Talk to me, Milo.'

'How do you fancy owning a dog?'

Slobodan was over in half an hour and looked admiringly round Lorimer's flat.

'Nice place, Milo. Real smart, yeah?' He rapped his knuckles on the helmet. 'Won't budge, eh?'

'No. This is Jupiter.'

Slobodan knelt by the sofa and gave Jupiter a thorough scratching, patting, going over. 'He's a nice old fella. Ain't you, boy? Going to come and live with Lobby, eh, old fella?' Jupiter put up with his ministrations uncomplainingly.

'Why did you put that helmet on, you great berk?' Slobodan asked.

'I felt like it.'

'Not like you, Milo, do something so daft.'

'Give me a minute to tidy some things away,' he said. While he had been waiting for his brother to arrive a vague plan of action had begun to establish itself in his mind. He collected crucial documents and his passport, threw some clothes, a few CDs and *The Book of Transfiguration* into a grip and was ready.

'Where to, bro?' Slobodan asked.

'Emergency. Kensington and Chelsea Hospital.'

It was a strange moment leaving number 11 and walking down Lupus Crescent with Slobodan and Jupiter. The world he saw was confined by the edges of the eye-holes, and he was aware of the blackness beyond the metal edge defining his field of vision, though he could no longer feel the weight of the helmet, as if the beaten bronze had fused with the bones of his skull and had become one, man and helmet, helmed-man, manhelmet, helmetman. Helmetman, cartoon hero, minor deity, toppler of flower vans, scourge of the foul-mouthed and ungallant, eliciting apologies for insulted damsels. He was pleased to see that Marlobe and Slushing-Voice had clearly been unable to right the overturned flower trolley, still lying on its side amidst a fritter of petals and vegetation and a widening pool of flower water. The helmeted warrior passed by his fallen prey and climbed aboard his burnished chariot.

'Going well?' Lorimer asked as the Cortina accelerated up Lupus Street.

'Like a dream. Built to last, these cars. Magic.'

Slobodan came with him to the reception area, where he was logged in with no comment and directed to sit in a waiting room with a groaning child and his mother and a young whimpering woman holding her limp wrist like a dead fish. He told Slobodan there was no need to wait and he thanked him sincerely.

'He'll be in a good home, Milo, no worries.'

'I know.'

'Funny, always fancied a dog. Thanks, mate.'

'He'll be no trouble.'

'Mercy can take him for walks.'

Mercy and Jupiter, Lorimer thought, that will be nice.

Slobodan left and Lorimer sat on, waiting. An ambulance arrived, sirens yelping, lights revolving, and a sheeted body on a trolley was rushed in and trundled through swinging double doors. The groaning child was seen, then the whimpering girl and finally it was his turn.

The cubicle was dazzlingly bright and he was faced with a dark-faced, tiny woman doctor, with big, slipping spectacles and a mass of shiny black hair loosely coiled and pinned on her head. Her name-tag said 'Dr Rathmanatathan'.

'Are you from Ceylon?' Lorimer asked as she jotted down a few details.

'Doncaster,' she said in a flat Northern accent. 'And it's currently known as Sri Lanka, these days, not Ceylon.'

'It used to be called Serendip, you know.'

She looked at him neutrally. 'So, what happened.'

'I put it on. I don't know why. It's a very valuable antique, almost three thousand years old.'

'It belongs to you?'

'Yes. I was feeling . . . feeling depressed and I just put it on. And obviously it won't come off.'

'Funnily enough that little boy had swallowed a tea-spoon. I asked him why and he said the same as you: he was feeling depressed so he swallowed a tea-spoon.' She stood up and came over to him. 'Popped it in his mouth and down it went.'

Standing, she was barely taller than he was, sitting. She gave the helmet a few tugs and saw how well it fitted. She peered into his eye-slits.

'We're going to have to cut it off, I'm afraid. Is it very expensive?'

'Yes. But never mind.'

He did feel oddly careless – care-less, literally. He would never, in any circumstances, have put this helmet on but the travails of the day had forced him into this act and he felt oddly privileged to have worn it for an hour or two. Walking around his flat, waiting for Slobodan, his mind had seemed strangely lucid and calm – probably because there was nothing he could do about the helmet-problem – but, more fancifully, he now wondered if it were something to do with the helmet itself, its very antiquity, the thought of the ancient warrior for whom it had been designed, some sort of transference –

He stopped himself: he was beginning to sound like David Watts. Sheer Achimota. There but for the grace of God.

The staff nurse, male, who came in with powerful clippers, said it was like slicing through stiff leather. He cut the helmet up the back, half way through the occipital bulge before, with a little easing, it came off.

'You could solder it back together,' Doctor Rathmanat-athan said, helpfully, handing the helmet to him.

The world was a suddenly much wider, less shadowed place and his head did feel different, lighter, swaying slightly on his neck. He touched his hair, it was damp, soaked with sweat.

'Perhaps I will,' Lorimer said, placing it in his bag, 'or

perhaps I'll leave it, to remind me of this evening. A souvenir.'

The staff nurse and Dr Rathmanatathan looked at him strangely, as if the thought had struck them that, actually, he might be mad.

'It still has value for me,' Lorimer said.

He thanked them both, shook their hands and asked reception to order him a mini-cab. There was much still left to do this evening. He told the driver to take him to the Institute of Lucid Dreams.

Chapter 20

'I think I may have got to the bottom of your problem,' Alan said. 'It's fascinating, highly complex and still, in its special Blackian way, highly ambiguous.' Alan began to pace about his lab as he elaborated on the metaphysical roots of Lorimer's sleep-disorder. 'Sleep is, in a way, Nature's preparation for death – a preparation which we experience every night. That's the real "*petit mort*" – not orgasm. A preparation for death and yet essential for life. Which is why –'

'Have you got a franking machine here?'

'No, but I've plenty of stamps.'

'You were saying –'

'Which is why your lucid dreams are so interesting, you see. In a non-Freudian, non-psychoanalytical sense. Lucid dreams are the human being's attempt to negate the death element implicit in sleep. For you they're a place where your dream-reality is controllable and anything nasty can be airbrushed away. The most frequent lucid dreamers are the worst sleepers – light sleepers, like you, and insomniacs. It's deep slumber, NREM sleep, that you unconsciously fear.'

'I just press "print", do I?'

'Yes. So, you see, Lorimer, for you, in a very profound sense, fear of deep sleep equals fear of death. But in the lucid dream you create a world where you hold sway, which you can control – the opposite of the real world, the waking world. The lucid dream is, in a way, a vision of a perfect life. I believe you light sleepers – and this may have been something you have biologically wrought upon yourself, you personally – have extra REM sleep because, unconsciously, you *want* to lucid dream, more than anything. You want to enter that perfect world where everything can be controlled. That's the key to your problem. Rid yourself of that desire and deep slumber will return. I can assure you.'

'You're very confident, Alan.'

'I haven't just been fooling around here, you know.'

'I would swop all my lucid dreams for a good night's sleep.'

'Ah, you say that, but unconsciously you prefer the opposite. Your lucid dreams offer you a glimpse of an impossible, ideal world. It's in your power to change it, but the lure of lucid dreams is hard to resist.'

Hard to resist calling all this arrant nonsense, Lorimer thought, but Alan was clearly passionate about his project and he did not want to start a row.

'Somebody once referred to this problem as "indigestion of the soul",' Lorimer said.

'That's not scientific,' Alan said. 'Sorry.'

'But, Alan, how will all this help me?'

'I haven't got all the data I need yet. When that's collected, collated and analysed, then I can tell you.'

'And that'll make me sleep better?'

'Knowledge is power, Lorimer. It will be up to you.'

He wandered away to make some coffee and Lorimer looked at what he had written. Alan was right, knowledge was power, of a sort, and partial knowledge bestowed limited power, true – but it was still up to him to exercise it or not.

He had typed out on one of the Institute's word processors a short history and interpretation of the Fedora Palace Affair, as he now mentally referred to it, and he thought he had caught its essence succinctly enough over the three pages he had compiled.

As far as he could determine there was an initial phase: a simple conspiracy to over-insure the hotel, and this was where Torquil came in as innocent dupe figure. The fool's errand, the fool proving more useful than a wise man. This was done – according to Bram Wiles's dates – prior to Gale-Harlequin's flotation on the stock market, to what end he was not entirely clear, but doubtless it looked impressive – a huge, new, very expensive luxury hotel – and made the company's assets seem healthier in the short term. He assumed that the building would be re-insured later for a figure that reflected its true worth. If, of course, the building was ever meant to be finished. It made a kind of sense: over-insuring was not a crime but there might have been an element of fraud in the desire to make Gale-Harlequin stock appear more desirable than was really the case. The floating and subsequent buyout of Gale-Harlequin was at the heart of all these manoeuvres. It merely had to look like the genuine article for a year or so – the time it took to almost build a new hotel. However, this clever but relatively straightforward plan went seriously awry through an event that no one could have predicted or pre-empted. All anticipations were seriously disturbed when a firm of sub-contractors, Edmund, Rintoul, started a small fire on an upper floor in order to escape penalty clause payments that were about to fall due. The small fire spread, became a large one, caused much damage, an insurance claim had to be filed and the anomalous nature of Gale-Harlequin's insurance policy with Fortress Sure was accidently revealed.

The processes of claim assessment and loss adjustment automatically moved into action. An adjustment of the loss was proposed and instantly accepted in order to have the incident blow over as quickly as possible, because the large cash-for-share takeover bid was in the offing from a firm called Racine Securities. And who benefited from the Racine Securities buyout? Why, the shareholders of Gale-Harlequin, all bona fide investors, it seemed, according to Bram Wiles, all except for one mysterious offshore entity called Ray Von TL.

Lorimer would bet good money that the figures behind Ray Von TL would include, amongst others, Francis Home, Dirk van Meer and, quite probably, Sir Simon Sherriffmuir.

Further, Dirk van Meer's Boomslang Properties bought the fire-damaged, partially demolished hotel at, Lorimer would guess, a very reasonable price.

Dirk van Meer, Lorimer would further wager, probably had a stake in Racine Securities. In other words, to untangle the knot somewhat, one part of his empire had simply bought a smaller part – money appeared to be changing hands, and large profits ensued for key participants.

Contemplating the outline of what went on, and who bought what, adding some smart guesswork to known fact, Lorimer concluded that this just about sketched out the outlines of the Fedora Palace Affair. Doubtless there were other ramifications he would never discover but some construction of this order began to shed a dim but revealing light on the mysterious events in which he had been peripherally involved.

What was more, he couldn't even swear that any of this was illegal, but the fact that he had been kicked out of GGH, had been set up *vis à vis* Rintoul, and was clearly functioning as scapegoat in waiting, made him almost sure that there were secrets here that important people wished to remain secret. It followed certain classic structures – notably the sending in of a fool – Torquil – confident that the fool would be true to his nature. Torquil was meant to foul up the insurance of the Fedora Palace and, with a little indirect nudging and pointing by Sir Simon, duly had.

Except, the other classic rule also applied: if you can think of a hundred things that can go wrong, and factor them into your plan, you will be struck down by the hundred and first. No one had calculated on the humdrum duplicity of a small firm of Peckham builders. But there had proved enough swift resourcefulness, enough strength in depth and power and influence to provide efficient damage-limitation: a culpable party was set up (Lorimer) and George Hogg bought off and brought in. An extra snout at the trough was a small price to pay. Gale, Home, van Meer and Sir Simon had all cleared at least ten million, so Lorimer had roughly calculated, probably more. God alone knew what Dirk van Meer was making out of the deals.

Lorimer printed ten copies of his 'Report into Certain Malpractices to do with the Insurance of the Fedora Palace Hotel' and placed them in envelopes he had already addressed to the Serious Fraud Office and the financial editors of the daily and Sunday editions of the broadsheet newspapers. Alan, as promised, produced a sheet of first-class stamps and Lorimer set about licking and pasting them down.

'Will you post these for me?' he asked. 'In the morning?'

'Are you sure you're doing the right thing?'

'No.'

'Well, that's all right, then. Of course I will.'

Lorimer had said only he was revealing a suspected fraud – he added in further explanation, 'Everyone's assuming I'll say nothing and I just hate being taken for granted.'

'You'll be cast out from paradise.'

'It doesn't seem quite so paradisaical these days. Anyway, I got what I wanted.'

Alan took the pile of envelopes from him and put them in his out-tray.

'I was sorry to hear about old Lady H.,' Alan said. 'But I think she was always a bit suspicious of me.'

'Never. Why do you think that?'

'Because . . .' Alan wiggled a spread palm. 'Once an old colonial always an old colonial.'

'Because you're black? Ridiculous.'

'There was always some reserve.'

'Nonsense. She liked you. She was proud to have a Doctor of Philosophy in the building.' Lorimer stood up. 'Where can I get hold of a mini-cab at this time of night?'

*399. **Irrationality**. I do not mind contradictions, paradoxes, puzzles and ambiguities. What is the point of 'minding' something as inevitable and entrenched in our nature as our digestive system is in our body? Of course we can be rational and sensible but often so much of what defines us is the opposite – irrational and nonsensical. I am defined by the fact that I consider Jill to be beautiful and Jane* *to be unattractive, by the fact that I prefer blue-coloured things to green, by my taste for tomato juice and disdain for tomato sauce, and that sometimes rain falling will make me sad and at other times make me happy. I can't explain these choices but they and their kind contribute to the person I am as much as anything more reasoned and considered. I am as much myself 'irrational' as I am 'rational'. If this is true for me then it must be true for Flavia. Perhaps we are all equally irrational as we blunder onwards. Perhaps, in the end, this is what really distinguishes us from complex, powerful and all-capable machines, from the robots and computers that run our lives for us. This is what makes us human.*

The Book of Transfiguration

The downstairs lights were on in his Silvertown house, he was excited to see and, unlocking the front door quietly, he smelt spices, cooked tomatoes, cigarette smoke. There was a bunch of freesias in a jar in the kitchen and a dirty plate in the sink. He put his bag down and crept upstairs, his heart struggling in its cavity as if desperate to break out. Pushing open his bedroom door a few inches he saw Flavia sleeping in his bed. She was naked and one breast was exposed, the nipple small, perfectly round and darkly pigmented.

Downstairs, he switched on the television and banged about in the kitchen making tea. In five minutes or so Flavia appeared, in a dressing gown, hair mussed, sleepy. Her hair was the colour of raven's wings, with a shimmer of inky blue and bottle green, making her skin seem so pale it was almost a bloodless white, the natural pink of her lips lurid and rose-red beside it. She accepted a mug of tea from him and sat there for a while, not saying much, letting consciousness reclaim her.

'How long have you been here?' he said.

'Since late last night. It's not exactly homey, is it?'

'No.'

'So, how was your day, darling?'

'Terrible.'

'I'm going to Vienna in the morning,' she said. 'I've got a job.'

'What?'

'A British Council touring production of *Othello*.'

'Are you Desdemona?'

'Of course.'

'Sounds nice. Shakespeare in Vienna.'

'Better than life at home, I can tell you.'

'He didn't hit you or anything, did he?'

'Not quite. He's just vile. Impossible.' She frowned, as if the notion had just struck her. 'I'm not going back.'

'Good.'

She reached out and took his hand. 'But I don't want to sleep with you tonight. Not tonight. I don't think it would be wise.'

'Of course.' Lorimer nodded many times, hoping his disappointment wouldn't show. 'I'll be in the spare room.'

She stood up and moved slowly to where he was sitting and put her arms around his head, folded her arms round his head and pulled his face to her belly. He closed his eyes and drew her warm bed-smell into his lungs, like a sleeping draught.

'Milo,' she said, and chuckled. He could hear her laugh reverberate through her body, vibrations on his face. She bent her neck and kissed his forehead.

'Will you call me when you get back from Vienna?' he said.

'Maybe. Maybe I'll stay out there for a while, let Gilbert stew.'

'I think we could be very happy.'

She pulled back his head so she could look at him better, her fingers gripping the hair behind his ears. She clicked her teeth together a few times and stared at him deeply.

'I think . . . I think you might be right. It was fate that brought us together, wasn't it?'

'I'm not quite so sure where I stand on fate these days. I would have tracked you down, one way or another.'

'But I might not have liked you.'

'Well, it's a point, I suppose.'

'Lucky for you I do, Milo, lucky for you.' She bent her head and kissed him again, gently, on the lips.

Lorimer unwrapped a new blanket and spread it on the spare bed in the little room upstairs under the roof. He took off his clothes and slid between the mattress and the prickly wool. He heard her in the corridor and for a brief moment fantasized that she might knock on his door – but after a few moments there was the sound of the toilet flushing.

He slept the night through, uninterrupted and completely dreamless. He woke at eight o'clock, parched and hungry, pulled on his trousers and stumbled downstairs where he found her note in her large and acutely slanting hand.

You can come with me to Vienna if you like. Air Austria, Heathrow, terminal 3, 11.45. But I can't promise you anything. I can't promise anything will last. You must know that – if you decide to come. F.

What was it with her, he thought, smiling, always these tests, these challenges? But he knew at once what he would do: this seemed far and away the best deal life had ever offered him and he accepted it unreflectingly and instantly. Unequivocally. He would go to Vienna and be with Flavia Malinverno – this would make him happy.

As he dressed he thought: I will be with her but she will not commit, she would not promise how long it would last. Well, neither could he. Neither could anyone, really. How long will anything last? How many miles can a pony gallop, as his grandmother would say. This shaky formula for his future happiness was as solid as anything else in this world, after all. There was no arguing with that.

400. Integumentary Systems. *The arming of a man began at the feet and as far as possible each piece subsequently put on overlapped that beneath it. The arming of a man, therefore, was carried out in the following order: sollerets or sabatons, jambs, knee-cops, cuisses, skirt of mail, gorget, breast and back plates, brassards, pauldrons, gauntlets and, finally, the helmet.*

Every living organism is separated from its environment by a covering, or integument, that delimits its body. It seems to me that the process of adding an extra integument is unique to our species and easily understandable – we all want extra protection for our soft and vulnerable bodies. But is it unique to our species? What other creature exhibits this same sense of precaution and seeks out this kind of protective armour? Molluscs, barnacles, mussels, oysters, tortoises, hedgehogs, armadillos, porcupines, rhinos all grow their own. Only the hermit crab, as far as I can recall, searches for empty shells, of whelks or periwinkles, or indeed any other hollow object and crawls inside, to serve as shelter and protection of the body. Homo sapiens and Eupagarus bernhardus – perhaps we are more closely related than we think. The hermit crab finds its suit of armour and keeps it on, but, as the crab grows, it periodically is obliged to leave its shell and travel the sandy undulations of the ocean floor, unprotected for a while, soft and vulnerable, until it finds a larger shell and crawls inside again.

The Book of Transfiguration

He called for a black cab and while he was waiting he took his ruined Greek helmet from his bag and placed it on the mantelpiece above the gas log-fire. From the front it looked perfect, no one could see the triangular slice dividing the back. He would put Lupus Crescent on the market, call Alan from Vienna, ask him to organize things, and pay Ivan back – and that would be the end of his helmet-collecting days.

He sat in the back of the cab, strangely serene as it left Albion Village, making his last long trajectory across the city. From Silvertown, to Silvertown Way, left at Canning Town flyover, through the Limehouse Link, past the Tower, Tower Hill, Lower Thames Street and on to the Embankment, under the Charing Cross railway bridge, on past Northumberland Avenue, left at Horseguards, right at Whitehall, on through Parliament Square, passing Vauxhall, Chelsea, Albert and Battersea Bridges as the cab motored along beside the restless brown river, then swinging round on to Finborough Road, cutting across Fulham and Old Brompton Road, on past Earls Court and into Talgarth Road, into the Great West Road then the A4 and climbing up on to the elevated section of the M4, the sprawling city spread below on either side, continuing west on the motorway until Junction 4 and then left into Heathrow Central Area and finally,

Terminal Three. This was one of the longest sweeps ever, from furthest east to furthest west, and he thought of all the many journeys he had made throughout his working life, crisscrossing the gigantic city, north and south, all the points of the compass, miles and miles, hours and hours of time . . .

Vienna was smaller, he thought, easier to handle, everything within walking distance. He and Flavia would stroll hand in hand from Stephansplatz to Schönlaterngasse, go to the opera, look at the Klimts and the Schieles, they might take a boat trip on the Danube, admire the topiary in the Augarten. They might stay on or set off on their travels together, he mused, pleasantly. Anything was possible, once they were there, anything.

He thought of other trajectories starting that morning: his ten letters moving from post box to sorting office and then making their individual routes to their respective addressees. And what would happen then? Nothing? A little ripple of controversy? A minor scandal? Some discreet fixing, words in important ears and then all forgotten? . . .

He wasn't entirely sure. If he did nothing, nothing would happen, Lorimer knew; and if and when he went back in a year, as they so warmly encouraged him, looking for his old job back, nothing would happen then. Sad smiles of regret, hands spread, shrugs of impotence. Times have changed, Lorimer, things have moved on, so sorry, restructurings, new priorities, that was then, this is now . . .

They had cut him loose and he was drifting away, just as they wished, but not so far for the moment that the finger of blame couldn't be angrily pointed at him if an emergency arose. But then, as more time intervened and short memories grew shorter, the happier and more relaxed they would be. 'Mud doesn't stick in our world,' Sir Simon had complacently but astutely observed. Lorimer could drift over the horizon as far as they were concerned: out of sight, very definitely out of mind.

He knew also that any power he held over them was limited and very short-term. The measure of it was that he had managed to compel Hogg to phone Mrs Vernon and his own 'punishment' was merely a sacking. He had some leverage but it would swiftly become nugatory. So now was the time to strike: he had added up two and two and had arrived at his version of four, just as Dirk Van Meer had surmised. But they thought he was dealt with now, silenced by false promises, drifting away out of their lives, seduced by the chimerical prospect of a return to the select club one day. But he was not so guileless and not quite dealt with, not yet. Now was time to see if some mud would stick: perhaps he could still disturb all anticipations.

As the cab swept up the elevated section of the M4 his eye was caught and held by a new advertising poster – a large white field and printed across it in black, lower case child's handwriting, 'sheer achimota'. David Watts was not wasting any time alerting the world to the coming of Sheer Achimota. Sheer Achimota would happen, that's what. Suddenly Sheer Achimota seemed finally to be working for him too, in his own life.

He bought his Air Austria ticket to Vienna and showed his passport at immigration. He looked for Flavia in the teeming shopping mall that was Terminal Three but he could see no sign of her. He waited five minutes outside the ladies' toilet but she did not emerge and small tremors of worry began to affect him. There were many people in the place, that was true, hundreds, it was all too easy to miss one another. Then the thought came to him, unwelcome: this couldn't be another of her crazy tricks, could it? Her unpredictable reversals? This whole *Othello* in Vienna number? Not another of her sly admonishments? No, surely not. Not Flavia. Not now. He thought of last night and it made him banish his doubts. He strode confidently to the information desk.

'I wonder if you could page my friend, Flavia Malinverno. She's somewhere in here and I can't find her. Flavia Malinverno.'

'Certainly, sir. And you are Mister –?'

'I'm –' he paused, thought fast. 'Just tell her it's Milo. Tell her Milo's here.'

He heard his new name – his old name – echo out among the bright shops and bars, the cafeterias and the burger franchises. She would hear it, he knew, and she would come; in fact he could see her in his mind's eye, looking up from whatever she was doing and smiling, and she would walk through the parting crowd towards him with her long, leggy stride, her easy grace, the light catching the restless iridescence of her hair, her smile widening, her keen eyes shining, as she sauntered through the shifting, parting crowd towards him – Milo.